Bound by WORDS

E.L. Koslo

TABLE OF CONTENTS

First edition July 2022
© Cherry Publishing
71-75 Shelton Street, Covent Garden,
London WC2H 9JQ, UK

ISBN 9781801163651

Bound By Words

E.L. Koslo

Cherry Publishing

Subscribe to our Newsletter and receive a free ebook! You'll also receive the latest updates on all of our upcoming publications!

You can subscribe according to the country you're from:

You are from...

US:
https://mailchi.mp/b78947827e5e/get-your-free-ebook

UK:
https://mailchi.mp/cherry-publishing/get-your-free-uk-copy

CANADA:
https://mailchi.mp/96b9df3ed1ca/newsletter-canada-cherry-publishing

AUSTRALIA:
https://mailchi.mp/f7093b3c6c1a/newsletter-australia-cherry-publishing

Dedication

To my husband, who spent tireless hours as my research assistant for this book, with the enthusiasm only a book husband could manage. (Mom, pretend you never read that. And no, I won't talk to you about book research.)

For content warnings, please check my website
http://elkoslo.com/words-series

This book deals with some heavy subject matter, so please check the warnings if you need them.

ONE

Kelly

Minneapolis

Peeking out the hotel suite door, I scanned the hallway, checking for traces of my mother. She was on a mission to ruin my fun today and had confiscated my mimosa for the third time. A girl had the right to get obnoxiously, depressively drunk on her baby brother's wedding day if she was so inclined.

Admittedly, it was 10:00 am, but we weren't getting into that. I'd sober up for the ceremony, but right now, I needed a damn drink.

"Sneaking out before she comes back?" Chase laughed from behind me. My sister-in-law to be was amazing, and we often ganged up on my little brother, Evan, to tease him, but her mother was cool and sophisticated, and she wasn't morally opposed to having two mimosas...in your hand at a time.

"Shut it," I hissed as I looked toward the door to my room down the hallway.

After my third wheel experience during the drive from Chicago, I'd forced Christine and Sam to stop at a liquor store before heading to the hotel. It was bad enough that I'd been forced to listen to their weird flirting ritual for six hours, but now I was going to be forced to do something worse...

Spend three hours in a spa with my mother while I was plucked, waxed, styled, and face painted within an inch of my life and shoved into a bridesmaid dress — that I actually loved. Chase had given me free rein, and I had a deep red, figure-hugging, satiny dream of a dress with lace cap sleeves that fit like a glove. If gloves were sexy...which, yeah...they might not be.

I was beginning to wonder if I might not be as well.

Usually, it wouldn't bother me to be attending a wedding without a date, but this time, the lack of a partner to support me was glaring. I'd never cared about being single, but when Evan had proposed to Chase, I realized that my life was nowhere near that point. Nor did I see that changing anytime soon.

5

Everyone around me was getting married or popping out babies, and here I was, no prospects other than the usual — overgrown, toddler-like, old enough to know better, usually divorced — executives from other companies in my building who sometimes pursued me. I was so tired of powerful men taking my mid-level managerial position within the tech company I worked for as an invitation to chat me up for an office romance. If I'd wanted to sleep my way to the top, I'd already have a better office. Not that there'd be a chance of that anyway because my boss had forbidden intraoffice dating.

The chime of a cell phone text message sounded behind me, and Chase cursed. "Go, go, go. They're on their way back up here."

"Shit!" I threw the door open, pulled my robe closed, and shuffled down the hall, trying not to ruin the toenails I'd just had painted. I had just enough time to get to my room and back before the fun police returned.

"Have a drink for me, you alcoholic!"

I tried to hold in a laugh at Isobel's loud command. She was obscenely pregnant and had spent the morning perched in a chair in the corner of Chase's hotel suite. Chase had been trying subtly to get information out of her as to the state of her and her sort-of boyfriend, Adrian's, relationship. She claimed they weren't serious, but the large bun in her oven spoke otherwise, as did the protective look he was giving her this morning when he escorted her to the bride's suite to get ready with the rest of the bridesmaids.

She may have been under the mistaken impression things between them weren't committed, but he wanted them to be. I vaguely remembered him being all over her at Chase and Evan's engagement in New York. Still, I had been a wee bit inebriated at the time while drinking copious amounts of free wine with Christine and trying to formulate ways to mount my sister-in-law's friend, Nathan.

Isobel had been pregnant at their engagement dinner in Minneapolis in the fall, but she'd hardly started showing back then. I'd been too busy trying to play wingwoman to a hopeless Sam to notice much past his relationship drama with Christine.

All I knew of my brother's editor was that I had been warned to stay away from him because he was a gigantic douche nozzle. I dealt with enough of those in my professional life daily and had no desire

6

to hook up with one who was so closely involved with my brother's career. Not that it was an option with his super-preggo not-girlfriend.

"Shit," I hissed as I tried to wiggle my key card out of the pocket of my robe with the heel of my hand, avoiding my almost-dry nails. Chase would kill me if I messed them up. She may have been a pretty chill bride, but I didn't want to risk activating bridezilla because of my teetotalling mother.

"Hurry," Chase ordered in a harsh whisper, and I panicked when I heard the chime of the elevator around the corner. I only had a few seconds to get inside my room before I was caught, and lord knew the lecture I'd get if I was.

"I'm trying," I whined as I managed to get the card wiggled up enough I could grab it with the tips of my fingers. The tie on my robe was slipping, so I tried to hold the lapels closed and unlock the door simultaneously without the full use of my fingers.

"Shit." The first swipe over the card reader flashed red, and I cursed, trying it again.

Muffled voices carried down the hallway, and I threw my shoulder into the door, slipping inside the narrow space and flattening myself against the surface. *Success.* Now, for the much-needed drink and then pretending I was just going to the bathroom when I rejoined the rest of the bridal party.

I tried to step forward and stopped short.

"Oh, fuck."

The robe was stuck in the door, and the tie had slipped enough that half of my robe was now on the other side of the heavy door, the front open and revealing the lacy red underwear that I'd splurged on with my New Year's bonus before I left Chicago. It wasn't likely that anyone would be seeing it, but it'd made me feel sexy when I'd put it on this morning. The vibrant shade of red matched my bridesmaid dress perfectly because, what other color would a bridesmaid wear for a Valentine's Day wedding?

My once reclusive, shy, previously completely inexperienced brother had greased a few palms and made his fiancée's wedding dreams come true. The royalties from their last book collaboration had made a quick wedding possible for the two authors whereas others often spent years planning. Hotels that didn't typically host weddings in their atriums suddenly had availability on Valentine's Day.

Gripping the side of my robe, I tugged experimentally, trying to see if I could slip the rest of the material through the door jamb. It remained stuck, which meant that I would have to open the door with my robe hanging agape and quickly try to disentangle myself, without simultaneously messing up the nails that had survived thus far and flashing any unsuspecting hotel guests in the hallway.

Pressing my ear to the door, I listened for signs of life, not hearing anything. It was go time.

The click of the door lever was loud as I pulled the door open and tried to pull the material of my robe through the tiny crack. No such luck. I tugged again, and nothing. Shit.

Pulling the door open wider, I peeked through the opening and saw that I'd somehow managed to hook the corner of my pocket on the door lever on the other side.

A soft chuckle from down the hallway startled me as I tried to tug it loose, and I glanced up, my eyes meeting those of someone I wasn't expecting to see.

"Oh God," I breathed out, fruitlessly using the pads of my fingers to try to pull my robe free while also trying to shield myself with the door enough that Nathan didn't get an eyeful of red lingerie.

"Do you need some help?"

"No!" I shouted as I watched him step away from a door a few down from mine, pocketing a room key card.

"Are you sure?" he smiled, and my eyes widened as he continued to head toward where I was trapped.

My fingertips fumbled on the slippery satin material, trying to pull it free before he reached me. Leave it to me to get my robe stuck around a door handle when the male embodiment of sex personified happened to be loitering in the hallway.

He looked good. Really, really, *really* good. My intoxicated self had thought he was handsome last summer when he'd dropped into the dinner party where Chase and my little brother Evan had gotten engaged at the end of their book tour. I hadn't known who he was, but I'd thought he was sexy as fuck with short dark hair and a smattering of facial hair.

He must have been one of those guys who grew a beard for winter because that smattering had filled in nicely, framing his full, soft-looking lips. His hair was a little longer, too, curling slightly at the ends.

"I'm good. You can go back to your room. Really. I got this." My voice was rushed as my fingers continued to slip on the material, the angle not helping as I tried to keep my body concealed behind the door.

"Kelly," he sighed, his voice clearly amused, small smile lines crinkling at the sides of his soft brown eyes. "Let me help you."

While I'd been there to help determine the seating arrangements, I'd obviously not been paying enough attention because I was sure I would've remembered Nathan being on the guest list. I knew that Evan had mentioned inviting their friends from Boston, but Nathan was the only one I'd met besides their editors, Isobel and Adrian.

This was a sign I needed to stop drinking because I should have remembered how sexy this man was from the last time we'd seen each other. I'd remembered he was attractive, but spending a few hours in each other's company when I knew he lived on the other side of the country hadn't formed a lasting attachment.

I didn't do long distance. It never worked. My brother was a prime example. Chase had all but abandoned her condo in Boston and moved into my brother's Connecticut farmhouse when she started dating him. Even Christine had moved to Chicago to be with Sam because they hadn't seen a future being a thousand miles apart.

"Stop tugging on it. You'll tear the material," Nathan instructed, his voice deep and authoritative. My exposed breasts tingled underneath their thin lace covering. That could have been because they were currently smashed up against a cold metal door — but I had a feeling it was the way Nathan's mouth looked when he said *stop.*

I'd heard some things — things no respectable sister should want to hear — about the friends who'd helped Evan and Chase with research for a few of their books. Nathan hadn't been named specifically, but I knew that was how they met him. He was into things. Things that had always piqued my curiosity but I had never had the guts to try. Things that were currently running through my imagination as Nathan's calloused hand closed over mine, gently prying my fingers from the silky material keeping me trapped against the door of my hotel room.

"Lean forward a bit," he murmured as he tried to get the opening of the pocket over the edge of the door lever.

"I can't," I whispered back, my voice raspy as I inhaled, the masculine scent of cedar filling my senses. He smelled like I'd imagine a lumberjack smelled, like the outdoors and trees...and what the hell was wrong with me? Focus, Kelly.

"Just a little," he encouraged, gently tugging the side of my robe, the material tightening across my hips. "Just slide forward a little bit, and I can get it over the tip."

That should not have sounded dirty but coming from his lips... *unf.* Goosebumps rose along my arms as he continued to invade my personal space.

"But..." I squeaked.

"Come on, Kell, you can handle it."

Oh, *fuck me.* No. Seriously. Someone needed to fuck me. You'd have thought I'd already taken a shot of the bourbon on my nightstand with how I was responding to his presence.

"Kelly," he coaxed, reaching around the edge of the door and tugging on the empty loop at the waist of my robe. "I promise I won't look. Not if you don't want me to."

"But what if I want you to?" I whispered and then slapped my hand over my mouth, wishing that I could just close myself behind this door and smack my forehead into the surface of it. Repeatedly.

"I'll pretend you didn't say that," he chuckled, tugging until my hip slipped past the edge of the door, the taut material that had been holding me in place suddenly slack against my back.

I stepped backward, my sandals sliding awkwardly across the floor, and I felt myself slip, pulling the door inward as I started to fall.

Nathan's eyes widened as he reached for me, but he wasn't quick enough as I landed — sprawled in the entryway — with my robe wide open and lingerie in full view before the door clicked closed a few feet away.

"Fuck, fuck, fuck," I whined as I tried to tamp down my mortification.

"Are you alright?" His muffled voice carried through the door as I sat there, my hip aching from where I'd landed, and my dignity squashed under my cold — almost bare — ass.

"I'm fine," I squeaked, wishing the ground would just swallow me whole.

Nathan had gotten an eyeful before the door had closed, and the look in those eyes had me wishing it was a vibrator on my nightstand instead of a bottle of Willet. *Now,* I needed a damn drink!

TWO

Nathan

Minneapolis

Well. That was one way to start off the weekend.

When I'd decided to come to Chase and Evan's wedding solo, I'd considered asking Marisa to go with me, but I couldn't keep getting her hopes up. We wanted different things in life, and it was better if I stopped leading her on. I could tell her it was casual as much as I wanted, but she'd read into being my date to a wedding. It was hard enough to put boundaries on our dynamic until she vetted a new Dom.

I don't know why I'd agreed to continue things until she had essentially found my replacement. Still, I'd made sure we documented the changes in our dynamic to reflect the discontinuation of our sexual and romantic relationship. It wasn't so easy to turn off the emotional part. We'd been together for over a year within our play dynamic and six months romantically, and while we'd agreed that the relationship wasn't strictly exclusive, I hadn't dated anyone else while I'd been with her.

It wasn't my style to sleep with multiple partners at a time. There wasn't necessarily anything wrong with it; I just tended to be more content with some version of sexual monogamy. Some of the other acquaintances in my lifestyle thought it was old-fashioned, but I knew where my boundaries were, which was basically why things hadn't worked out with Marisa.

That wasn't to say I didn't enjoy watching others at parties or engaging in one off rope play without bringing sex into the equation, but I didn't like to share in that sense. My mentor, Emory, once called me a greedy motherfucker, but once he'd met his partner, Talia, he'd understood me and embraced it without looking back. Monogamy within a kinky relationship was much more common than either of us had initially realized and many widely embraced it and grew stable loving relationships. You could still be kinky as fuck and have some boundaries in place.

A knock at my door interrupted where I'd been unpacking, and I dropped my socks back into the suitcase to finish later.

When I opened the door, Emory was standing on the other side with a drink in his hand, Talia hot on his heels with a glass of wine in hers.

"See, I told you he'd be here," she laughed as she perched herself on the edge of my bed. Despite spending most of our morning in and out of airplanes, she still looked perfectly put together, her dark hair pulled back into a sleek ponytail and her makeup as flawless as ever on her dark skin.

"Yup, here I am, all by myself."

"Oh, quit," Tal laughed, rolling her eyes at me. "You act like you're the only one flying solo this weekend. I'm sure Chase has a single cousin around here somewhere. These Midwesterners seem to breed like rabbits. It wouldn't hurt you to have a weekend fling."

"Yeah, not sure that's in the cards."

After I'd essentially broken up with Marisa, I'd fallen back into a bad habit with Grace, a Domme who I'd played with infrequently over the last few years. We were the farthest thing from exclusive in our arrangement, and we'd technically never had sex, but for some reason, I couldn't seem to stay away from her when I needed a rope session. Which was more frequently when I was between sexual relationships.

She was a rigger too, or at least she had been before she'd developed her penchant for humiliation. But she was different when she played with me. Softer. The façade she wore around others dropped a little, and it was just about the two of us and the rope.

"Don't tell me you..." Emory trailed off with a shake of his head. "You did, didn't you?"

My jaw clenched, and I wished I had a drink in my hand.

"When are you going to realize that there are plenty of other partners out there who are just as talented a rigger as she is?"

"I know." I'd tried out a few of them, but I couldn't replicate the feelings she evoked in me. It was probably the dirty, degrading things she whispered in my ear once I was her bound captive sometimes. At first, I'd thought I'd hate it, but then I started to crave it. You'd think someone who'd been in the scene for over a decade wouldn't have an undiscovered kink, but here we were.

"Why do you keep doing this to yourself?" Tal added, tsking at me over the rim of her wineglass. "You know she's just manipulating you."

I did. I did know that Grace was manipulating me, but it was an addiction. She toned down her usual blatant degradation, and she'd figured out how to get under my skin. I knew I should stop — finally tell her no for once — but I kept answering her texts, which were eerily timed to when I felt vulnerable. It was all consensual, and I agreed to her terms of our one-off dynamic freely, but it still felt like there was something missing. She wasn't a bad person. It was me that was starting to drift.

"Because she knows what she's doing," I shrugged. It was as simple as that. I craved the release of being tied, and she was good at it. Sometimes she was too good at it. But I'd drawn the line early on in our arrangement at being in any sort of romantic relationship with Grace. I knew she was non-monogamous and that she was into much harder things than I was able to provide as a bottom, so I couldn't — and wouldn't — commit to something more with her.

We'd kissed infrequently, and in a scene, I'd climaxed, but no penetration of any kind had ever happened between us. It was a mutually beneficial arrangement. Nothing more.

"Your dependency on her is keeping you from finding something more fulfilling."

"No," I shook my head. "My refusal to change my boundaries is why I haven't been able to find something more."

"I know that Mar wanted a baby, and you couldn't provide that, but you're not getting any younger, Nate. This screwing around for fun thing has to be getting old."

"That's not an issue either."

There'd been no screwing around. I'd lost the taste for vanilla relationships and one-night-stands a while ago. I wanted someone who could fulfill all my needs, and if it meant I was celibate until then, so be it.

Besides, if I was going to do something reckless this weekend, I had a feeling it'd be with the dark-haired beauty down the hall. The momentary glimpse of red lace on her creamy skin I'd gotten before the door slammed closed had been seared on my subconscious. Kelly Stineman was insanely gorgeous, and it'd taken all my self-control not to insist she let me confirm with my own eyes — and possibly my hands — that she was fine after the fall inside the door to her room.

She'd landed hard. Legs splayed, her soft pink lips dropped open in shock as I stood there like an idiot a few feet away. I'd been so distracted by trying to be a gentleman and averting my eyes when she'd clearly been embarrassed about getting her robe stuck on the door handle to react to her falling. How she managed to get trapped like that, I had no idea, but I'd found the situation a little humorous until she'd fallen.

Then I'd been torn between concern and raging attraction — and other raging things — as I took in all her barely concealed curves a few feet away.

She'd looked shocked to see me standing in the hallway when she peeked around the door, but there was a flash of recognition in her eyes as well. She remembered me.

We'd only met once, at dinner while I was in Manhattan for a business meeting on a project for my firm, but she'd left a lasting impression. I'd thought she was adorable — while hilariously intoxicated — and I'd felt comfortable with her all evening.

I'd initially thought it'd be awkward, Chase and Evan extending a last-minute invitation when they'd heard I was in the city, but spending time with their interns, Sam and Christine, and Evan's sister, Kelly, had made the evening enjoyable.

She was sarcastic and funny, teasing me without hesitation during the evening, and I found myself wishing Chicago was closer to Boston. We'd exchanged phone numbers at the end of the night, but when things got serious with Marisa, we'd lost touch. It'd felt like a betrayal to keep up long-distance casual texting with a woman I was attracted to.

It was never sexual or anything like that, but I'd picked up on the vibe that she'd been into me, and I'd been equally intrigued by her.

"What the...?" Tal asked, tilting her head to look at me. "What's that face? You look half constipated, half aroused. That had better not be about Grace."

"No. It's not about Grace," I sighed, wishing she didn't keep coming up as a topic of conversation. I knew that she was my toxic indulgence, but I also knew that they didn't truly judge me for it. They just wished I'd search for another rope top. "Not everything is about Grace."

"Thank fucking God," Emory chuckled, leaning against the desk near my floor-to-ceiling windows. I'd barely had a chance to admire the view of downtown Minneapolis from my window, but in a sense, it was just another city covered with snow. Boston had looked much the same when we left practically before dawn this morning.

It was too bad Chase hadn't wanted a destination wedding in February instead. Which had my mind going dangerous places imagining Kelly in a bikini. Not that her lingerie choices had left much up to the imagination, I knew exactly how gorgeous she'd look in swimwear. All luscious curves and sun kissed skin. I bet she'd have sexy shoulder freckles that I'd like to trace with my tongue...

"What time do we need to be down there for the ceremony?" I asked, checking my watch. It was nearly noon back at home. I'd forgotten to change the time on my wristwatch on the plane. It was my grandfather's old Tag Heuer, an old-school relic, but it was my go-to in formal situations. I knew everyone had a smartwatch nowadays, but you couldn't beat the look of a traditional watch when you wore a suit. Which, for me, wasn't very often.

Most of my days were spent in a pair of heavy-duty work pants; a button-up shirt rolled to my elbows, steel-toed boots, and a hard hat. As a commercial construction manager, my job meant I bounced back and forth between the main office with the architects and on-site with my project foremen. I loved it; I'd always loved building things, but it was non-stop. It'd been hard enough to clear vacation time in my schedule to take Monday off to travel, but I hated spending less than twenty-four hours in a new place. Not that Minneapolis in the dead of winter was a vacation hot spot.

"I think by 4:00," Emory responded, scrolling through something on his phone. "The ceremony is supposed to start at 5:00 pm, and the reception is in the ballroom downstairs."

"Then you need to tell me where you got those drinks so I can catch up."

Unpacking was forgotten as Talia, Emory and I sat in the hotel bar, nursing our drinks and catching up after we'd changed into something a little more formal. I'd even bitten the bullet and shaved off my beard, my face feeling surprisingly naked.

Sometimes our lives dragged us all in different directions, and it felt good to spend time with them on neutral ground with none of the usual pressures of our lives.

16

"I have no idea how you do it," I shook my head as I looked over at Emory. He had the patience of a freaking saint. As a professional photographer, his day job brought all kinds of bratty women into his life. It'd literally kill me to put up with that much shit and not let out my Dominant inner traits. "I'd want to bend every single one of them over my knee."

"Oh, trust me, it's not easy," he laughed as Talia playfully scowled in my direction at the implication Emory should bend a supermodel over his knee. Still, we both knew he was only interested in her. "But I happen to like my job, despite the constant need for a mute button. I've honestly learned to tune it out. And I'm at a point where they know to keep the dramatic shit to a minimum. I've apparently got a reputation of being a hardass."

"Imagine that," Talia giggled, leaning her head against his shoulder. When they'd met, I'd thought they'd make an unlikely couple, but when she was in the right headspace, she was his perfect match in his playroom, even if she was a totally different person when they weren't in a scene. But the truth was, they were both her, just different parts of the same person matching the different parts of his personality. Emory in Dom mode was a little more intimidating than the photographer in gossip mode.

That was what I wanted, a person that fit all the parts of me and me with them, without judgment, without pretense, and without lying about ourselves. I wanted a partner, and I just hadn't found her yet. Settling for less or compromising what I wanted would just end up with me breaking someone, like my father had broken my mother.

"So, as I was saying," Emory continued before I interrupted him. "She's standing there in five-inch heels, glaring at my lighting assistant, no idea that I'd already told the rest of the set to wrap for the day. She'd been so focused on him saying she needed to turn slightly to get the right angle, thinking he was calling her fat. The body image of some of these women is mind-blowing. Her shoes weighed more than she did soaking wet, but he tells her to move, so she doesn't have a glare on the side of her face, and suddenly she's been fat-shamed."

"Man, give me carpenters in hardhats with saws any day, and I will gladly take all their shit."

17

"Alright, as riveting as this conversation about roughnecks and supermodels is, we should get in there. I don't want to get stuck in the back," Talia interjected.

"You love it when you get stuck in the back," Emory quipped, wrapping an arm around Talia's waist and leaning down to growl into her neck.

"Wow," I laughed. "You need to slow down, my friend."

Emory looked up from Tal's neck, winking at me before he placed his empty glass on the bar, sliding a hundred-dollar bill across the polished surface.

I threw down a few twenties to cover my tab and grabbed a mint from a bowl on the bar, popping it into my mouth as Emory offered his arm to Talia.

"You mean you're not going to escort me in too?" I batted my eyelashes, sighing dramatically as I followed behind them.

"He's all yours," Talia joked as she winked over her shoulder at me. "But just a warning, he likes to bite."

"TMI, Tal, TMI."

"Oh, please," she rolled her eyes before she faced forward again. "It's not like you haven't seen it all before."

She was right, but there was a time and a place, and I found myself getting curiously anxious for this wedding to start.

While we'd spent the better part of the last four hours in the hotel bar after getting changed, my mind had drifted to a certain groom's older sister more than I cared to admit.

I was dying to see the dress that would cover that lingerie. Whatever it was, I knew she'd fill it out to perfection.

"You've got that look on your face again," Tal teased as I found myself scanning the hallway as we headed to the hotel atrium where the wedding was being held.

"Hate to break it to you, Tal, but this is unfortunately just my face."

"Whatever, drama queen. I'll get it out of you soon enough," she warned. And I had a feeling I'd be getting teased about having the hots for a particular bridesmaid for weeks to come. Not that it mattered, because while we were in the same place this weekend, Kelly and I lived worlds apart. In more ways than one.

We found seats on the aisle, right in the middle of the bride's side, behind an older woman who was unsuccessfully trying to wrangle a red-headed little pixie in a frilly pink dress. Her hair was a fiery halo, a pink satin bow haphazardly hanging from the end of one curl of hair as she bounced up and down in the seat in front of me.

Objectively, I could appreciate that she was adorable, but I had absolutely zero desire to have one of those. Talia made faces at the little girl, cooing in her direction as Emory looked on with a gentle smile on his face. It was only a matter of time until they too succumbed to societal conventions, declared a monogamous legal union, and started creating their own little hyperactive spawn.

That was never going to be in the cards for me — at least the kids part — and I was perfectly fine with it. I was better at being an uncle anyway, where I could give the child back at the end of a visit.

As the seats filled and Evan appeared with his groomsmen at the front of the aisle; a man with equally bright red hair scooped up the little girl and held her in the crook of his arm as he took his place at the front.

"She was so cute," Talia smiled, sighing happily as she leaned back into Emory's arm. "Did you see those dimples?"

"Don't get any ideas," he teased, but I knew he'd do whatever Talia wanted.

The light music changed before I could get into one of my overthinking spirals, and people took their seats, clearing the aisle as the doors to the atrium opened.

The crowd stood, facing the double doors as a tall — heavily pregnant — blonde woman in a pink dress started her way down the aisle, followed by a pretty brunette with glasses in a matching dress and a man in a suit with a hot pink bow tie and hair color accented to match. And then there she was...

Kelly fidgeted with the flowers in her hand as she looked down at the red velvet aisle and then glanced back up toward the crowd as it was her turn to join the procession. She looked gorgeous. Although that word somehow didn't seem to encompass her appearance. Her long hair had been pulled up into a sweeping braided bun, soft curls framing her face. Her eyes seemed brighter, the fresh-faced beauty from this morning accentuated by smokey eye makeup and bright red lips I was dying to bite.

I was fucked.

Talia was right; maybe I did need to get out of my head for the weekend. Have a fling. Enjoy the company of a beautiful woman without worrying about all my baggage at home. But I wasn't going to sleep with some random woman.

If anything happened, it'd be with the radiant goddess who was a few feet away from me, staring right at me with a light blush staining her high cheekbones before she looked down nervously, and then right back at me from underneath her long dark eyelashes.

I hoped my mouth wasn't hanging open as she walked past my seat on the aisle, but as she floated past me in a clingy red dress, glancing briefly at me over her shoulder as she passed, I knew I'd seek her out before the night was over.

THREE

Kelly

Minneapolis

I should have known he'd fill out a suit impressively. I'd seen him in semi-casual dress clothes in New York, but Nathan in a full tailored suit, with his hair combed back off his face and that jaw fully exposed, nearly made me face-plant in the middle of the aisle in front of all my relatives.

My job as the maid of (dis)honor had been a surprise, but I'd taken it on with excitement; I'd always wanted a sister. Chase had chosen her sister-in-law, Elle, her brother-in-law, Miguel, and her editor Isobel as her other bridesmaids/dude.

"How much you wanna bet they try to sneak off?" Miguel whispered as we stood off to the side of the stained-glass windows in the lobby of the expensive hotel venue, watching Chase and Evan get about a thousand pictures taken.

"Who says they haven't already?" I'd seen them disappear into a conference room for ten minutes after the ceremony before the photographer told us to meet at the front of the hotel. I wasn't sure exactly what they did in there, but Evan came out with a dazed expression on his face, and Chase had spent a solid five minutes in front of the bathroom mirror afterward fixing her makeup before the photographer had tracked her down.

"Ew," Miguel laughed with a pinched face. "Not that your brother isn't total eye candy, but those two will fuck anywhere."

"Ew," I echoed, gagging in my mouth a little. I mean, I knew we were blessed with good genes, but no one needed to hear that their brother had sex appeal across both genders. Or just that he was sexually desirable in general. He'd always be the skinny loser to whom I'd gifted a bottle of industrial-sized lube and a Costco-sized box of condoms on his fifteenth birthday. I hadn't even known a person's face could turn that red, but it'd been worth my paycheck to see it.

21

But I loved that little anxious shit like no one else in the world. Well, maybe Chase loved him a little bit more, but I loved him with a totally non-incestuous sibling tolerance that was more than the norm.

Which was why it physically hurt how much I was jealous of him today. I'd been the one my parents had pinned their hopes to with hitting life goals on time, and I'd been in a holding pattern for years. A year, specifically, but they hadn't known how close they'd been to all our lives changing; no one did. Part of me wished I'd never figured out what was going on.

"Hey," Miguel bumped my shoulder, drawing my attention back to him. "No pouting today. I know you're feeling a little usurped with Mr. Tall, Handsome and Awkward over there finally putting a ring on it, but you're hot as fuck today, and you need to own it."

"Yeah, because my brother's wedding is crawling with guys to impress," I sighed dramatically. "This isn't your Instagram feed."

"*Excuse me*, on behalf of the hottest guy here and his almost equally attractive husband; you are not allowed to question the attractiveness of the guests at this wedding. The Rodgers clan has about a bajillion cousins, and I'm sure we can find one sexy ginger in the bunch to give you a whirl on the dance floor. Or maybe a roll in the sheets. Seems like a waste to have that king-sized bed all to yourself."

Shaking my head at his blatant appraisal of his in-laws' extended family, I laughed, despite my need to get my hands on a cocktail. My quick shot of bourbon in the hotel room after I'd mortified myself had been my last of the morning, my nerves too shot to enjoy getting drunk with Elle and Miguel once we'd moved to the spa.

"Yeah, that just sounds awkward." I cringed, thinking about being teased for eternity by Chase for hooking up with one of her cousins. No thanks; I wasn't quite that desperate.

But I felt my neck flush as I thought about my brief interaction with Nathan today. He'd looked downright predatory in the few seconds our eyes had met this morning before the door slammed closed between us, and then that same heat had been in his eyes as I passed him on my way down the aisle.

"We're up, space cadet." Miguel nudged me before he went to retrieve his husband from where he was standing with his brother and sister-in-law. I'd stayed away from them most of the morning —

well, at least from Ethan and Sadie. The little girl was adorable, and I'd fawned over her when they'd been at my parent's house last summer, but the ache in my chest after the news I'd gotten a few months ago made it hard to enjoy being around their little family. You always wanted what you couldn't have, even if you weren't sure you wanted it to begin with.

"Alright, I'm coming," I groaned as I blew out a breath and prepared to plaster on my fakest of photogenic smiles.

"Not in public, Kelly. Geez, have some self-control," Miguel cackled as he stole his niece and headed for the photographer.

My brain didn't have room for my mind to wander when I was being bossed around by the wedding photographer, but as soon as he dismissed the bridal party to get ready for our entrance into the reception, my pulse started pounding. Nathan would be in that reception, and he'd already seen me half naked today, so I wasn't sure if I was excited or terrified he might try to talk to me. Probably both. *Definitely* both.

"Save me a dance, bish," Miguel whispered as he passed me on his way to the front of the wedding party formation. He and his husband, Drew, were leading us in. I was near the back of the formation, the last one in before the bride and groom were announced, and the only one without a partner. Isobel had offered up Adrian, but she'd been getting progressively paler as the day went on, so I didn't want to steal her boyfriend when she was clearly exhausted.

"Yup," I nodded, going over the dance steps Miguel had demonstrated for our grand entrance in my head. I just had to make it across the dance floor without doing something stupid, and I was home free.

My mother was thrilled I was such a great big sister, but I was just tired. And seeing all the happy couples in front of me wasn't helping. It made me feel that much more alone.

The doors to the ballroom swung open, and the opening notes of the music started, so I shook my hands out and put on the mask I'd been wearing for months. Fake it till you make it...or at least until you're alone when you can fall apart.

Miguel and Drew owned it, strutting in and sliding across the dance floor, to the amusement of all the wedding guests. Elle and

Ethan followed — with Sadie stealing the show by blowing people kisses, Isobel waddled in — Adrian hovering and spinning her before leading her to the head table. Then it was my turn.

I stepped into the open doors, gesturing dramatically along with the cue of the music. When I glanced to my side, Nathan was leaning back in his chair at a table near the door, arms folded across his broad chest and his eyes locked on me.

Something about the way he was looking at me made me feel powerful — and sexy — so when I blew out a breath and faced the dance floor, I put a little extra swing in my hips and sashayed across the floor. When I reached the center of the dance floor where my partner was waiting, I took Miguel's hand, letting him spin me around before Drew grasped my other hand and stole me from his husband before dipping me dramatically.

"That was perfect," Drew laughed as he righted me, spinning me to the edge of the dance floor where the wedding party was all seated at a long table.

"You killed it," Miguel beamed as I took my seat beside him.

"At least I didn't fall on my ass like I did in our practice this morning," I panted, my adrenaline still running a little high.

"Well, if that demonstration doesn't get you laid, then I don't know what will," he chuckled as he reached forward to grasp his champagne glass, wiggling his eyebrows at me.

"Let it go, Miguel," I warned, trying to get him to drop the subject before Evan and Chase made their way to the table. If they got wind of his mission to find me a one-night-stand, I'd never live it down. Evan already gave me more shit lately since his little sexual awakening, which the thought of made me throw up in my mouth a little. I mean, I loved Chase, but I did not need any details about what she did with my brother's dick.

"Someone is watching you," Miguel whispered as he leaned in toward me.

My eyes shot up, and I scanned the room, heat rushing through me as they stopped on Nathan, who was now leaning against the bar staring straight at me.

"He's cute," Miguel teased as he shimmied in his seat.

"Who's cute?" Drew asked as he placed his hand around the back of Miguel's chair and leaned in so he could hear what we were saying.

"Hottie at the bar in the black suit. Yum."

Drew glanced at the bar and then turned back toward me with wide eyes, mouthing "Dayum."

"Quit staring at him," I hissed as I turned my attention to the DJ, who was announcing the bride and groom.

I watched them raise their joined hands in the doorway to the ballroom, Evan twirling Chase under his arm before he grasped her around the waist and dipped her dramatically, kissing her with way too much tongue to be appropriate around all their relatives.

Glancing back at the bar, Nathan was still there, still watching me. I flashed him a small smile, and he lifted his glass in my direction before he downed the contents and pushed off the counter, heading in my direction.

"Oh, God. Oh no…"

My eyes widened as a hand clamped down on my thigh, drawing my attention to Isobel's whimpering voice from where she was seated next to me.

"Oh, shit." From the way her face was contorted, I could tell that something was wrong. Her fingers tightened on my leg, and a low moan came out of her mouth as Adrian turned back toward her from his conversation with Ethan on his other side.

"Are you alright?" I asked as I placed my hand on top of hers.

"I think my water just broke," she whimpered as I looked down and saw a wet spot starting to spread across the pink satin of her dress.

"Holy…" I looked up, making eye contact with Adrian, who looked just as startled as I did.

"Babe? Is she coming?"

"I think so…" she panted, grimacing as her hand tightened on my leg.

"But it's not time yet. We were supposed to be back home."

As I watched her try to breathe through a contraction, a hush had fallen over the rest of the wedding party as they realized what was going on.

"Grab her wrap, hot shot," Miguel instructed as he gestured at a shell-shocked Adrian.

"Fuck, sorry, babe." He seemed to come out of the panicked fog then, quickly pulling Isobel's heavy velvet wrap off the back of her chair and throwing it over his girlfriend's shoulders.

25

"Do you think you can stand?" I asked as her fingers relaxed and her breathing slowed.

"Maybe."

"Let's get you up then." Grasping her elbow, I pulled her up as I stood, holding on tightly as she wobbled a little.

Adrian pulled out her chair and shifted the heavy velvet around her waist as he bent slightly, pulling her up into his arms.

Well, damn. I knew Evan joked about him being a gym rat, but he didn't even look to be straining while he held his heavily pregnant — whatever they were.

"I've got yah, babe," he assured her in his heavy Boston accent as he nodded to the table. "Grab her clutch and follow me to the front, would yah?"

By the time we got to the corner of the dance floor, Chase and Evan had realized what was going on, rushing over to see if they could help.

"I'm fine. I promise. I'm so sorry," Isobel apologized as Adrian started to carry her toward the exit, with most of the wedding party as his entourage.

"Don't apologize," Chase waved away her worries. "Is there anything we can do to help?"

"I didn't mean to ruin your wedding reception. I thought we still had a few weeks," Isobel whimpered as Adrian whispered reassurances in her ear.

By the time we got to the valet stand, Sam had already run ahead to flag down someone and arranged for them to bring around the rental car.

"Do you guys even know how to get to the hospital?" Chase asked, looking mildly panicked.

"Don't worry," Drew interrupted, taking the keys from the valet once he pulled up. "Miguel and I got this."

"Wait? What?" Now Miguel was the one looking panicked as he looked between the panting pregnant woman and his husband. "I am not delivering a baby. No, no. That was not part of my agreeing to be a dude of dishonor."

"It'll be fine," Drew assured him as he moved to open the back door of the SUV. "We'll get them checked in and come back to the reception. She's not going to have the baby in the back seat."

"That better be a fricking guarantee."

Adrian moved forward, interrupting Miguel's little freak out, gently settling Isobel into the back seat and reaching around to fasten her seatbelt. He jogged around to the passenger door on the far side of the car, jumping in and slamming his door.

"Let's go." Drew jerked his head toward the car, and Miguel flashed me a look of pure terror.

"Go," I nodded, knowing that if they waited too much longer, he *might* be delivering a baby on the side of the highway. I wasn't sure how long she'd been in labor, but Isobel had seemed mildly uncomfortable all day, looking back on it.

As the car pulled away, the group headed back into the hotel. Chase giggled as Evan wrapped his arms around her from behind and whispered in her ear. She looked like a princess, her sleek ivory gown hugging her curves and the wild mane of golden curls laced with jeweled pins sparkling in the lighting of the lobby.

As I looked around, everyone was paired off — Evan and Chase, Ethan and Elle, Sam and Christine, and then there was me. With nobody.

Blowing out a heavy breath, my eyes burned as tears pricked at the corners of my eyes. I was *not* going to cry. At least, not yet.

My body moved on autopilot as we returned to the head table, the DJ calling the room to order once the bride and groom had reappeared. Then the nerves kicked in earnest. Now I knew why Elle and Miguel were all too happy to let me be the maid of honor...well, technically Elle was the matron of honor, and Miguel had dubbed himself a dude of (dis)honor because he said he was too young to be a matron. Anyway, it was because I now had to stand in front of several hundred guests and speak about my love for my little brother.

I'd written a speech — of course, I had. I took assignments seriously, well...most of the time. But now, I was trying to filter through the mush in my brain to recall all the sappy things I'd written.

As I watched both my father and Chase's struggle to hold it together as they looked proudly at the newly married couple during their speeches, my mood darkened. Then Ethan got up there and talked about growing up with this intense desire to protect his baby sister and how he knew from the first time he met Evan that he didn't need to worry anymore. I was gutted as he handed me the microphone, my mind full of static.

The room quieted as I took a deep breath and closed my eyes for a moment, trying to get ahold of myself.

Warm fingers squeezed my left hand, and I opened my eyes, looking down to a slightly disheveled Miguel taking his seat. He winked and nodded at the microphone, so I took another deep breath and faced the crowded ballroom.

"For those of you who haven't had the misfortune of meeting me, I'm Kelly, Evan's older — much prettier — sister. Well, unless you ask Chase, she seems to think this guy is cute or something," I laughed, hooking my thumb at Evan.

"Or something," Chase said loudly, and the crowd chuckled.

"As the first born, I was used to being the center of attention. As a toddler — if you ask our parents — I had a rather severe reaction to them bringing a baby back from the hospital on my third birthday. I told them I'd asked for a Barbie doll, not a baby brother, and they could take him back to the store to exchange him. As you can see, they didn't listen to me." I paused, glancing over at my parents. My dad was laughing, and my mom was shaking her head at me with a smile on her face.

"Most of the time, I'm glad that siblings are non-returnable. Evan has grown on me over the years, both in height and like an incurable rash. He was forced to follow in my shadow throughout most of his childhood, teachers exclaiming how different we were to my parents when the loud, talkative, high-energy child was followed up with her quiet, vastly more socially compliant brother who never got in trouble for bossing his classmates around or refusing to stop talking."

"Despite being forced to deal with my reputation, Evan was always supportive — except for that one time he refused to let me dress him up like a Ken doll for Halloween." Chase laughed loudly, and Evan's cheeks turned pink. I didn't even want to know why with those two.

"Evan was always the quiet sibling, but I didn't mind because it meant I had a captive audience. He tolerated a lot of teasing from me over the years, and until recently, he took it with a stoic acceptance. When he called me last year asking for a ride from the airport, he seemed different — not only because he was wearing leather pants — but I couldn't quite put my finger on why. Then I sat and listened to Chase read an excerpt from the first book they wrote together. I could immediately tell that Evan had written part of the passage she read, his usual eloquence shining through."

"As we sat there and listened, I watched his face as he observed her speaking, his expression one I'd never seen from him before. I could see the amount of pride he felt as she held the entire audience captivated with her voice, but it wasn't until she finished that I realized what his expression was." I glanced over at Evan, smiling at the soft grin on his face. He was in a room surrounded by people, and he was utterly relaxed. "Evan has had trouble being in a crowd since we were kids, always tending to avoid social situations that placed him in large groups. I'd seen him during author events early in his career, and he tended to look more like he was being led to slaughter."

"When Chase opened the floor to questions, talking about her writing experience with Evan, I realized that Evan had finally done something first. While he'd spent his entire life getting to do everything second, he'd managed to beat me to one thing — well, I guess now two since we're here today. Evan was the first of the two of us to fall in love."

"Even though they'd only known each other for a few months, and he'd spent the night prior sick after recovering from a panic attack, I knew before I'd even met her that Evan was desperately in love with Chase. It was written all over his face, kind of like it is now."

"In typical sibling fashion, I teased him about it, but in watching them over the last half a year, I've seen a completely different person in my little brother. Chase has not only brought him out of his shell but she's also calmed him in a way that even his writing doesn't manage. She supports him unconditionally, not letting him take himself too seriously. And he's shown me — much like our father has — how a man should treat his partner. With grace and compassion, and most of all love."

"If..." I paused, swallowing past the lump in my throat. "If I'm ever lucky enough to find a man like my little brother — well, not exactly like my little brother, cause ew. If I'm ever lucky enough to find a man who looks at me with the love that Evan holds for Chase, he's taught me that it's worth the risk to hold onto it, to cherish it, and to take risks to protect it."

"So, I'd like you to join me in a toast." Holding up my champagne flute, I scanned the crowd, my eyes momentarily pausing as they locked with Nathan's across the room. He nodded, smiling faintly, causing my throat to tense.

"May we all find someone in life to love us as much as these two love each other, and may we do everything in our power to hold onto it with all our might."

Turning to face the bride and groom, I tipped my glass at them, trying to keep myself from crying. "To Evan and Chase, who deserve every moment of happiness life has to give them, and may they have a long and happy life together."

Evan's lips twisted as he smiled at me, using the back of his hand to swipe at the corner of one eye. Dammit, that bastard was going to make me cry.

I flipped off the switch to the microphone, setting it on the table before I raised my champagne flute in the air, catching sight of the proud smiles my parents had on their faces before I brought it to my lips and downed the contents.

Dinner came out then, and I forced myself to eat something, listening to Miguel recount their mad dash to the hospital. Thankfully, Isobel did not give birth in the back of the rental car. Still, she did curse at Adrian half the ride to the hospital and told a male nurse she didn't care who she needed to blow, but they had better send a damned anesthesiologist to her room as soon as humanly possible.

The ache in my chest started up again, and I forced myself to plaster on a smile as the dancing started, watching Chase and Evan spin around the dance floor with envy. As soon as I could slip away, I'd be making a beeline for the bar. Maybe sobering up before the wedding had been a bad idea, because I needed some liquid courage to make it through the rest of the night without completely breaking down.

FOUR

Nathan

Minneapolis

My cover had been blown.

"Just go talk to her," Talia whispered as she flicked the side of my neck. I'd been leaning against the bar, watching the bridal party on the dance floor. Kelly was being spun around the dance floor by her father; at least, I assumed it was her father because he was the older version of Evan only with darker hair liberally laced with grays.

"I'm not going to talk to her." I wanted to — God, did I want to — but I couldn't. After my inattentiveness had blown up their book release party last year, I'd finally gotten to a good point in my friendship with Evan. He never held it against me, but I'd felt like shit after we'd tracked him down and again when I'd realized that he'd had a full-blown panic attack.

I knew what it was like to have to walk on eggshells to have to avoid someone's triggers, my entire adolescence one big minefield. I typically prided myself on being considerate of other people's limitations. My whole life was constructed on maintaining and respecting boundaries.

Watching Kelly Stineman from across a crowded ballroom was as good as it was going to get for me, no matter how disappointed my dick was at my restraint. The image of her in that red lingerie was burned into my retinas for the foreseeable future.

But it wasn't just her physical beauty that appealed to me. I'd been captivated by her speech. Evan may have been the one who wrote novels for a living, but she'd talked with an open heart and candid honesty that was hard to do in a room full of people. She was charming in a way that pulled you in to listen to every word that slipped past those luscious red lips of hers.

Smart, funny, persuasive women had always been my weak spot, and Kelly was quickly checking all the boxes of what I wanted in a partner. But that didn't matter because she wasn't an option. She was in Chicago, and I was in Boston, and my entire life was there.

31

We'd barely spoken, we didn't know each other, our interactions before brief and superficial, but I couldn't keep my eyes off her.

"Seriously, go." Talia pushed my shoulder, and I turned to give her a pointed look. "Sorry, fine. Be stubborn, but you've got to stop staring at her if you're not going to do anything about it. You're rapidly descending into creepy voyeur territory."

"We both know why I can't." My response was terse. "I'll leave the voyeurism up to you."

"My word, you're so freaking dramatic," she laughed. "Go ask her for a dance, no one's asking for you to marry her."

"Don't you have your own date to harass?"

"It's much more entertaining to sit here and tease you," she grinned.

"I'm going to tell Emory you're being a brat again," I warned.

"And he won't be surprised. We're not playing this weekend, so I can be as obnoxious as I want without repercussions."

"To him, maybe. I don't recall signing up to be the target of this obnoxious behavior."

The music changed, and when I glanced back over to the dance floor, she was gone. The wedding party had returned to their seats — but hers was empty — and other wedding guests were starting to fill the dance floor.

"Where did she go?" Talia asked as she saw where my attention had been redirected.

"How am I supposed to know?"

"It's a wonder you ever get laid with your attitude," she teased as she rolled her eyes at me.

"It's a wonder you can walk with how much you're running your mouth this weekend. Emory's hand is bound to get cramped up with all the spankings you're earning yourself."

"He likes me feisty," she giggled, and then sobered up as Emory rejoined us.

"What are you two staring at?" he asked as he pulled Talia into his side with an arm around her waist.

"Nathan has the hots for Evan's sister."

"I do not."

Emory raised an eyebrow at me. I hated that he didn't even need to speak to compel people to tell him things; his face conveyed everything.

"Fine. I think she's attractive."

"Yes, because I stare obsessively at people I find attractive all day," Talia sighed.

"Tal, I know you've got a free pass, but give the poor guy a break. He's clearly enamored with her," Emory chuckled as he placed a kiss on Talia's temple. Once upon a time, he'd been my wingman, not his sassy partner's.

"Fuck the both of you," I grumbled, tipping my glass up and draining the contents before signaling to the bartender for a refill.

"Don't threaten me with a good time if you're not going to follow through," Talia giggled, and then she gasped. I knew enough about their amorous behavior not to look back at them, but I had a feeling Emory's hand would be sore tomorrow. They may not have been playing this weekend, but I knew they had difficulty keeping it clean in public. It'd be disgusting if I wasn't envious of their connection.

"I think he's got his sights set on something besides watching us tonight," Emory murmured as Talia leaned back into his embrace. He was right. I did have my sights set on something — someone — else, and the more scotch I sipped, the better talking to Kelly about the lingerie I knew she had on under that sexy dress sounded.

"He's not even listening to us anymore," Talia giggled.

"He needs to stop worrying about what other people think of him." Emory was right. Evan's friendship was important to me, but there was something about his alluring sister I couldn't resist. Talking to her wouldn't hurt. It was all the other thoughts that were running through my mind regarding her that might make things complicated.

"This hesitance isn't because of Marisa, is it?" Talia asked with a hand on my arm.

"No. This is me."

While Marisa had made me a little gun shy of dating after things had fallen apart, that wasn't what had been keeping me from pursuing a new relationship. I was hesitant to disclose what I knew was a deal-breaker with some women early in the relationship. It was also the steps I'd already taken to ensure that it wouldn't be an issue any longer. At least not on my end.

People assumed since I was the youngest of three — well technically younger middle child of four — that I'd be quick to jump on the family-making train, but that couldn't be further from the truth. It'd already made things awkward with Marisa, and once that dynamic was over, I dreaded going through the vetting process with another potential partner.

I just wanted to enjoy being with a woman again. Learning what made her tick, laughing, talking about inconsequential things. Making her cum...listening to the sounds she made...fucking her until she was wild underneath me.

OK, maybe I needed to get laid.

"We're going to dance," Talia announced, and I came out of my haze, scanning the dance floor for the object of my temporary obsession.

"We are?" Emory was looking over at her with a look of skeptical indifference, but I knew he'd indulge her.

"We are," she nodded, grasping his hand, and tugging him away from the bar. He pulled back on her hand, and she smiled, flawlessly spinning into his chest with a giggle, and I knew I was being left to my own devices for the rest of the night.

The music changed to a slow ballad, and I downed the rest of my drink before I dropped a few bills into the tip jar and walked to the edge of the dance floor. The older man from before was dancing with someone else now, and I didn't see Kelly's dark, shiny, upswept hair in the sea of guests embracing. Evan was entirely wrapped up in Chase, whispering things in her ear, and I knew now was my chance to find Kelly while everyone else was distracted.

If nothing else, I wanted to tell her she didn't need to be embarrassed about our run-in this morning in the hallway. While I hadn't expected to get quite the eyeful I did with her little robe incident, she had absolutely nothing to be self-conscious about. She was all curves and soft skin, dark brown doe eyes, and silky, long, dark hair. I'd always had a thing for women with long hair, and I was dying to pull all those pins out of her hair and wrap that braid around my fist.

I could already imagine the noise she'd make while I held her in place.

As the music shifted into another slow song, I made my way to the doors back to the lobby, scanning the small groups of people dotted around the seating areas, coming up short once again. She'd disappeared while I was distracted, but I wasn't letting her escape me that easily. She had to be around here somewhere.

34

The elevators were empty as I quickly hopped on, riding up to our floor, listening for signs of life coming from the room down the hall. I knocked a few times, hoping she was just changing her shoes or something, but there was no response.

When I finally gave up and moved back to my room, I slipped into the bathroom, pulling out my emergency stash and stowing a few condoms in my back pocket. While I wasn't trying to find her purely to proposition her for sex, I also wasn't going in unprepared if the opportunity presented itself.

The lobby was quiet as I descended back to the main floor, Kelly still nowhere to be found. The ballroom was the same. Her family was all there, still enjoying the party, the dance floor packed, and the liquor flowing, but she wasn't with them. I wondered if all the happy couples had gotten to her as well. It was hard to be one of the few single people at a wedding, a place I'd been in when my siblings had paired off and gotten married.

Weddings could be incredibly romantic, especially one held on Valentine's Day, but when you didn't have someone to share the atmosphere with, it was even more lonely. I hated to think of Kelly escaping somewhere by herself because she couldn't stomach being left out. At first I'd been worried my staring would be noticed by her date, but there hadn't even been an empty chair beside her at the head table. She was here without a plus one, just like I was.

I moved out into the hallway that bordered the courtyard; the thin layer of snow outside was illuminated by the soft pink lights that had been strung in the trees. It reminded me of the first time I'd seen Kelly, her flushed cheeks lit by the fairy lights that Evan had covered the courtyard at the Met Cloisters in during that dinner in New York. I hadn't let myself acknowledge it at the time, but there was something even then that had drawn me to her. And her unsubtle comments to Christine about how she'd like to climb me sent a thrill through me at the time I'd quickly tamped down because of my commitments elsewhere.

Now that those weren't an issue, that attraction flared to life as I caught a glimpse of dark red velvet and white fur at the edge of one of the outside windows.

I had a feeling I'd just found my runaway bridesmaid, and I didn't think I had the strength to stay away from her any longer when I glimpsed her profile and saw her wet cheeks glistening on the other side   of   the   glass.

FIVE

Kelly

Minneapolis

Angrily swiping at the tears that gathered in the corners of my eyes, I pulled my cloak tighter around my shoulders and tried to ignore the soft instrumental music that drifted through the open doors of the venue. I should be in there — at my own brother's wedding — having fun, not throwing a pity party for one. I'd blame it on my period, but it wasn't due for weeks, and I'd been feeling this way for months. Ever since...

Sniffling, I tried to stop the tears, hating that I was so upset over my brother tying himself to the love of his life. It just didn't seem fair to me. Evan was over four years younger than I was, and his life was more put together than mine.

And when Miguel had regaled everyone within earshot of the story of Isobel going into labor, and the mad dash to the hospital, I couldn't hold in tears anymore. I found myself escaping out into the cold after my obligations as maid of honor were complete. I hadn't even been paying attention while my dad talked to me on the dance floor.

Sure, I looked like I had my life together. My job was well-paid, I lived in a nice condo a few blocks from Madison Avenue, and I had a luxury car that I rarely drove parked in an underground parking space that I paid way too much for, but those were just things.

My last serious boyfriend was almost a literal year ago, and even he was dating someone new now. Thirty-two — almost thirty-three — shouldn't feel ancient, but I'd had goals ten years ago, and it seemed none of the personal ones were going to be accomplished anytime soon.

Maybe spending the morning with Isobel had been messing with my head, making me think about things I couldn't have. I found myself imagining what it would be like if one thing had gone different last year, but focusing on something like that would only make me miserable.

The part that bothered me about Evan finally getting married was that I couldn't even find a date for his wedding. No one took me seriously enough to look past the outside package.

"Kelly?"

Shit. This was just great. The man saw me half-naked this morning, which was embarrassing enough. This was just the icing on the cake.

"Go away, Nathan."

His deep chuckle made the hair on the back of my neck stand up as I turned away from him, swiping my fingers underneath my eyes. We'd had a brief flirtation months ago, when Chase and Evan had gotten engaged, and we'd exchanged a few friendly text messages, but even those had faded away, kind of like my sex life.

"What's bothering you? You slipped out without anyone noticing. I thought you'd be in there tearing up the dance floor."

I clenched my eyes closed as I willed away my reaction to his voice, that deep timbre setting off something in me that I responded to on some primal level.

"And yet you noticed," I muttered. "Just enjoying the lovely night." I shivered, my voice cracking as I tried to press myself into the window I was leaning against. Maybe I could just disappear into it, and he'd leave me alone to wallow.

"You're so full of shit," he chuckled as he stepped forward, placing one hand above my head on the glass and using his pointer finger on the other to tilt my chin toward him. "What's wrong? Did your date stand you up?"

I hated that he was so tall, it made me feel vulnerable, and I didn't like feeling at a disadvantage. I also didn't like the way his chestnut-colored eyes glowed in the dim lighting, or the neatly styled hair and clean-shaven jaw he sported that was so different than this morning. He looked utterly handsome, and I was a mess.

"Leave me alone," I sighed, averting my eyes, and he clucked his tongue at me.

"Cut the shit, Kelly." My breath caught at the authoritative undertone of his voice, my nipples pebbling under the thin layers of my satin dress. I tried to convince myself it was just the cold, but *damn*, his raw whisper had me shaking from something entirely different. "You don't need to shut me out just because I saw you in your lingerie. If I pushed away everyone who saw me half naked, I wouldn't have any friends left."

"What do you want?" I exhaled as I looked back up into his eyes, challenging him to be honest with me. "Didn't I embarrass myself enough around you this morning?"

"Aren't you a little ray of sunshine?" he laughed humorlessly. "You thought that was embarrassing? I haven't been able to stop thinking about it all day." He paused, his gaze trailing down the front of my dress. "You looked sexy as hell, although I'm sure you'll probably have a hell of a bruise with how hard you went down."

I rolled my eyes, and his grip on my chin tightened, jerking my gaze back in his direction. He narrowed his eyes at me, one eyebrow arching.

"You seem to be doing a pretty damn good job of making a girl feel like she's a desperate mess around you. I can't manage to keep myself from making an ass of myself, and then you laughed at me falling on my actual ass."

The muscles around the sharp cut of his jawline flexed as he tilted my head backward, leaning further into my personal space, one of his feet slipping in between mine and spreading them apart so he could get even closer. "I laughed at the situation, not how you looked. That enticing body hidden under that dress makes me want things that I shouldn't. But I know this is probably my only shot to get you alone, so here I am."

I could smell the alcohol on his breath, but he didn't seem drunk, his dark eyes entirely focused on my face.

"I don't even know what that means." I rolled my eyes again and tried to push him back from me, but he didn't budge. His fingers loosened momentarily before he slipped his warm hand along the side of my neck.

"Stop doing that," he growled as he leaned forward, his dark eyes flaring angrily as he met my challenging gaze.

"Doing what?" Why was my voice so breathy? Damn him.

"Rolling your eyes. It makes me want to bend you over my knee."
Whoa.

"Sorry, I'm not into the whole Daddy thing, *stud*," I sassed, hissing a little as the grip on the side of my neck tightened momentarily.

"I don't want to be your fucking *Daddy*," he growled with disgust. I'd obviously hit a sore spot with my choice of words. He was doing that jaw-clenching thing again, but it'd been hot when he said the word *fucking*. "And I didn't give you permission to call me that."

"Then what do you want?"

His face softened for a moment, his head tilting slightly as he drew in a breath, his chest pressing forward into mine. "I want you to tell me why you're out here crying when I've been trying to find you for the last half hour. I'm worried about you."

"Yeah, right," I scoffed. "Sort of like you've been meaning to return that text I sent you six months ago before I finally realized that you just weren't that interested in me. Because no one is interested in me. I can't even fucking swing a date to my little brother's wedding. He hates people, and he even found someone to marry him."

I hadn't meant to blurt all that out, but I couldn't take it back now, and I watched as a few emotions flitted across his expression: amusement, confusion, pity. That one made me pause. I didn't want his pity or anyone else's.

"Kelly," he sighed, leaning forward, so his lips stopped just barely brushing my ear. "I'm more than interested in you, but I shouldn't be."

Geez, again with the cryptic shit. I knew what he was into. I wasn't naïve. I may joke around and say stupid things, but I wasn't a moron.

"You think I care about that?" I whispered. It seemed that he, too, was used to people judging the book by its cover.

He sighed, his warm breath ghosting along my cheek, "You don't know what you're getting yourself into. My life is complicated."

"Oh, come on," I chuckled, my heart pounding as I placed my hand on his firm chest. "You think a little kink is going to scare me off? I think I can handle myself."

Technically, I'd never actually been involved with someone who used playful spanking, much less the kind I imagined he engaged in, but I had an open mind. I was a big girl; I could handle a little rough sex and being told what to do. At least I had hoped I'd get the chance to try when I'd met him before, but he'd shut that down when he ghosted me.

"What you see in movies doesn't begin to cover it," he whispered, his bottom lip barely grazing my ear lobe. "Books can come close, but even those can't cover the depth of what you'll feel while you're completely surrendering yourself to another person to bring you what you need. A person who knows everything about you. A person who is so focused on your pleasure that they deny themselves to make it better for you."

He paused, releasing his hand, but he didn't move away. "I shouldn't even be touching you, but I can't seem to help myself."

"Then show me," I challenged, my voice breathy and my chest heaving. His solid form was immovable against me, his body heat burning me despite the chill in the air. "If it's that intense, why don't you show me and back up all those intimidating words."

"Oh, beautiful girl, the things I'd like to do to this mouth of yours..." His thumb softly drifted across my bottom lip, pulling it forward softly before his hand disappeared.

"Uh-huh..." I could just imagine what those hands would feel like on the rest of my bare skin, tracing, taunting, pushing past all my boundaries, on me, inside of me, his voice just as rough in my ear as it was now. "I'm listening."

"Are you sure you can handle me, sunshine?" His lips traced along the soft skin behind my ear, slowly tracing down my neck until they reached the delicate lace that tapered off into the cap sleeve covering my shoulder. My back arched into him as I gasped, my hands gripping the open sides of his jacket. He was barely touching me, but that voice and those luscious lips of his were making me forget why I was out here in the first place. "Can I call you that? I keep taking liberties with you that I shouldn't. You should tell me to leave you alone."

"Yeah, that's alright," I nodded as I tried to make my voice sound convincing, but the stuttering moan gave me away. "And I don't want you to leave me alone."

Nathan's hand slipped into the loose hair under my bun as he pulled lightly, angling my head back so he could trace his nose along the neckline of my dress, tugging it lightly with his teeth. His soft hair grazed my neck, and I keened softly, already completely under his spell.

"This sexy dress, and what I know is beneath is making it hard for me to keep my hands off you," he whispered, his voice rough.

41

If this is what it felt like when he was barely touching me, his lips only tracing the exposed skin on my chest and neck, I wasn't sure I would survive him unleashing the full impact of his prowess on me. I already felt like I could combust, my skin hypersensitive of each little nip and kiss, each gentle swipe of his tongue causing erotic images of the two of us to dance behind my eyelids.

"Would you like to see what you *can* handle, sunshine?"

My voice wouldn't work, my lips opening and closing several times before I nodded, my hand coming forward to cradle the back of his head. His lips stopped, the hand on my neck loosening before Nathan let go, quickly reaching back to grasp my hand, raising my arm, and pinning my wrist to the glass next to my head in one smooth motion.

"It's my turn to touch." It was an innocent enough statement, but the way he'd rendered me immobile — his body holding me in place — let me know that he was in control. He wanted to lead. And I was desperate to let him. "Use your words, Kelly. Tell me what you want."

"Take me to your room," I whispered, more than ready to let him do whatever he wanted to me, even though I knew it was impulsive and dangerous. I typically wasn't the one to suggest such a thing, but he needed to be naked. Like *right* now.

"Gladly." His dark chuckle made the hair on my neck stand up again, his grip on my wrist squeezing slightly before he released it, slowly tracing his fingers down the inside of my arm and along my side, gripping my hip and spinning me in front of him as he pushed off the window he'd had me pressed against. "But you need to tell me this is what you really want."

"It is," I promised, my voice breathy but sure. "I want this...I want you."

"Then let's go. Walk," he urged as he pressed his hand against the center of my back.

As we reached the side door to the hotel that I'd escaped out of less than an hour ago, I paused, hoping that I wouldn't run into any of my relatives as we snuck into the building.

That'd be a fun conversation, 'Oh, yeah. Hi, Aunt Karen. This is Nathan. I'm pretty sure he's going to take me back to his hotel room and do unspeakable things to my body after he ties me up, but I'll catch up with you later. Enjoy the cake!'

"As much as I'd be happy to give you a demonstration out here, sunshine, I don't think that you're quite ready for observers. Although I'm sure you would be fire to watch come undone in a room full of people."

My breath caught as he reached around me to pull open the door, waiting for me to walk through. My feet seemed rooted to the spot as I peered inside and scanned the lobby quickly, plotting the fastest route to the elevators.

Thankfully, my parents had decided to get an upgraded room, so theirs was nowhere near mine or Nathan's. They knew I was far from an innocent flower, but doing the walk of shame past your parents in the morning wasn't on anyone's list of priorities, regardless of your age.

"Let's go," he laughed as he slipped around me and reached back, firmly grasping my wrist and tugging me inside behind him. "Just stay behind me. I've got you."

I hid my face in the back of his jacket as he slowly maneuvered across the room, careful to avoid the small group of people in the hallway near the ballroom. By the time he reached the elevators, my heart was ready to beat out of my chest. Maybe this wasn't such a good idea.

"Don't get all shy on me now, sunshine," he whispered as he loosely grasped my hips, flattening his body against the back of mine as we stood in front of the elevator doors. "We're just getting started. Tell me to stop, and I'll just escort you to your door. I won't even offer to tuck you in."

Glancing over my shoulder, I looked back into his eyes, and his pupils dilated as he slowly peeked the tip of his tongue out to wet his top lip. My lips parted slightly, watching the motion and I let out a quiet gasp as the tips of his fingers tightened on my hips, pressing me forward as the swish of the doors opening sounded.

"In we go." He lifted me and took a few short steps into the small space, setting me down in the middle of the small area as he reached back to press a button on the control panel. The doors closed, and I found myself pulled firmly against his solid chest, my wrists held securely behind my back, his mouth at my ear.

"Tell me now what's off-limits, because once I get you out of this sexy as fuck dress, there are all kinds of things I want to do to you."

Clenching my bound hands into fists, I bit back a moan at the barely concealed restraint in his voice, like he might want me just as much as I wanted him.

I don't know what possessed me to say it, but the words slipped out of my mouth without consulting my brain first. "Nothing. I'm yours however you want me. I'll do whatever you want."

A low growl built in his chest, vibrating through me; my eyes dropped closed as shivers caused goosebumps to cover my exposed skin. "You might regret telling me that."

I might...but I was determined to see this through. I wasn't ready to give up the way it felt to be pressed against him, and I was sure the feeling would intensify when all the layers of fabric preventing our skin from touching were gone.

Absently listening to the chime that sounded every time we passed another floor on our journey upward, I let out a harsh breath at the sixth one, and the elevator softly halted. Nathan released my hands as he stepped backward through the open doors, patiently waiting as I turned around and joined him in the hallway.

I was afraid to speak as he grasped my hand and tugged me down the hallway behind him, my heels struggling to keep up with his long strides.

He stopped in front of the door to his room, only a few down from mine, and gently released his hold on me as he reached into the inner pocket of his jacket and extracted the black key card.

One quick swipe against the card reader, and he was disappearing inside, his hand tugging me inside impatiently. My opportunity to check out his room was brief before he'd stripped off his jacket, loosened his tie, and grasped the end of my cloak, yanking it from my shoulders and gracefully dropping it to the floor at his feet.

He took two steps forward, and I flattened my back against the closed-door as both of his large hands caged me in, settling on the wood just to either side of my head. His tongue peeked out again, wetting his lips as he stared down at me, his eyes intense as he slowly closed the distance between us. "I want to taste your sweet mouth. Can I kiss you?"

My heart sped faster as he watched me, not moving any closer without my consent.

"I don't know, can you?" I teased, watching his eyes flare with annoyance, enjoying the little thrill that ran through me at the sight.

"There are plenty of things I can do without kissing you," he taunted. "But I'm not going to touch you unless you ask for it."

Nathan's lips hovered, just out of reach as his warm breath fanned across my lips. His face was the picture of patience as he waited for me to make a move. I could try to play it cool and call his bluff, but we both knew I was borderline desperate; at least it felt like that.

"Kiss me," I begged. My voice was a breathy whimper, knowing there wasn't a reason to fight this.

Soft lips grazed mine momentarily before he tilted his head and then pushed forward again, his tongue coaxing my lips apart as he stole my breath. My palms flattened against the wood on either side of my hips, desperate to grab ahold of him, but after his reaction out in the courtyard, I wasn't sure how he'd take me touching him.

The measured intensity of his kiss was firm but sensual, our lips parting fractionally before he sealed his mouth over mine and drove me into a frenzy with his tongue. My nails bit into the wood beneath my hands, my chest tight before I finally tilted my head and gasped as his lips blazed a trail down my neck, pausing briefly to suck on my collarbone. "I fucking love it when you beg."

"Oh God," I moaned as one of his large hands left the door and quickly pulled down the zipper at the back of my dress, the soft satin and lace falling to the floor in a puddle at my feet with a few tugs of his fingers.

His hand pressed on the center of my back, pulling me up against his chest as he returned to my mouth, resuming his fevered exploration of my lips with his kiss.

When our lips parted this time, he barely gave me a chance to suck in a shallow breath before I was crushed to him, one of his large hands grasping the back of my thigh as he held me up against his chest and turned into the room. It only took a few strides to cross the space toward the bed, and then he was laying me down against the cool sheets, his large body following me up onto the mattress as I hurried back toward the pillows.

"These are hot," he chuckled as he grasped my ankle and slowly pulled my heel loose, dropping it off the side of the bed and repeating the action with the other. "But let's take them off for now. Though, I might let you mark my ass with them later if you're interested."

Unable to respond because I was panting so hard, I nodded, watching as he leaned back on his heels and began to unbutton the cuffs of his dress shirt. He rolled them up to his elbows and loosened his tie before pulling it over his head, slowly crawling over the top of me with the silk grasped in his hand.

"I want to restrain your hands, but only with your consent. Tell me to stop, and this ends," he whispered, looking down to me for confirmation. I nodded, and he shook his head slowly, "Not how this works, sunshine. I need the words. Red means stop."

"Don't stop," I whispered, and an almost predatory grin pulled at his lips, his teeth slowly scraping against his bottom lip.

"Oh, I don't plan to, not unless you say so…" His voice was rough as he leaned forward to whisper in my ear. "Now be a good girl and place your hands above your head."

My eyes widened as he leaned back, slowly kissing my lips as one of his hands traced down my arm, his fingers gripping my wrist and coaxing my hand above my head. I followed suit with the other automatically, and he released me from his kiss, quickly slipping the soft silk of his tie around my wrists. He loosely bound them before he leaned back, dragging both of his warm palms down the inside of my arms, along my sides, his thumbs barely grazing my red lace-covered nipples before they continued their route south.

"Such a pretty, sexy girl. And so fucking soft. Fuck, I could touch you all night."

He made eye contact as he slowly peeled my lace thong from my hips, sliding it down my legs as he leaned back and stepped toward the end of the bed. His hand briefly cupped my ankle, urging my leg outward before he climbed back onto the bed between my outstretched legs.

"And look how wet you are, sunshine," he groaned as he looked down to where I was exposed. "I can see you dripping from here. There wasn't any use fighting this, was there? It's clear you want this as much as I do. Don't you?"

"Oh God, don't stop."

Soft involuntary moans filled the air as his palms pressed flat against my knees, pushing them apart as those large hands resumed their travels north, stopping just short of where I wanted him to touch.

"Please," I panted, my voice almost desperate sounding as his thumbs traced the inside of my thighs, just barely grazing where I was eager for him to explore. "Touch me."

"Hmmm," he growled, and I pressed my head back into the pillow. My fingers grasped the soft cotton above my head from their bound position. They clenched the material as he pressed his thumb into me, dipping in experimentally before he sat back on his heels and sucked the digit between his lips. "So sweet."

"Please," I begged again, hating how my voice sounded, but I couldn't help it. I wanted him — on me, inside me, touching me, teasing me. My hips squirmed against the bed, desperate for any friction as I waited for him to have his way with me.

"So impatient," he taunted in that husky tone, my eyes closing at the rough whisper. "My sunshine is desperate for me to touch her. You can't stop squirming. Empty and aching for me to fill you up."

Normally, a guy giving me such a childish nickname would have driven me insane, but the way his lips moved when he said it made me want to hear him say it more. The only thing I wanted more was to see him moan my name — lips parted in pleasure, but it appeared I was far from in charge during this encounter.

"Would you like me to kiss you here?" he asked, his thumb dipping inside of me again, causing me to arch my back, seeking more friction, wanting to be filled with something more substantial. At least I hoped it was more substantial – the tenting in his dress slacks indicated it might be. Please let him have a decently sized dick or at least the knowledge of what to do with it.

"Do you want me to lick and suck this pretty little pussy until you're sobbing for me to let you cum?"

Holy...yes please.

SIX

Nathan

Minneapolis

As I gazed down at Kelly, watching her chest heave, I knew I shouldn't be doing this. This encounter was skirting the boundaries I'd constructed around myself. I didn't do vanilla. Every failed attempt at a so-called 'normal' relationship over the past ten years had cemented that for me, but there was something about her that made me forget about all the reasons I had to stay away.

Even when romantic feelings had developed, most recently with Marisa — who played with me as Mara — there had been a distinct dynamic to our relationship when we weren't playing. She had a hard time getting herself out of the submissive mindset in her real life, and I needed someone who gave outside the playroom as much as I delivered when it was my turn to be in charge inside the playroom. It led me to feeling unfulfilled because she wasn't comfortable pushing to the edge of my boundaries. That was how I'd gotten mixed up with Grace.

Don't get me wrong, my mouth could get just as filthy as the best of them, but I respected my partners, and Grace skirted that line with everyone she ever worked with. She respected me when she saw me as a peer, but the second I submitted to her, she knew she had the upper hand, and she flaunted it. She was never abusive or intentionally sadistic toward me, but I still was left feeling torn by the scenes we created. I liked the release she provided, but it wasn't the style I'd typically prefer. Before her, I'd never felt shame when I was in a scene. While for some people that intensified their experience, it left me feeling empty in a way I couldn't even explain to myself.

When I was with Kelly, even for the few hours I'd talked and laughed with her at that dinner in New York; I'd admired her sharp wit and her smart mouth. It made me feel things I didn't think I could handle. Like I might have a connection with someone beyond my need to control every facet of our interactions in and out of the bedroom, but I'd already been involved with Marisa at that point. Pursuing Kelly would have compromised my dynamic, so I'd kept things friendly despite my initial attraction.

I had a hard time stepping away from being in charge in every facet of my life. My job gave me a certain amount of power over my crew that fed my need to micromanage. Buildings could tower or crumble at the snap of my fingers, and I craved the rush it gave me when we finished a job ahead of schedule. Much like I craved the high of a scene that went off flawlessly.

"Nathan." My breath caught at her rough whisper, eyes dropping to her stretched out in front of me. She was squirming against the sheets as she waited for me to touch her more. Her eyes were wary, but I could see the excitement in them as she watched me refocus my attention on her. Right. Focus on the almost naked woman you have tied up, Nathan.

This was part of my problem. I had a hard time being mindful of the present — often getting caught in my own thoughts. Analyzing things from every perspective. Part of that was why I had difficulty staying out of the scene. I craved the way it kept me focused. Mindful of where I was and my partner.

"Hmmm," I hummed, a low growl building as I watched her breasts rise and fall with each labored breath. It was a sound I'd been told made women wet, and it seemed to be working right now as I watched her lips part and her eyes dilate in the dim light.

"Are you going to touch me? I *do* want you to kiss me...down there..." Her voice wavered just slightly, but I could tell it was from excitement, not a hesitation to participate.

The flare of defiance in her eyes when I didn't respond right away had me clenching my fingers into her thighs. She was going to be my undoing. It was hard to separate the Dominant part of my personality from the man. It'd been at least five years since I had a partner who was a novice, or in this case, someone as vanilla as I suspected Kelly to be. She may have talked a good game, but she truly didn't know what being with me was getting herself into. Not that this would progress further than this weekend. Or that she'd know half the twisted things her delectable body made me think.

It wasn't that I needed to have a partner involved in all the social parts of the scene, but having a checklist on the table let me know exactly what to expect and what she needed from me to get the most out of our interactions. Boundaries were important to me, and I found myself simultaneously intrigued and scared shitless that I had no idea what Kelly's were. Did I see how far I could push her, or did I try to keep things tame for her sake? I could handle vanilla with a little bit of spice.

"Nathan, please." And she was begging again. *Fuck.* She seemed to know all my weaknesses. "Touch me, please."

"Shhh," I ordered, and I watched as her fingers clenched around the pillow above her head, her hips shifting under my hands. "Stop moving."

Her movements halted, and she gave me a slight nod, her teeth pulling her bottom lip into her mouth. Arching an eyebrow at her, I could tell from the subtle flex in her arms that she was trying to be a good girl and hold still for me. I could work with that.

"Exactly like that, such a good girl. Now, sunshine, I'm expecting you to listen to exactly what I'm about to tell you. Nod if you understand."

Her eyes widened, making my inner caveman roar with anticipation. "Yes."

"I didn't ask for you to talk." Her mouth snapped shut at my correction, and I gave her an appraising look. I rubbed my hands up and down her tense thighs at her nod. "That's a good girl, sunshine."

Waiting a few moments, just to make sure she could continue to be a good listener, I watched her body for subtle cues. Her breaths were heavy, just short of panting, eyes slightly dilated and focused on me, but her jaw was soft. *Good.* Arms remained stretched above her head, perfectly manicured hands gripping the pillow loosely in between her fingers, but not enough to strain. Nice. She was gorgeous in her natural submission.

"If you'd like me to continue," I started as my thumbs rubbed circles just shy of touching her wetness, "I need you to be a very good girl and hold still for me. If you squirm, I stop. Do we understand?"

Her lips parted, but then she snapped them closed again, waiting for me, good girl. "A nod will work."

At her subtle shift in confirmation on the pillow, I knew she might have trouble with this next part, but it'd be worth it for her if she could manage it. "You need to try to stay as still as you can until I

50

tell you otherwise, and when I give you a command, you obey. Understand?"

Another nod. She was a natural.

"That's a very good girl, sunshine." She let out a sound that almost sounded like a purr as her legs shifted in my hands. "One red from you, and we stop. You need to use your voice if you don't like something. Yellow, I slow down. Green means…"

Her eyes widened, and she whispered, "Green…so green."

Closing my eyes to center myself, I slowly caressed her thighs again, feeling the taut muscles relax under my palms. She was so sensual without even realizing it, and the fact that she was already communicating with me was a green flag. The last attempt I'd had at vanilla sex, the woman had told me to shut up when I tried to talk to her about her limits. I didn't even look back as I'd left her apartment with a semi hard dick and a red mark on my cheek from where she'd slapped me after I told her I was going to leave if she didn't grow up.

Something about the Dom/sub dynamic made it easier for me to relax and just do what felt good for both myself and my partner. They knew ahead of time what to expect, and I knew exactly what they needed from me and how. There wasn't a subject that was off-limits in that kind of relationship with my partner, and even if something was a hard limit, we still discussed it without making the other feel like they were pressured into doing something.

When I opened my eyes, I saw Kelly watching me, the anticipation clear in hers. She wanted this, and she wanted me, and I could put the Dominant part of my personality aside a little to make her feel good. I could make her feel *so* good.

"You're stunning, sunshine," I whispered, my hands pushing her thighs up as I shifted down the mattress. "You smell amazing, and your skin is so…so soft. That tease I saw of you this morning had me hard half the day." And imagining what she'd look like if she crawled across the floor toward me in that lingerie…or maybe out of it.

She let out a satisfied sigh as I leaned down toward where I knew she really wanted me and began to kiss across her stomach and the tops of her thighs. Her body relaxed as I kissed and caressed her, teasing her a little as I kept my touch light, pausing to nip at her hip bones before I used my thumbs to spread her wide.

"You look delicious, sunshine." She bit down on her bottom lip, and I could see a blush spread across her cheeks as I praised her, but I could tell she liked it. She was such a good girl. A praise kink was one I loved to fulfill. "There's no need to be embarrassed."

She looked away, her hips shifting slightly, but she was trying not to move.

The flushed quality of her soft, fair skin was enticing, and I couldn't help fantasizing about what it'd look like with faint pink marks from my hand — or maybe with my cum splashed across her pert breasts — her eyes hungry as she looked up at me from her knees.

"Are you ready?" I asked, confirming that she did want this before I dove in. Consent was tricky when you were improvising, so I wanted to make sure she felt comfortable enough to communicate with me, even while in the moment. "I'm dying to touch you, but not unless you want me to."

Her chest heaved as she gave me a small nod, licking her lips before she whispered, "Green."

Leaning forward a little, I reached behind her back and released the clasp on her bra, slowly pushing the soft lace up her arms as far as her bound hands would allow. Soft pink nipples stood at attention, just begging for my tongue, but a quick pinch would have to do until later.

"Ahh," she moaned softly, her eyes closing as I leaned back down to blow my hot breath across her sensitive flesh. Placing my thumb at the top of her mound, I made sure to expose the part of her I intended to worship first.

One palm held her thigh still as I made my first slow lick, her back arching enticingly as I pressed my lips a little more firmly and really started to test her. Her labored breaths were like music to my ears as I worked her up into a frenzy, sliding one finger into her warmth as I licked and sucked. My other hand traveled up her chest, cupping and massaging her breast as I began to slowly fuck her with my finger.

Her eyes slipped closed, and her fingers tightened on the pillow above her head as I worked her up, trying to keep my touch gentle, so she didn't cum, but give her just enough that it felt amazing. The subtle rocking of her hips with my motions made the situation in my dress slacks almost uncomfortably tight, but this was about her. About what I could give her.

"Mmmm," I hummed against her as I could feel her muscles start to pulse inside subtly; she was close. She was so warm and wet and smelled so sweet. I watched with rapt interest as she got right to the edge, so close to cumming, but not quite there yet.

Pulling my finger out, I sucked on her clit one last time, enjoying the way she tried to hold in a moan. We'd have to work on her breath control.

I clenched my jaw to keep from laughing as her eyes blinked open, and she looked at me with disbelief as I sat up. Her mouth opened and closed a few times as I began to kiss my way up her thighs and finally got a taste of those luscious nipples. Her feet shifted against the mattress as I nipped at her and then kissed my way up her neck.

"Still with me, sunshine? Use your words if you'd like."

Kelly pinned me with a determined stare as I crouched over her, not quite touching, completely clothed. I wondered if she'd ever had a man take his time, get her close, and then back off, teasing her into an orgasm so explosive she couldn't feel her face as she shattered below him.

I was guessing not. Some men rushed through the foreplay like it wasn't something to be cherished with their partners.

"Please touch me again," she breathed out, lifting her head slightly toward me and looking at my lips.

"Would you like me to kiss you?" I whispered as my cock pulsed at the thought of her tasting herself off my lips.

"Please," she nodded as she lifted her neck again, straining to try to reach me.

One of my hands reached forward to grasp the tail of the tie, stretching her arms against the headboard as I leaned in and kissed her softly, coaxing hers open with the tip of my tongue. She moaned and shifted a little as I pressed in further, turning my head to deepen it, kissing her frantically until I had to pull away to breathe. There was something so hot about a woman not being afraid to kiss me after I'd pleasured her.

"What do you need?" I breathed in her ear as I nipped at the lobe, loving the catch in her breath as I gripped the tail of the tie a little tighter and pressed my clothed hips down into her.

"Uh…" she whimpered as I kissed along the side of her neck.

"Tell me, Kelly."

She moaned in my ear as I ground myself against her, wishing I could feel her against my skin. My cock throbbed as she pressed up against me and hooked one of her legs around my calf.

"Use your words, beautiful, and I'll give you whatever you want."

"Touch me," she whispered, her voice hoarse, "make me cum."

Fuck. Now that, I could do. If she were mine, I'd edge her until she couldn't take it anymore, but I didn't know what her limits were. Knowing that this was probably the only opportunity I would get to worship this gorgeous body of hers, I was going to throw my typical restraint out of the window and just do to her what I'd fleetingly imagined the last few months.

She thought I was ignoring her, but I'd been trying to stay away from her. Even through text messages, I knew that I would quickly become attached, which was dangerous for me. I was involved with Grace, and while she had multiple partners, I knew she didn't like her subs being shared. If I started dating someone from across the country, she would have an opinion on that, and I wasn't ready to let go of the release she provided me. I also hadn't known then that my relationship with Marisa would fall apart.

Kelly was writhing against me as I kissed my way back down her body, biting her taut nipples and getting the most beautiful moan in response. By the time I settled in between her legs, her cries were increasing in pitch, turning to choked gasps as I plunged two fingers inside and curled them, massaging her until I could feel her clench.

"That's it, sunshine. You're such a good girl. Look at me, let me see your eyes," I coaxed as she moaned again, her back arching up from the mattress as she tried to maintain eye contact with me. "Not yet, just a little longer."

"Oh God," she moaned loudly as her eyes slipped closed and her hips undulated against my hand. I resumed sucking on her clit softly, rolling the tip of my tongue around the sensitive flesh, teasing her nerves as my fingers continued to plunge in and out of her.

"Kelly, look at me," I commanded, my voice low as I looked up toward her from between the V of her legs. She gasped as I felt her clench against my fingers again, and I knew she was right on edge. "Right fucking now, sunshine. Cum."

Her eyes opened again, and I watched the slight changes in her pupil as she plunged over the edge, pulsing against me. Milking my fingers in the most sensual way.

"Oh, Nathan, don't stop. Oh my God," she sobbed as I continued to coax her further into her release. Her back arched as she moaned again, and I knew if I kept this up, she could probably have multiples. Leaning down, I latched onto her clit and grazed it with my teeth before sucking it into my mouth. After a few more nips and a little more suction, I could tell she was on the edge again. I sped up the movements of my hand, coaxing her body until her toes curled against the mattress, and she thrust her hips up, practically screaming my name.

"Oh, fuck, Nathan. Oh…"

Slowing my movements, I kissed my way up her stomach, pausing to caress her breasts as I kissed her neck softly. She was spectacular. "That was amazing. Such a gorgeous girl. You did so well."

"Mmmm," she hummed with her eyes closed, sated against the pillows.

"Are you ready for more?" I whispered as I crawled up the mattress and laid down next to her, my fingertip tracing a line from her neck, across the peak of her breast and lower, softly touching her skin. Her hips jerked as I slipped my finger inside, softly fucking her with it as she began to shift against the soft sheets again.

"How…" she panted as she turned her head to look over at me. "How are you still clothed?"

I couldn't help but chuckle at her, silly girl. Now I was convinced she'd never had a man take his time with her. "There's no rush."

"Well," she sighed as she shifted to turn onto her side. "I'm kind of curious what you look like underneath all those clothes. You've known what I look like all day."

"That I have. And what a visual it was to see you like that. Legs wide open, all that lace. Your gorgeous unblemished skin." I grinned, leaning forward, and kissing her lightly as I released her hands. Pressing my thumbs into her palms, I rubbed lightly, slowly tracing my fingers down her wrists and her forearms, massaging out the stiffness as I leaned back and pulled her into my chest. "Let's give you a little break from that. How are you feeling?"

An adorable little sly grin pulled at her lips as she looked down and toyed with one of the buttons on my dress shirt. "Is it bad that I enjoyed that?"

"Why would that be bad?" I chuckled as I tilted her chin up so I could see into her eyes. "You did amazingly well. Have you..." I trailed off as she shook her head.

"No, I've never been tied up."

"Hmm...Thank you. For trusting me with something like that. You did great." I tucked her head into my chest, running my fingers across her shoulders and pulling the straps of her bra loose, and tossing it to the floor behind her. We'd only seen the tip of the iceberg, but she'd done well with a simple restraint. Would she be shocked or aroused at my playroom in Boston, where I had a cabinet full of rigging equipment and restraints? A grid most people thought was for décor hanging from the ceiling, reinforced to hold the weight of a grown adult, or maybe two.

"Hah," she laughed against my shoulder, "I'm pretty sure I should be the one thanking you."

She traced her hands up my shirt to my shoulders, seeming hesitant as her fingertips touched the skin just above my collar. "You can touch me, sunshine."

"I wasn't sure...outside in the courtyard you seemed uncomfortable when I touched your neck."

I shook my head, leaning back so I could look at her face. "I was trying to show restraint. It wasn't you touching me. I just knew we needed to find somewhere more private, or I would go insane. You have no idea what your touch was doing to me, making me throb for you. Can't you tell how hard you make me?"

"Hmm," she hummed as she slipped her hand up my neck and she traced my bottom lip with the fingers on the other hand.

Playfully nipping at her fingertips, I hummed out a little growl and rolled her backward, grasping both of her hands above her head, interlacing our fingers as I covered her body with mine. "You're so unfuckingbelievably sensual. You have no idea how hot that is."

She plunged her tongue into my mouth as our lips collided, hips pressed together, her feet sliding along the material of my dress pants. Panting as she turned her head to the side, leaning over slightly to whisper in my ear. "I need you to fuck me, Nathan. Please, I want to feel you."

"Oh fuck," I groaned as I released her hands and leaned back, sitting up on my knees as I started to unbutton my shirt. She leaned forward slightly, making quick work of unbuckling my belt, unbuttoning my trousers, and yanking down my zipper. I stilled her hands as I grasped the edge of my belt buckle, whipping it out of the pant loops in one practiced swoop. Her eyes widened as she laid back against the pillows, watching as I folded the leather strap in half, snapping it twice before I tossed it off the edge of the bed to the floor.

"That was cute. Very intimidating." She raised an amused eyebrow as she watched me finish unbuttoning my shirt, shrugging it off my shoulders, and reaching back to pull it off. Her eyes felt like a caress as she gazed at my naked torso, studying the small cluster of tattoos across my ribcage and along my forearm. They weren't as large or detailed as others in the scene, simply a small group of birds, tribal art, and some text.

"Can I?" she asked as she held her hand up toward me. I hated that I'd made her wary of touching me earlier — when I was trying to hold myself back — but the fact she was checking in with me meant that she respected my boundaries. That was the kind of consideration in the bedroom that often couldn't be taught.

Grasping her hand, I tugged her forward, placing her palm on my chest as she rose to her knees. Soft fingers traced my skin as I looked down at her studying the marks on my body, her gentle touch igniting the need to claim deep inside of me. When she leaned down to kiss the skin over my heart, I cupped her jaw, lifting her face as I kissed her softly at first, and then more aggressively as she flattened her breasts against my chest. The feel of her soft skin against mine was even more potent than I thought it would be.

Kelly's small hands shoved at the waistband of my pants as I held her in place, stealing her breath with my tongue. A groan built in my chest as she plunged her small hand into my open waistband and grasped me firmly in her fist.

"Fuck," I panted as I looked up toward the ceiling.

"That's the idea," she laughed as she pressed her hand to the center of my chest and pushed lightly. "We definitely need to fuck."

Laughing at her candid demeanor returning and the subtle ways she was trying to get me to submit to her movements, I shook my head and stepped off the side of the bed, quickly removing my shoes and socks and pushing my pants to the floor. I pulled protection from the back pocket and then climbed back on the bed, throwing it toward the pillow as I grasped her neck and kissed her again, finally feeling her fully skin to skin. It'd been so long since a partner was in sync with me, asserting their own wants as we dropped to the pillows, and she climbed on top of me.

"Is this OK?" she asked as she leaned forward and grasped the condom, tearing it open with her fingers.

"You can take whatever you want, sunshine." I grinned as a wicked little smile pulled at her lips.

She placed one hand on my chest, leaning forward to whisper into my ear. "You might regret telling me that," she growled my own words in my ear, reaching down between us to stroke my hard cock as she nipped at my bottom lip.

Maybe she was channeling her Domme side a bit. It made the Switch inside of me desperate to have her telling me what to do. She'd be glorious with a whip. She was already impressive, sitting astride my hips with my aching cock in her hands.

"I doubt it," I whispered against her lips as I kissed her. "Use me, gorgeous. I can't wait to see you ride my cock."

She made quick work of sheathing me, and I reached down with one hand to hold myself still as she lined up and lowered herself onto me.

"Goddamn," I moaned as she pressed herself down completely, rocking a little bit as she settled against my thighs. She was so fucking tight and wet, and it was amazing. "This is fucking bliss. God, keep going. Just like that."

"You like that, stud?" she whispered as she planted her hands on either side of my head, forcing her hips to mine in a steady rhythm that had me closing my eyes and panting as I grasped her waist.

"Fuck yes," I groaned as she swiveled her hips and sped up, moaning against my lips as she used me to pleasure herself. It was fucking amazing watching her ride me as she wanted without hesitation. She could go as long and as hard as she wanted. "Bounce on my cock, sunshine. Use me to make yourself feel good."

"Oh, Nathan," she groaned as she leaned back, arching her back, her chest thrust out as she placed a hand behind her on my thigh to brace herself. I reached up and grasped one of her tits as she roughly rocked herself against me, lightly pinching her nipple, slowly increasing the pressure as her moans got louder.

Her hips faltered momentarily, and I could tell she was getting close. Deciding to help her out a little, I leaned up from the bed, cradling the backs of her shoulders as I sat up and pulled her flush with my chest. "That's it, sunshine, cum for me," I growled in her ear as she cried out, gasping, and pulsing against me after a few more rough thrusts.

"I'm not done with you yet," I whispered in her ear as she came down, her fingers grasping the hair at the back of my head as she fought to catch her breath. "Get on your hands and knees."

Helping her to climb off me, I ran my palm down the length of her back, pausing to squeeze that peach of an ass as she pushed herself up onto all fours. Rising to my own knees behind her, I lined up and pushed back inside of her warmth, my eyes closing as I groaned when I felt how wet she was.

"Scream for me," I moaned as I started thrusting into her, watching with rapt interest as her fingers grasped the pillowcase above her head. Her back arched as I pounded into her, my hands gripping her hips tightly. "Let everyone know how good it feels to have my cock making you cum, over and over and over. Fuck, you're so fucking tight."

"Fuck," she whined as I felt her body tense, her head dropping to the pillow as she leaned further forward. "It feels so good."

I stretched myself over her back, kissing along her shoulders and her neck as I ground myself into her, reveling in her gasps and whimpers. "I need you to cum for me again," I commanded as I reached beneath her and found where we were joined, pressing into her firmly and circling as her moans increased in volume. "Milk me with that pussy."

"Oh…oh, fuck…oh…oh…" she moaned as she bit down on the pillowcase, her body shuddering in my arms.

"That's a good girl, fuck…yes," I moaned as I snapped my hips forward harder, her moans increasing in volume as I fucked her roughly through her orgasm, chasing my own.

"Please," she whispered as she pressed back into my movements, and I groaned as I lightly nipped the back of her shoulder, pulsing into her. "Oh, God."

Blowing out a breath, I pulled out and collapsed back onto the pillow at her side, pulling Kelly tightly against my chest and pushing the loose hairs back from her forehead with my fingertip. She was stunning, and I dreaded having to leave her after this weekend.

I wanted to keep seeing her, but I needed to go back to Boston, and she needed to go back to Chicago. Her life was there, and mine was back home, with all the responsibilities and commitments I desperately wanted to throw away just to spend more time wrapped up in her.

"Breathe for me," I whispered into her forehead as I kissed her lightly, tracing my fingers over the back of her neck and down her back, nestling her into my chest as tightly as I could.

"I can't feel my lips," she giggled against my chest — voice slightly strained — her fingers tracing my collarbone. "I think you fucked me numb."

My inner voice roared with her appraisal, but I needed to ensure she was alright with what we'd done. It was intense, and I knew that she'd not been restrained before. And from the way she'd responded, she liked the dirty talk too. While it was a far cry from an actual scene, I didn't want her regretting what had happened between us once the endorphins wore off. I'd gone slow for her benefit, but I had a feeling she'd beg for more if she knew I was holding back.

"How do you feel? You can be honest with me," I encouraged as I traced the soft skin of her back. Her fingers toyed with my hair as she laid her cheek against my chest, her legs entangled with mine.

"I feel like I don't want to go home."

"I was just thinking the same thing," I whispered back as I tightened my arm around her waist, desperately wishing I had a way to keep her. The feel of my hand slowly caressing her back was just as calming for me as it likely was for her. She was so warm, and soft, and pliant in my arms. "My tickets are for Sunday night."

She looked up at me, her eyes soft, expression open. "I'm supposed to drive home Monday."

"Hmm…so we've got time."

"I also feel like I want to do that again," she smiled as she leaned forward to kiss my chest. "And then maybe again another time as well, just to make sure we cover all our bases."

Chuckling against her hair, I flattened my palm against her back, slowly tracing it down until I could grasp that ass of hers and pull her hips flush with mine. "You can cover me with whatever you want. All my bases are yours to claim."

"Oh really?" she giggled as she pressed herself against me as tightly as she could. "We'll have to see what room service can deliver this late."

"I could use a second helping of dessert," I whispered as I leaned down and nipped at her ear, pulling her up my body. My hand pressed between her legs, and I dipped a finger into her from behind, feeling myself awaken as her hand grasped my shoulder, her nails digging into my skin. She was still so wet, so ready for me. "You have no idea how fucking good you taste on my tongue."

I still couldn't see a way to have more than just this weekend with her, but I was going to make the most of the time we had left. As she squirmed against my chest, her body so responsive to my touch, I knew I had to have her as many times as I could before this was over.

"Get the fuck up here and sit on my face."

She giggled as I dragged her up my body, caressing her thighs as she looked down at me with a nervous smile. There was something about her that had me addicted already, and I knew she could easily destroy my life with more of those smiles.

SEVEN

Kelly

Chicago

Glancing down at my phone, I pulled open my text messages, as I often found myself doing, scrolling through the last text from Nathan, hating that our relationship seemed to start and end in the same weekend. It'd been almost two months since we'd spoken, but he still lingered in my thoughts.

Nathan: I hope your drive tomorrow goes well. My flight just got in. Please take care of yourself. x

Instead of responding, I'd cried myself to sleep that night, all alone in my hotel bed, wishing I was somewhere else, *with* someone else. I was dreading the loneliness settling in, and I found myself regretting that I had ghosted him as he'd initially done to me after we met, but we both knew it'd never work. Our lives were too different, and they were a thousand miles apart. He hadn't texted me since then either, but I couldn't imagine him giving me a second thought.

I should be socializing, enjoying the night out with my colleagues, but I couldn't muster my normal enthusiasm with my two best friends missing. My boss Tom and his wife Charley were probably already asleep, the two of them exhausted as the end of her pregnancy neared.

I'd been forced into an after-hours department dinner after the successful launch of the web infrastructure of a huge client. When several of my co-workers moved to the bar down the street, I'd tried to beg off, but they'd guilt tripped me into coming with them.

So far they'd been grinding on random men on the small dance floor at the back of the bar while I'd been alternating between scrolling through my email and watching grown professionals behave badly.

The office douchebag, Trent, had been hitting on the newer female employees again, and it was painful to watch him continually get shot down when he started not so humbly bragging about himself.

He'd tried his moves on me several times in the last few years, and I was glad he was leaving me alone for once.

As I scrolled through the notes Tom had emailed me regarding his upcoming paternity leave, a hand settled at the small of my back and startled me.

"You're supposed to be having fun." The hair on the back of my neck stood up as I tried to lean away from the touch, turning to glare at Trent. "What're you drinking? I'll buy you another one." He nodded toward my empty glass; the one old fashioned I'd indulged in drained with a rapidly melting ice cube in the bottom.

"I'm good. I don't need another one. Just some water." Not wanting to be outright rude to him, knowing that he could get belligerent if he thought he was being dismissed, I turned on my stool, dislodging his hand from my back subtly in the process.

He waved toward the bartender, catching his attention as I scooted my stool away, hopefully discouraging his wandering hands.

"The lady will take another, put both on my tab." Trent gestured to my empty glass.

Frowning at his inability to listen, I placed my hand over my empty glass. "I'm done. Just a glass of water, please." The bartender glanced between us, taking in my tense posture and grabbed my empty glass, placing it beneath the bar top. He pulled out a clean glass, filled it with ice and used the tap to fill it with water.

Trent scowled at the bartender as he gave me a wink and disappeared to the next waiting customer. "Oh, come on, I know we have to work, but it'd wouldn't kill you to relax a little."

"I've got a lot on my plate and can't afford to be hungover tomorrow. I know where my limits are."

"Hmmm," he nodded, leaning in close as his fingers grazed the back of my hand where it rested on the bar. "We could always get out of here and I can make sure to tuck you into bed early."

While I was sure those kinds of lines worked for him, I wasn't interested, and certainly not when I watched him try to work the room for the last hour and get shot down. I wasn't desperate or lonely enough to fall for his charm, what little he did have. And I definitely didn't want him to know where I lived.

"I think I'm fine on my own." Grabbing my water, I downed half the glass and pulled up the Uber app on my phone, requesting a ride. There was no way I'd risk walking to the closest L station without

Tom to keep me company when Trent was clearly hitting on me, again. I didn't think he'd try something, but I'd heard enough stories to be wary of his temper tantrums. "Early day tomorrow, but I know how to tuck myself in."

"Doesn't it get lonely pining after a man who isn't available?"

Fuck. Just because I spent a lot of time with Tom didn't mean that I was interested in him like that. People around the office had thought I was dating Thomas a few years ago, but he reminded me too much of Evan back then. He was awkward and kept to himself, preferring to email people rather than speaking face-to-face. He'd changed a lot in the last five years, but sometimes I still got glimpses of the slightly insecure twenty-seven-year-old he'd been when I first met him.

"He's my friend, and he's married — to my other friend. Don't believe every piece of office gossip you hear — or start."

"Could have fooled me. He seemed pretty adamant that you take over as interim department head while he was out. There were plenty of other people who were just as qualified that would have appreciated having a chance, but he didn't even take open requests."

"Trent, just...don't. Don't start this fight. I've been with the company just as long as Tom has and have seniority over you and everyone else in our division. This wasn't nepotism, this was hierarchy, and I have several more years under my belt than you do." And was almost a decade older than him.

Trent had joined the company two years ago, fresh out of grad school and his work ethic was solid, but he was an arrogant jerk who had bragged about every successful project he'd worked on since he started. His questionable behavior around the women of our office hadn't earned him any friends either.

"Nepotism, my ass," he grumbled and opened his mouth to respond further, but luckily my phone chimed indicating my ride was here.

"As lovely as this has been, my ride awaits." Gathering up my purse and work bag, I slid a twenty across the bar to cover my drink and took off toward the exit before Trent could follow.

When I looked back as I stepped through the entrance, he was glaring at me from his place at the bar, clearly not liking that I'd blown him off again, but some people just couldn't take the hint.

The next morning, I came in early and got to work, going through all the notes in my inbox and trying to ignore the text thread from Nathan. He'd been a frequent star in my dreams as of late, and I knew I needed to forget what happened, or at least move on. But two months later, I was still desperately single, and my only prospects were the office asshole and my vibrator. As I unlocked my phone again, I scanned through the last messages, wishing we'd left the line of communication open.

"Hey."

Startling, I locked the screen and tossed my phone onto a folder sitting on my desk. Right...I should be working. Not daydreaming about the best sex I'd ever had, with a man who was so sexy I couldn't think straight, who also lived halfway across the country and was probably off seducing other women with his dangerous neckties. That'd be bad to do while on the clock.

"Hey!" I knew my voice was overly bright, and Thomas would see right through me, but I needed to stop obsessing over Nathan. Move on with my life. Like that was even possible. "How are you? Charley about to pop yet?"

Thomas was technically my boss, but we'd started at the tech company we worked for around the same time. His wife was hugely pregnant, but still adorable, one of those women who glow with pregnancy and only had a modest bump that made you think she was five months pregnant, not nearly full term. She'd recently gone on maternity leave, her job as a Human Resources manager in our company being temporarily filled until she could get back to work in a few months. She was also a managing partner's daughter, but luckily, she didn't flaunt her status as the boss' daughter, often poking fun at his expense. Her bright and bubbly nature was the antithesis of her stoic father.

"Any time now," he laughed, tapping his hand on the frame of the door. "Can I check in with you real quick? I know you've got it handled, but contracts are signed with the Jacobsen Group, and I need to make sure you're up to speed before I'm out for the next few weeks."

"Sure," I nodded. "Your office or mine?"

He stepped toward my desk, tossing the folder that he'd been holding onto the center and sitting down on the edge of my desk. I was lucky that he wasn't a hardass like some other department heads. Charley even joked that I was his work wife since we seemed to contact each other constantly for various time-sensitive projects.

"These are the latest updates on what their people sent over for the infrastructure they'd like built with their online ordering system. I talked with the guys in IT, and they've guaranteed that they can get the work done on time, but you know how it goes with debugging. I need you to stay on their asses while I'm gone, make sure that no one drops any balls here. Or Deacon will have *my* balls."

"Pfft. Like your father-in-law will do anything other than scold his golden boy," I laughed as he leaned in and playfully kicked the corner of my chair. He knew I was right, though; he'd been the star in our group of new hires, quickly rising to the top and securing a promotion. A few people in the office joked it was because he was dating Charley, but her dad hadn't known they were involved with each other until after he'd been promoted. "Don't worry. I'll keep your balls jiggling...I mean juggling."

"Don't even start me on that," he rolled his eyes. "He made me change assistants again."

Ugh. Deacon was one paranoid motherfucker. He was a great boss, but after his secretary tried to file a sexual harassment lawsuit against him because he wouldn't promote her without any real professional qualifications, he was cautious about any interoffice flirting of any sort. It was an unspoken rule that HR had to know you intended to date a co-worker — NEVER a subordinate or superior — before you even smiled at the person the first time. It'd cut down on the interoffice fucking that sometimes happened, but it was still awkward if Deacon caught you casually talking to another co-worker.

We often socialized together outside of the office — like the bar outing last night — and I knew there were people slyly hooking up, but it wasn't like the on-call room in *Gray's Anatomy* in the copy room anymore. He'd also installed cameras in the hallways outside the executive offices, which was slightly creepy. But in his defense, when a twenty-year-old gold digger threatens your livelihood, a little caution was understandable.

"What was wrong with Gianna?" She was the least likely person I'd see to go after Thomas. She was quite open that she liked to lick tacos on the weekend, so he wasn't even on her radar. He was cute, but no lesbian was going to jump ship to get in his pants suddenly.

"He said that she was *too* friendly."

"What?" I frowned as I tilted my head to the side. "What in the actual fuck is that nonsense? I thought you liked working with her?"

"I did," he shrugged. "She was great. Organized, friendly with my clients, didn't take shit from the programmers, but you know how he is. He reassigned her to Coleen."

Holding in the snort was hard, but I somehow managed to do it. Coleen was pan, so that was bound to be an interesting match-up because I knew for a fact that she liked dark-haired snarky individuals, which Gianna was both. Now, *there* might be an office romance brewing.

"So much for trying to prevent something inappropriate," I laughed as he grinned at me.

"I know, right?" he laughed as he leaned in toward me. "Charley said the same damn thing."

"Is there anything I can do for you guys?" I knew he was nervous about being out of the office for the next several weeks, and there were a few assholes — cough, Trent — who were unhappy I was the one taking the helm for our division while he was gone, but we had it handled. Thomas had given me a full debrief on all our outstanding clientele, and he'd even made me a long-ass list covering all the possible project parts I'd need to check in on.

"Nah," he shook his head. "She's in full-on nesting mode. This baby is going to come home to the cleanest house imaginable and shit all over the white stuff she insisted we needed in the nursery."

"Ew, gross, Tom."

"Oh, come on," he laughed. "I've been around my nieces. Babies are gross. If there is one thing I've learned from my sister, don't put white on children under the age of ten. It's just a hot mess waiting to happen."

"Noted," I shook my head at him. "Not that I'll probably ever need that information. Maybe I can pass it along to Chase someday."

"Kell, stop," he sighed. "Some lucky guy is going to come to sweep you off your feet, and you'll settle in the burbs near your parents and have a dozen smart-mouthed little clones of yourself."

"Not likely." Ever. "But sure…I'll get right on that."

"How are the newlyweds?" he asked as he leaned forward to whisper. "Any advance copies of their new book on hand?"

"Quit using me to get to my brother," I laughed as I pushed on his shoulder. "Just because your wife gets off to their dirty books doesn't mean you can use me to feed her addiction."

He cracked up laughing, his foot pushing my chair out, my hand gripping the desk right next to his to keep myself from tipping backward. "Careful there, big boy."

"Hey, Kelly…oh…"

My eyes widened at Trent standing in the office doorway. He was one of the assholes who was not happy with my position being higher up the food chain than his. He also didn't like that I turned him down on multiple occasions because he creeped me the fuck out, like his unsubtle advances at the bar last night.

"Hi, Trent," I frowned as he looked between Thomas and me, his eyes narrowing on our hands next to each other on the desk. "What can I do for you?"

"Oh, uh. If you guys are *busy* I can come back later."

"No, man," Thomas told him as he stood from my desk and tapped the folder he'd given me. "Just making sure Kelly has everything she needs for when I'm out. Don't give her too much of a hard time when she's your boss for a few weeks."

I could tell by the way his lips twisted at Thomas' words that Trent was not thrilled with me being in charge — as if his very vocal protests in our last staff meeting weren't already enough.

"Yeah. I'll make sure to take it easy on her." His tone was hard, probably unlike the thing in his pants could get, if office gossip was anything to go by.

"I'll be checking in by email with her, so make sure to relay anything you need me to go over through her."

Oh, shit. By the way his eyebrows rose, I could tell that he was not happy about Thomas telling him that he had to go through me. While I appreciated that Thomas reinforced that I was in charge in his absence, Trent was clearly unhappy with me.

Probably because when I'd turned him down more than a dozen times in the last three years like I had last night, he was an arrogant jerk every single time. His ego had a hard time seeing when a woman was not interested in him. He was likely one dick punch (from me) or sexual harassment complaint (from every other person with a vagina in the office) away from being fired, but he continued to make us all miserable until he pushed it too far.

He was also permanently attached to Deacon's right ass cheek. If Trent's terrible self-tanning lotion didn't make him look like an Oompa Loompa, you'd be able to see how brown the tip of his nose was from all the time he spent with it up our boss' ass.

"I'll run any questions I have while you're gone through Deacon, but I'm sure Kelly will do fine while you're off with your *wife* and your *baby.*"

Motherfucker…this again.

"Yeah, poor Thomas off with his super-hot wife and adorable new baby and me here for eighteen hours a day picking up the slack."

Thomas grunted, probably trying to hold in a laugh, but I was so tired of the men in this office thinking I was a decorative prop. I gave my life to this job, and it wasn't like I had anything else to distract me from kicking ass at it. An entitled douche canoe with a God complex wasn't going to put me down to make himself feel better for being hung like a chipmunk.

"Anyway, good talk, Trent." Thomas cleared his throat as he stood from the desk. Trent stepped to the side but lingered in the doorway as Tom left, eyeing me suspiciously as he gripped the edge of my door frame in his tiny hand.

"Was there something you wanted?" I asked as I scooted my chair back up to my desk, opening the folder Tom had left me. "If you hadn't noticed, my plate is kind of full."

"Your mouth too," he muttered, and my jaw clenched, my hand tensing on the paper in my hand.

"Excuse me?"

"Well, it has to be good for something," he smirked as he started to push my door closed. "I'm sure you're a greedy little bitch."

"Are you fucking kidding me? Don't you dare close that door," I hissed, pushing back from my desk, standing from my chair, and straightening out my skirt.

"What are you going to do about it?" Trent taunted as he took a menacing step toward my desk. "Just because that big mouth of yours has gotten you in Tom's good graces doesn't mean anyone else in this office has to respect you. Whores like you are replaceable."

"What the fuck is wrong with you? Is this because I wouldn't let you take me home last night?" As he stopped in front of my desk, I shook my head as he reached over to pick up my abandoned folder.

69

Slamming my hand down on the edge of it, I leaned into his face, trying my best to keep my voice quiet. "This is work that was assigned to me by our supervisor. It'd be in your best interests if you took your hands off this confidential paperwork and went back to your office. If you leave now, I'll even skip my trip to HR to file a harassment complaint about the blatant lies and inappropriate language that came out of your big mouth a few seconds ago."

"Bitch," he hissed as he released the folder.

"Yup, that's me. A total bitch, but for the next few weeks, I'm the bitch you're reporting to, so get used to it."

He growled, narrowing his eyes at me as he leaned in, his breath stale with coffee wafting into my personal space. "You think I don't know how you got where you are? Maybe Deacon didn't need to worry about that gold-digging assistant of his. He's got a little skank ready to get on her knees and open her mouth to further her career a few doors down from his office."

"Get out," I growled through clenched teeth. I didn't have time to deal with his shit, but I wasn't about to sit here and take his abuse. "Walk back through that door and stay the fuck out of my way while Thomas is gone, or I'll make your life hell. You're taking it too far this time."

He shook his head, backing off and heading for the door, tucking his middle finger behind his back as he stopped in the open doorway.

"Good luck keeping shit together. You're going to need it."

"Fucking dick," I sighed, my hands shaking as I collapsed back into my chair.

While I knew I should be drafting a report to HR about his increasingly aggressive behavior toward me, I also knew that I didn't have time.

We were already on a crunch to get one of my client's internal web infrastructures into place before the end of the quarter, but adding the preliminary planning from the Jacobsen account on top of it would keep me here half the night. I could easily work from home after hours, but the servers here were faster, and if I was going to do a final test of the system, I needed the extra boost.

My unpleasant interaction with Trent was forgotten as I lost myself in work, my lunch sitting uneaten in the mini fridge in the corner. Most people hated working until their eyes crossed, but it helped keep my mind off the other things in my life that weren't going to plan. And not having anyone at home to give a crap if I was still at work made it easier to keep going.

"Kelly," the speaker on my phone chimed with an interoffice page, and I pulled off my blue-light blocking glasses, hitting the speakerphone button to connect with Deacon's assistant, Angela.

"Yeah, I'm here," I responded, distracted as I continued to verify I had all the changes the clients had requested completed before I moved on to proofing the copy on the next part of the site.

"Deacon would like to speak to you in his office."

"Right now?" I asked as I took my hand off the mouse and sat back in my chair.

"Yes. He's leaving for the day in an hour, and he needs to speak to you at your earliest convenience."

We both knew 'at your earliest convenience' meant, 'right the fuck now.'

"I'll be right there. Give me three minutes."

"I'll let him know," she confirmed before I heard the chime that the speaker had disconnected.

Fuck me. What did he want at 4:00 pm on a Friday?

I closed out my computer, locking the system down and putting the files I'd been working on in the locked drawer in my desk. Thomas often thought I was paranoid for making sure my projects were never left out unattended, but I didn't trust a few people, namely Trent, to stay out of my office while I wasn't in it.

My suit blazer was hanging on the back of my office door, so I quickly pulled the wrinkles out of my blouse and pulled it on, carefully arranging my sleeves to peek out at the edge of the cuff. I kicked off my flats, trading them in for the uncomfortable heels I kept hidden behind my door, and let out a deep breath before I walked down the hallway to Deacon's corner office.

I was no stranger to the walk, but usually, it was with Tom by my side as we headed to an executive meeting, never because I was being summoned by myself.

"Go on through," Angela instructed, only glancing up at me momentarily before returning her attention to her computer screen. She wasn't always the most talkative person — reminding me of an older uptight school administrator — but she'd never been outright frosty before.

71

Knocking to alert him to my presence, I pushed open Deacon's office door and paused as I took in the woman sitting in the chair in front of his desk. Charley's temporary maternity replacement, Helen, looked over her shoulder at me, an eyebrow arched high on her pointed face. She was the former head of Human Resources for our entire company, but she'd retired last year to spend more time with her grandkids. You'd think that'd make her a warm and fuzzy type with cat sweaters and mints in her purse, but she was scary as hell, and I'd seen her make grown men cry.

"Have a seat, Ms. Stineman." Deacon nodded at the other open chair, and my palms started to sweat as I took my seat and tucked my legs to the side.

"This is my last meeting for the day, so let me make this as brief as I can. We've received an anonymous complaint that you've been sexually harassing your co-workers."

My mouth moved, but I couldn't quite formulate words. Was this a joke?

"Excuse me?"

"While Thomas has assured me that the accusations made against you are false, I have no choice but to send you on a sabbatical for the next eight weeks while we conduct an internal investigation into some of the other accusations this person made."

What the actual fuck? I had no idea where this was even coming from. I rarely talked to my co-workers about anything other than work, much less doing something to constitute harassment. I sat stunned, trying to figure out what was going on before my mind raced back to earlier.

"Was it Trent?" I knew I should have taken a break and filed the complaint after his behavior in my office earlier in the day, but I didn't think he'd resort to something like this. Allegations of sexual harassment, regardless of your gender, were serious business in any corporate culture. This had the potential to not only cost my job, but now my entire future stood on shaky ground. If they fired me, word would spread and I'd be tainted, untouchable.

"I'm afraid we are not allowed to divulge any additional details until we've completed our investigation into your behavior in the workplace." Helen's quiet voice was sympathetic, but she was still looking at me like I was a naughty kid sitting in the principal's office, which I felt like right now.

"I'd like to file a complaint. Mr. Alsop cornered me in my office this afternoon and insinuated that I was having an affair with your son-in-law. He threatened me and said some very sexually inappropriate things to me. He's also propositioned me out of the office several times."

Deacon sat down at his desk, shaking his head as he blew out a breath. "Is there a reason you didn't go to Helen when the incident occurred today? Or even tell Tom what was going on?"

Closing my eyes, I cursed my hatred of conflict and my singular focus when I was on a deadline. "I had a project that needed my full attention, but I should have made time to talk to her. It's not the first time Trent's said something inappropriate to me, but he was abnormally aggressive in his comments this morning."

"This doesn't change your mandatory sabbatical, but we will take action on this in your absence." Deacon's voice was compassionate, but he was still resolute.

"That's it? I'm being banned from the office because he lied to Human Resources?"

"Ms. Stineman," Deacon cleared his throat. "We take any allegations of misconduct very seriously in this office. At this point, you still have your job, and once the investigation is concluded, if we determine there is no merit to the complaint made against you, you may return to your normal job functions. I'd hold off on obtaining legal counsel, but if there is any merit to these allegations, we may have to take action including termination."

Fuck.

"What am I supposed to do for eight weeks? Thomas is out on paternity leave, and I'm supposed to be taking his clients while he's gone. I have deadlines, and…"

"Ms. Stineman," Helen cleared her throat. "You will be given limited access to the company server, and you'll be able to continue working on your non-emergent projects while you're on partial leave. Deacon will assign you work while you're out of the office."

Deacon nodded, looking at me sympathetically. While he liked Trent, I could tell he struggled, given his history with false accusations. "You've been a very dedicated employee, Kelly. That's why we aren't seeking termination at this point, but we can't give you special treatment either."

"What about Trent?" That fucker better not keep his position in the office by smearing my name with our employer because he was an insecure dick.

"If your allegations are founded..." Helen began.

"If?" I questioned, my hands clenching the armrests on my chair. "He's trying to ruin my career and he just gets to keep going without any repercussions? He said that I kept my job by working from my knees."

"Kelly," Helen placed her hand on my forearm, and I looked over at her. "He'll likely be put on leave as well. But we need to get all the paperwork filled out."

Maybe Deacon had been onto something with all the cameras inside and outside his office. Trent's advances had always happened in my office or the break room, always when we were alone. I'd dealt with his shit, but now I felt like I didn't have any real evidence of his behavior toward me. It was my word against his. And he'd been the first one to fire shots. This was a nightmare.

"Tom has assured me that you can handle a majority of his projects remotely," Deacon said. "We'll make sure you have the necessary files available while you're gone, and I'll take care of checking on the clients that you aren't assigned."

Nodding, I could still feel my blood pressure rising. This was bullshit, but I couldn't do a damn thing about it. That asshole was so egotistical that Trent had sabotaged my entire career to avoid having to report to me for a few weeks. Other than fend off his inappropriate behavior, I hadn't done anything to him.

"Let's head down to my office and fill out the necessary paperwork for your complaint, and then security should be able to escort you out from your office to your car in the garage when we're done."

Great, I'd fill out paperwork with Helen to save my job, and then security would escort me out because that didn't give everyone the impression that I'd done something wrong.

The next hour was done in a haze, me recounting as much of what Trent had said to me as possible to Helen, as well as any other incidents I could recall, with dates and the things he'd said. I should have documented it better, but I just thought he was a jerk, not that he'd try to get me fired. I was too trusting. My gut feelings about him had been right all along.

By the time I was sitting in my car in the underground parking structure, I was shaking. My laptop bag was crammed full of paperwork in my passenger seat. Security had locked my office door and asked for my copy of the key, riding the elevator with me to the underground garage and helping me load my belongings into my car. At least I'd driven to the office today. I couldn't even imagine trying to take the train home with the two large file boxes in my trunk.

I don't know how long I sat there, but when my phone started buzzing in the cup holder, I was startled, quickly wiping my cheeks before picking it up.

"Hello?"

"Hey." My sister-in-law's cheerful voice carried through the line, and I hated that I cringed when I realized it was her. I could have looked at the caller ID and declined the call, but my brain wasn't exactly firing on all cylinders. Or any cylinders. I was just numb. And fucking screwed. "Just wanted to check in with you before we left for the city. I know we said that you could come visit when we got back, but we might be spending a little longer in the city than we anticipated."

"Alright." There, that sounded normal. Maybe she wouldn't be able to tell that I was crying. Or that my life had essentially turned into an epic dumpster fire in the past three hours. *I* was having a hard time believing what my life had turned into in the last three hours.

What the hell was I going to do with myself for the next eight weeks?

What if I lost my job?

What if I couldn't find a new one?

Fuck. I was panicking.

"Are you alright? Your breathing sounds weird. Are you at the gym?"

"I'm..." I choked, bringing my fist to my mouth, and biting down on my knuckle for a moment as I tried to pull myself together.

"Kelly? Do I need to get Evan? You're kind of freaking me out."

"No!" I shouted, my voice echoing in the confined space in my car. "No. No, I'm fine. I'm not hurt. I'm just..." I paused, not even knowing what emotion I was feeling right now.

"Are you sure? I know we're supposed to fly out tomorrow afternoon, but we've got travel insurance if you need us to postpone the trip. We've waited this long for a honeymoon. A few more days won't make a difference."

The tears I'd been trying to hold back escaped my eyes at the concern in her voice, trailing down my cheeks as a sob escaped my lips. "I think I need help."

EIGHT

Nathan

Boston

Absently scratching the matted, slightly sweaty hair on the back of my neck, I placed my hard hat on the desk in my portable office, pulling my personal phone from my pocket as it buzzed against my thigh. I typically didn't check it during the day, but it'd been buzzing for the last ten minutes with text notifications.

There were a half dozen from my mother and sister, but I wasn't replying to those. They'd expect a call if I responded, and that wasn't happening. One from another rigger asked if I'd be free for a demonstration class, but I'd been shying away from those lately. I wasn't in the right headspace to be teaching right now. Sometimes you needed to step away from the scene between partners to get perspective on what you wanted.

It was the last one that made me pause.

G: My office. Two hours.

Typically, a text from Grace would have sent my pulse racing, the anticipation of release amping me up for our next scene together, but I'd had a hard time mustering any excitement about our interactions in the past few months. She'd been tolerant of my avoidance, as long as I saw her every few weeks, but I knew she was growing impatient with me. Blowing off her check-ins and attempts to gauge my wellbeing were violating our play agreement, but I had zero desire to share my growing frustrations with life with her. I knew she could be a good impartial friend if I let her, but I didn't want to open that type of bond further in our play. I had a feeling our arrangement for one-off rope play would be ending soon. I just hated to be the one to initiate it.

When I'd taken on Marisa as a sub, she'd been indignant, aiming little barbed comments at me whenever we saw each other at events. Grace had eventually settled down once I'd started playing with her again after a few months, but for someone who insisted on no commitments, she was a possessive person.

77

Marisa had ended our dynamic immediately upon my return to Boston after the wedding in Febraury. I'd felt relieved to see her moving on, but she'd been close-lipped about her new Dom and what her future was. Meanwhile, I'd been fixated on my brief time with Kelly, and I found myself comparing every woman I met to her. It didn't lend well to trying to find a new partner.

Emory had known something was bothering me the last few months, but he'd been traveling more — taking Talia with him to Europe — and I'd withdrawn into the projects at work. If I could just do one thing right, it'd make all the other things seem less stressful.

My mother had been contacting me more, the anniversary of my father's death looming over all of us, but I'd been avoiding her. It wasn't fair, and I wasn't being a good son, but my sister could shoulder her emotional neediness for a while. I was tapped out.

My adolescence had been spent picking her up off the floor after one of her episodes, and I couldn't handle it with everything else going on right now. I was tired, and I just needed a break.

Nathan: Any instructions?

It took her a few minutes to reply, but I was sure it was so she could keep me on edge.

G: Sensory deprivation scene in reclined suspension. We can discuss logistics when you arrive. I have a scene list drafted. Take a shower before you come.

Knowing she'd be irritated with me later if I did, I didn't leave her on read for long.

Nathan: Yes, ma'am. Any requests on products?

G: The cedar. That's a good boy for asking for instructions.

Somehow, even though I knew she was praising me in her text, it still felt condescending, and the sense of shame I'd recently been feeling after a scene with her was rearing its head early. That didn't lend well to me being able to drop into sub-space.

It figured that she always insisted on me showering because she said I smelled like sawdust or sweat or a construction site, but then she wanted me to use products that made me smell like a forest. I knew it was standard protocol before a scene, but she liked to remind me of things I already knew because it kept her in the dominant position of power. I let her do it because we agreed upon it, but it still didn't feel natural to submit to her completely.

She also wanted me to shave the beard I'd grown out since the wedding, but that wasn't happening. Grace got to play with my body, and since we seldom kissed and my beard never made contact with her body, she could get over it. Body hair wasn't in our agreement, and I wasn't one of her pleasure subs.

Over the next hour, I checked the worksite for progress and any potential delays in the schedule, distracted by what I knew was coming later. Grace had been taunting me on my reluctance in vetting a new sub. While she acted like she didn't want to share me, I also think it pleased her that I could flip the switch and bring out my Dominant side with the right partner. She loved it when her partners got attention.

My rigging skills rivaled Emory's, and she liked that people in the rope community respected me. While Grace thrived on bending people to her will, she loved any kind of attention that made her seem important. Collecting prized pets appeared to be the way she went about it recently. The more clout a person had in their real life, the more she craved the ability to bring them to their knees to serve her. While our relationship wasn't a traditional dynamic, she still made sure people knew I was involved with her.

I hated to admit it, but if you were into degradation, humiliation, or impact play, Grace was the pinnacle of Dommes. She wasn't for everyone, but she did know what she was doing. She'd started as a rigger, but now she only rope-played with me. I wasn't sure if I should be honored that I was the only one she used to keep her rope skills sharp, but that shouldn't be the reason I gave myself to stay in an arrangement that wasn't healthy or working for me.

I just wasn't sure if she was the rope top for me anymore, and the more those feelings grew, the more I knew I needed to end it. Emory had been right that Grace was manipulating me, but as long as she kept the cravings for restraint inside of me at bay, I'd tolerated it.

G: Don't be late.

Rolling my eyes at the reminder, I left the worksite, locking up my office and telling my foreman I was headed out for the day. I knew he could handle closing down the site, and he'd be doing it full time in a month or so anyway — at least while I was on vacation.

My seniority in the commercial construction company I worked for ensured me four weeks of vacation every year, and I was taking them all at once.

Evan had called me shortly after their wedding asking if I had any connections in Connecticut. He wanted to build a guest house on their property and was having trouble lining up someone to manage the exterior construction. The company that had built his house was booked up for months, and he didn't want to wait a year to get started.

After making some calls, I volunteered to get the building up, letting him hire local contractors to pour the foundation for me. He'd have another contractor come in after me to complete the interior and the finish carpentry. It'd been almost a decade since I worked on a crew, but my first experience in construction had been building houses for Habitat for Humanity as a teenager.

My grandfather's residential construction company had been sold several years ago after he died because I didn't want to leave Boston to take over, but I'd kept some of the equipment and part of his property in Connecticut. My older brother was an accountant and didn't have any desire to work with his hands, and my sister was a stay-at-home mom with an investment banker for a husband and had likely still never held a drill in her life. She'd been Daddy's little princess, staying inside the house with my mom while my dad taught us boys how to use power tools.

I'd apprenticed with my grandfather's company while I was an undergrad. Still, commercial construction had always appealed to me more, despite his disappointment when I changed directions with my degree in construction management. Part of me wondered what would have happened had I come back home and taken over when he wanted to retire, but I couldn't imagine leaving my life in the city permanently.

It'd been too hard to think about returning home after he died, especially since it meant I'd be closer to my mother and the family skeletons I'd been trying to avoid — my father's ghost being one of them. It was too hard to face the company he'd worked for every day of his adult life up until his death, especially knowing that he'd used it as an excuse to cover up his second family.

My half-brother was long gone, taking off right after high school, and while it killed my grandfather that he'd never looked back after he'd raised him since he was a toddler, I couldn't stomach dealing with the proof of my father's lies.

While I was sure a psychologist would tie my involvement with the kink community into my daddy issues and trauma response, I'd always been fascinated with rope. I was the first in my scout troop to get through the entire knot tying manual and earn a merit badge, and when I was older, I'd helped a summer camp set up a ropes course for my Eagle project. It didn't matter what kind of rope it was; I was into it.

In my junior year at university, a casual acquaintance had seen a handmade net hanging on the wall above my bed in my apartment and had introduced me to shibari. I started with self-tying and didn't look back. It wasn't until I met Emory in a community photography class and we became lab partners that I'd started to delve into the local kink community.

Emory had, surprisingly enough, been an instructor at an intro to partner tying workshop I attended when I was twenty, and I'd begged him to mentor me. He'd been hesitant at first, but we'd been close ever since.

He was how I'd initially met Grace, and after avoiding her for a solid ten years while I threw myself into the community, I'd eventually relented and done a scene with her when she was in a pinch during one of her showcases.

She'd known about my Switch tendencies and my rope skills and sweet-talked — well, as sweet as Mistress Grace ever got — me into trying to rope model for her.

Emory was one of the few rigger Doms I trusted to tie me, so it'd been a new experience with her. One I'd been trying to shake ever since. I'd modeled in educational workshops for some other local Dommes, but they didn't cause the same sensations I felt when I was in a scene with Grace. No matter how much I wanted to deny it, she got under my skin.

G: You're going to be late.

Nathan: I apologize. Coming in now.

G: Change of plans, report to the suspension set right away. I'll talk to you once you're dressed.

Well, that was new. Grace tended to present scene lists and discussions in her remote office, much like I'd assume she put together presentations in her boardroom on the thirteenth floor. She was the HBIC (Head Bitch in Charge) of a commercial real estate

81

firm and owned the entire office building. We'd never gone into a scene together blind.

Her regular employees had no idea that a portion of the bottom level of the building, off the loading dock, housed an expansive set of offices designed for her to hold local kink showcases and run her side gig as a Dominatrix for hire. For the right price, she would mentor a select few in the scene. While Emory and I gave our time freely to local kink education when we had the availability, Grace leveraged her experience into a lucrative extra source of income.

If any of her regular employees were in the know as to her extracurricular activities, she'd slapped an NDA on them so fast their head had spun. Much like hers had when she discovered I was the project manager on that portion of the building while it was under construction.

At first, I hadn't known if her desire to get me to rope model for her had been a way to keep me quiet or if she was interested in me.

A majority of the sexual relationships I'd had with other kinksters had been while I was in the Dominant position. My relationship with Grace was no different. Almost two years into our arrangement and my dick had never been in any of her orifices. Not that I hadn't fantasized about cramming my cock into her mouth as a means to muzzle her. But that was a fantasy neither one of us would ever allow to happen. While she was a beautiful woman, I wasn't attracted to her like that, and I think she liked the chase. If I gave in to her, it'd be less exciting, and she'd have to find another rope bottom.

When I let myself into the carefully camouflaged door with my digital key card, the lights were dimmed in the main salon area. It looked like any other boring office complex waiting area when it wasn't full of scantily clad men and women and all the other excesses Grace liked to indulge in at her parties. She never allowed drugs and rarely allowed alcohol, but everything else was fair game.

Grace was nowhere in sight as I punched in my personal door code, the electronic deadbolt disengaging for the rigging set. It was impressive, and with my knowledge as a rope top, it'd been fun to tie in an industrial feel to the room along with a concrete reinforced suspension grate that ran the entire length of the ceiling. The leather bed in the corner was made up with blood-red sheets, but I noticed a pile of items next to the bed with my name neatly scrawled across the card in her sloping cursive writing.

Soft music came through the overhead speakers as I picked up the note, fingering the set of leather quick release cuffs on top of the pile.

Naughty Nate,

You've been keeping things from me. Cuffs and cage on. Wait for me on the settee on the stage.

Mistress G

Shaking my head at her cryptic message, I quickly stripped down, pulling on the leather cock cage she liked to put me in when she was feeling particularly sadistic, and pulled a loose set of mesh athletic shorts on over my hips. She'd seen me naked before, but there was something that made me feel safer when I wasn't quite so exposed. It also prevented rope chafing in some sensitive areas I preferred to keep unmarred. I was a big guy, which meant my weight created deeper marks where the weight suspension was concentrated on the ropes.

The floor was cold as I crossed the room, stretching out my arms and arching my back as I settled onto my knees in front of the settee she liked me to lean on when she started. The heavy pulley and rigging rope were already hanging above my head, so I knew she was planning to suspend me completely, but I knew she liked to work me into a scene.

A set of wireless earbuds sat on the soft velvet, along with a loose silk gag and a blackout eyemask. Grace was nothing if not a prepared rope top.

Popping the earbuds in, I closed my eyes, leaning forward onto the cushion at my chest. The gag wasn't enough to cut off my speech, just enough to get the point across that I would not talk during this session. While some of her other 'pets' wore studded collars and had ball gags in their mouths, she'd been accommodating of my refusal to wear such items. I was often surprised at her willingness to bend her desires to accommodate my needs. She was manipulative sometimes, but she was typically very respectful of her subs. At least outside of a scene and what they'd consented to.

Soft instrumental music played while I waited, my forehead leaning against the soft velvet in front of me, my posture relaxed.

The leather cuffs sat beside me on the cushion, waiting for her to put them on.

She didn't leave me waiting for long, the hair standing up on the back of my neck as a sharp pinch started at my shoulder and carried on down my back. I'd felt it enough times to know it was her nails trailing across my skin, the sharp points leaving a trail of sensation in their wake. I was still and quiet as she grasped my wrists and fastened on the leather cuffs loosely, just enough that it gave the illusion of restraint but not enough to cut off any circulation.

Her fingertips trailed over my back, tugging on the waistband of my shorts, the cool air rushing in briefly as she ensured I'd put on all the items she'd left out for me.

"We're going to start with some impact play today. Do you consent?" she asked as the soft tails of her whip trailed down my shoulders.

Pushing the gag out slightly with my tongue, I nodded and said, "Yes, ma'am," through the soft material.

The music in my ears changed slightly, a seductive pulsing beat starting as the first hit of the whip across my shoulders made me jump slightly. I held my posture still as she continued, striking me as the song's chorus swelled and then using her warm hands to rub out the sting.

Endorphins flowed through me as she continued, and I struggled to keep myself calm, my cock twitching against the confines of the leather straps it was buckled into. Part of me was glad I was blindfolded, because I typically had a hard time containing my arousal when it was combined with the image of her in full Dominatrix attire.

Grace loved the showmanship, often dressing in revealing leather harnesses or tight lace, pleather, and latex. The time she spent away from this building was clearly spent with her trainer, and her toned body left many kinksters in the community panting after her.

The handful of people who knew of my arrangement with her found it hard to believe I wasn't one of her pleasure pets, but I wasn't crossing that line with her no matter how attractive she was.

Driving bass started to morph back into something soft, but an ominous bass beat started as she gripped the hair at the back of my neck and pulled upward. I stood, remaining still as she circled me, her fingers pulling up the edge of the blindfold as she caressed the side of my face.

"Are you ready to begin?" she asked softly as she rubbed her thumb across the skin of my lips that peeked out beneath the loose gag. I knew from experience that I was to remain quiet and nodded, keeping my gaze over her shoulder.

Grace walked me to the ropes hanging from the ceiling and started to overlap them around my torso, creating a clean series of criss-crossing ropes that would align with my spine once she coaxed me up from my standing position.

I kept my posture neutral as she worked, slowly but efficiently binding my arms in front of me before she had me lean back into the hold of the rope, the familiar sensation of floating starting as she wrapped the ropes around my thighs and tightened them until they held my weight. She checked in with me at regular intervals, asking me questions that I responded to non-verbally with a shake or nod of my head.

Rigging wasn't a quick kink, sometimes taking hours to get the rope model into the desired position. Grace shifted my weight, urging me in this direction and that as she fine-tuned the hold she had me in. Once my full weight was supported by the ropes, she pulled the blindfold fully back on, checking her ties before she left me to get used to the hold.

"I'll be close. There's something I think you need to listen to."

Stretching my limbs within the confines of the rope, I felt myself sinking into that state of euphoria, tingles running along my skin as I shifted, figuring out which position created the most intense feelings. The soft music morphed into something a little more ominous as I settled deeper into the tie, the seductive bass starting back up again.

A guttural feminine moan filled my ears, a shiver running down my spine as my eyes blinked open beneath the blindfold. The music softened as the audio of the woman increased in my ears, the sound of slapping flesh accompanying the dulcet tones of her voice as she cried out again.

There was something familiar about the sound, but I had difficulty identifying it as I shifted against my bonds, causing arousal to pull at my groin as her moans increased in intensity. Apparently, whatever secrets I'd kept from Grace meant that she was feeling a bit sadistic as I fought the swelling of my cock. The leather pinched as I hardened, and no amount of thinking about grotesque things decreased my arousal as the moans got louder.

"You like that, don't you, my little cum slut?" a rough voice whispered, the sound sending a shot of adrenaline through my system. "You like it when I fuck you. Greedy for me to fill you up."

The low-grade pain of being confined kept me from falling back into sub-space as I listened, ensnared by the sounds in my ears. I didn't recognize the male voice but was a captive audience as I listened to the scene play out. Grace wanted me to listen to this for a reason, so I tried to calm my breathing and focus.

"It's too bad I can't put another baby in you," he groaned as a low smack filled my ears. "Such a naughty girl fucking me with another man's baby in your belly."

What the fuck was this?

"Oh God. Yes, Daddy. Fuck me harder."

I almost choked against the gag between my lips at the feminine voice. I knew that voice. *She* knew better than to call me Daddy, but Marisa had begged me to fuck her harder in that raspy moan dozens of times during the last year.

My fingers clenched, my muscles straining against the rope as I tapped my thigh, indicating I wanted out of the hold. Grace couldn't be far, she never left me during a session, but I didn't know what she was getting at.

My feet hit the floor as the ropes released, my legs wobbly as I fought to keep my balance. I tried to make myself stay still as I waited for her to untie me but growled as my arms rose above my head, keeping me bound as the rest of the ropes released.

"You've been keeping secrets." Grace's low voice was almost growly as she pulled one of the earbuds free, her hot breath on the side of my neck. "You know who was in that scene and why I called you here today."

A subtle shake of my head was the only way I could respond while I was bound like this, but the adrenaline coursing through my veins made it hard for me to keep the anger that was swelling in my system at bay. I didn't want to get myself too worked up, the last thing I needed was to pass out in a hold, but Marisa wasn't involved with Grace, at least she hadn't been, and that audio was beyond fucked up.

I knew Marisa had a breeding kink, but knowing my limits, her giving this audio to Grace was too much.

"When she came to me in January, telling me about how your dynamic was falling apart and she needed a mentor, I never anticipated uncovering the secrets you've been keeping from me, Nathan."

My teeth clicked together at the disgust in Grace's voice.

"I hadn't wanted to help her at first, but you know I can't resist protecting my mentees. When she told me she was pregnant with your baby, and you turned her away a few weeks ago, I realized how much of a liar you truly were."

Pushing my tongue against the gag across my lips, I used my teeth to tug it down, my voice rough as I croaked out the one word I'd never used in her presence. I hadn't needed to safeword in a scene in almost a decade, but this was too much.

"*Dovetail.*"

"I'm disappointed in you, Nate," Grace chided as the ropes binding my arms came loose, and the blindfold over my eyes disappeared. "You never struck me as the type to abandon his responsibilities. You know how I feel about loyalty and respect."

"What the fuck is going on?" I growled, turning toward Grace as I shook off the ropes at my feet and she unbuckled the cuffs on my wrists.

"You never told me you'd gotten your little plaything pregnant."

My nails dug into my palms as the audio kept playing in my ear, the pitch of Marisa's moans increasing as the sound of slapping flesh got louder.

"Turn that the fuck off," I yelled as I reached up and ripped the gag from my chin, flinging the scrap of fabric at Grace.

She narrowed her eyes at me, taking a step toward where I was standing, her whip on the floor at our feet.

"Don't even fucking think about it. This scene is over. We're over. I'm not playing these fucking mind games with you."

"Oh, come on, *Daddy*," she cooed sarcastically, reaching for me. I stepped away from her, turning so I could unclasp the leather digging into my now deflated cock.

"Don't." Whatever twisted game she was playing, I wanted no part of it. I wasn't sure how she'd gotten the mistaken impression I'd impregnated Marisa, especially since I hadn't had sex with her since before Thanksgiving. "I don't know what she told you, but both of you are beyond fucked up. She is not pregnant with my kid."

"I think we both know that there's a possibility it could be, Nathan."

The audio shifted from the animalistic sounds of a couple...coupling...and I listened as the soft cries of another audio clip started from Grace's phone. With how many times Marisa had broken down crying at the end of our relationship, I knew it was a recording of her.

"I don't know why he won't talk to me. I can't get him to answer my calls. I don't want this baby to grow up without a father, Grace. But Nathan wants nothing to do with me. I need your help. You can help him see that we need to be together. That we can be a family."

Grace reached forward to touch my hand. "Even with precautions, things can happen. All it takes is one time. You need to do the right thing. I know there's a compassionate man in here, please don't make a mistake like this. You can't take it back."

Part of my resolve faltered at the pain in Grace's voice. I knew her history and that she was always seeking validation because of the rough childhood she'd had in foster care until she was adopted. I could see how Marisa's lies would have tugged at her heart strings, but my anger at being manipulated was overriding any sympathy I may have harbored.

"No," I growled. "It doesn't just take one time. Because I can't get anyone pregnant. So whatever twisted game you're playing with her, I want no part of. That is not my fucking kid, and if you want to see the test results after my successful vasectomy, I'd be happy to show them to you. But this ends now. This was a fucked-up way to try to trap me into whatever in the fuck you two concocted."

"Wait," Grace's tone changed, her surprised eyes darting to mine, but I refused to look at her anymore. "You mean...?"

"It doesn't matter because we're fucking done. Rip up my contract. Lose my phone number. Stay the fuck away from me. Both of you." I couldn't believe Grace could make such a huge breach of trust with someone she played with. There were expectations that came along with being in the Dominant position, even in play only arrangements, and she'd failed me today.

"Nathan, wait." She tried to reach for my arm as I walked past her, but I shook her off, grabbing my things from the bed across the room

88

and throwing my key card in her direction as I wrenched the door open. "If he's not yours, what's going on?"

"I don't know," I told her, backing away, "But that sounds like something you need to take up with Marisa. You fucked up today, and I can't be a part of this any longer."

My hands were shaking as I pulled up the app to request an Uber, needing to get as far away from here as quickly as possible.

The poor guy looked at me strangely when he picked me up at the curb a few minutes later. I was sure I looked crazy, shirtless and barefoot, holding a pile of clothes in early April, but it wasn't his job to judge me. I hoped Chase and Evan didn't mind me heading down early to survey their lot while they were on their honeymoon because there was no way I was staying in the city another night. I needed out of here. This was the last time Grace manipulated me like I was one   of   her   little   pawns.

NINE

Kelly

Boston

By the time my plane landed in Boston, I was wiped. Chase had made my flight arrangements before they'd flown out the day before, my shock at the events of the previous day making it hard for me to concentrate on much more than getting my car back to my apartment before I lost it and sobbed in the bathtub with a pint of ice cream.

I was sure I fit every cliché of a scorned woman as I broke down that evening. When the pounding on my door and the blaring alarm on my phone sounded at dawn this morning, I'd dutifully opened the door and let Sam and Christine into my apartment. I even managed to put on a pot of coffee before I tried to pull myself together.

Christine had offered to accompany me on the flight, telling me it'd be a good excuse to visit her Nana, but I just wanted to be alone. Every time I thought about things, I'd started crying, and I didn't want to embarrass myself by turning into a blubbering mess on the three-hour flight. A spicy paperback in my carry-on would distract me sufficiently enough to keep my mind off things because I was not prepared to deal with it all.

They left me at the airport in Chicago with tight hugs and Sam threatening to exact some justice upon Trent, but we both knew he was too nice to beat the shit out of someone. I just wanted it all to go away.

I'd tried to contact Thomas as I waited at the gate, but his phone was turned off, and Charley's rang through to voicemail. Deacon had made it sound like Tom knew what was going on, but with her due date so close, I wouldn't bother them. The baby was here already for all I knew, but I was afraid to reach out again. He'd trusted me to keep things going in his absence, and I somehow felt like I'd failed him.

I knew it wasn't my fault, but now I was replaying every interaction I'd ever had with the men in my office, searching for

90

anything that could be misconstrued as suggestive or inappropriate. I was friendly, but I rarely dated and never anyone from the office. And I didn't interact with the clients beyond professional emails.

I'd taken numerous ethics trainings courses throughout my career and even taught at a sexual harassment seminar. I knew where to draw professional boundaries, but I'd still been blindsided by one jackass with a sexist superiority complex.

After I'd made the trek through Logan airport when I landed in Boston and gathered my two suitcases from luggage claim, I requested an Uber, pulling my coat hood up as I dashed through the early spring mist into the waiting sedan.

It was lunchtime by the time I reached Chase's condo, my stomach growling as I dragged my bags into the elevator. I wasn't sure what my plan was as I unlocked the front door and wrestled my damp luggage into the entryway.

The place was still furnished, Chase and Evan often staying here when they needed to be in the city to meet with their editors or attend book signings. But there was an empty quality to it, almost like a hotel but with wedding pictures of my brother on the wall instead of generic landscapes.

I knew it likely would be with my unplanned trip, but the refrigerator was bare, only a few condiments in the door, a bottle of white wine, and a pitcher of filtered water inside.

I felt weird sleeping in the bed they shared — even if this wasn't their primary residence — so I grabbed fresh sheets from the tiny hall closet, tucking them into the couch cushions. Finally sitting down, I pulled up a food delivery app and started browsing the restaurants in the area.

The drive to their house in Connecticut was only a few hours, but I'd never driven it by myself. I didn't want to risk getting lost in the rain, so I decided that maybe I'd spend a few nights in the condo before I made the drive down. It'd probably be a good idea to download all my projects to my laptop from the server in case the internet service was spotty at their farmhouse.

Since I didn't have any other plans, I ordered Chinese delivery, changed into my pajamas despite it not being dark yet, and pulled up Netflix on the television in the living room.

Throwing myself into other people's lives, I watched some terrible romantic comedies, finally uncorking the wine and pouring myself a glass. I knew alcohol was never the answer to anyone's problems, but spending another night obsessing about my derailed future wasn't going to help either.

By the time the sun finally did set, I was snuggled under a blanket, remote in hand with a nice buzz going on as I watched the main character from *Emily in Paris* make questionable life choices. At least I wasn't the only one who didn't know what to do with their future.

Seeing Emily with Gabriel made me think of Nathan. Knowing I was in the same city made the impulse to drunk dial him tempting, but I'd be more likely to cry on him in my current state than be an attractive hookup. Not that he'd touch me again. I had a feeling our brief affair had been an isolated experience for the both of us. Neither of us had made any promises when we parted ways, and the deserted text message thread indicated he wasn't exactly anxious to hear from me.

I needed to get my life together before dragging a man back into things. Maybe it was better if I left our brief affair in Minneapolis as just that. A whirlwind wedding affair. A whirlwind wedding affair that'd included the best sex I'd ever had in my life, repeatedly. It had just gotten more intense as the weekend went on, but we both agreed it was only for the time we were in the hotel room.

After my third glass of wine, I snuggled into my blanket fort, comfortably numb as I let my eyes close. I wasn't in any state to be making any major life decisions.

Sunlight filtered in through the living room curtains as I cracked open my eyes. Despite the mostly empty bottle of wine on the coffee table, I didn't feel too terrible. Maybe a bit dehydrated, but rested overall.

The clock on my phone showed I'd been asleep for nearly twelve hours. I usually never slept past 9:00 am — even on the weekends — but as my stomach growled, I didn't regret turning off all the alarms on my phone last night.

It wasn't like I had anywhere to be, and Helen had advised me to take the rest of the week to get settled before I started to work remotely. For the first time in years, I had absolutely nothing to do. And nowhere to go. At least not in any hurry.

Chase had texted me Isobel's contact information, but I didn't want to disturb her. She was still supposed to be on maternity leave for a few more weeks and likely had better things to do than babysit Evan's older sister while she had a not quite mid-life crisis.

Chase had told me she often dealt with difficult male editors — her non-boyfriend included — but I knew I wouldn't contact her. Part of me still ached when I thought of what my life might have been like by now, and seeing further reminders of what my future wasn't going to hold wouldn't help me get out of this funk. It'd just add a steaming addition to my already large enough pile of crap.

Christine: You get on the road yet?

My phone buzzed on the coffee table, Christine's name flashing across the screen. I knew she had appointed herself my babysitter, but I didn't want anyone's pity.

Kelly: Nope. Got another hot date with Netflix. I'll head down tomorrow.

It wasn't like I had anywhere to be. I could spend another day hiding from the world. It was not that driving to the middle of the countryside wasn't hiding from the world, but it involved putting on real pants. Pants were so overrated.

Christine: You sure you don't want to stay with Nana? She's got plenty of room, and Piet is a fabulous cook.

While I appreciated the offer, I also didn't want to spend my exile playing the third wheel to an octogenarian and her silver fox boy toy.

Kelly: I'm good. I promise.

At least I would be after I ordered more takeout and found another bottle of wine.

The second bottle of wine the delivery driver brought didn't go down quite as smoothly as the first. I should have stuck with the white. I should've also stopped drinking, but I had the toxic habit of self-medicating with the cursed fermented devil grapes when I was stressed out, lonely, or horny... maybe I needed to step away from wine for the rest of this forced sabbatical.

It was an unattractive habit, but no one was here to criticize me for my life choices right now. My parents didn't even know I'd left Chicago. We only saw each other a few times a month, so I was hoping to have at least a week before I had to explain why my life was falling apart around me while I hid in my brother's house.

I was beginning to see the appeal of Evan's need for solitude after everything that happened with that slag, Serena. Now it'd just turned into his love nest with Chase where they escaped to write their scandalous books that entertained my mother's book club. Maybe I could claim squatters' rights and refuse to leave their house. Moving into the new guest house once it was completed was sounding like an attainable new life goal for me. But first, I had to get there.

Evan's Audi was parked in the underground garage attached to Chase's building, looking like it'd never been driven. He'd probably kill me if he knew I not only had a travel mug of black coffee but a flaky croissant I'd obtained from the bakery down the street in his precious vehicle.

I was surprised that there weren't any remnants of their trip up to the city left behind, but I was sure Evan had carefully cleaned out his baby before they'd caught a cab to the airport. He always was a little on the OCD side. A stark contrast to my loosely organized hot mess.

I almost felt sorry for Deacon having to sort through my unorthodox filing system in my absence, but then I thought about how he'd forced me on this break, and I didn't feel sorry for him in the slightest. It wasn't his fault, per se, but his policy ensured I had a mandatory lock-out period. It didn't matter that I was innocent — until he'd obtained enough proof of that, I was going to be shut out. Fed enough scraps of work to keep me busy until they tugged me back in or sent me packing. Being in limbo sucked.

Luckily, I'd missed morning rush hour by the time I started on my drive out of the city, and soon the skyscrapers and brick buildings were replaced with rolling fields dotted with puddles from the recent rain and lots and lots of nothing but nature...and cows.

Don't get me wrong, I was sure that come summer it'd be gorgeous, but as rain clouds gathered on the horizon and the lingering wine headache made my temples throb, I had a hard time finding beauty in anything.

The drizzle had turned into a torrential downpour by the time I reached the turnoff that led deep into the wooded area where Evan had built his house. I didn't know how he did it, Chase, either. I'd never survive this far outside of a big city.

It was so dark, and the only lights were those of the car headlights and the nearly blinding floodlight on the front porch that clicked on when I parked in front of the house. I knew I should get the car secured in the detached garage, but I decided getting warm and passing out early were higher on my priority list.

Leaving my suitcase in the car, I ran through the rain, shielding my eyes from the onslaught. My hair was plastered to my head when I reached the front door and punched in the code on the lock with near-frozen fingers.

The inside was just as cold, the security system chirping at me as I pushed the door closed. Quickly typing in the code, the beeping stopped, and I toed off my wet shoes before I went in search of the thermostat.

None of this 68-degree bullshit. I was turning the thermostat up to 72 until this place didn't feel like an icebox.

Eyeing the fireplace hopefully, I crossed the room to peer into the basket beside it, but it was empty with only a few bark scraps in the bottom of it. I suspected it was the real deal, not a gas model I could turn on with the flick of a switch like the one in my condo.

My phone chimed from my coat pocket, so I wiped my wet hands on my leggings before I pulled it out.

Chase: Got an alert from the security system. You get in alright? Local weather said there were some storms in the area.

Yeah…you could say that. Monsoon season had made its way to rural Connecticut.

Kelly: Yup. Safe and sound. Don't tell Evan I changed his thermostat.

Chase: Don't worry. Your secret is safe with me. Don't hesitate to text if you need anything.

Kelly: Aren't you supposed to be honeymooning?

Chase: We are. Your brother is passed out.

A winking emoji, a smirking emoji, and an eggplant came through next, and I cringed when I realized that they had clearly already been enjoying their honeymoon suite. Gross.

Kelly: TMI.

Chase: You asked.

Kelly: Go back to defiling my little brother now and spare me the details, please. Thank you for letting me stay at your house.

Chase: No problem. Get some rest. The freezer is fully stocked. Help yourself.

My prowess in the kitchen involved following the directions on the meal prep kits I had delivered each week or using an app to order takeout when I worked late. The latter of which was done more frequently than was probably healthy.

Since Evan's location was so remote, I knew he'd expanded upon our mother's basic cooking tutorials she'd forced on us before college and had become quite the home chef. It was part of why I knew Chase had readily agreed to move here. I had to admit I'd likely follow a man who could cook to the middle of nowhere, too, if the food was good enough. And the dick, but that was my little brother, so I was going to pretend they were celibate spouses who never touched each other.

After I'd pulled out a container full of the most flavorful pot roast I'd ever tasted — *sorry, mom* — I peeked out the front windows to see if the rain had died down.

It hadn't.

Thankfully my slightly hungover travel attire consisted of a pair of soft joggers and a long-sleeved tunic that almost reached my knees. Retrieving my pajamas could wait until the monsoon passed.

The past few times I'd visited Evan, I'd had trouble sleeping because it was so quiet. As I pulled the thick comforter over my shoulders in the guest bed, I didn't have that problem — I was passed out within moments of my head hitting the pillow.

Thwack

Two-day-long hangovers weren't a thing, right?

I mean. I hadn't been that drunk the other night when I rationalized that leaving a glass' worth of wine in the bottle before leaving town was wasteful. It was my duty as a house guest to kill the bottle. I *had* to do it.

Thwack

Squinting at my Apple Watch, I realized that it was dead, the screen black as I tapped the face. Right. Chargers were in my suitcase.

Luckily, I'd charged my phone on the drive down, and it still had half a charge.

Thwack

The screen read 10:00 am. So at least I'd gotten some solid, not wine-induced sleep.

Thwack

Realizing the noise wasn't coming from my overtaxed brain, I reluctantly pulled myself out of bed, pleased that the house seemed to have warmed up overnight.

Thwack

A quick peek out the windows overlooking the back of the house later, I failed to identify the source of the obnoxious cracking sound.

Thwack

As I passed the mirror on the dresser, I cringed as I took in the nest my hair had dried into after running through the rain and not brushing it before I fell asleep. Great. Now, I looked like a wild hermit lady hiding in the woods. At least I was embracing the part.

Thwack

The persistent noise continued as I crept into the living room, flattening myself against the wall as I made my way toward the large picture windows that faced the front of the house.

Thwack

As I peered around the edge of the frame, using the curtains to conceal myself, a hulking figure came into view across the gravel drive.

Thwack

My heart raced as the glint of an ax head reflected in the bright morning sunlight, almost twinkling as it paused midair and then disappeared as the arms of the figure quickly vanished out of sight.

Thwack

If I weren't so freaked out, it'd be kind of hot, but my hands shook as I reached into my pocket and fumbled with my phone.

There was an x in the top right corner as I unlocked the screen. Shit, no signal. I hated that it was spotty sometimes out here.

As the little symbol for the Wi-Fi signal blinked on, I pulled open my text messages.

Kelly: You've got some dirty lumberjack squatting at your house.

Chase: What the hell are you talking about? Where are you?

Kelly: Hidden next to the front windows at the farmhouse, he's out in the yard with an ax. I can't get a signal on my phone to call for help.

Chase: Then how are you texting me?

Kelly: And I'm the dumb one. Wi-fi, bish. My iMessage still works. Send help!

Chase: Has he come up to the house?

97

Kelly: No...
Chase: What does he look like?
Kelly: Shaggy chin length brown hair, half pulled into a bun, full beard.

Again, if I weren't so freaked out, the beard would be hot. I was starting to wonder if I had some latent lumberjack fantasies that I'd been repressing.

Chase: I think you should talk to him.
Kelly: Are you fucking crazy?
Chase: Trust me.
Kelly: No. He's not wearing my face like a trophy. This is how serial killer documentaries start.
Chase: And I'm the one who has the overactive imagination.
Kelly: Um...you just have a naughty imagination.

The figure propped the ax up against the stump he'd been using to chop with and reached into his back pocket, pulling a phone up to his ear.

Chase: He's coming up to the house.

As the text scrolled across the screen, I saw the man turn toward where I was standing. I jerked back abruptly, rolling myself with my back against the wall.

Kelly: WTF? Are you psychic?
Chase: Evan called him. He was supposed to let you know he was there.

My eyes widened at her message, and my fingers flew across the screen, formulating my response.

Kelly: You told an ax murderer to come to introduce himself?
Chase: Answer the door, drama queen.

"Fuck, fuck, fuck," I squeaked as a loud knock sounded on the front door.

Kelly: I'm writing you out of my will.
Chase: You have a will?
Kelly: No...but you're no longer in it.
Chase: Go!

"Ugh, I don't wanna." My voice was a low whine as I reluctantly dragged myself across the room, pausing at the window above the entryway table and trying — unsuccessfully — to tame my wild hair again.

But it wasn't like it mattered to some backwoods lumberjack. He could have three teeth for all I knew. I doubted he was the hunky woodman of my dirty fantasies.

Except...when I opened the door, it wasn't some unknown backwoods lumberjack. And he had a full set of perfectly straight, white teeth. And he had already featured in many of my recent fantasies.

Nathan stood with his hands braced on the top of the doorframe — with a sexy as fuck beard, and a smirk on his lips — as he looked down at me.

"Hello, sunshine."

And that was when I panicked and slammed the door in his ridiculously, ruggedly attractive face — catching the hem of my tunic in the doorframe in the process.

Because, of course, I did.

"Fuck."

TEN

Nathan

Boston

Since I'd checked on my active worksites the day before, it wasn't difficult to move my vacation up a few weeks and pass the rest of my projects onto someone else within the office. A few late-night emails later, I was free to leave Boston. I'd already packed a bag, planning on taking off first thing in the morning to my inherited property in Connecticut. It was a short drive to Ashford, the closest town to Evan's location, which was why I hadn't hesitated to offer my help.

Grace had tried to call, but I declined everything, sending her calls to voicemail. I was not giving her another in since she hadn't even talked to me before pulling the stunt she had. Even one-off play arrangements weren't the place for mind games, and while our play involved a certain amount of power exchange, what she had done had crossed so many lines.

Yesterday's scene had been a total mindfuck, and I wasn't playing this game with them. Marisa and I had parted ways, and it was staying that way. I knew without a doubt that was not my child, and I was not getting roped into some crazy baby mama drama. I worried about the state of her mental health, but she wasn't my sub anymore, so I had to let her figure out her life on her own. She was an adult, and she had a child to worry about now. I hoped for its sake that she got her life together.

I'd been — mostly — honest with Grace about our relationship, and since sex wasn't on the table with us, it hadn't been her business for me to include my fertility status. She knew I didn't want kids and that they were a hard limit. That was enough for our relationship. The decision I'd made for myself a few years ago was none of her business.

My sleep was broken, every little noise of the city another prick against my subconscious, making it hard to relax. I knew I could practice my meditation techniques, but something about the betrayal

100

of someone who you'd let in and trusted was too much for me. I never wanted to turn into my mother — an empty, anxious shell of a person, but Marisa's betrayal of my limits was hard to overlook.

For her to try to trap me into whatever her game was with Grace as an accomplice was unforgivable. If our dynamic hadn't already run its course, I would have ended it immediately; we were done. Marisa was lucky I wasn't contacting people I knew within the community to get her banned from every invitation list possible. Grace may have been an uninformed accomplice, but she knew better, and I knew she was likely beating herself up that she'd violated the trust we'd built up between us with her acting as my Domme.

As I tossed and turned, my mind wired despite the weariness in my body, I tried to make sense of Marisa's actions. I knew she wanted children. I respected that, but I'd told her very candidly when we were still in the vetting process that it was a hard limit and non-negotiable for me. I hadn't told her about the vasectomy, but the fact it was a hard limit should have been enough for her to respect my choices.

If the situation had been reversed, I either would have walked away if it was a deal-breaker before we'd even set up our contract, or I would have respected my partner's wishes. She knew I wanted a romantic partner to play with, but not at the expense of my wants and needs. She clearly had no issues with deceiving herself and me about what she truly wanted.

It didn't bother me that she was sleeping with other men while we were together because we hadn't put exclusivity in our arrangement if she was safe. It was the fact that she thought she could rope me into impregnating her, and she'd lied about the birth control she wasn't using. If I hadn't already been tested after we parted ways, I'd be concerned about what she could've potentially exposed me to. Another reason that I insisted on protecting myself.

Everything about our relationship was now muddied. All I knew was that I needed to be firm about what I needed with whoever I got involved with next. I was tired of liars and tired of games. All I wanted was for someone to support me and the ability to do the same for them.

Even though she had nothing whatsoever to do with the shit that had gone down, my mind drifted to Kelly and the bubble we'd created in that hotel room. Maybe it was because I was headed to her brother's house that she was at the forefront of my mind. The weekend I spent with her was the most effortless interaction I'd had with a woman in years. Even with the limited time, she'd been transparent about not only her sexual wants and desires but also her life.

In between all the sex, she'd listened to me talk about work, and she'd shared with me about her workaholic tendencies. The Dom in me had wanted to scold her for not taking care of herself, but I knew we weren't in a dynamic, so I'd kept my mouth shut. I knew she could flourish with the right relationship and support, but it wasn't my place to be that person for her.

By the time the sun started to rise over the building across the street through my window, I had hopped out of bed because I just wanted to get moving. After I'd gotten out of the shower — trying to groom my beard and my longer than typical hair — my phone buzzed on the counter.

Emory: Tal and I are back in town. Want to grab dinner tonight?

While I needed to fill them in on yesterday's events, I knew I wasn't in the mood to hear their 'I told you so' commentary about Grace and Marisa. They'd been supportive of both relationships for my sake, but I knew they had opinions on both women they didn't express to my face. I know there were things I'd kept to myself about their relationship when they'd first met.

Nathan: Can't. Heading to Evan's to start framing.

The heavy spring rains we'd been having in the region lately would likely hinder my progress, but the foundation was solid when I'd been down there in the fall. I also had a copy of the blueprints Evan had commissioned from one of the architectural firms who often partnered my company.

I knew it would take longer going down now because it wasn't like I could just make building materials appear with a snap of my fingers, but I had enough materials on hand that I could get started while I tried to move up my orders on everything else. There was also likely a fair amount of brush I needed to clear out of the wooded area surrounding the foundation.

Emory: Thought you weren't starting until they got back from their trip?

Nathan: I wasn't. Plans changed.

Emory: Are you going to share with the class?

I knew he'd have questions, but I just needed to throw myself into a project right now and not dwell on how I couldn't change other people's behavior even if it were bound to lead them on the road to self-destruction. I learned the hard way a long time ago it wasn't my job to save people.

Nathan: Not at the moment. I can fill you in when I get back. If Marisa contacts you, don't engage.

Emory: What did she do? Do I need to send Tal to cut a bitch?

Nathan: No, not worth your time. I'm done. Just walking away.

Emory: I thought you already had.

Nathan: Cutting all ties.

Emory: With Grace too? Aren't they training together?

So he'd known about the mentorship, and I hadn't had a clue. I knew I'd been distracted since we got back to town after the wedding, but you'd think I would have heard about it from someone in our circle.

Nathan: Don't have an answer for that one. Just taking a step back for now.

Emory: Do we have a problem with G?

Nathan: Just some communication issues I don't know if I want to invest the time to work through. I ended our arrangement. That's enough for now.

Emory: You sure you don't need to talk?

Nathan: Not yet. I'll let you know when I'm ready for a postmortem.

Emory: You know we won't push. Text when you get there, or Tal will worry about you.

Nathan: Only her?

Emory: You know I only keep you around because she has those lumberjack voyeur fantasies.

Nathan: Fuck you, dude. You're just jealous you can't pull off plaid and a full beard like I can.

Emory: So jealous I can't stand it.

Emory: Seriously, whatever you need, we're here for you.

Every day for nearly the last two decades, I'd wondered what my life would look like if I hadn't decided to follow my instincts and jump into the kink community. But even with the disappointment I'd experienced over the years when dynamics and play arrangements ended, I knew I'd never find another friend or mentor like Em. He was my favorite human being, in a purely platonic way, despite Talia using me as fodder for their fantasy flirting sometimes.

Nathan: I know. Thank you.

The masculine urge to blast loud, angry music was intense as I climbed into my Jeep, but I knew it wouldn't be cathartic or healthy, so I opted to lose myself in an audiobook on the drive down. While I'd never admitted it to her or her husband, I enjoyed Chase's books and had been working my way through her backlist by sneaking in her audiobooks when I had the time.

Romance novels hadn't appealed to me before — Evan's works were more in my target genre — but there was something about how she developed these complex characters that drew me in. I was sure it'd give Emory another excuse to tease me about being a hopeless romantic, but he wouldn't strictly be wrong. I did want the romance, too, someone to take care of and who tried to take care of me in return. It was lonely trying to be the partner who had their shit together. I wanted to be a hot mess with someone and have them love me despite my flaws.

With my fortieth birthday approaching, I was worried I'd be single forever.

Gravel crunched under my tires as I slowed my speed and turned down the narrow drive to my grandfather's old property. The farmhouse right on the road had been sold with a small plot of land, neither of my siblings wanting it, but I'd retained the deed to his acreage and the large warehouse-like barn I'd filled with his equipment before we'd sold off his construction business.

My brother had thought it was pointless for me to keep the workshop, but I hadn't wanted to let it go. Maybe it was because it was the last link I had to our grandfather and subsequently our father. I sometimes wondered if I'd made a mistake walking away from the family business, but it also allowed me to stay close to my roots.

Carpentry had been my first love — another result of scouting, and my grandfather. Sometimes I drove down here on the weekends to start a new project, the most recent one a new dining room set for my mother's house. It was nearly complete, the chairs glued, sanded, and cleaned for staining, covered with cloth tarps as they awaited the mahogany stain I'd picked out. The tabletop was done, propped up on a set of sawhorses, but I hadn't liked the legs I'd been trying to fine-tune the turning on. I was out of practice, and I knew old Bradley Sr. wouldn't approve of how I neglected my skills, but it still made me feel close to him to use his workshop.

The trailer was a little dusty as I unlocked the old Airstream, but after a thorough wipe down, it was clean enough for me. I opened the side door of the building, hitching it to the Jeep so I had someplace to sleep while I worked. There weren't any hotels close enough to make the expense and commute time worth it, and it was weird to be a guest in someone's house for extended periods. Evan had permitted me to clear some of the trees closer to the house, so I had somewhere to park it long term, but he'd told me I could put it in his detached garage until I could get some gravel down once I'd cleared the space.

The rain let up briefly as I made the half-hour drive to their house, carefully backing the trailer into the garage, leaving space for the Jeep beside it. Evan's car was in Boston, and I knew Chase's had been sold a few months ago because she'd been having some transmission issues. It wasn't like they needed two cars anyway; Evan continued to stick close to home often, and they rarely spent any significant time apart.

While I was sure some people thought they were on the co-dependent side, I knew it wasn't because they needed each other to survive. They genuinely wanted to be in each other's lives. Emory and Talia were the same way. I'd never been able to find that, and part of me wanted it desperately.

Before the rain started back up, I quickly made a trip into Ashford, filling up my cooler with food staples and some non-perishables. Chase had texted that they had a freezer full of pre-made meals, but I'd picked up some tricks over the years to keep myself fed without solely relying on takeout. Not that it was an option with the closest restaurants nearly an hour away.

It was dark by the time I got back to the house, the rain starting to pour down in sheets. The lane to the house was dark, the floodlight only flicking on once I'd pulled up to the garage door. I could see the merits of living like this, but I still preferred the convenience of living in a major city like Boston.

Knowing that I'd likely be wearing myself out over the next few days, I quickly hooked the Airstream up to the external power supply in the garage, set up my small generator to charge as well, and stowed my groceries to put away once the fridge had cooled down.

Falling asleep didn't come as quickly as I would have liked, so I popped in my headphones to continue listening to the book I'd started on the drive down.

Somewhere between meet-cute where the heroine embarrassed herself in front of the love interest and their first kiss, I passed out — dreaming of soft lips, dark brown hair, and Kelly's raspy moan.

There was a light layer of fog in the air when I opened the side door to the garage the next day, the heavy mist making the woods around the property look slightly ominous.

Connecting to the Wi-Fi with the password Chase had sent me, I quickly checked the weather, making sure the rain was planning to stay away so I could get some work done this morning.

While the forecast for the rest of the week looked to be filled with scattered thunderstorms and possibly some ice, as soon as the fog cleared, it was supposed to be another clear, chilly New England spring day.

I still needed to pack the trailer full of most of my tools and equipment, but I'd brought along my trusty ax and a chainsaw to work on clearing the brush while the weather was questionable. There was a reason this job wasn't supposed to start until things had begun to dry out in May, but there was no way I was remaining in Boston while things were so tense.

I knew it was avoidant behavior, and I would have to talk this out with Grace eventually, but I was protecting myself right now. I needed space to make sense of what I wanted going forward. She'd broken my trust, so entering another one-off play relationship with her was out of the question, but I didn't want to burn bridges with her because someone else fed her lies.

Marisa worried me more than I wanted to admit. She'd always been a little emotionally fragile, but I kept reminding myself that she was an adult, and I wasn't her savior. She'd freely ended our dynamic, and she hadn't tried to contact me since, despite the lies she'd told Grace. She may have believed there was a chance that her child was mine, but I knew that it wasn't. Out of an abundance of caution, I had myself retested every year, and I was medically sterile. My most recent test results from January proved I was STD free and shooting blanks. Not that there'd been much shooting since February.

The fog was starting to clear as I grabbed my ax and work gloves, throwing my wayward hair into a half bun before I stepped out the side door. It was cold, but I left my beanie off, tucking it into my back pocket. As soon as I started working, I knew that I'd get too hot to keep it on.

The soil sunk a little under my work boots as I stepped into the wooded area just past the poured concrete driveway. While I knew it meant I wasn't likely to be able to start framing within the next few days, I found I didn't mind. The fresh air and the quiet surroundings were already working their magic as I felt my mind and body relax. It was worth the delays just to get away from everything that had been bothering me.

I would otherwise never have been able to shake the anxious feeling that staying in Boston had caused after the other day at Grace's building. My phone was silent again, her persistent calls tapering off after I didn't respond. Marisa still hadn't tried to contact me, but it was only a matter of time once she realized her attention-seeking behavior with Grace hadn't worked.

Thwack

As the ax lodged itself into the side of a small tree trunk, I surveyed the area, figuring out the easiest place to work. There was the rotting, jagged stump of an old tree about ten feet into the woods, but I'd need to get my chainsaw out to turn it into a flat work surface.

I paused as I made my way back to the driveway, frowning as I noticed a familiar Audi parked close to the house. It hadn't been there last night once I got back from the store, and I didn't recall hearing anyone outside last night. But the wind of the thunderstorm had likely drowned out the arrival of a car pulling up.

Pulling my phone from my pocket, I checked the time, noting it was just after 7:00 am. I wasn't sure what the time difference was, but I sent Evan a text anyway.

Nathan: Is there a reason your car is parked in the driveway?

I snapped a picture, making sure to include the Connecticut license plate, just in case I was wrong about the owner.

Moving back to the garage, I pulled out the case for my chainsaw, ensuring the oil inside hadn't gone bad since I'd used it last. Evan had a can of gas sitting in the corner, so I filled it up quickly, screwing on the cap and pressing the primer switch before I tugged on the cord a few times, the motor whirring to life.

I flicked the kill switch, exiting the garage and watching the house for signs of life as I crossed the driveway. There weren't any lights on, and the curtains were drawn in the main bedroom, but they'd been closed when I arrived yesterday.

The chainsaw whirred to life as I pulled the cord a few times to restart it, the blade spinning smoothly as I pressed the hand trigger. I hoped the noise wouldn't wake whoever the house guest was, but I didn't care enough to delay getting started. The break in the weather would only last so long, so I needed to get to work.

Placing my noise-canceling earbuds in, I cranked up my music as I got started, quickly shaping the stump into a flat work surface, and using the chainsaw to cut down the surrounding trees. Beads of sweat gathered in my hair and along the sides of my face as I worked, the air cooling me just enough not to become uncomfortably overheated.

Quickly slicing the small trees into manageable sections, I started a pile off to the side of the large stump. It'd take me a while to get all the lumber split, but Evan would have quite the stockpile of firewood once I was finished.

I laid the chainsaw down at the edge of the driveway, grabbing my ax again as I set up my first log on the stump.

Pulling my work gloves off, I wiped them on my sawdust-covered jeans, trying to brush off the worst of the sweat so I could get a good grip. I'd have preferred to keep them off while I worked, but I'd had plenty of blisters on my palms over the years from ax handles and didn't want to tear up my hands to build the calluses back up.

Tilting my head side to side, I cracked my neck before I braced my legs, pulling my arms above my head and bringing the ax down in the center of the log, a satisfying crack sounding as the sides split apart on the second hit.

The pulsing beats in my ears made it easy for me to drop into the zone, working through the pile of logs to the side of the now ax-marred stump. Stretching my arms across my chest, I pulled on the muscles, enjoying the satisfying burn it caused. I shook out my hands, clenching my fists to alleviate the humming I felt from the repeated impacts of the ax against the wood.

I picked the ax up again, continuing until I felt my phone vibrating in my pocket. Leaning the ax against the stump, I pulled it out of my pocket, frowning when I saw Evan's name scrolling across the screen. I'd expected him to text me back, not call, but I pulled off a glove, swiping the screen to answer the call.

"What's up, man?" I asked as the music cut off in my earbuds once the call connected.

"Just enjoying the time away," he chuckled, and I could hear Chase's voice in the background. "I know. I'm telling him. Calm down. It'll be fine," he laughed, his voice muffled.

"What are you telling me? Is it about the person who parked your car in the driveway late last night?"

"Yeah, about that," he sighed, and I heard Chase's giggle carry through the phone again. "It hopefully shouldn't be a problem, but my sister is staying at the house."

"Kelly?" I cleared my throat, hating the way my voice had cracked on her name.

"Yeah. She had an emergency come up with her job, and she needed to get away for a while. She shouldn't be in your way, but would you mind letting her know you're there?"

"Yeah, no problem." I scratched the back of my head as he pulled the phone away from his ear again, and I heard Chase laughing in the background while she talked too quickly for me to make out the words.

"Would you mind going up to the house now?" he chuckled, and I heard more laughter from Chase. "She's kind of freaking out and thinks you're a serial killer with an ax."

Glancing over my shoulder, I laughed as I saw the curtains in the front window twitch, knowing that she was watching me.

"Does she know it's me?"

Evan covered the receiver again as he talked to Chase. "That's just mean," he laughed, but he didn't sound angry.

"No, she doesn't know it's you, but she knows you're a friend of ours."

"Alright, I'll go up and talk to her. I think she's watching me from the front windows. I'm sure having a strange guy with an ax and a chainsaw in the yard was quite a rude awakening this morning." I was kind of surprised she hadn't woken up earlier when I had the chainsaw out, but I knew the guest bedroom was on the lake side of the house.

"Thanks, man. As I said, Kelly shouldn't bother you, but Chase felt bad telling her she couldn't stay there while we were gone."

"Is everything alright with her?" I hoped my tone seemed casual, trying to keep the concern out of it. Since they hadn't said anything when we talked about me starting work a few weeks ago, I had a feeling this trip wasn't planned. I also knew it had to be something major bringing her here because Kelly told me she rarely took vacation time.

"Yeah, she'll be fine. Something happened at work, so she needs to work remotely for two months. But I think she'll probably only be at the house for a little while. Not sure if she plans to stay once we get back in a few weeks, but..." he trailed off. "Anyway. I've gotta go. Thanks for giving her a heads up."

Tucking my phone back into my pocket, I pulled off my other work glove, throwing them both beside my ax as I turned toward the house. I hadn't seen any more movement from the curtains, but she had to know I was headed her way. Part of me was slightly offended that she couldn't just come outside and talk to me, but I could understand her being worried about a strange man loitering outside with an ax. That *was* how serial killer documentaries started.

Knocking on the door twice, I waited, rolling my neck as I braced my hands against the top of the door frame, leaning forward to stretch the tense muscles in my back. I sighed as a few loud pops sounded and the tension that'd been building in my back eased, my muscles relaxing slightly.

Well, my muscles *were* relaxed until the door swung open. Kelly was standing there with wide eyes, clutching the edge of the door, her mouth opening and closing once before she made this adorable squeaking sound.

"Hello, sunshine," I grinned, shaking my head slightly at her disheveled appearance. And that was when Kelly slammed the door in my face.

A muffled "fuck" sounded from the other side of the door, and I laughed, leaning forward to put my ear against the wood.

"You alright in there, Kelly?"

Clearly, Chase hadn't told her that the blood-thirsty lumberjack was me. You couldn't fake that kind of shock. It was fucking adorable, watching her eyes widen as she saw me standing there.

"Go away," she moaned with a light thump on the door, which I assumed was her head.

A piece of fabric was trapped in the door jamb, so I tried the knob, but it was locked.

"I think you're stuck," I chuckled. "If you open the door, I can help you get free." I tried for a joke when she didn't respond. "At least you're not practically naked this time."

Another thump sounded on the door with a low curse I couldn't make out, and then it started to open slowly, the fabric dropping out of sight.

"What do you want?" she whispered as she peeked around the edge of the door.

"Just letting you know I was out here working. Evan and Chase told me you thought a serial killer lumberjack was roaming the property."

She narrowed her eyes, slowly trailing them down before they returned to my face. I knew I was covered in sawdust, the mist from the fog that still hadn't cleared, and sweat. I was sure I smelled ripe too, but the look in her eyes was not disgust.

It was curiosity mixed with blatant appreciation. She'd checked me out enough times while we were together last summer, and then again in February, that I knew what it looked like when Kelly liked what she saw.

"Well," she waved her hand out the gap in the door in a shooing motion. "You can get back to your jacking. I mean lumberjacking now. I don't want to keep you from your wood."

I bit the inside of my lip to keep from laughing as she shook her head, her brain clearly not firing on all cylinders.

"I'm guessing someone hasn't had their coffee yet?"

"No," she mumbled as she sighed, the door slipping open a little bit more. "All that whacking woke me up."

Deciding to overlook another accidental innuendo coming out of her mouth, I nodded, shifting my weight.

"Do you want to come in and have a cup with me? Maybe you can figure out my brother's complicated coffee press. Don't know why he can't have a Keurig like a normal person."

She turned and walked back into the house, making her way toward the kitchen. I paused for a moment and then stepped inside, closing the door behind me.

"I'd love to."

ELEVEN

Kelly

Connecticut

It really was unfair how men somehow managed to look more attractive when they were disheveled and sweaty. I looked like a red-faced tomato in spandex after any type of physical exertion, but Nathan, covered in sawdust and sweaty plaid, looked like some rugged spokesmodel for a cologne ad.

"How've you been?" Nathan asked as he joined me in the kitchen, leaning against the fridge.

"Fine," I sighed as I opened and closed several cabinets, searching for the coffee beans. I knew Chase practically needed an IV caffeine drip every morning, so the coffee had to be somewhere, but apparently not where any normal person would keep it.

"Would you mind if we didn't beat around the bush?"

I turned, frowning at him as he took a seat at one of the barstools on the other side of the kitchen island.

"I'm not sure what you mean." My brain still wasn't completely awake, and now that the adrenaline had started wearing off from when I thought there was a strange lumberjack roaming the property, I was just tired.

"Why are you here?"

Fuck. Sighing, I closed the cabinet I'd been looking in and turned, leaning against the counter, and glancing up at Nathan's concerned face.

"Why are *you* here?"

His eyebrow arched at my accusatory tone, but he shook his head and smiled.

"I'm here to work on the guest house. Not sure what Evan and Chase told you, but they had issues finding a contractor, and I agreed to get the framing done so they could have finish contractors come in and do the rest this summer."

Nodding, I picked at the edge of my sleeve with my fingers. That meant he wasn't leaving any time soon.

"Where exactly are you staying? I didn't see any of your stuff in the house when I got in last night. And Chase never told me you'd even be here."

He stood up without a word, moving to the refrigerator and opening the freezer. He dug around for a moment and then pulled something out, closing the door and holding it in my direction. "Here."

My fingers grasped the cold package, frowning when I realized it was a half-empty bag of coffee beans.

"They're so weird," I sighed. I hadn't even thought to look in there. Most mornings, my coffee was either made at work by one of the executive assistants or provided by my Keurig into a travel mug on the way out the door. I hadn't used a coffee maker that required grinding beans since I lived with my parents during the summer while I was in college.

"It's perfectly normal to put your coffee in the freezer for a few weeks."

"Ah, so you're one of those," I teased, turning to the complicated-looking coffee maker, frowning at it for a moment before I plugged it into the wall and pulled it to the edge of the counter.

"One of what? That could mean all kinds of things, sunshine," he chuckled, placing his hand on my hip and lightly pushing me to the side.

I moved out of his way, taking a few steps back, and turning to lean against the front of the sink while he pulled open the top of the machine. He read something on a label inside and then opened the bag of coffee beans, using the scoop inside to measure out a few servings.

"A coffee purist. Someone who makes their own using real beans."

"And that's a bad thing?" He shook his head as he glanced in my direction, a smile forming on his full lips.

I'd forgotten how attractive he was. Or maybe I'd blocked it out because I knew that what we'd shared after the wedding was short-lived. There was no point in getting attached if nothing could come of the situation. Well, things *came* alright that weekend, just not a developing, ongoing relationship.

"Taking your time with things shouldn't be considered a shortcoming."

Heat flared through me at the thought of what else he liked to take his time with. He'd been more attentive than I'd been expecting. I had wrongly assumed that him being a Dominant, or whatever, meant that he liked to be in charge and have women do things for him. With how he'd practically worshiped my body at points, almost protesting the one time I wanted to go down on him in the shower, I knew that wasn't the case. Not in the least.

"You still didn't answer my question, Kelly. How are you doing?"

I knew I'd deflected by throwing his question back at him, but I didn't know how much of my fucked-up situation to share. Was he going to think I was a terrible person if I told him the truth? I didn't do anything wrong, but he didn't know that. Having a gut reaction to things like mentioning sexual harassment was natural. I'd judge someone if I knew they were working remotely for that reason. It wouldn't be intentional, and I'd like to think I'd listen to their side of things, but it was a very polarizing topic.

"I'm not sure how to answer that."

"You could start by telling me why you're here. I'm going to assume since they're gone during this visit that Chase and Evan aren't the reason you're in their house right now."

He closed the top of the coffee maker, pressing a few buttons before he made sure the carafe was seated correctly. When he was done, he stepped toward me, leaning against the edge of the island opposite me and crossing his arms on his chest.

"You're not going to leave me alone if I tell you it's none of your business, are you?"

He frowned, shaking his head slightly. "If you don't want to talk to me, I'm not going to pry into your personal business, but I have to say, I'm worried about you. You told me you rarely take vacations as a self-proclaimed workaholic, and yet you're here, hiding out at your brother's house working remotely."

"How much did they tell you?" I knew he was starting to get close to Evan, his presence at the wedding enough indication of their friendship, but I wasn't sure how much they shared.

"They told me you'd be here for a few weeks working remotely because something happened at work."

Just enough to put me on the spot, but not enough to tell him the gravity of the situation.

"Can we leave it at that for now?"

He nodded, reaching forward to grasp my hand, running his thumb across the back of my fingers. "That's fine, but I'm here if you need to talk."

Clenching my jaw, I nodded my head, my nose burning as tears formed in my eyes. I inhaled harshly as I tried to look away quickly, but of course, he saw my reaction.

"Hey," he murmured, stepping forward and cupping the back of my head, pulling me into his chest. "It's alright. I'm not going to pry, but if you're this upset about it, talking might help."

Nathan's chest was warm as I laid my head against his shoulder. I was sure once we'd separated, I'd be covered in sawdust, but it felt good to have him hold me, one hand tangled into the mess of my hair and the other loosely wrapped around my waist.

Closing my eyes, I nodded, but I still didn't have the words to explain the mess I'd gotten myself into by hesitating to report Trent.

Nathan didn't say a word, just breathed deeply as his thumb stroked my waist, the motion sending shockwaves of pleasure through my system. I practically melted into his embrace, enjoying the comfort he was trying to provide. He didn't care what had happened. He was here for me because he thought I needed him. It made me ache in a way I hadn't expected.

I wasn't sure if it was because we'd slept — or not *slept* — together, or if he was just that genuinely nice of a guy, but it felt good to have someone who cared that I was upset.

The quiet sound of the coffee percolating was the only noise in the kitchen, and I snuggled deeper into his embrace, enjoying the soft sigh he made when I grasped the material of his shirt on his lower back.

"You don't have to tell me anything," he whispered as his fingers burrowed under my hair, tilting my head back so he could look down at me. "But I hope you know you can tell me everything if you want to."

My eyes searched his, and my heart started to beat faster at the sincerity in his expression. He'd told me back then that he wanted things from me that he shouldn't. And right now, looking up into his soft brown eyes, I knew that there were things I *needed* from him desperately that I shouldn't.

"Thank you," I whispered, pushing up onto my tiptoes and kissing the corner of his mouth. His beard tickled my cheek, the sensation so different than what it'd been like to be this close to him before.

"Anytime, sunshine," he smiled softly, moving his hand around to cup my jaw. "I hope you know I mean that."

The beep of the coffee maker startled me, and I took a step back before I could respond, aimlessly brushing my hands down my front as I retreated backward.

"Sorry." He smiled as he gestured toward the sawdust that he'd unintentionally transferred to my tunic during the hug. "Didn't mean to cover you in that."

I tried to shut down the memory of something he'd said in that hotel room about covering me in something else, but I could feel my face flame as he looked at me curiously before turning toward the coffee maker.

"I won't even ask what has you blushing like that," he chuckled as he grabbed two mugs from a cabinet and began to fill them.

"How do you like it?" he asked as he reached for the canister of sweetener packets on the counter. Again, my filthy brain conjured images of him behind me, his fist wrapped around my braid as he pounded into me, asking me if I liked it rough.

"Your coffee, Kelly. How do you like your coffee?" He shook his head again with a little chuckle as my cheeks flushed. I crossed the space between us, grabbing a single Stevia packet and emptying it into one of the mugs. Then I pulled a caramel creamer tub out of the basket on the counter, emptying it into the cup before I started opening drawers, looking for a spoon.

"I would have done that for you. All you had to do was ask." He smirked as he turned to lean against the counter, bringing his mug up to his lips for a sip. "You don't have to do everything yourself, Kell. Let other people be nice to you."

"You know I don't like to ask for help," I teased as I retreated to my spot by the sink.

"Oh, I'm well aware of that," he laughed. "But you don't always need to. Let someone in some time, and you might be surprised how good it feels."

"I know how good it feels to let someone inside," I retorted, my eyes widening at the double entendre. By the way his nostrils flared and the way his hips shifted against the counter behind him, I knew he remembered how good something felt inside as well.

"Can we talk about why you're here now?" I begged as the heat in the air between us started to make me nervous.

"I already told you why I'm here," he smiled, casually taking a sip of his coffee, the charged moment between us starting to fade.

"Now, who's being avoidant?" I challenged. "I know Evan said you weren't supposed to start working until early in the summer."

"Fine. Some shit happened in Boston, and I needed to get out of there to clear my head. I'll admit my timing wasn't ideal with the crappy weather forecast for the next few weeks, but I needed a break."

I nodded, knowing it wasn't fair to pry when I was being tight-lipped about my situation.

"That's it? No more questions?" he teased before he tilted his mug up and drained the last of its contents. He took a step toward me, his smile widening as I swallowed hard, shifting over to attempt to get out of his way.

Nathan's hand grasped the side of my hip, holding me in place as he gently set his mug down in the sink. "You don't need to move on my account, sunshine. I'm happy to lean around you."

"Geez," I scoffed as I tried to hide my face behind my mug. "I forgot how much of a flirt you are."

"Did you now?" he teased, using his finger to brush a stray lock of hair behind my ear. "Because I didn't forget a damn thing about you."

My hands trembled against my mug as I continued to hide my face. I wasn't prepared for this. Never once had I factored running into Nathan in my plans to hide for the next few weeks.

"I need to get back to work before the rain starts again." His voice was soft, and his fingers flexed on my hip as he hesitated. "It's really good to see you, Kelly. I've thought about you a lot over the last few months."

A jerky nod was all I could manage as he took a step back, his eyes trailing down my body as he retreated to the other side of the island. I looked down, breaking eye contact as he turned around and headed back toward the front door.

"Can I come to check on you later?" he asked quietly as he stopped in the entryway.

I nodded, my face still half-hidden behind the coffee mug I had clenched in my hands.

Nathan smiled in response as he pulled the door open, looking back at me briefly as he stepped outside.

"Wait," I called as the door started to close, quickly setting my mug down on the counter and taking a few steps in his direction. He stopped, pushing the door back open with a soft smile on his face.

"Yes?"

"Would you like to eat dinner with me?"

He hesitated, and my stomach dropped. Of course, it was a stupid idea.

"Never mind." I waved him away with my hand. "I'm sure you've got other things you need to be doing, and I don't even know where you're staying. It might be out of the way for you to come back here."

"Can I answer your question now?" he chuckled as he leaned against the door frame with his arms folded across his chest.

Nodding, I gripped the edge of the countertop, trying to keep myself from running away, suddenly terrified at the thought he might reject my offer.

"What time do you want me back here?" He smiled, and I felt myself relax.

"Whenever is good for you. I'm not actually going to cook. I wouldn't subject you to that," I laughed nervously. "Evan has a whole bunch of pre-assembled meals in the freezer. Surely I can't screw up reheating one for each of us. I haven't had a chance to drive into town to grocery shop. So I don't have much to drink or anything, but if you'd like to join me, I'd appreciate the company."

"Breathe, sunshine," he chuckled from the doorway.

Narrowing my eyes at him, I let out a little growl at his teasing. I was acting like a nervous wreck this morning — but with our history, he gave me the jitters.

"Fine, whatever. I'll just eat by myself."

"I didn't say that," he laughed. "Although this display of nerves from you is fucking adorable. But I'll be here around eight if that works for you? I might need to drive back to my property to shower after I'm done working. The sun is supposed to start going down around seven, so I'd like to get as much done as I can in case the rain moves back in."

"You can use me," I blurted. *Fuck.* "I mean the shower here."

Nathan's smirk faltered, a loud laugh escaping his mouth. "I don't want to inconvenience you. It's not a problem to go use the utility shower in my barn."

Running my hands down my face, hating that I could tell how red my cheeks were from the heat coming off them, I nodded. "OK. Whatever you want to do. But there's two here, so you don't even need to use me — I mean mine. Evan has a big walk-in shower in the main bathroom you can use. You're bigger. I mean, it's bigger than mine."

Nathan was unsuccessfully trying to smother his laughter by biting his lip. I needed to get my shit together if he was going to be here the entire time I was. A girl could only embarrass herself so many times in front of a guy.

"If you don't mind, I'll knock around seven once I get my things together from the trailer. I appreciate the offer."

"What trailer?" I frowned, glancing toward the windows that overlooked the driveway.

"It's in the garage." He jerked his head back toward the building outside. "It's where I'm staying while I'm working."

"Is that comfortable? I mean, I'm sure we can fit you in here somewhere if you want to come inside."

He laughed again, his mind clearly going into the gutter mine had been residing in throughout half this encounter.

"You know what I meant!" I shot back, trying to hold in my laughter.

"Not sure I did, sunshine. Where exactly would you be fitting me?" he challenged, one eyebrow rising into his forehead. "You know I'd love to come inside."

"Fuck off," I growled, shaking my head as I walked toward the door. He already knew I said ridiculous things when I was nervous. Lord knows the crazy things I'd said during that weekend in the hotel room. I didn't even know I was capable of half the things I said and did with him.

Which was not helping my situation at all right now.

"Not unless you ask nicely, sunshine," he murmured as I walked into the entryway, loosely gripping the edge of the open front door. One of the dirty work boots he'd put back on a few moments ago

120

was propping the door open as he leaned against the frame, his smirk making it clear he was enjoying my inability to speak around him.

"Fine, I take it back. Stay out in the cold garage by yourself, and I won't have to worry about the hassle of wearing pajamas in here."

"But you wear them so well," he teased, once again letting his eyes trail down my body. How he could flirt with me when I knew I looked like a hot mess was beyond me, but I had to admit I was enjoying it.

"Well, I look even better out of them." Slapping my hand over my mouth, I shook my head, not having intended to say that aloud. "Sorry, that was inappropriate," I mumbled through my fingers as he started to chuckle.

He grasped my hand, pulling it loose and squeezing my fingertips before he dropped it gently. "Don't be embarrassed, Kell. You know I like this side of you. Don't ever change."

My cheeks flooded again, a tingle running up my spine at his words.

"Just come let me know if you need me to run to the store later this afternoon," he continued. "I'm looking forward to spending more time with you. Even if you do keep looking at me like a piece of meat."

"Oh, shut it," I snapped as I tried to push him out the door. "Go back to playing with your wood."

A surprised laugh burst out of Nathan's mouth as he shook his head, pushing himself off the door frame and nodding in my direction before he crossed the driveway.

I paused to look at him for a moment, enjoying the way his hips swung as he strutted toward the woods, bending over to pick up his ax from where he'd left it propped.

He turned to face me, a smirk on his face when he caught me watching. He threw his hand up in a wave. "Have fun watching me handling my wood!" he yelled, and I quickly slammed the door, his loud   laughter   echoing   outside.

TWELVE

Nathan

Connecticut

Despite knowing that Kelly was watching, I still felt a thrill crawl up my spine every time I glanced toward the front windows of the house while I was working. I'd caught glimpses of her throughout the day and had to force myself to concentrate.

Becoming distracted while holding a sharp object in my hands was not only a potential hazard but downright stupid. I'd barred people from a worksite before for letting their personal lives distract them from paying attention to their often-dangerous jobs and the machinery they handled.

Ever since my brief phone conversation with Evan, I'd found myself analyzing the timing of everything. At first glance, it appeared to be a coincidence that we'd be in the same place at the same time, much like the wedding. But it felt like something bigger was at play here.

Kelly had been placed in my path twice when I felt listless. Who was I to question fate or divine intervention or whatever it was that kept drawing us together? While the weekend we spent together had a short shelf life, it seemed we'd be together for at least the next few weeks this time. Was this a test of some sort?

She had seemed flustered to see me, and her fumbling this morning had been downright endearing. She had the potential to be quite the firecracker if she'd relax a little and let me inside that head of hers. Her outer beauty paled in comparison to glimpses of her personality that she'd revealed. A sense of humor was something I found completely and utterly sexy, but we'd have to work on the self-deprecation. I had a feeling Kelly was harder on herself than she needed to be.

The only flaw I saw in reading more into the situation was her hesitation to trust me. She'd outright refused to tell me what happened with her job, and the pain in her eyes at the mention of it made my mind race with possibilities of what might have happened.

None of those scenarios were good. And if someone there hurt her in any way...

The very thought of it ignited something primal and protective inside of me. I'd fly to Chicago and fuck someone up if they'd done something to her. I knew all kinds of methods to torture someone; give me a rope and a pocketknife, and I'd make sure they wished they'd never been born.

A glance at my watch showed it was already nearing 7:00 pm. My shoulders burned with the exertion of clearing the space next to the driveway and around the foundation. It wasn't easy work by any means, but I felt accomplished as I looked over toward the large pile of firewood next to the garage that I'd loosely covered with a tarp. There was a pile of brush I'd need to dispose of as well, but the woodchipper back at the barn would chew through that in no time.

The lights in the house flicked on as the sun began to set in the west, the reds and pinks of the sky reflecting off the corner of the lake I could see down the hill from the house.

Evan had chosen well with this location, and if I ever wanted to move out of the city permanently, I could see myself wanting something like this. Quiet, undisturbed, beautiful surroundings. It didn't surprise me that this was where Evan and Chase chose to do most of their writing.

Kelly briefly appeared in the front window, running a brush through her wet hair as she scanned the area around the house. I was far enough into the wooded area she likely couldn't see me, but I could see the emotions flickering across her face from here.

Kelly might have thought she was vanilla, but I'd seen some voyeuristic tendencies in the way she watched people, mostly because I'd watched her intently throughout the weekend of the wedding. As her dark eyes scanned the woods again, I found myself thinking dangerous thoughts about what other little hidden kinks she might have.

I already knew she didn't mind being restrained and took direction well. She had also granted me glimpses of hidden dominant personality traits I'd love to see come to light. If coached correctly, she had the potential to bring men to their knees — literally. I just wasn't sure if that were something she'd want or something I hoped she'd let blossom within herself for selfish reasons.

When she stepped away from the window, moving toward the kitchen, I realized she was likely waiting to see if I'd make an appearance. She *had* offered the use of one of the showers in the house, and it'd be rude to refuse her hospitality. At least, that was the excuse I was using for the need to spend more time with her that had been rising in me since Evan mentioned her name. I knew he said she wouldn't be a problem while I was trying to work, but he had no idea about the secret fixation I had with his sister that had come roaring back to life as soon as she opened that door all grumpy and sleep-rumpled.

Gathering up my tools on the way back to the garage, I stowed away my chainsaw and ax, making sure the blades were clean and dry as any good workman should.

It was nearing 7:30 when I got my toiletries and clean clothes thrown into a small duffel bag and knocked on the front door.

"You're late," Kelly smiled while she held the door open. "It's not nice to keep a lady waiting."

"I apologize." Stepping closer, I leaned in to place a small kiss at the corner of her jaw. "I'll try better next time."

"Awfully presumptive to assume I'll be inviting you in again," she laughed, closing the door as I stepped into the house.

"We're both here for the next several weeks. Seems foolish to spend all that time by ourselves. But if you don't want me around, just say so, and I'll leave you alone." She nodded, trying to suppress a smile, but I was onto her. "But I think we both know you like having me here. So there's no point in lying about it."

"Quite sure of yourself, aren't you?"

"Only because I saw you loitering around the window several times today ogling me."

"I wasn't," she stuttered, turning her face away from me as a soft blush appeared on her cheeks. "I was just looking out the window. I wasn't looking *for* you. Arrogant much?"

"Not typically, but the phrase 'takes one to know one' comes to mind. And I think you've got some voyeuristic tendencies in you. You like to watch, don't you Kelly?"

"Does everything have to be about kink with you?" She rolled her eyes, crossing her arms, which caused her breasts to push up against the   neckline   of   her   sweater.

She was trying to deflect, but I saw the way she swallowed hard when I whispered the comment about her watching.

"No. But once you know how to look at people's behavior, it's not hard to pick out what someone's kinks might be."

"Well," she sighed dramatically, waving her hand toward the hallway. "Why don't you go clean yourself up, and then you can tell me all about your kinks."

"Putting me in the spotlight, huh?"

She stepped back toward the kitchen, rolling her eyes, and arching a brow at me. "Maybe you'll stop asking me so many questions if I get you talking about yourself. Let's be realistic here. You're probably more interesting to talk about anyway."

"Don't," I shook my head as I stepped into her personal space and tilted her chin toward me with the tips of my fingers. I was sure I was getting her dirty, but I found I didn't care. "Don't put yourself down. Don't do that. If I weren't interested in spending time with you and listening to what you have to say, I wouldn't be here."

The nervous look in her eyes softened as they darted between mine. I wasn't sure what she found there, but she nodded her head hesitantly. "OK. I won't. I'm sor…"

"Don't apologize either."

She stared up at me hesitantly for a few seconds before she stepped back, bumping into the edge of the kitchen island, and grasping the edge of the countertop to steady herself. "The main bedroom is at the end of that hall. Help yourself to whatever you need. I left a towel on the counter for you."

"Thanks," I nodded, secretly enjoying the way she watched me walk down the hallway. I could feel her eyes on me. As I turned to look back at her from the doorway, I caught her looking in my direction, causing her to jerk her head to the side like she hadn't been following my movements.

"I'll just get the food going," she shouted as I walked out of sight, chuckling to myself as I moved toward the bathroom.

The hot water in the walk-in shower felt good on my sore muscles, and by the time I was scrubbed clean and dried off, my stomach had started to growl. The protein bar I'd wolfed down midday had done nothing to keep my stomach full, and I was glad Kelly had saved me from trying to muster the energy to cook something for myself in the small microwave or on the old propane stove in the Airstream.

"You look refreshed," Kelly smiled as she looked up from the corner of the large couch in the open living room. "Food is heated up. I wasn't sure what you liked, so I grabbed a few different things. Whatever we don't eat, I can always reheat for lunch tomorrow. Although I should probably make a trip into town sooner rather than later, or I'm going to burn through Chase's whole stash of freezer meals, and then she'll murder me."

"I highly doubt your brother or Chase would be upset with you taking advantage of their hospitality." Running my fingers through my damp hair, I combed it back from my face. I'd forgotten to grab a hair tie, and I was sure it'd dry into a curly mess by the time the evening was through. A haircut hadn't even been on my radar when I was fleeing Boston, although I knew I was more than several months overdue for one. It was on the longer side when Kelly saw me months ago, and now it was almost to my chin.

"Well, you underestimate how much my sister-in-law despises cooking. Why else do you think she was quick to move in with Evan?"

"Maybe because she enjoyed his company?" I laughed.

"Hardly," Kelly giggled. "You have met Evan, right?"

"I'm not sure that's entirely fair. He's a cool guy, a little quiet, but he's pretty funny once you get to know him. They seem to get along well. You know, considering the whole living together, and getting married and writing books together thing."

"Yeah, yeah." She waved her hand in the air dismissively. "Tell me all about how perfectly nauseating they are together. Like that isn't the topic of half my conversations with my mother since they met."

Kelly stood, smoothing out the long sweater she was wearing, the edge of the neckline falling to one side to expose the soft skin of her shoulder. It was clear from the outline of her body underneath that sweater that she wasn't wearing a bra again. My fists clenched at my sides as I fought the urge to pull her into my arms and kiss all that soft, exposed skin.

"Let's eat before it gets cold, and can we please not talk about how perfect my brother is for the rest of the night? I'd rather not."

Frowning at the weariness in her voice, I nodded, following her toward the kitchen, where several covered plastic containers sat spread out on this island. "Looks good. Thank you for inviting me for dinner."

She glanced over her shoulder, shrugging with a shy smile on her face before she turned back to the food she was uncovering. "What can I say? I felt sorry for you."

"Such a mouth on you." A loud laugh escaped my mouth as she bit the corner of her lip and glanced back at me with mirth in her eyes.

"You like it."

Nodding, I smiled back at her. "I do." There were all kinds of things I found myself liking about Kelly. Her sass was definitely one of them. For once, the slightly bratty behavior didn't make me want to try to tame it out of her. I found myself wanting to encourage it and see her turn the tables on me. I found her spark to be one of her sexiest qualities. Well…that and her amazing ass.

"Eyes up here, stud," she giggled as she bumped her hip into mine.

Grabbing a plate, I dished up even portions from the containers of each dish onto both plates, enjoying the way she eyed me from where she'd leaned back against the edge of the counter.

"Where would you like to sit?" I asked as I picked up both plates, glancing toward the small table near the sliding glass door and then the cozy living room area in front of the fireplace. The fire wasn't lit, but that could be easily remedied.

"Do you mind if we sit on the couch? I'll feel less like I have to entertain you that way."

"Oh, pour on the flattery, sunshine. Let me know how you really feel about spending time with me."

"I think your ego is big enough, Nate. You don't need me to feed it."

"Ouch," I faked being wounded by her barb, frowning as I followed her into the living room, waiting for her to take a seat before handing her the plate I'd fixed for her.

"You know I'm perfectly capable of plating up my own food," she teased as she settled back into the corner of the cushions, folding her legs underneath herself, covering her legs with a blanket, and balancing the plate on her knees.

"I do," I nodded. "And maybe you should let someone serve you for a change instead of trying to do everything by yourself." I'd be happy to do her bidding for more than just making sure she had a meal.

"Aren't you going to sit down?" she asked as I leaned over to rest my plate on the coffee table.

"Do you know where they keep the matches?" I nodded to the fireplace.

"On the mantel, but you don't need to worry about that. There isn't any firewood anyway," she said, motioning to the empty basket on the hearth.

"I've got this," I winked as I moved back to the entryway.

"You don't need to bother," she called after me.

I kept moving, grabbing my coat, and heading toward the garage. I pulled a few dry pieces of wood from the pile in the corner and then filled a bucket with freshly cut timber from the stacks outside. The least I could do as repayment for dinner was to start a fire. Not that she likely couldn't do it for herself, but I felt compelled to take care of her.

"Your food is going to get cold," she scolded as I walked past her and settled down on my knees in front of the fireplace. Reaching up to grab the matches off the mantelpiece, I opened the grate and stacked the dry wood inside, pulling a few pieces of newspaper from the basket off to the side and crumpling them up.

"It'll reheat," I shrugged as I kept working, lighting the paper with a match, and slowly coaxing the flames higher. "I get distracted and don't end up eating while my food's hot half the time anyway." After a few minutes, I sat back, watching the blue and orange flames dance, heat starting to move out into the room. I checked that the flue was completely open before I closed the grate.

"Well, aren't you quite the Boy Scout," Kelly teased as I picked up my abandoned plate, sitting down opposite her on the couch. Her plate was mostly empty, discarded on the corner of the coffee table while she cradled a glass of wine she must have poured when I was outside.

"Actually. I am. But this is hardly building a campfire in the wilderness with two sticks."

"Which I'm assuming you've done." She was watching me as I ate, a calculating smile playing across her lips. I wasn't sure if it was

128

time or the alcohol making her more comfortable with my presence, but I'd take it over the anxious fumbling of this morning.

"Wouldn't be much of an Eagle Scout if I hadn't. We had to learn all kinds of survival skills at summer camp."

"The only thing I remember from Girl Scouts was coercing my neighbors into buying more cookies than they needed so I could get a T-shirt."

"I could see you being highly persuasive." It was the truth. If Kelly wanted to, she could convince me to do all kinds of things. Not that it'd take much convincing.

"I have my moments," she shrugged, slowly sipping from her glass.

We sat in a semi-charged silence as I finished off the contents of my plate. I set it on the coffee table before leaning back into the couch corner opposite her and stretching my arm out along the back. "Have you decided whether you're going to tell me why you're here?"

Might as well try to ask while she was more relaxed than earlier today. I was still curious, and while I wouldn't force her to tell me anything, I wanted to know.

"You're not going to let that go, are you?"

Pausing for a moment, I decided just to lay my cards on the table. "I can let it go if that's what you really want. But is it? Do you want me to let it go? It seems like you've bottled something up, and it might help to tell a neutral party."

From the myriad of emotions that crossed her face, I could tell she did want to let me in, and I wasn't going to coerce her into anything against her will, but she had to know that I was concerned. This visit was as out of character for her as it was for me, and while I was enjoying being in the same place as her again, if she needed support to process going through something difficult in her life, I wanted to be that for her.

"Why do you care so much?" Her voice was quiet and guarded; her grip on her glass indicated I was making her feel uncomfortable. That was the last thing I wanted.

"Because I care about you, and if you're going through something difficult, I want to be here for you to lean on."

"Hah," she scoffed. "You hardly know me."

"I think we both know that's not true, sunshine. We didn't just fuck in that hotel room, and you know it. I talked to you about things I rarely talk about, and you did the same, so don't pretend that you know my feelings toward you. Because I can assure you, you don't."

"Me whining about working too much and being upset my brother found someone to spend his life with before me are hardly deep philosophical conversations."

"Cut the shit, Kelly. You're deflecting again, and I know how you get when you feel exposed. Or did you forget those whispered conversations in the middle of the night about how you weren't sure anyone in your life took you seriously? This is me trying to take you seriously, so let me. Let me in."

She frowned, placing her glass down on the coffee table and settling back into her corner with the blanket in her lap grasped tightly in her fingers. "Because they still don't. Which is why I'm in this fucking mess."

"Talk to me."

"Why? What's the point?" I watched as a single tear tracked down the side of her face and decided that I was going to take matters into my own hands, literally.

"Come here," I scooted toward her, holding my hand out as she continued to avoid looking at me.

"You don't…"

"Don't tell me what I do and don't want. Get in my fucking lap and let me hug you, sunshine. You're hurting, and there's no reason to try to shoulder everything on your own." She laughed, scooting toward me, and hesitantly leaning against my side. "Come on, don't be shy. I've seen you naked. Get on my damn lap."

"You're bossy today," she huffed, looking into my eyes as she scooted a little closer.

"This is nothing, sweetheart."

Once she was pressed into my side, I wrapped my arms around her, pulling her fully into my lap and tucking her head underneath my chin. Sometimes you just needed a fucking hug, and I was going to give it to her.

"Nathan…" she started, trying to scoot herself off my lap.

"Just relax and talk to me. It might be easier if you aren't looking at me. I'm not going to judge you, but I can't help you if you keep shutting me out. I know you don't think we know each other well, but I know you, Kelly. You take on everything by yourself, and you need to learn to let some of that go and accept help — and comfort — from people when they offer it."

"I don't even know where to start," she whispered, letting out a stuttering breath as she relaxed against my chest. I slowly ran my hand down her loose hair, burrowing my fingers underneath so I could rub the tense muscles in her neck. "Part of this is my fault, and I can't figure out where I went wrong."

"Start at the beginning. Or the end. Whatever you want to tell me, I'll listen."

And then she started to talk. She told me more about her job and how she'd worked her ass off to be where she was in her department, reporting directly to the department head. I felt a stab of jealousy as she talked about her friendship with Tom but then settled down when she told me he was married and likely a new father by now.

But even I knew that didn't mean anything. Being married and being a father didn't make you some upstanding person. From the fucked-up things I learned about my father after his death, I knew that. No sixteen-year-old should have the rug pulled out from their seemingly boring life as I had.

When Kelly started talking about her co-worker, Trent, my hackles rose, knowing I wouldn't like what she would tell me next.

"It started with little things. Snide comments about accounts that I'd worked on or my friendship with Tom. Undermining my work in staff meetings and giving me dirty looks when I got praised by our supervisors. I don't know when things changed from the harmless stuff..."

"Kelly, those aren't simply harmless things. He was downright rude to you from the beginning, it seemed, and you took it. You should never let someone make you feel like your hard work doesn't mean anything." From her description of this guy, I already wanted to pin him to the nearest wall and ask him what his problem was with successful women. It seemed that he was never taught how to behave like a gentleman.

"I'm not one of those people who needs everyone to like them. I knew he was jealous that I got more attention for my work, but I just chalked it up to him being upset I wouldn't go out with him."

131

"Wait," I stopped her again, leaning back and tilting her face up so she'd look at me. "This started after you turned down advances from him?"

"Well," she shrugged, almost looking embarrassed. "They weren't sexual advances or anything like that at first. But he'd ask me to get a drink with him after work sometimes, and I turned him down. If the department went out together, I always tried to stay away from him. I just didn't like him. He was so into himself it was a turn-off. He also had his lips suction-cupped to Deacon's ass. A brown nose wasn't a good look for him."

"You said at first," I prompted, trying to keep myself calm. I'd dealt with men, and women for that matter, like Trent. They always seemed harmless at first, and then, before you knew it, they escalated. We'd had a carpenter on one of my crews who would hit on the female architects when they'd come on-site, trying to play off sexist comments as jokes. Eventually, he'd made a physical pass at the wrong woman, and she filed a complaint against him. He was off the site within a week, and I hadn't worked with him since.

"Then he started making derogatory comments about my friendship with Tom. He was convinced something was going on with the two of us behind his wife's back. He even told Charley about how we spent too much time together. She knew I wasn't interested in her husband, but it made things awkward for a while."

"Hmm," I hummed, knowing that sometimes those speculations were true, and sometimes they weren't. I had a feeling in Kelly's case; they weren't.

"I wasn't," she quickly said, sitting up slightly to make eye contact. "I was never involved with Tom like that. He reminded me of Evan."

"What happened?" I could tell she'd been building up to something big.

"Trent didn't like that I was being left in charge during Tom's paternity leave. He was very vocal about how unqualified I was to lead the rest of our team. A few people defended me, but he still hated the idea of reporting to me, even for a few weeks."

"What did he do?" My blood pressure started to rise as she clung to my shirt, her heart hammering against my chest. Grasping her hand, I leaned down to kiss her knuckles and then the top of her head. "He did something, didn't he?"

"He told me that I kept my job because of the skills I had while on my knees. He cornered me in my office and said some other nasty things, and I kicked him out, threatening to go to HR about his behavior."

"And did you?"

"No," she whispered, her voice breaking. My arms tightened around her shoulders as I tucked my face into her hair, feeling her body tremble. "I know I should have, but I was working on a project with a deadline, and I didn't want to seem like I was overreacting to it. I guess I thought it would show him I was weak or something if I couldn't handle it on my own. He went to HR that afternoon and told them I'd sexually harassed *him*. And now I can't go back to the office or interact with anyone for the next eight weeks because he's trying to ruin my career. I didn't even do anything to him, ever. I'd never..." her voice broke as she gripped my shirt in her fist, burrowing her face into the fabric.

What an epic asshole. Who did shit like that because their ego couldn't take a woman who'd shot them down supervising them for a few weeks?

"I'm so sorry," I whispered into her hair, pulling her closer. Kelly shifted, her knees settling on either side of my thighs as she tucked herself fully into my chest, laying her head on my shoulder. "I'm sorry he did that to you, sunshine. What he did to you was not OK. I know how hard you work, and I can't believe he'd let his jealousy cloud how much of an asset you are to that department."

She sniffled, holding onto my arms, her nose buried into my neck, puffs of warmth spreading along my skin as she breathed heavily. I held her, softly running my hands through her hair as she clung to me for comfort. Eventually, her body relaxed, and the tension drained from her muscles. I almost thought she was asleep until I felt one of her hands burrow its way underneath the back of my shirt, softly tickling the skin of my lower back, making sensations run through me that I couldn't control.

"Touch me," she whispered into my neck as she wiggled on my lap, her lips dragging along the edge of my beard.

"What are you doing?" I whispered, laughing a little as she nipped at my pulse point. "I'm supposed to be comforting you, silly girl."

"I know another way you can comfort me," she whispered, sitting up a little straighter and kissing a path from my neck to my ear. I shuddered beneath her, trying to control myself, but I could only do so much to fight off the sensations a wiggling, warm, sensual woman kissing up my neck was causing.

"Kelly," I scolded, but it turned into a groan as she rocked against me, biting down on my earlobe as her hand wandered into the back of my jeans. "What are you trying to do?"

"I'm obviously not doing it right if you're asking that," she laughed as she leaned back, scraping her fingernails through the hair at the edge of my jaw.

"I know what you're doing, sunshine," I laughed, grasping her waist with my hands as she rocked forward, causing me to grunt as I leaned my head against the back of the couch. "But I don't know what you want from me."

"I want you to make me forget," she breathed out softly, her eyes wide and vulnerable as she let out a deep breath. "I want you to make me forget my own name."

"Kelly." Her name was a harsh whisper as my fingers tightened, a surprised gasp escaping her mouth as I tried to hold her still.

"I want you to make me cum, Nathan."

Fuck...

How   had   comforting   her   turned   into   this?

THIRTEEN

Kelly

Connecticut

I was almost afraid Nathan would turn me down as his grip on my waist tightened, my thighs clenching in response. He was still staring at me with his head thrown back, his chest heaving as he tried to hold me still. I wasn't sure at what point the soft caresses of his hand on the back of my head and his comforting hold turned into something more for me, but suddenly I couldn't help remembering how good we'd felt together and how much I wanted to feel that again. Not to forget about all the shit that'd happened to me in the last few days, but to remember how it felt to be with *him*.

"I'm..." His voice cut off on a pained groan as he closed his eyes, shifting underneath me. I could feel how hard he was between my legs, but I could also see I'd caught him by surprise. He'd just been trying to be a good friend, a confidant for what I'd been going through.

"I'm sorry," I whispered as I looked down, feeling tears forming at the corners of my eyes as I tried to climb off his lap.

"Stop," he groaned again as he leaned forward, bringing his chest flush with mine and looking down into my eyes. "I don't want to be some guy you use to forget your problems," he whispered. "Don't start something if that's all this is to you."

Bringing my hand up to his cheek, I softly stroked the skin along the edge of his beard, hating that I was screwing this up too.

"I'm sorry. That's not why I..." I trailed off, looking down to the side. "Being with you made me feel more alive than I ever have in my life. I wanted to feel that way again."

Something flashed in his eyes, and I sat still, feeling his warm breath against my temple as I waited. "Tell me you want *me*, Kelly. Not just what I make you feel."

"I've wanted you for months, Nathan, but I thought I'd never see you again," I whispered as I closed my eyes.

One of his hands left my waist, slowly ascending my back before he gripped the end of my hair in his fist, tilting my head back, so I was forced to look into his eyes. "What do you want from me?"

My mouth opened and closed, and I felt my resolve falter as his eyes continued to search mine for something. "I…"

"What do you fucking want, Kelly? Tell me." His voice was strained, but there was no mistaking the fact that he felt this intense energy between us. I could feel him hard in between my legs. I'd forgotten what it'd felt like to be with him like this. Like I was holding onto a live wire and waiting for it to spark.

"I want you to make me cum," I whispered, closing my eyes, and letting out a shuddering breath. "I want to feel you between my legs, inside me. Covering me. I want you to make me cum so hard I can't stop shaking. I want *you* and the way you make me feel."

Something about confessing what I wanted with my eyes closed made it easier to say it aloud. To tell him what I'd been thinking probably since I saw him standing in that doorway this morning.

"Fuck," his rough whisper was the only response I got before his palm grasped the back of my neck, pulling me toward him as he crushed his lips to mine. I ground against him desperately, the ache inside of me growing as I rocked against him, feeling how hard he was already.

My fingers shook as I tried to pry the buttons on his shirt loose while he absolutely took possession of my mouth, his tongue curling around mine in a way that made me clench. I remembered what it felt like to have that tongue on my body, and I wanted it with a ferocity I couldn't describe.

"Help me get these off," I whispered as I pulled away from his lips, tugging at the button and zipper of his jeans.

"God, you're fucking impatient," he laughed as I stood up and shoved down my leggings and panties, reaching forward to help him tug down his jeans. I hadn't invited him here tonight to have sex with me, I hadn't even considered it as an option until a few seconds ago. But as his cock sprung free, and he kicked his jeans off, his plaid shirt hanging open as he sat panting against the back of the couch, I couldn't think of doing anything else.

"Are you complaining?" I laughed as I climbed back into his lap, grasping him loosely in my hand as I rose to my knees.

"Fuck, no," he groaned as he grasped my jaw with his hand, pulling my mouth back to his as I hovered over him. "Fuck," he groaned loudly as he gripped my waist, halting my movements.

"Is this...? Is this OK?" I asked quietly, my voice breathy as I felt him poised at my entrance. Every other time I'd been with him we'd used protection, but I wanted to feel him.

"Should we use something?" he asked, his voice a harsh whisper. "Fuck. I've been tested. I'm safe."

"I have too. I..." I paused, wondering how much detail he needed on why birth control wasn't an issue with me.

"What's wrong?" he asked, loosening his fingers on my jaw, and wrapping his palm around the back of my neck. "We don't have to if you don't want...I think I have some condoms in my trailer if you're worried about that. I wasn't exactly expecting this."

"We don't need them if you don't want..." I trailed off, suddenly feeling emotional about something else that had gone wrong in my life.

"Hey," he shook his head as he sat up, forcing me to sit back against his knees. Talk about ruining the moment. "I wasn't expecting this, but if you don't want to, there are other ways I can make you cum."

"It's not that. I want you more than I can even describe. God, I'm ruining this," I shook my head, starting to rise from his lap.

"Fuck that," he groaned, grasping my hips, and keeping me in place as he placed a quick kiss on my temple. "You haven't ruined a damn thing, sunshine. Now talk to me."

Avoiding his eyes, I whispered the thing I'd been trying to deny for the last six months, the other reason I had to keep him at arms-length. "I can't have kids. That's why we don't need anything if we're both safe because you couldn't get me pregnant anyway. I'm broken."

"Kelly," his voice was a rough whisper as he cupped my cheeks, leaning down to kiss me softly. "You are far from broken. And you didn't ruin anything. You have no idea how much I want you or why. It doesn't change anything for me."

"But..." I whimpered as he leaned in to cut me off with his lips again, slowly coaxing me into a sensual, open-mouthed kiss as my eyes slipped closed.

He released my cheeks, his hands framing my hips and urging me forward as he leaned back against the couch. I lost myself into the sensation of his lips tugging at mine, his tongue invading my mouth with firm strokes as my hands wove into his hair. We broke apart, gasping for air against each other's lips, his eyes watching me as his fingers flexed on my hips.

"Stay with me, sunshine. I've got you."

Nathan held me still as he rocked up from the couch, pressing inside of me. I moaned into his mouth, pushing down and taking him fully inside of my body. That intensely full feeling made my body quake as I rocked against him, his firm grip on my hips urging me into an almost frantic pace that had me teetering on the edge before I knew it.

"Fuck, you feel so good," Nathan groaned against my lips as I leaned my forehead against his, panting into his mouth as I began to swivel my hips. "I forgot how good you felt."

"Isn't that my line?" I whimpered as I ground against him, feeling my orgasm building as he pushed up into me with firm thrusts, making stars dance behind my eyelids every time they slipped closed from the pleasure.

"Look at me," he groaned as his fingertips bit into the flesh of my hips, pulling me onto him with rough strokes. "I want to see your eyes when you come all over my cock."

"Oh fuck," I moaned as my back arched.

"That's right. Use me to make yourself cum," he whispered as his thumb pressed against my clit, a loud moan tearing out of me as I felt myself start to fall over the edge.

My heart was practically beating out of my chest as I ground against his lap, impaling myself on him over and over until the pressure became too intense to bear. I recalled that being with him had been intense, but as his dark eyes stared up at me, I hadn't remembered it being quite like this. I wasn't this desperate, this forward, or this wanton before. I didn't do this. I didn't have one-night-stands or fuck my brother's friends or sleep with men I hadn't seen in months. Something about being with Nathan made me want him, and I was powerless to stop it.

"Eyes on mine," he snapped with a growl as they started to close, the pleasure making it too hard to keep them open. "Focus, sunshine, look at me while I make you cum."

His pelvis thrust up from the couch, pushing into me over and over as he held my hips tightly in place. I couldn't help the string of loud moans that tore out of me as I felt myself finally fall, clenching against him.

"Fuck, yes," he groaned as he continued to manipulate my body. Nathan pulled me into each of his rough thrusts as my fingernails dug into the soft flannel covering his shoulders while I came hard, my climaxes stretching into one after the other as his punishing pace didn't slow. "Keep cumming on my cock," he growled as he pulled me forward, sucking on my lower lip roughly as he thrust two more times and then groaned into my mouth, pulsing between my legs.

"Holy shit," I giggled as I collapsed forward, laying my head on his shoulder. My lips rested against his sweaty neck as his arms tightened around me.

"Damn, girl," he laughed as he turned his head and pressed a kiss to my temple, his hands creeping down until they were tucked against my skin underneath my sweater. "That wasn't even on my radar when you asked me to come to dinner."

We were both half-dressed, sweaty messes as we clung to each other, but I didn't feel ashamed about having sex with him again. Some part of me felt like I should, knowing that I'd basically just used him to get off, but he'd been right there with me. Fucking the hell out of me even though I was the one on top. I hadn't lied when I told him that I wanted him. He'd been in my thoughts constantly since February.

"You alright?" he whispered into my hair a few minutes later, his fingers slowly trailing down my back.

"I think so," I responded quietly, leaning forward to kiss his neck. "That was intense."

He laughed, pulling me tighter to his chest. "Fuck, the things I want to do to you, sunshine. That was only a little taste."

My heart leaped as he tucked his face into my hair, thinking about how he'd said that before. I knew there was this whole other side to him I'd only seen glimpses of, but I wanted more. We hadn't had the time before, so I hadn't asked, but we would be here for the next several weeks. Maybe it was time to push past some boundaries and try the things he wanted to do to me.

"Tell me what you want to do to me?" I whispered against his neck.

He was quiet for a few moments, his hands still on my back. I thought maybe he'd try to brush me off again, but he didn't.

"I wish we were in Boston. I'd show you my playroom. There are all kinds of fun things we could play with there. You'd look so good tied to my bed. I have this blue rope that'd look fucking amazing against your skin. I can just imagine it looped around you, revealing glimpses of that curvy body."

"What would you do to me while I was tied up?" My pulse hammered as his fingers started up their teasing patterns on my lower back again, his once spent cock starting to awaken inside of me.

"Depends on how well you listen to me, sunshine. If you were a good girl, I'd let you suck my cock while I knelt above you, watching your eyes water as you took all of me down your throat until I took pity on you and fucked that tight pussy. Then I'd free you, and we could cuddle until we were ready to go again."

I clenched, causing him to groan against my ear as I listened to his filthy words, imagining the scene he'd described in vivid detail in my imagination.

"If you were a bad girl, I'd spank you with my hand until you were dripping, teasing you with my fingers and my tongue until you were *so* close to letting go and then stopping, watching you squirm against the ropes until they left impressions on your skin. I'd keep you right there on edge for hours, making you frantic to cum but not letting you. Not until you were begging me to fuck you. Sobbing for me to plunge my cock into you." He punctuated his words with a flex of his hips, and I moaned against his neck as I rocked in his lap. It seemed telling me about his fantasies had gotten him worked up, and I had to admit, it'd done the same to me.

"What else?" I asked, breathless, as I moved languidly against him, enjoying the low groan in my ear as he pushed up into the undulations of my hips.

"Then I'd blindfold you and bend you over my leather spanking bench, tying your hands to the legs while I teased you with a vibrator, making you cum again and again while you counted out your orgasms, one by one, until you were so wet it'd be dripping down your thighs."

His hands cupped my back, pulling me forward as I swiveled my hips, moaning as he hit places inside of me that made me clench with anticipation. I'd never been so turned on by someone's words before.

"Anything else?" I moaned as I nipped at his earlobe, earning a low, strangled groan as he thrust his hips in time with mine.

"Then I'd cuff you to my cross and spank you again with a paddle until your ass cheeks were red and you were begging for me to take you hard and fast. I'd fuck you until you were screaming my name, desperate for me to let you cum again."

"Oh God," I whimpered in his ear as I ground against him, feeling the telltale fluttering of my impending release.

"Would you like that, dirty girl?" he growled in my ear as he pulled me down into his lap, roughly pushing up into me. "Do you want me to fuck you so hard you can't walk?"

"Oh Nathan, yes," I moaned as I buried my face in his neck, so close to cumming.

"Off," he pulled my hips back, and I dug my fingernails into his shoulders as he tried to lift me from his lap. "Lie over the arm of the couch," he whispered, his voice rough as he turned me, his hand pushing the center of my back as he urged me to lie down. My chest was heaving as I felt his fingers rub my clit from behind, my pussy clenching on nothing. I was almost frantic for him to be back inside of me.

"Look at you, so fucking sexy. So desperate for me to fuck you. Feel how wet you are."

"Oh God, now," I moaned as he dipped his fingers inside, the sound of them thrusting inside of me almost obscene with how wet I was from his words and what we'd done before.

"I almost forgot how impatient you are, squirming that tight little ass against my hand." I jumped as his palm connected with my skin, the initial burst of pain blossoming into something more as his large hand massaged my ass, the fingers of his other hand still slowly thrusting inside of me.

"Please," I whimpered as I pushed back against him, almost pleading.

"The sound of you fucking begging is like music to my ears, sunshine. Do it again. Beg me."

"Fuck," I moaned into the upholstery, my fingers digging into the cushion beneath my head.

"That doesn't sound like begging," he teased as his hand came down again, the sound of it smacking my flesh loud in the otherwise quiet living room.

I couldn't believe I was getting spanked after having some very intense sex on my brother's couch. That should have bothered me, but as Nathan's fingers twisted and his thumb pressed down on my clit, I found I didn't care one bit. I could only think about Nathan putting his cock back inside me and making me cum.

"Fuck me," I moaned, arching my back, and pushing against his movements.

"So greedy," he laughed darkly. Tapping me lightly with his palm, he grabbed my ass, squeezing. "You know what I want. Beg."

"Please," I whispered hoarsely, whimpering as he pulled out his fingers. I didn't have time to protest as he grasped my hips, pushing himself inside of me with one rough stroke.

"God, you're so fucking tight," he groaned, slowly thrusting inside, only to retreat and then immediately plunge forward again. "You have no idea how many nights I spent with my cock in my fist trying to remember what it felt like to be inside of you like this. But it was never quite like this. Taking you raw is a special kind of torture that will haunt me for years."

As his pace increased, speech was impossible, only loud moans escaping my lips as he pushed inside me, over and over.

"That's it, let me hear you scream," he panted as he leaned over my back, roughly pulling me into his punishing thrusts. "Cum all over me, sunshine. Squeeze my cock. Make me fill this greedy pussy."

My entire body spasmed, milking him hard as I let go, screaming my release into the cushion in front of my face.

"Fuck, yes," Nathan growled as his fingers dug into the flesh of my hips, holding me in place as he thrust harder, finally stilling, and groaning loudly as he came inside of me.

I was panting as he slipped from my body, pulling me down against the couch cushions and laying down next to me, wrapping his strong arms around my back.

"That was amazing," he whispered into my hair, softly drawing his hand over the sweater still covering my back. "You're so fucking sexy, Kelly. That was…"

His voice trailed off as I nuzzled his chest, soaking in the closeness of his embrace. I kept waiting for the regret to set in, the panic that I'd let things get out of hand. That I'd told him too much or shouldn't have asked him those things, but it never came.

As my eyes closed and I drifted off to sleep, I listened to the strong thrum of his heartbeat and let myself relax, knowing I was safe with him.

FOURTEEN

Nathan

Connecticut

Kelly didn't stir as I pulled her into my arms, standing from the couch and carrying her toward the guest bedroom where I knew she was staying during her time here. I felt a pang of sadness when I thought that even our time in this house had an expiration date.

We may have more time together this go-round, but in a few weeks, after she'd completely destroyed me, I'd have to let her go back to her life in Chicago.

My blood still boiled as I thought about what that fucking douche bag Trent had done to her. Kelly might flirt and say borderline inappropriate things to me, but her career was her entire life. There wasn't a doubt in my mind she behaved professionally while she was in the office. The thought of her sexually harassing someone was laughable at best.

As I leaned over to pull the covers down, her fingers gripped the hair at the back of my head, a whimper escaping her lips. Some primal part of me loved the possessive way she touched me, digging her fingers into my skin or hair, unashamedly using me to bring herself both comfort and pleasure.

"Don't go," she whimpered with her eyes closed as I laid her head down on the pillow, sitting on the edge of the bed as I tucked the blankets around her body.

"I'll be right back," I whispered as I leaned forward, gently kissing her on the forehead before I stood. As I watched her chest rise and fall steadily, I fought the urge to climb under the covers with her.

She didn't stir as I crept out of her bedroom, gathering up our discarded clothing on the way to the kitchen. Pulling on my boxers and my jeans, I surveyed our mess from earlier.

First, I folded her pants, smiling at the unassuming pair of pink cotton panties she'd been wearing underneath her dark leggings. I'd had quite a few fantasies about the red lingerie she'd been wearing at the wedding, but these had their own allure. She truly hadn't invited me over tonight to seduce me. It'd just spontaneously happened, and it was fucking phenomenal. I knew I shouldn't encourage her using sex as a coping mechanism, but I had a hard time exercising self-restraint around her.

My thoughts throughout the day had often strayed to what might happen between us, but my musings hadn't led to us sleeping together quite this quickly. The weekend of the wedding was an escape for both of us, and I felt like the next few weeks could be too, but I found myself wanting to learn more about her now than just what she sounded like mid-climax.

Something about her fragility as she finally confided in me had me desperate to do anything to make her smile. I'd thought joking around with her would do the trick, but her riding me through several orgasms had gotten the job done as well.

As I worked to clean up the kitchen, I found myself plotting how I could continue to make her smile over the next few weeks, but then I stopped short.

While my talk of tying her up and spanking her had aroused her, I knew I couldn't go there with her casually. It would be irresponsible of me to draw her into my kinky fantasies and not do it the right way.

Without intending to, I'd already been interacting with her like I intended to vet her. The conversations we'd had in the hotel, getting her to open up to me tonight, it was all me trying to get closer to her emotionally. I was invested, and I'd hate to sabotage that by jumping into things with my dick instead of my head.

I could spend the next few weeks fucking her at every opportunity, but that wouldn't be healthy for either of us, no matter how mutually enjoyable it'd be.

Once I was done cleaning, stacking the clean dishes in the drying rack, I wiped my hands on a kitchen towel and made a plan. Tomorrow I'd plant the seed of her filling out a limits checklist and talk to her about safewords.

My options for play here were limited. It wasn't like I carried around a kinky survival kit in my car, just waiting to tie up random women as sex objects. I was pretty sure they called those kinds of people serial rapists. I'd already assured her once that I wasn't some blood-thirsty logger, didn't need her questioning my motives.

But, there was a hardware store in town. I could pick up a few things we could play with when I went into town for my supply order.

Talia would be happy to mail me things, but that'd likely take a week, so I'd have to improvise until then. I might never need them, but I wanted to make sure I was prepared in the event Kelly wanted to play. I fired off a text, knowing Tal probably wouldn't reply until the morning. Emory had told me he often confiscated her phone in the evenings so she would actually sleep.

Nathan: Can you get some things together to send me? I'll text you the address tomorrow if I need you to send it.

Her response was almost immediate.

Talia: What kind of things?

I could just picture her rubbing her hands together with glee imagining what I was requesting.

Nathan: Lube, beginner plug set, bondage tape, silk restraints, blindfold, sensory play kit, soy candles, massage oils.

The dots indicating her typing a response popped up, and I leaned against the counter as I waited for her response.

Talia: Found yourself a plaything out in the woods? Or just playing with yourself?

She followed it up with a string of crying laughing emojis, and I knew she was having a good laugh at my expense.

Nathan: Something like that.

Talia: Oh, come on. Tell me something.

Nathan: Quit being nosy.

Talia: Is it someone I know? How the hell did you pick up someone in one day?

Nathan: Sort of. She just kind of showed up.

The dots appeared, then reappeared a few times before they went away.

Tucking my phone into my pocket, I quickly pulled on my boots, threw my coat on over my open shirt, and jogged over to the garage. I pulled my laptop out of the locked compartment in the trailer, taking it with me as I returned to the house.

After logging onto the internet, it only took me a half-hour to compile a list of what I needed, using the wireless connection to the printer in the living room to print it out.

My phone buzzed in my pocket as I walked down the hallway to the guest bedroom, unbuttoning my pants on the way.

Talia: Are you seducing Evan's sister again?

I laughed at her phrasing. If anyone seduced someone earlier, it'd been Kelly. I hadn't put up much of a fight, but she'd been the one to initiate things.

Nathan: Mind your own business.

Talia: That wasn't a no. Please be careful with her. Chase will kill us all if she thinks you're taking advantage.

Nathan: I know. But it's different with her.

Talia: Just don't mistake great sex and physical compatibility for more. I know you're smarter than that.

As I sat down on the edge of the bed, pushing the hair covering Kelly's face behind her ear, I blew out a breath before I texted my response.

Nathan: I'll be careful, but I can't just walk away from her this time. There's no mistaking this is more.

Sun streaming through a break in the curtains woke me up, and I stifled a yawn against the back of my hand as I ran the fingers of my other hand through the tips of Kelly's hair as it lay on my bare chest.

She'd curled into me as soon as I climbed under the covers with her last night, and it appeared she'd stayed there all night.

"Wake up, sleepy sunshine," I whispered as I shifted down the bed, placing a kiss on her forehead as she moaned sleepily into my neck.

"What time is it?" she yawned as her eyes blinked open, a little wrinkle forming between her eyebrows.

"A little after eight," I replied, squinting at the digital clock on the dresser across the room. "It's getting late."

"Ugh. It's still seven for me," she groaned, trying to pull the covers over her head.

"Nope," I laughed, prying the blanket out of her hand and throwing it back. "We've both got things on the agenda today, and it's time to get up."

"Noo," she whined as she tried to burrow into my chest, hiding behind the curtain of her hair.

"Come on, sunshine. I'll even make your coffee. Although we need to have a chat about your hydration regimen."

"You suck."

"Not at the moment, but if you play your cards right…" I teased as I ran my fingertips down her back and underneath her loose sweater. She wiggled against me as I tickled her sides lightly, laughing against my skin.

"Stop that. It tickles."

"That's the point. Get up, sweet girl, before I'm forced to spank you."

"Mmm," she hummed, turning to rest her chin on my chest, looking up at me with sleepy eyes. "Is that supposed to be a threat or a promise?"

"It's about to be both," I warned as I dug my fingertips into her sides, eliciting more sleepy giggles as she squirmed against me.

I could feel other parts of myself enjoying her movements, but I wasn't going to be distracted by her intoxicating presence this morning. *Down boy.*

"Get your ass out of this bed right now, sunshine."

She paused, her wide eyes flashing up to mine. "Yes, sir."

Fuck me.

"Don't call me that unless you mean it," I warned. Something about those two words rolling off her tongue had me excited in a way that was hard to contain.

"Maybe I do mean it." Her voice was quiet, the look on her face more serious than it'd been in the moments prior.

Cupping her cheek, I rubbed my thumb over her bottom lip, swallowing hard. "Then we need to have a serious conversation this morning. It's time to get up, sunshine."

She nodded, her fingers tracing a random pattern on my chest. "Why do you call me sunshine?"

I blew out a breath, knowing my answer might scare her a little.

"It started off with my sarcastic comment about you being a ray of sunshine. But really, it's because when I think of things that are warm, and addictive, and larger than life…I think of you," I whispered, combing my fingers through her hair. "And I'm fairly certain any joy in my life would cease to exist right now without you in it."

Her lip trembled as she looked at me with glassy eyes before she hid her face against my chest and squeezed her arms against my sides.

"Hey," I whispered, placing a finger underneath her chin, and coaxing her to look at me. "I didn't mean to make you upset, but I'm not going to lie to you."

"I don't know what I'm doing, Nathan," she whimpered, laying her head against my chest. "My life is a dumpster fire right now, but I know I'll regret it if I try to convince myself to stay away from you."

"So, don't. Let me in, sweet girl. We could be so good together."

She nodded, turning to kiss my chest softly. "I'm trying."

"That's all I'm asking. Now, let's get up. I'll make you breakfast."

She rolled off my chest, throwing her arm over her eyes and huffing out a labored breath.

"Come find me when you're ready." Shifting myself onto my side, I arched my back, wincing as my stiff back muscles protested the movement. It was a bitch getting old.

"I need a few minutes." Kelly mumbled from beneath her arm, her voice quiet.

"Take your time." I nodded. "But don't take too long, or I'm coming back in here to get you, and you won't like it."

She moaned, pulling the blanket over her face.

Laughing at her response, I pulled on my jeans and grabbed my shirt from the dresser by the door, shrugging it on. As I stepped into the hallway, she called out after me.

"Don't threaten me with a good time because I probably will like it."

"Oh, I can assure you that withholding orgasms isn't going to be fun," I hollered back. "At least not for you."

"Now you're just being cruel," she yelled. "You're a mean, mean man."

"And don't you forget it," I laughed, heading toward the front door to get the eggs from my trailer.

…

Kelly was waiting for me in the kitchen, angrily stabbing at the coffee maker while I emptied my arms onto the island. We'd definitely need to make a supply run soon, but I had bacon, eggs, and enough veggies to make a decent omelet.

"Did a grocery store magically appear in my brother's garage?" She yawned as she adorably rubbed a hand next to her eye.

"Not quite," I chuckled as I stepped around her and started peering in the lower cabinets, searching for a frying pan. "Boy Scout, remember?"

"Hmm," she nodded. "But you weren't prepared last night."

Finding what I was looking for, I pulled out the pan and gently placed it on the stove top before taking a step toward Kelly.

"I wasn't," I nodded, caging her in against the counter and dropping my face into the soft curve of her shoulder. "I thought I'd be able to resist you for one night. Clearly, I was mistaken."

She let out a quiet moan as I sucked softly on her warm skin, arching toward me as her hand slipped around the back of my neck.

"You're putting me in the mood to eat something other than eggs," I whispered in her ear, reveling in the way she arched toward my chest, rubbing herself against me. She was so sensual without even trying, just doing what felt good to her body. None of it was choreographed to gain my attention, and she was just responding to the way I made her feel. It was intoxicating to have that much influence over her reactions to me.

"What's stopping you?" she gasped as my fingers slipped between her thighs, rubbing lightly against the tiny sleep shorts she'd thrown on. I think I almost preferred her in only the soft sweater she wore last night and nothing else.

"We need to eat." Placing one last lingering kiss on her neck, I stepped back, her eyes flashing to mine with part surprise, part annoyance. The sadistic part of me wanted her to protest, to let out a little of that bratty energy I picked up on sometimes, but she simply blew out a breath and rubbed her thighs together.

"You're a tease," she huffed, her arms crossing over her chest, her nipples highlighted against the soft material of her long-sleeved top. The fabric kept falling off one shoulder, revealing enough unmarred creamy skin for me to deduce she didn't have a bra on.

"I'm only a tease if I don't intend to follow through eventually. It might not be right now, but I promise you, by the end of the week, I'll be back between those pretty thighs."

She growled, narrowing her eyes at me as I set up my workspace next to the gas range, spreading out my ingredients and pulling a knife free from the wooden block on the counter.

"Something to say, sunshine?"

I had to admit, her pouting was adorable, but I couldn't blame her for being frustrated. The next few days would be a test for both of us, but I knew it was necessary. I couldn't start to build a relationship with her, especially not one where we played together, based on only having mind-blowing sex. We needed to have some conversations, and she needed to do some real soul-searching to see if this was something she wanted to do with me.

With a time limit seemingly always hanging over our heads, I didn't want to diminish our time together by making mistakes. And I'd already made so many. Kelly was vulnerable right now, and part of me knew I needed to tread carefully. If we'd met under other circumstances and she was going through what she was going through right now, I would push for us to remain friends until her life had settled down.

I didn't want to take advantage of her. She'd all but admitted she was using me for comfort, and while I was glad she felt comfortable enough to tell me what she needed, sex was not a cure all for her problems. It had the potential to muddy the waters between us, and I didn't want to close the door on a relationship with her before it'd even begun.

"You're being all cryptic this morning, and I'm not sure I like it."

She was right. And perceptive, but I felt like I needed to ease her into this conversation.

"That's not my intention, but our topic of conversation is hardly material one discusses over omelets and mimosas."

"There are mimosas?" Her stormy expression cleared as she glanced around the kitchen, that small wrinkle forming between her eyebrows again.

"Well, not technically, unless virgin cocktails count."

"Pretty sure a virgin mimosa is just orange juice there, stud," she laughed as she opened the refrigerator and pulled out the carton I'd tucked in there earlier. "And you won't give me your *cock*tail, so I guess I'll have to settle for this."

While she poured two generous glasses of juice, I got to work, dicing vegetables and meat, mixing them in a small bowl on the counter. The pan sizzled as I dropped a few tablespoons of butter into it along with several strips of bacon. Kelly watched quietly, occasionally taking a sip from her juice as she leaned against the island.

"At least one of us isn't hopeless in the kitchen," she remarked as I used a pair of tongs to pull out the crisped bacon, before slowly pouring the beaten egg mixture into the sizzling pan.

"Can't get through the day in my line of work without a decent breakfast."

She laughed, propping her bare toes on one of the drawer pulls in the bank of drawers next to where I was working. The muscles in her toned calf flexed as she shifted her weight, and a loud pop from the pan drew my attention back to my task. "I thought you were just the management."

"I started as a drywaller and then moved into finish carpentry before I ever had a degree. Construction is in my blood. Literally. With as many times as I've cut my hands open over the years."

"Ah, not just a pretty face then," she teased, smiling as I glanced back toward her.

"Well, I don't think I was ever just a pretty face — at least not compared to someone as stunning as you, sunshine."

"Aren't you flirty this morning?" she cooed, shifting her weight, so my eyes were drawn back to her long legs again. Typically the women I gravitated toward were petite with slight builds, they made the perfect rope models, but Kelly's long frame and curvy hips were a sight to behold.

I could just picture the marks and indentations my ropes would leave against her fair skin, criss-crossing over her toned muscles and flawless complexion. She was so different than the women I'd played with in the past, but there was something so alluring about that. She was new and fresh, slightly forbidden, and entirely consuming.

"I'm not typically a fan of my eggs being burned around the edges," she laughed, pointing toward the skillet I'd nearly forgotten about. "But seeing as I'm not doing the cooking, I shouldn't complain."

"Something tells me that knowing you shouldn't do something isn't a deterrent for you."

"Are you calling *me* impulsive, Mr. Harrison?"

"Well, you're certainly not predictable, that's for sure." My attention returned to our breakfast, the first omelet a little crispy around the edges but otherwise perfectly done. While my mother had been the one to teach me how to cook initially, my grandfather had taken over my cooking lessons before I went to college, teaching me dishes he'd picked up over the years.

My mother had always fed a family, but Bradley Sr. had been widowed in his forties, leaving him to fend for himself and his teenage son. His lessons were more on the practical side, and I felt lucky that he'd taken me under his wing after everything that'd happened. Maybe he saw me as an opportunity to rewrite the ways he thought he'd failed his own son.

"Hey." Kelly hopped down from her perch at the island, reaching up to tuck my wayward hair behind my ear. "Where did my playful Nathan go?"

"I'm here," I smiled, knowing that I was getting caught up in my head again. Maybe that was why I'd never settled down. I didn't want to make the same mistakes my father did and the ones his father thought he made. "Sorry, I just get distracted sometimes."

"Hmm, you can talk to me about it if you want to. I mean, I won't force you, but I'm listening if you need me."

While oddly reminiscent of my own from the day before, her words were comforting, and I had to respect that she was leaving it to me to share my burdens. I'd had so many women who thought they could fix me, but some things you couldn't force. It'd taken me over twenty years to finally let go and forgive my father for everything that he'd done. For all the ways he'd destroyed my childhood memories; for the events of his last two years alive.

"Let's eat first. Then we can have the serious discussions." I nodded toward the couch, not wanting to bother with setting the table. It seemed easier to sit side by side somewhere comfortably to talk this morning.

"Sounds ominous."

Shaking my head, I led her to the living room with both plates in my hands, waiting until she was seated to pass off her food and take a seat next to her. "Not scary, just important."

"Mmmm," she hummed as she took her first bite, closing her eyes with a smile on her face. "I know kidnapping is frowned upon, but I think you need to come to be my personal chef in Chicago."

"Not exactly my wheelhouse, but I'm not opposed to a visit…or two." *Hopefully many more.*

"Good to know," she smiled as she kept eating, humming with every bite. If I didn't have to control myself, I would have already stripped her down, eaten her for breakfast this morning, and maybe fed her a little sausage of my own.

Trying to discreetly rearrange your erection while enjoying breakfast with a beautiful woman was an almost unbearable test of restraint. I felt like I was edging myself, denying my intense attraction to Kelly. My common sense managed to keep my baser instincts at bay — just barely — until she finished, laying her empty plate on the coffee table, and turning to face me.

"So what's this important discussion we need to have?"

Placing my empty plate next to hers, I leaned back into the cushion, spreading my arm along the back, grazing a fingertip against her bare shoulder.

"What are your thoughts on learning about my lifestyle?"

Her eyes widened, her mouth dropping open slightly as she shifted on the cushion, my eyes falling to where her nipples had puckered against her shirt. Well, that was a favorable reaction.

"Like *with* you?"

"Yes, like with me. In a dynamic of sorts. You seemed to have a very visceral reaction to my words last night, and I wanted to see if that was something you wanted to explore further."

"In a what?"

"A dynamic. A relationship — likely temporary — where I teach you a little bit more about kink. Since our physical chemistry is so intense, I thought maybe you'd be interested in playing with me a little while you're here."

"Here?" she asked, eyes wide. "As in my brother's house? Don't you need special equipment or something to do this?"

"Not always," I smiled, loving the way she was squirming in her seat. The idea clearly intrigued her, most likely to an arousing extent, and I clenched my fist in my lap to keep from reaching over to see just how excited she may be. Her nipples were already attempting to burrow through the fabric covering them, and my mouth watered at the thought of how slick her pussy would be against my fingers.

"Uh," she cleared her throat, looking away from me, her body shuddering slightly as I saw goosebumps break out across her shoulder. *Lovely.* I traced the puckered skin with the tip of my finger, my pulse racing at the quiet gasp that fell from her lips. I hadn't intended to touch her while we talked, but I couldn't resist.

"How…I mean, what?"

"Breathe, sunshine," I whispered as I leaned toward her, brushing a strand of hair from her shoulder before I softly kissed her skin. "You don't need to be nervous."

"Right now?" she squeaked as her head fell back against the cushion, her chest pressing forward at my gentle touch. She was still so responsive to me, which made the precarious situation in my pants even more dangerous. I couldn't lose control with her. I didn't have her consent to play yet, and I didn't fully know what she needed from me.

"No," I whispered, shifting backward, and settling into the opposite corner of the couch, out of touching distance from her. "There are some things we need to discuss first, and you'd need to fill out a limits checklist before we can truly talk about what you're interested in."

She blinked, drawing her legs up in front of her and hugging them to her chest. I recognized it as a defensive posture, but however she needed to cope with this was valid. I wasn't a threat to her, I just wanted to bring her pleasure.

"And you just carry one of those around with you in your Jeep?" she asked, her typical sarcasm flaring as she stared over at my relaxed posture.

"Well, I do have my standard documents stored in a Dropbox account, so yes, I do just carry them around with me in a way."

"Waiting for unsuspecting women to fall for your charm?"

Frowning, I watched her, taking in her tense posture and the way she was gnawing on the corner of her lip. I'd made her uncomfortable, or at least nervous. It was hard to decide which. I knew I hadn't misinterpreted her attraction to me sexually, but maybe she'd just been caught up in the moment last night.

"It's alright if this isn't what you want. I'm not interested in pressuring you into anything. But this is part of who I am, what *I* need, so if it's not for you, then we need to keep our hands to ourselves from now on." *Please don't let that be what you want.*

Her eyes widened again, and she blew out a labored breath, her cheeks puffing out slightly as she tried to relax her posture.

"We can return to being friends, or friendly acquaintances or whatever, for the length of my stay. I'd still like to get to know you, Kelly."

"You just won't have sex with me again."

"Correct." As much as it'd fucking kill me. And as much as I'd likely lock myself in my trailer at night and fantasize about being with her with my cock in my hand. If this weren't what she wanted, I'd have to leave her alone. The big question was if I could follow through and keep my hands off her. My self-restraint had been obliterated in seconds the night before.

She sat quietly, avoiding looking at me by fixating on the fireplace across the room. This wasn't how I'd anticipated this discussion going, but it was a lot of information for her to take in. Maybe she was still not in a headspace where she could process something like this. Walking away now would be the responsible thing for me to do. I needed to give her space to heal from what'd happened to her in the last week, not try to convince her to enter a dynamic with me. No matter how phenomenal I knew she'd likely be, or how I could picture her thriving in a relationship with me.

It wasn't my choice to make.

"It's OK, sunshine. I shouldn't have offered. Let's just leave this alone. Would you still like to eat dinner with me this evening? I can run to town if you give me a shopping list."

Starting to rise from the couch, I reached for our discarded plates. I'd just clean up my mess from breakfast and give her some space. Clearly, I'd overstepped.

"Wait," she whispered as she gripped my wrist. "Please don't go. Show me this list."

As I looked back over my shoulder toward her, I saw the nerves she'd been holding fade away, a look of fierce determination taking over her striking features. Maybe I'd underestimated her.

FIFTEEN

Kelly

Connecticut

Nathan stopped, glancing over his shoulder at me before setting our plates back on the coffee table. Slowly turning toward me, he pinned me down with a significant look. While he didn't say a word, I could tell he was trying to see how serious I was about this.

When he'd mentioned a checklist, I'd panicked, realizing that maybe I was in over my head with him a little. I was intrigued, and the words he'd said the night before had gotten me so turned on it was crazy, but entering a relationship like that with him — even temporarily — was intimidating as fuck.

"You're serious about this?"

Swallowing past the nervous lump in my throat, I nodded. "Yes, I'm serious. Nervous, but serious."

His body relaxed as he sat back down at the opposite end of the couch, careful not to touch me. My shoulder still tingled from the lingering kiss he'd placed there moments ago, but I didn't doubt his commitment to keeping his hands to himself for the time being. The needy part of me wanted to throw caution to the wind and crawl across the cushions and into his lap, using my tongue to prove how serious I was about exploring this with him, but I knew he'd shut that down before I could even get my lips near his.

"Nervous is understandable, sunshine. I'm a little nervous myself, but I want you to take this seriously."

Nodding, I cleared my throat, picking at the sleeve of my long-sleeved top. "I will. I promise. Now, how exactly do we do this? Is there a contract I have to sign first? A non-disclosure agreement or something? Do I need to get a physical or a wax or something?"

He chuckled, shaking his head at me with a little roll of his eyes.

"Kelly, this isn't some '*Fifty Shades*' nonsense. We both need to go into this with our eyes open. The checklist is necessary, but I trust you enough to keep this strictly between us. If you want a written contract drawn up, that's pretty standard, but it won't be legally binding. It'll simply detail our arrangement and the terms we agree on for our dynamic."

"But..." I started, but he held up his hand, interrupting me.

"I'm not going to play with you until we've had a frank discussion about your needs and mine because we're equals in this equation, but I'm not interested in owning you." He smiled. "Maybe just controlling you a little."

"And we can't..." I trailed off, tilting my head, and making a vaguely suggestive gesture with my hands.

"You know that I want you," Nathan laughed, clearly amused by my reactions. "I'm not going to deny that. I'm just making sure you understand that I'm not entering a dynamic with you without going through at least a checklist and a conversation about limits. This isn't a lifestyle to jump into without preparation. If you truly want to learn more, I'll make sure you have the resources, but I'm not touching you like that without at least implicit consent and some planning."

I frowned, realizing this lifestyle might not be as spontaneous as I assumed. "But I thought this was something where you're in charge, and you tell me what I should like."

"And *that* is why I'm not touching you as a true Dominant right now. You've got a lot to learn, and I can only help you with so much. If you truly want to dive further into this, I'll put you in contact with Talia, but I can't be your mentor *and* your lover. It doesn't work that way."

I nodded, thinking for a moment. What he was saying made sense, but I'd never considered playing like this with anyone but him. Did I really need a mentor? "And I need one of these mentors?"

"It depends, but I'll at least introduce you two, and she can be someone who you can feel comfortable asking questions you don't want to ask me. If you decide this lifestyle is something you want after..." Nathan trailed off. I didn't want him to finish that sentence because I couldn't imagine doing this with anyone but him.

"How is that going to work with us out here and Talia in Boston? Does she even know we're...*together*...like that?" My cheeks heated up a little at the idea of letting someone else into this relationship or whatever it was this was evolving into.

"She already knows you're here. But we can set up a private video call if that's alright with you. Or maybe you could go back to Boston with me once you're done here?" he asked, looking a little nervous.

"If that's something you want, of course, I'm not sure how invested you are in doing this with me."

"How will this…" I motioned between the two of us, "…work after I leave? Can we even do something like this long-term if we're a thousand miles apart?"

He nodded, pursing his lips. "There are people who have long-distance dynamics. We'd need to work out a schedule of when it'd be feasible to see each other in person, but I'm interested in seeing this play out. Our natural chemistry is something that I think could work well for us. This isn't just about sex, sunshine, or even just playing. A real relationship with me would be the foundation for all of this. It can be a deep friendship or more. I'm not going to set limits on how this unfolds. But we'd remain in constant contact."

"And that's what you want?" I asked, looking at my lap. We still only knew parts of each other, but I'd talked to him about things so far that I usually kept closely shielded around others.

The only other person who knew I was infertile was my last boyfriend, Tyler, who had promptly left me after finding out my chances of conceiving after my miscarriage were nil. We found out my uterus was inhospitable — at least according to my gynecologist and several specialists — and he'd pushed me away. I knew I still needed to tell Nathan everything, but the way he'd looked at me last night, telling me I wasn't broken, it'd meant everything.

"Come here, Kelly." He held out his hands, pulling me across the couch and settling me into his lap. I laid my head against his shoulder as he wrapped his arms around me, whispering into my hair. "Of course, I want you."

"I want you, too," I whispered, playing with the collar of his shirt.

"So, talk to me, tell me about what you want out of this. Tell me about you." His warm body beneath mine made it easier to let go of my nerves.

"I liked what you did with the tie." Like wasn't a strong enough word to describe the experience, but judging from his deep chuckle, he got the idea.

"That wasn't even scratching the surface, sunshine. Bondage isn't something to be taken lightly. I studied for years to get to the skill level I'm at. It's intense and can be scary, and you need to be in the right mindset to develop a scene with me. That kind of play isn't spontaneous, and you must be prepared for the drop that can happen afterward. Aftercare can help you lessen it, but it's going to mess with your head the first few times."

I nodded, listening to the quiet rumble of his voice. He was back into his somber persona, trying to clarify that this was something I needed to take seriously. "I think I can handle that."

"You say that now, but once you see the imprints that rope leaves on your skin and the bruises I may unintentionally inflict on you, you might curl up in a ball inside the bathroom crying so hard you can't hear me calling your name, much less acknowledge the fact that anyone is there at all." His low voice had a bit of a bitter tone, and I knew that things he'd experienced in the past hadn't gone to plan.

"Sounds like you're speaking from experience."

"Maybe I am. But I know that there isn't anything that feels like a scene that goes off flawlessly." My neck tingled as his warm breath washed across my skin. "It can also crush you on a soul-deep level when one goes wrong no matter how much you've talked about what's going to happen."

Chewing on my bottom lip, I contemplated his words. I couldn't tell if he was trying to scare me or maybe talk me out of this. "Are you trying to persuade me not to do this? I understand this will be different than what we've done before. What *I've* done before."

"I just want to make it clear that while it can be exhilarating to give someone that much power over your body, it can also be a little terrifying. The amount of trust you would need to have in me would be something different than you've probably shared with any other lover."

Nodding, I leaned back, cupping his cheek, "You aren't any other lover to me."

"Kelly…" he smiled, turning his face to kiss my palm.

"I mean it. I feel close to you even if you won't touch me. That first night…" I trailed off, goosebumps forming at the thought of everything that had transpired between us, from the tie to the shower where he helped gently wash the layers of hairspray from my hair, to having to say goodbye to him and wanting more. Then everything that'd happened last night. It was overwhelming, but I wanted more.

"Was intense, and you liked it, which is why you need to know what you want from me. I'm not a mind reader, and I'll make mistakes, but I need you to trust me not to hurt you. Emotionally or physically," he smiled, a naughty grin overtaking his features. "Unless you ask me to."

"You mean like spanking me?" I laughed, remembering what it'd felt like to have his large palm connect with my skin.

"Yes, but there are times when I'm going to need to correct your behavior for your own good, and you will know it's coming, but I need you to trust that it's all for you. I don't like punishing my subs, but crossing some boundaries, will warrant correction. And spanking is only a small way to get my point across."

"Even if I tell you to stop?" I probably would tell him I wanted more, but I wasn't sure how much I could take.

"It doesn't work like that, Kell. If you use the safe word, I stop, help you come down, and the scene is done, but..." He paused, shifting his hips as he held me.

"But?"

He turned me to face him, leaning back into the couch cushion as he balanced me on his thighs. "But then we'll need to talk about it. You will have to be completely honest with me about why you put a stop to things. And if you want to walk away from the dynamic because of that conversation, then I'll have to let you."

Nathan talked like we already had an expiration, or he expected me to walk away from him. Yes, it was intimidating, but I was committed to exploring this with him. "You make it sound like I have more power than you."

"It's not about one of us having more power, sunshine. It's a power exchange. It's about trust, and if you don't trust me, you shouldn't agree to that power exchange." He paused, looking into my eyes. "And I shouldn't ask for it."

Staring at the soft flannel of his shirt, I contemplated his words, knowing that this whole situation involved a tremendous amount of trust between the two of us. I could see it developing already, but it was a lot to process all at once.

"And if I don't want to be in a dynamic with you?" I did, but I needed him to answer the question, even if I already knew the answer.

"Then I can't be like that with you."

Walking away from Nathan or him walking away from me was the last thing I wanted at this stage, but I could see where he was coming from.

"You could try to have a vanilla relationship with me."

"No…" He shook his head, placing a finger under my chin and tilting my head so I'd look at him. "I know what I need in a sexual and romantic relationship, and I've matured enough to know that a relationship that neglects to meet all my needs is doomed to fail."

"Then what happens…?" *when I go back home, and you forget about me.*

"If our dynamic ends, it's because you aren't getting what you need from me, or you don't trust me. Neither of those lends well to a romantic relationship."

Thinking about the end of this before we'd even really begun was like a knife to the heart, and I felt myself getting a little choked up thinking about it. "So, it'd be over?"

He nodded. "It'd be over."

"Oh." My breath caught as a single tear escaped my eye before I could stop it.

"Hey," he whispered as he pulled me forward, tucking my head beneath his chin. "Sunshine, stop, don't cry. I'm not going into this saying it has an end, but if being with me romantically, or as your Dom, or even if you decide you'd like to switch — which I would be thrilled with, by the way — is too much for you to handle, then we need to stop trying to force it. It'd kill me if you resented me. It'd kill me even more if something I did made you hate me, or worse, yourself."

"This is more intense than I thought it'd be," I whispered, feeling calmer as I listened to the steady beat of his heart.

"It *is* intense," he agreed. "But it's also what I need. And I can't pretend to shut off that part of myself, even for you. Even if I find myself falling…"

His voice trailed off, but his heart started to pound as the quiet drew out between us. I was already beginning to fall for him too. I knew it was fast, and it'd likely blow up in my face, but this *thing* between us was about more than just the way our bodies fit together. I felt different with him, more than I'd ever felt with anyone else.

"You find yourself falling?" I whispered into his shoulder, afraid to look at him.

"For you," he sighed. "You have to know that. It's part of why I walked away from you after the wedding. I wanted you, and I had

162

some very serious feelings by the end of that weekend, but I knew it wasn't fair to try to keep you."

"You're making it hard for me to resist you," I whispered, reaching a finger up to trace the smooth skin of his neck where his beard ended.

"Then you'd better start reading because I'm going to need that list from you sooner rather than later," he chuckled. "But seriously, take as much time as you need. I've got a checklist printed out for you to look at and a list of websites I want you to read through. You can also ask me anything. I'm an open book."

"So, bossy," I giggled, leaning up and blowing out a stuttering breath as I made eye contact with him.

He smiled, reaching up to cup my cheek. "You don't even know. Not even a little bit, sunshine."

Leaning into his touch, I nodded. "But I'd like to."

"That's a good start, but first, you figure out what you need from me, and I'll see if I can deliver." His thumb trailed across my bottom lip, and I blinked, trying to keep myself from melting into a puddle of goo in his lap.

"You've already delivered plenty," I winked, trying to move back to the playful banter we'd shared before.

Nathan shook his head, his eyes rolling as he caught onto my game. "Such a dirty mind, Kelly."

"Such a dirty mouth, Nathan." I wiggled my eyebrows, and he laughed, pulling me forward into a sweet kiss that seemed to seal the agreement between us.

SIXTEEN

Nathan

Connecticut

For all her avoidance telling me why she was here initially, Kelly proved to be a very dutiful and dedicated student. She'd spent the last few days tucked into the corner of the couch, spending her free time studying the long list of websites that I'd compiled for her.

We ate most of our meals together, spent the nights talking about ourselves and getting to know one another — avoiding anything potentially sexual, of course — and while I went out to continue clearing the foundation between breaks in the weather, she studied like she was preparing to take an exam.

I hadn't expected her to dive into the subject with quite the enthusiasm she had, but it was making it hard to keep my hands to myself. Seeing her completely absorbed in learning about my lifestyle was sexy as fuck.

"Are you ever going to show me *your* checklist?" she asked, stretching her leg across the couch cushion separating us, trailing her toes against the side of my thigh.

"Sunshine," I scolded, gently lifting her foot from my leg before she could trail it any higher and see how hard I'd been for her over the past several days. I had a feeling if even one of her petite little toes made contact that I'd likely maul her, which wouldn't do either of us any good — even if it'd feel fucking amazing to sink my cock into her tight little pussy.

"What?" she asked, a mask of innocence on her features, but I could see the naughty glint in her eyes as she looked at me. "It's only fair for you to show me yours if you intend to look at mine."

"You'll see it when you've got yours completed." I already had a copy sitting on the counter inside the trailer, knowing that I'd need to give it to her once she was done.

"You're no fun," she pouted, narrowing her eyes at me. "I want to see what you like."

"And you will once you're done. I don't want my list to influence you, so we'll exchange them when you're ready."

"Fine," she sighed, shaking her head at me as she looked back to the tablet in her lap. "I guess I'll just have to discuss these things with you later."

I shifted against the couch, tilting my head to try to see what she was reading. I'd told her she was free to ask questions, but she hadn't so far. Just reading and taking notes in a little purple notebook she kept next to her, but her checklist was still blank. Whatever information she'd researched so far hadn't led her to fill it out yet. Not that I'd look at it until she was ready, but it made me endlessly curious every time I saw the papers on the corner of the coffee table, pen perched on top, the lines and checkboxes still blank.

"You can ask me whatever you need to," I clarified, still unable to see what she'd be staring at on her tablet for the last few moments. "Have you even looked at the checklist again?"

"Yes, I've looked at it," she nodded, not looking up from her reading.

"Is there a reason that you haven't started filling it out?" I asked, knowing it'd continue to drive me insane if I didn't. I was dying to see her responses to some things, but I knew it was hers to share when she wanted. She was taking her assignment a lot more seriously than I'd anticipated. Given a majority of my previous partners weren't novices in the kink community, they'd had their checklist ready to share with me within the first few days of getting it.

"I already know what I'm going to fill out for, probably..." she hummed, looking up at the ceiling and biting the corner of her lip for a moment while I waited impatiently. "Seventy to eighty percent of it, but there are still some things I'm looking into."

"Such as?"

She smiled, sitting up a little straighter and looking over at me with a mischievous glint in her dark eyes. "What about this one?" she tapped on her tablet screen, briefly turning it in my direction. "CNC. What does that stand for?"

Fuck. If I weren't already sitting here with a perpetual hard-on, I would have been rock solid in an instant. As it was, I was just left uncomfortably shifting my hips as my cock tried to break out the fly of my jeans. "Consensual Non-Consent."

"Yeah, I read inside the parentheses," she laughed, clearly enjoying my reaction to her. "What does that *really* mean?"

Taking a deep breath, I mulled over my answer. "It means that you are consenting to a sexual encounter that simulates non-consensual contact. It's like giving your partner blanket consent to do whatever they want to you as long as they don't violate the limits you've established. It can be for a single scene or ongoing, it depends upon what has been negotiated."

"Like a rape fantasy?" she asked, and I glanced at her face, unable to interpret her neutral expression.

"Not really," I shook my head. This whole subject was one that different groups couldn't seem to agree on. Some people thought consensual rape play was part of CNC, but others often disagreed. "CNC is a little more complicated than that. I personally have never trusted someone enough to consider something like blanket consent. Rape play is more fantasy role play. It involves a lot of boundary setting and it isn't quite as spontaneous as some other types of role play. It skirts a fine line with consent and involves an enormous amount of trust."

She nodded, seemingly satisfied with my answer, even though it was only covering part of the subject. "Have you...?"

"Dabbled in rape play. Yes." I nodded, enjoying the way she shifted against her own cushion. Maybe she wasn't as unaffected by my presence as she'd seemed.

"As the top or the bottom?"

I knew she was digging because she wanted a genuine answer, but I wasn't going to go into details about my past experiences with it because they'd been with other people. They weren't relevant to *our* budding dynamic. "Technically both. But not in the way you're probably thinking."

"You're not going to give me any details, are you?"

"No," I smiled, shaking my head. She was a nosy little thing. "Play between consenting partners is confidential in a dynamic. And every situation is unique. Play with a previous partner wouldn't necessarily apply to you...or anyone else. Your limits will be different. What turns you on may not work for someone else. That's why you always plan out scenes ahead of time."

Kelly was quiet for a few moments, looking thoughtfully back at her tablet. I continued sifting through my emails on my phone while she kept reading, but I knew she'd have more questions now that she'd started to ask them.

"Doesn't all that planning make it boring?"

Setting my phone down on the table, I turned, pulling her feet up into my lap and rubbing the center of one of her arches with my thumbs. She let out a little moan in response, making me throb, but I tried to focus on answering her question. "No. It makes it possible for both partners to have set expectations. You won't know what will happen exactly when in a scene unless that's what you ask for, but they act as guidelines, so you know what's allowed."

She frowned, nodding a little. "Isn't that what safe words are for? So you know what's not allowed."

Ah, rookie mistake, thinking that the safe word was something you *wanted* to use. "The last thing I want to happen in a scene is for my submissive to use her safeword."

"Why?"

"Because that means I failed in meeting her needs, or she felt uncomfortable with me to the point of breaking. I pushed something past what she was comfortable with, and she needed it to stop immediately." Using a safeword had rarely happened for me, but sometimes things came up in a scene that neither of us had expected. Sort of like Grace deciding to ambush me. Which I still needed to talk to Kelly about. And, explicitly, 'the vasectomy'. It just hadn't come up yet.

"But what if she didn't know that it was a limit?"

"That's what safewords are designed for, to stop something you didn't anticipate. It should always be there to use, but if your play partner disregards your agreed upon boundaries, they aren't respecting your dynamic or your relationship. Pushing things to that point because of poor planning isn't acceptable. At least not to me." Emory had taught me to try to anticipate every aspect of a scene. It was better to over-plan than to get myself or my submissive into a situation that would damage our dynamic.

"You like to be in control, don't you?" It was easy to tell from the calculating way she watched my reactions that she was studying me.

"Sometimes." I shrugged.

"And other times?" Some of her questions almost felt like an interrogation, but I was pleased she took the initiative to start conversations like this.

"I crave the release someone else can grant me. Sub-space is like a shelter for me. A place I can let everything go. Let someone else take the reins for a while. It's kind of like a euphoric release where your mind floats. It's a little different for everyone, but it can be intense, and a little addictive. I've usually only been able to get there when I'm bound."

She nodded, picking up her notebook and writing something down. It almost reminded me of how Chase documented everything when she observed play parties, but I wasn't telling Kelly that.

"And that's what you want from me? To be able to provide that for you?"

Nodding, I switched feet and smiled at the way she arched her back as I dug my thumbs into her sole. "Only if that's what you want."

"And if I don't?" I held my breath, studying her face. She hadn't indicated she was opposed to switching roles within the dynamic. I'd already explained to her that I was a Switch during our weekend together. She knew I wasn't only a Dominant player in this lifestyle.

"That's what you need to figure out," I replied evenly. "This isn't just about me and what I want. What you want matters too. This won't work without both of us getting what we need."

She nodded, letting me continue to massage her feet as she returned her focus to the tablet.

When her stomach started grumbling twenty minutes later, I knew she'd been neglecting herself.

"Did you eat lunch while I was outside today?" This would be the real test if this kind of relationship would work. All of the subtle ways a soft Dominant helped their submissive take care of themselves. Would she think I was annoying for reminding her to eat or stay hydrated? Play depleted a lot of energy from your body, so you needed to be well-rested, well-fed, and hydrated.

"I must have forgotten," she grimaced as she reached over to place the tablet on the edge of the coffee table.

"You need to be taking better care of yourself."

She squinted at me with her head tilted to the side as she gauged my intentions. "Are you trying to act like my father now? Should I call you Daddy?"

A low growl built in my throat as I stood from the couch, her feet falling to the empty cushion as I ran my hands through my hair. "First, yes, you *do* need to take better care of yourself. I expect you to eat regular meals and drink enough water every day to avoid being dehydrated."

She giggled, swinging her legs around to sit up. "You're easy to get wound up."

"This isn't funny, and second, please don't call me *Daddy*. That's not an honorific I like to use." I knew she was baiting me, but that word just pushed a button inside my brain that made my skin crawl.

"OK," she nodded. And I knew before she opened her mouth what she would ask next. "Are you going to tell me why?"

Closing my eyes, I exhaled, knowing the explanation would take a while, and we needed to figure out dinner. "Let's just say I have some daddy issues and revisit this topic at a later date."

"But you will tell me?"

I nodded. "Once you're ready to tell me more about what's going on with your fertility issues."

"Oh," she nodded, looking at her lap. "Is that...? I mean..."

"Relax, sunshine. I didn't mean this was a tit for tat, but I don't think you're ready to dive that deep yet."

She gave me another jerky nod in response, avoiding eye contact. "Is that going to be a deal-breaker for you? Me not being able to have children?"

"Look at me." She hesitated, pulling at a loose thread on her shirt. "Kelly."

There were tears in her eyes as she looked toward where I was standing. "Just tell me now if it is."

Taking a step toward her, I cupped her cheek, brushing away an errant tear. "No. Quite the opposite, actually. I'm more content to be an uncle than ever to be a father. It's not in the cards for me, and I've done things to assure that. I promise I'll tell you more when we're ready."

"Alright," she nodded, taking my proffered hand to stand, and following me toward the kitchen.

"Now, let's feed the beast in your stomach before it breaks out."

She shook her head at me, but it lightened things between us as we scrounged for something to heat up, the pre-made meals starting to dwindle. We'd need to make a trip into town soon.

Once we were tucked into the guest bed later, the questions started again. Kelly hadn't wanted to be alone, and the thought of returning to the small bed in the trailer alone without her wasn't appealing. I thought it'd be awkward to cuddle up with her every night without sex being involved, but I liked listening to her voice while we lay in the dark.

"What's your safeword?" she whispered. "Let me guess, something rugged like chainsaw or ax-master."

"Not quite," I chuckled. "It's dovetail."

"Like the joint?" she asked, propping her chin on my chest as she looked up at me. The moonlight coming through the window illuminated her features enough I could read her expressions, and she could apparently read mine as well. "Don't look so shocked. My gramps was into woodworking. That's the strongest type of joint, right?"

A genuine smile pulled across my lips as I traced a finger across her shoulder blades. "You are full of surprises, sunshine. And yes. It is one of the strongest joints in furniture making."

"So, why did you choose it? The strength aspect, or…" Her voice trailed off as I shook my head.

"No, I chose it because it involves two pieces that by themselves have weaknesses and empty spaces, but when you join them together, they form something so strong it's almost impossible to pull apart."

She was quiet for a few moments, staring down at my bare skin as she played with my chest hair.

"Oh…wow. That's…"

Suddenly feeling a little self-conscious, I decided to go for self-deprecating. I hadn't had a sub ask me *why* I chose that word before. "Cheesy, I know."

"No, it's beautiful," she argued, kissing the skin above my nipple. "Your words are beautiful, Nathan. That…that gave me goosebumps."

She wasn't lying as I felt her flesh pebbled underneath my fingertips. "Have you thought of what you want to use for yours?"

170

"Well, now everything I was considering sounds stupid in comparison," she laughed, "but I'm working on it."

"It needs to be something you'll remember under any circumstance," I told her, but I had a feeling she likely already knew that. "Hopefully, you'll never need to use it, but make sure it's something you remember."

"I'll do that," she whispered before she laid her head down on my chest again.

"We should go into town tomorrow. Otherwise we'll run out of food in a few days."

She sighed, nodding as she let out a big yawn. "Alright."

"And I need to get some things from the hardware store." She didn't ask what, but hopefully, they'd have a decent selection of ropes. I also needed to check on the status of my lumber order.

Kissing the top of her head, I listened to her quiet breaths, relaxing once they deepened as she drifted off to sleep. Her warm body and steady heartbeat against my side lulled me off to slumber right after her.

SEVENTEEN

Kelly

Ashford, Connecticut

As the door chimed over my head, I scanned the small grocery store, hoping I could find everything I needed. I knew Evan lived here pretty much full time, but I'd been spoiled with grocery delivery living in downtown Chicago.

A clerk was busy ringing up another customer, throwing a cursory nod in my direction as I grabbed a basket from the stack next to the entrance.

Nathan had told me I had forty-five minutes to get what I needed before he'd be done at the hardware store down the block.

Fishing my AirPods case from my coat pocket, I popped them in my ears and started down the far aisle, a soft feminine voice in my ear after I pressed play on my phone.

I knew Nathan was patiently waiting while I finished my checklist, but I was doing another type of research this morning, courtesy of my sister-in-law.

She'd been where I was once, a novice desperate to learn more, so listening to her first book on the subject might give me some insight as to how things worked. At least with fictional characters. I knew it wasn't reality, but I thought it might help.

My eyes dragged over the shelves, my fingers brushing familiar items and placing them in my basket as I listened intently to the story of Michael and Kayla.

Kayla was brave, not backing down from the intimidating executive who had pinned her down with a menacing stare as she entered his home for the first time. I wished I had her kind of courage. I hadn't finished the checklist yet because I had no idea exactly what I wanted. There was so much information and so many things I didn't know.

Fantasizing about something and doing them were two entirely different things, and while my imagination was a dirty bitch, I was afraid real-life Kelly was just a big bore.

Would Nathan be disappointed if I wasn't as adventurous as I tried to appear?

What if he wanted to try something I didn't?

I knew he said he'd respect my boundaries, but I had no idea what they were. What if I asked him to try something, and I hated it?

This was too much pressure.

I listened intently as the story played out, continuing to work my way up and down the aisles. Michael was an intimidating hero, alpha to the core, with very set methods, and he didn't leave much room for humor in his interactions with Kayla. I couldn't picture Nathan in that kind of role. He definitely had some alpha tendencies, but he was warm and kind, funny and playful. I found myself wishing I could see more of his Dominant side. I had a feeling he could be just as authoritative as Michael if he wanted to, but I was having a hard time reconciling the scenes in my ears with what I'd seen of his behavior.

As I rounded a corner, a hand closed on my shoulder, causing me to jump, my heart beating out of my chest.

"I thought you were going to be longer." My voice was strained as I willed myself to calm down. I had nothing to be ashamed about. I was a grown woman. I could discreetly listen to smut in public if I wanted to.

"Well, last time I checked, it was long enough, but if it's not doing it for you..." He trailed off with a smirk.

"Oh, shut up."

His eyes momentarily flashed with heat, but he smiled, reaching up to rub his knuckle across my cheek.

Nathan was the last person I'd expect to judge me, but I was still embarrassed I'd been caught unawares because I was so engrossed in listening to the spicy things that had come out of my sister-in-law's imagination. I had absolutely no idea how Evan swung marrying such a badass.

"Why are your cheeks all pink?" Nathan frowned. "You aren't feeling ill, are you?"

Nope. Just horny as fuck. But I wasn't telling him that. Especially not in the middle of a tiny grocery store in a town where everyone literally knew every other person. I didn't live here, but Chase and Evan did, so I didn't want it getting back to them that Evan's sister was a thirsty ho.

"I'm fine. Just fine. Absolutely fine," I rambled, earning an amused smirk from Nathan. It shouldn't be news to him that I was a giant dork. "You don't need to worry about me. How are you? Did you get the wood you needed? I mean, get the lumber order moved up?"

His smile widened as he crossed his arms over his chest, the soft blue plaid stretching enticingly over his biceps.

"My wood is just fine. It should arrive on time," he laughed. "Did you get everything you need here?"

"Yup. Got it all." I nodded, shoving my phone in my pocket along with my loose AirPods.

"You ready to head back to the house? I'd like to get some things set up so I can take advantage of a dry day tomorrow to get more of that brush cleared and get some framing done."

I nodded, my heart finally calm after he'd startled me. Thank God he hadn't asked what I'd been listening to. I was a terrible liar, and he knew it. In the short amount of time we'd spent together, he was already picking up on my tells.

"Lead the way."

He started toward the cash register, motioning for me to put the basket on the counter once we reached the front.

"Find everything you needed today?" the cashier asked as she looked between us with a gentle smile.

"Yup," I nodded. Already calculating the amount of time it'd take us to get back to the house to continue the audiobook where I left off. I'd just gotten to the good part, and I was feeling a little desperate for some relief.

Knowing Nathan would be occupied the rest of the afternoon would make it easy for me to sneak off and listen while I was pretending to get work done. I did need to do actual work, but I could multitask, right? I was sure plenty of people listened to straight-up smut while they were at work. There was nothing to be ashamed about.

"I got this," Nathan whispered as he reached toward his back pocket.

"Absolutely not." I shook my head. Half the stuff in the basket was just for me. I wasn't making him pay for my snacks, even if he could easily afford it.

174

"I didn't offer because I thought I had to. I'm trying to do something nice for you. And I'll be eating this too." His voice was low so that the cashier couldn't hear, but she was watching us curiously.

"And while I appreciate it, I can pay for the groceries. But thank you," I whispered, reaching into my pocket for the wallet I'd shoved in there before we left the house.

Nathan shrugged, watching me inquisitively. I swear he stared at me sometimes like I was a complicated math equation he was trying to solve. I hated to break it to him that I wasn't that deep.

"Michael stroked Kayla's hair, lingering on the tight braid that ran down the expanse of creamy, soft skin left exposed on her bare back."

My wide eyes met Nathan's, his flashing with something that looked like recognition as the audiobook narrator's voice sounded loudly from my pocket.

Oh shit.

"'Such a beautiful pet.' His deep voice murmured as he watched her chest rise and fall, her beautiful pink nipples straining in the cool air of his playroom. As goosebumps spread across her skin, he wrapped the tail of the braid around his fist, tilting her head backward as a small moan escaped her lips."

"Holy shit." My mouth dropped open as I lost the hold on my wallet, watching as it fell to the floor while I tried to get a grip on my phone.

"As the tension tightened on her hair, Kayla's eyes closed, another moan escaping as Michael held her captive. From her position on her knees, she tried fruitlessly not to move, but as the pain radiated from her scalp, mixed with the rush of pleasure that followed, her legs flexed, her thighs rubbing together.

'Such a greedy little pet,' Michael murmured. 'Already shamelessly rubbing her legs together as she waits for my coc-'"

The sound cut off, but the damage had already been done.

"Oh!" The cashier chimed in, much to my mortification. "I know that book!"

"Do you now?" Nathan smiled as he glanced between my flushed cheeks and the bright eyes of the excited clerk.

"Yes!" She chirped. "And the author lives in town. She autographed my book last year. She's so nice. And that new husband

175

of hers, phew." She fanned herself, giving a dramatic pant. "He's super quiet but so handsome. You know what they say about those quiet ones."

"I don't know. What do they say?" Nathan tilted his head, studying her name tag. "Elizabeth. I'm curious now."

"Stop it," I hissed under my breath as I bumped my hip against his.

"That they're the biggest," she paused, leaning forward to cup her hand next to her mouth, "...freaks in bed."

"Kill me now," I sighed as Nathan laughed loudly.

"Yup, it's always those quiet ones you have to worry about."

"Excuse me for a moment," I mumbled as I bent down to pick up my wallet. *While I vomit in my mouth a little...*

Nathan chatted with the cashier as I unzipped my wallet and pulled out my credit card.

"Oh, honey. It's already been taken care of by your ruggedly handsome friend here," the cashier waved away my hand as I offered her the card.

Glaring at Nathan, I grabbed one of the paper sacks from the counter, turning toward the door without a word.

"You two have a wonderful weekend," the clerk called out after us. "Come back and see us anytime!"

Nathan rushed ahead to open the door for me, smirking as he held it in place, the other bag tucked under his arm. "After you."

"Bite me," I growled as I briskly walked the short distance to where his Jeep was parked. I was tempted to kick one of the tires but decided the poor car hadn't done anything to embarrass me.

"Don't ask for things you don't want," he laughed as he stepped around me, opening the back door so I could put my bag down in the backseat.

"Kiss my ass," I taunted, pushing my hand into his shoulder as I attempted to walk around him. He captured my hand, holding it to his chest as I glared at him. He was enjoying the fact that I was totally embarrassed.

"We both know I'll gladly do that wherever and whenever you want, sunshine. But I don't think you're quite ready to explore your exhibitionist side. Let's get back to the house first. Then I'll gladly worship that ass."

"Don't tease me with things you aren't planning to deliver on, *Nathan*."

The easy grin on his face morphed into something a little more calculating, maybe even sinister, as he backed me up against the passenger door. "Oh, I can fucking deliver."

My head fell back onto the window, the cold glass a stark contrast to the heat I felt as he caged me in, his entire body pressing me into the side of the car.

"You're playing with fire, little girl. You talk a big game, but I'm not sure you can handle what I want to do to you."

The whimper that escaped my mouth was involuntary, but he was right. I'd been doing a lot of taunting lately that I wasn't sure I could back up with actions.

Nathan pulled back, pinning me down with an intense stare as he watched me. I averted my eyes, suddenly embarrassed at the way I'd been acting toward him.

"Look at me," he whispered, tilting my chin up, his breath steaming the air between us.

"I'm sorry," I whispered, closing my eyes. "I don't know what I'm doing. This isn't me."

His lips touched mine softly, slowly coaxing them to move with his in a languid kiss that had me melting against him. As he wove his fingers into my hair, I sighed against his lips, kissing him back until we were both breathless.

"Relax. You're doing just fine. This is about doing what feels good to you, sunshine. If giving me shit in the middle of the grocery store because you're embarrassed you got caught listening to Chase's smutty billionaire novel feels good, then go for it."

"I'm not..." I trailed off, my face flaming. "Wait!"

He was smiling as my head jerked up to meet his amused gaze. "Yes?"

"How did you know what Chase's book was about?"

"Hmm?" He deflected, stepping back, and reaching around me to open the passenger door. "Is that what I said? The cashier said something about..."

"Nathan," I growled, narrowing my eyes at him as he helped me climb into the passenger seat. He reached around me, grasping the seatbelt as he whispered in my ear.

"Because that particular audiobook is one of my favorites."

My breath caught as he leaned back, his eyes studying my face as he clicked the seatbelt into place. "But…"

"Hold that thought," he murmured as he leaned in to kiss my forehead, his fingers cupping the side of my neck as he lingered.

My heart thumped erratically as I watched him jog around to the driver's side, the gust of cold air that preceded him making me shiver in my seat. Or maybe it was the naughty little grin pulling at his lips as he quickly buckled his seatbelt, turning the key in the ignition.

I wasn't sure what to say as he leaned forward and turned off the radio, holding his outstretched hand out in my direction.

"Unlock your phone and hand it to me, please."

I opened my mouth to protest but then stopped, reaching into my pocket to pull out my phone.

The audiobook app was still pulled up, and my finger hovered over the x in the corner.

"Don't even think about it." Nathan's hand closed over mine, gently pulling the phone from my grasp.

I shifted in my seat, licking my lips as he glanced at me briefly, lifting one eyebrow as he reached forward and clipped my phone into the mount he had on his dashboard.

"This is my favorite part," he murmured as he pressed play, the deep voice of the male audiobook narrator filling the enclosed cabin of the Jeep.

"Michael circled Kayla, his eyes following her subtle movements as she tried to calm her breathing. Taking slow, measured steps as he watched her try to relax her body, her shoulders softening."

I could suddenly relate to Kayla on an acute level because I was suddenly having a hard time relaxing as Nathan pulled out onto the main road, the crunch of the gravel under his tires the only sound besides the dulcet baritone of the voice actor.

"She truly was a beautiful example of femininity. Soft, fair skin. Long flowing hair pinned up into a neat bun at the base of her graceful neck.

Her ample chest heaved slightly as she kept her breaths even, but he loved to watch the gentle jiggle of her breasts with each inhale. That slightly rounded stomach that tapered into full hips and an absolutely mouthwatering ass he wanted to grab at every opportunity."

178

Risking a look at Nathan, I watched as his hands tightened on the steering wheel, his chest heaving as we listened to the story unfolding from the speaker. He wanted me to think he was unaffected, but he shifted in his seat as a quiet moan slipped from the speakers, his eyes momentarily meeting mine before he focused on the road once again.

"His fingertips teased her nipples, watching as they pulled into tight buds, the skin surrounding them pulling taut. Michael watched as her jaw clenched, her fingers twitching on her thighs as she let out a quiet breath."

My own nipples felt tight underneath my sweater, aching like I imagined Kayla's did under Michael's attention.

"'Let me hear how much you're enjoying this, pet,' he murmured as his fingernail trailed over one of the aroused peaks.

'Oh,' Kayla breathed out softly, a quiet moan filling his ears as she arched her back, pressing her chest into his ministrations."

Nathan wasn't the only one shifting in his seat as Michael teased and caressed Kayla, his strong hands drawing down her body until they settled between her legs.

"Fuck," Nathan grunted softly as the female narrator moaned, his hips shifting in his seat.

I watched him, noticing how white his knuckles were against the black leather of the steering wheel. His grip was so tight I had no doubt he could rip the damn thing off.

As I observed him out of the corner of my eye, only half listening, it appeared his plan to tease me on the ride home was having an undesired side effect.

Something about the way he was squirming as the scene played on made my feelings of embarrassment shift into something different. A rush of adrenaline raced through me as I realized that maybe my dirty audiobook had turned the tables on Nathan's control.

He jumped as my hand settled on his thigh, his fingers clenching against the wheel so tightly the leather creaked. Scooting closer, I pressed up against the center console, wishing it wasn't there so I could press myself into his side.

"What do you think you're doing?" His voice was harsh, but I could tell he was just trying to keep himself restrained.

"I think someone has gotten himself a little worked up." My hand trailed higher on his thigh, grasping his concealed erection and

179

squeezing as he quietly growled under his breath. "Did listening to Chase's spicy book make you this hard?"

"Fuck, Kelly," he hissed as his hand covered mine. For a second, I thought he'd try to remove it, but as he pressed down on the back of my hand, thrusting his hips toward it, I knew he was just trying to maintain control.

"Well, you told me no one was going to be fucking Kelly today, so which is it?" I taunted, a thrill rolling up my spine as he turned and narrowed his eyes.

"Such a mouth on you," he groaned, his head leaning back momentarily as I began to stroke the outline of his arousal through the denim of his jeans.

"And I'm going to show you what this mouth is capable of. Pull over." Nathan looked over at me with a pained look, frowning. "Now, stud. Or I can just start sucking you off while you drive, your choice."

He was panting as I quickly unbuckled his belt, yanking down the zipper and pushing my hand inside. His hard cock pulsed against my palm as I explored him through the thin material of his boxer briefs.

"Alright, I warned you," I taunted as I pulled down his boxers, revealing his hard shaft. My mouth watered as I leaned over, suckling the head as Nathan cursed loudly.

The Jeep jerked to a stop, the tires crunching loudly on the gravel as Nathan's hand gathered my hair in his fist. He pressed the release button on my seat belt, and I leaned over the console, engulfing his erection.

"Holy fucking shit," he groaned as his cock hit the back of my throat, and I swallowed, causing his hips to buck into my movements. My eyes watered as I slowly let up, my hand cupping the base before I started a quick rhythm of taking him as deep as I could manage.

"God, sunshine. Suck that cock. I want to hear you choke on it. All the way down," he moaned. "Relax your throat. Yes...fuck. So fucking good."

Empowered by his gruff words, I took him deep, swallowing hard as he hit the back of my throat, doubling my efforts as his moans increased in volume. I was vaguely aware of the audiobook continuing in the background, but as Nathan's hand pressed on the back of my head, forcing him to the back of my throat, I had a hard time paying attention to anything but the man in the car with me.

"Fuck, that's it. Take it all," he groaned as his hips started thrusting into my movements. "Can't wait to fill that naughty mouth of yours."

His trembling legs indicated how close he was, and I sped up, choking on his length as he held my head in place, thrusting into my mouth. "Swallow my cum, Kelly. Every single fucking drop."

"Mmmm," I moaned as I felt him start to pulse in my mouth, his cock spurting his release into the back of my throat. I swallowed quickly, squeezing the base of him as he came, his cock throbbing against my fingers and tongue.

"Fuck. Yes. All of it. Good girl. Just like that," he praised in a husky moan as his hands fell away from my hair. I knew some women hated it when men tried to direct them during a blow job, but the praise at the end after you rocked their world made you feel powerful.

Nathan's eyes were closed, his chest heaving as I leaned back into my seat, discreetly wiping the corner of my mouth.

"Someone is proud of themselves," he chuckled as he opened his eyes, a lazy smile on his face.

"Fuck yes, I am. That was some of my best work," I giggled, and he narrowed his eyes.

"I'm still not going to fuck you, sunshine. Not yet."

I squirmed in my seat, my panties more than wet and my nipples tight buds under my shirt. He may have thought that sounded like a threat. But the 'yet' part was what I was focusing on.

"We'll see."

"At this rate, the only thing you'll be seeing is a red handprint on your ass if you don't quit tempting me."

"Again with the promises," I giggled as I turned to face forward again, securing my seatbelt back into place.

As his laugh filled the car, I couldn't keep the smile from my face. This was the most fun I'd ever had with a man in my entire life.

Now, I had a checklist to finish.

EIGHTEEN

Nathan

Connecticut

Kelly didn't say another word the entire ride home, grinning like the cat that ate the canary while humming to herself. I took mercy on the both of us and returned her phone after turning off the audiobook and reverting to the radio — not that I'd been able to focus on the music. That hadn't turned out as I expected it to. The little minx had turned the tables on me, and I'd been pleasantly surprised at how she'd behaved. She'd taken my comment about doing what felt good to heart.

While I hadn't been able to let myself submit to her, she'd shown me a part of herself that could be developed into budding Domme behavior. Kelly already had all the traits of a switch, and it was almost eerie how similar we were, but different in all the right ways. When she'd called me stud again and told me to pull over, it'd gotten me so hard I'm not sure what I would have done if she'd just been teasing me.

Instead, she'd nearly sucked the life out of me when she deepthroated my cock. That was another thing I wasn't expecting. Marisa hadn't been a huge fan of performing oral sex, so it'd been a few years since a woman had sucked my dick as if her life depended on it, and Kelly surpassed any other lover I'd ever had in less than five minutes. She seemed to be blowing — pun fully fucking intended — all my previous partners out of the water without even trying. Our chemistry was already off the charts, and we hadn't even gotten properly started yet.

"You're quiet," she observed as I made the final turn toward the house, the trees slowly easing apart as the paved driveway came into view. I'd made some solid progress in the past few days, but Kelly was a distraction. A very welcome distraction, but a distraction nonetheless. With nasty weather forecast, I knew I needed to buckle down and get the side of the driveway cleared, so it was ready when they delivered my gravel next week. It'd be easier if they could drop

182

it where I wanted it rather than having to transfer it later. Although the thought of Kelly watching me from her voyeuristic perch at the front windows while I lifted shovels full of heavy gravel with my shirt unbuttoned had its merits.

"I think you sucked the words right out of me," I laughed as I put the Jeep in park, turning off the ignition. "I'm still processing this newly revealed skill of yours."

Kelly giggled as she unbuckled her seatbelt, still looking adorably smug. She should; I agreed that it was some of her best work. Damn. Now I was never going to get anything done knowing she was capable of that.

"I do what I can. Must admit it was rather fun watching you squirm beforehand, though. Never pegged you for a guy who listens to dirty romance novels. Should I be worried you're using me to get closer to my sister-in-law to feed your secret addiction?"

"Go inside before I make good on my promise to spank you." I nodded toward the house as she stepped out the passenger door.

"Yes, sir," she saluted, and I held in a groan. I knew she was taking a few liberties with the use of honorifics before we'd established a dynamic, but I'd called her sunshine from the beginning, so I had no room to judge. And I liked hearing her call me stud and Sir in the same conversation.

Shaking my head as I watched her head across the driveway, I gathered the overflowing shopping bags from the back seat and followed her inside the house. I knew I needed to get some more work done, but I'd also received an email tracking alert that a package requiring a signature was due to arrive this afternoon.

Talia hadn't been messing around and had gotten the things I'd asked her for express shipped sooner than I'd expected. Knowing that I now owed her a huge favor should have worried me, but it just meant I was that much closer to play time with Kelly, so I'd gladly do Tal's bidding.

While I was sure Kelly would find it amusing, I didn't want her to see the things I'd ordered before she was ready. Most of the things in the box were intended for her to use on me, but she didn't know that yet. This whole week had turned into an exercise in patience, and I wasn't sure how much more I could take.

...

Unfortunately, the weather service had initially underestimated the storm that rolled in the next morning. They'd predicted large amounts of rainfall along with sustained thirty miles per hour winds, but it'd changed overnight to rain, followed by sleet and freezing rain that'd turn into ice and a solid six inches of potential snow.

While a little on the short side, that was not the six inches Kelly nor I wanted to hang around. Although, it would mean more time spent inside the house with her.

And we'd *clearly* need to continue sharing the same bed to preserve body heat.

And the best way to generate body heat *was* with direct skin-to-skin contact.

*But...*that'd destroy my resolve to keep the sexual part of our relationship on the back burner until she was done with the studious examination of her potential kinks.

I did admire her dedication, though, exploring other means of research through listening to that audiobook. Maybe Kelly wasn't as vanilla as she'd initially come across. She just needed the right partner to unlock this side of her. And I'd gladly strip her bare to help with the process.

While I'd have loved to continue fantasizing about Kelly, I needed to buckle down and start preparing for the inevitable storm.

My morning was spent securing my equipment in my trailer, ensuring I hadn't left anything out that would be lost to the weather.

Deciding it wasn't worth risking it, I hitched my equipment trailer to the Jeep after a quick breakfast. I made the drive back to my barn, securing it inside and ensuring all the exterior doors were locked tight before returning to Evan's.

Kelly was spending the morning trying to get caught up on work emails. I didn't want to disturb her in case the internet went down. It was an unlikely possibility, but sometimes these late spring storms came in with a vengeance and left you without power or stranded.

She'd been quiet about how working remotely had been going, but I knew she spent hours at her laptop while I was outside preparing the foundation so I could start framing as soon as the weather cleared again.

It was hard not to dwell on the future of her career. While I was a little biased, that company would be foolish to let her go. As she'd been proving with her research into more private matters, she was dedicated to whatever she set her mind to. Her career had been her focus for so long I worried about the mental toll this whole situation was taking on her. While our betrayals were different, we were both struggling with some pretty heavy things.

Waiting for Marisa to reappear often worried me; not knowing what was going on with her was daunting. Was she planning on trying to pass her child off as mine? Would she cause problems for me once I got back to Boston? Would something like this damage Kelly's relationship with me if she found out since she couldn't have children?

Ominous dark gray clouds started rolling in as I drove past the sign for Ashford, the light rain changing into a driving downpour that almost blew the Jeep sideways with the wind.

Knowing that the full force of the bad weather wasn't going to hold off for long, I parked close to the side of the garage, hurrying into the house, and grabbing the keys to Evan's car, deciding it was safer inside the garage.

Kelly looked up briefly as I rushed inside and promptly turned around, but I needed to hurry if I wanted to finish before the ice started coming down.

As I checked the side manual locks on the rolling garage door, I pulled up the radar on the weather map, cursing at the mass of red and purple that was headed in our direction.

"Fuck," I grunted as I tried to push open the side door against the wind, barely holding onto the handle as it threatened to rip wide open.

I checked the tarps on the firewood against the side of the garage, tightening all the straps before I moved inside and started making sure my generator was filled with gas.

Part of me felt like I was being paranoid, rushing around like the storm of the century was about to hit, but as I saw a heavy metal outdoor chair roll across the yard, I knew things were about to get real.

The rain pelted my waterproof work coat as I raced to the rear of the house, making sure the furniture was stacked securely, and the weatherproof covers were tight, so things didn't blow into the half-frozen lake.

Power was still on in the house, so I wasn't worried about Kelly, but as I returned to the garage to pack up the rest of my food into one of the coolers, the overhead lights flickered.

"Nathan!" Kelly's voice startled me, and I looked up as she struggled to hold the side door, her coat flapping in the wind.

"What are you doing, sunshine?"

The hood of her coat had kept her from getting drenched, but she was shaking as she crossed the space between us, the leggings she was wearing underneath clearly doing nothing to keep out the chill.

"It sounded like it was getting worse out here, so I wanted to help you. What can I do? Put me to work."

My caveman side wanted to tell her to go back inside, but I knew she was perfectly capable of helping me, despite her unpractical sneakers.

"Can you lift that cooler? It needs to go inside. There's a bag of ice in the freezer we should empty into it."

She nodded, pulling up her hood, hefting the cooler up by the plastic handles, and moving toward the door. I followed, holding it open for her and making sure it closed before grabbing the bag of extra batteries I'd pulled out of my equipment trailer earlier.

"You're out here running around like it's Armageddon," she laughed as she hoisted the cooler into the middle of the kitchen island. "Are you sure I can't help with anything else?"

"You can make sure that the freezer is full of anything we don't plan on eating within the next day or so. If the power goes out, we need to keep it closed to keep it cold."

Her eyes flashed to mine, concern etched into her features. "The storm is going to knock the power out?"

Not wanting to send her into a panic, I shrugged, but as the wind started to howl outside, rain beating against the front windows, the lights flickered again, answering my question.

"What else do you want me to do?" she asked, her voice trembling a little.

"Stay inside, maybe look for some supplies? I know you don't live here, but surely they've got some things easily accessible we can use. Like a lighter and some candles?"

She nodded, still looking a little worried as she braced her hands against the island.

"Hey," I soothed, wiping my damp hands on my jeans before I walked toward her. "Everything will be fine. I'm probably just being over-cautious. We'll just plan on hunkering down tonight to ride it out."

Her nervous smile turned into a naughty smirk as I reached forward to cup her cheek.

"*Ride* it out, huh? Sounds promising."

This girl. So surprisingly naughty.

"Behave," I scolded, leaning in to kiss her forehead, stopping to enjoy having her close for a moment.

"Is that what you really want?" Kelly asked as she tilted her head back, her dark eyes searching my face. As I leaned in to kiss her, she shifted up into her toes, closing the distance between us.

"No, sunshine, it's not," I whispered against her lips, wanting to do nothing more than strip off her heavy coat and lay her across the kitchen island naked.

But my fantasy was abruptly ended as a loud crack outside the house shook the windows, and the power blinked off, leaving us in a dim kitchen, the sunlight struggling to break through the storm.

"Fuck," I groaned, quickly stealing one more kiss before I stepped away, willing down my body's response to her closeness. "I'll be back. Please stay inside. I'll worry about you if you try to come back out."

"Please hurry back," she nodded as she reached forward to squeeze my hand. "I'll worry about you out there too."

"I'll be fine," I assured her, my lips pecking her cheek before I pulled my hood up and rushed out the front door, worried about what this storm would bring.

NINETEEN

Kelly

Connecticut

It wasn't like I hadn't dealt with power outages before. Wind and thunderstorms, sometimes even ice storms knocked out the power all the time back in the Midwest. Well, maybe not *all* the time, but enough that I remembered sitting with Evan in our living room huddled around in a makeshift blanket fort with flashlights as children. But I didn't know where Evan kept anything, so I was left with a half-dead smart phone as my flashlight.

Nathan had gone back outside ten minutes ago and still hadn't reappeared. It made me nervous for him to be out in the storm, but I knew he had a generator on-site for his power tools. I was sure he was outside doing something handy. My accident-prone ass was staying in here. Knowing my luck, I'd slip in the mud or on a sheet of ice and end up in the pond.

Death by a lightning strike or accidental drowning in a shallow body of half-frozen water was not on my list of priorities.

The kitchen had been a bust. I thought I'd at least find a lighter or another box of matches, but the only thing I'd turned up was an engraved wooden spoon.

It was probably still where I'd dropped it on the kitchen floor after I'd seen the words on the back.

Please Spank Responsibly

If it were in anyone else's kitchen, I would have laughed my ass off, but finding it in my little brother's kitchen was fucking weird. Chase was all about immersive research, and I knew exactly what that spoon had been used for. *Ew.*

I didn't know if he was the one on the giving or receiving end, but dwelling on it would just lead to me wanting to vomit at the thought of my brother being paddled with a wooden spoon.

"Kelly?" Nathan's deep voice carried down the hallway, almost drowned out by the noise of the wind outside.

"I'm in here!" I yelled back, hoping he'd figure out I'd ducked into the main bedroom to try to find something that would give us a little more light than my iPhone.

"What are you doing?" When I turned around, my breath caught at Nathan leaning against the door jamb of the master closet. His shirt was plastered to his chest, water droplets in his hair and running down the sides of his face and neck.

In the dim light, he looked intimidating, and I could see how he'd be able to pull off a rape fantasy scene convincingly. Being trapped in a house with no power in a thunderstorm seemed like the perfect setup to an intruder breaking in to seek cover.

"Kelly?"

"Hmm...?" My vivid imagination had started to run a scenario through my brain where he had me trapped against the kitchen island with my hands tied behind my back. Somehow, I'd been magically changed into a skirt, and he'd find out I was bare underneath and scold me for being such a temptation.

My weak cries would cut off as he placed his hand over my mouth and told me to be quiet or he'd have to fill my mouth with something. His hard cock would be pressed up against my skirt, throbbing against the thin material covering me.

I'd tremble in fear as I heard the sound of his belt buckle in the quiet room and try to scream against his fingers. His huge cock would thrust into me, pounding the orgasm out of me as I tried to fight back against him, surely leaving bruises I'd feel for days on the front of my thighs.

He'd just chuckle, pinning me to the island with his large frame as he made me scream from the pleasure and pain combined until I was so delirious from multiple orgasms that I'd pass out...

"You're staring."

"What?" Shaking my head to clear it, I refocused on where Nathan was standing with his arms crossed on his broad chest and a sexy smirk pulling at the corners of his lips. Lips that had made me cum harder than any man I'd been with before. *Shit.*

"What has you so distracted?" he chuckled as he took a step forward, causing me to stumble back into the shelf behind me, my phone dropping to the floor.

"I'm looking for candles or a flashlight or something."

"Do you think maybe it's in there?" He nodded at a box over my head, and I looked back, noticing the small letters spelling out *SUPPLIES* in red sharpie.

"Well, that'd be the obvious place to look, wouldn't it?" I'd completely missed the words when I'd walked in here a few minutes ago. Likely due to the fact he'd turned me into a sex-obsessed nymphomaniac who was currently a livewire of arousal because he wouldn't touch me until I gave him that checklist.

"Let me get it down from there. We don't know how heavy it is."

I nodded, ready to step out of his way, but he'd already moved forward, reaching above my head, the wet fabric covering his chest brushing against my cheek as he tried to pull the box down. He smelled like fresh rain and something uniquely him, but it wasn't helping the situation in my pants from my little trip to the imagination station a few moments ago.

"That's weird," I frowned as I noticed that the box was taped shut. Why would a box of supplies be taped shut?

"Let me put this down. I've got a knife in my pocket."

"Oh," I laughed as I followed him out into the bedroom, where he carefully placed the box on the edge of the bed. "You mean you aren't just happy to see me?"

He turned back toward me, his face barely illuminated, but I could still see his naughty grin. "You already know it's a little bit bigger than a pocketknife, Kelly." I stopped a foot away, my mouth opening slightly as he leaned in my direction. "But you're not wearing a bra, so, of course, I'm happy to see you."

"Just cut open the damn box already, so we don't have to spend all night in the dark."

He frowned, pausing as he looked over to where I was now, crossing my arms over my chest to cover the nipples that'd awakened with his blatant ogling. "Are you afraid of the dark?"

"No."

He tilted his head to the side.

"Would you quit? I'm not afraid of the dark. I just don't want to use all my phone battery to see." And I was jumpy because I was horny as fuck.

"Hmm… I already brought one of the work lights inside. It runs off the same batteries as my power drills."

"Well, aren't you Mister Prepared?" I chuckled, the sarcasm in my voice heavy. "Pocket knives, battery-powered lights, you *are* just a regular Boy Scout."

"Where do you think I learned the fine art of knot tying. And I'm not a regular Boy Scout. I'm an Eagle Scout."

The smirk was back, combined with a naughty wink, before he looked back down at the box, pushing the button on the side of his knife to reveal a wicked-looking blade. It was several inches long and gleamed in the light. It'd make an intimidating prop in my earlier scenario. *Fuck.*

He carefully peeled back the flaps of the box, eyes widening as he peeked inside. He frowned as he closed one side and shined the small pocket flashlight he had attached to his pants at the label on the box.

"Well, I don't think we'll be finding a flashlight in this box," he laughed as he quickly nested the flaps together and picked the box back up. He mumbled something under his breath that vaguely sounded like *Fleshlight*, but that couldn't be right. Could it?

"Wait," I put my hand out, keeping him from walking around me. What the hell kind of supplies were in that box if it wasn't emergency supplies?

Although my brother was boring as fuck, knowing him, it was likely extra notebooks and a supply of red pens. Surely it wouldn't be something a little more adventurous. Fleshlights were sex toys, right?

"Don't worry about it," Nathan laughed, but now my interest was piqued.

Grabbing my phone, I aimed the flashlight toward the label, frowning when I vaguely recognized the name.

"Who is Talia Stephenson?" I wracked my brain for how I knew that name, and then it clicked. "Isn't that your friend? The one who you said you could get in touch with if I had any questions about...." I trailed off as I connected all the dots. "What's in the box, Nathan?"

"I'm sure your brother and Chase wouldn't appreciate us going through their things while we're guests in their house."

"Oh, fuck that," I laughed, wrapping my hands around the side of the box and trying to pull it out of Nathan's grasp. "You're showing me what's in this box."

191

"Kelly," he warned, but I was already tugging on it, stumbling back a step as I pulled it from his arms. "Don't. This isn't our business."

"Try and stop me," I taunted as I turned and rushed toward the closet, trying to close the door behind me with my foot.

Nathan's large hand grasped the edge of the door and pushed it open, squeezing in the gap before pressing it closed.

"If that checklist of yours were done, that little stunt would have earned you a trip over my knee," he warned, his eyes more serious than he'd been moments before.

I shivered when I realized he implied I would have earned a punishment by taking the box from him, and the idea didn't scare me.

"And I might have liked it," I teased as I propped the box up against a shelf and pulled open the flaps. "Whoa."

My eyes widened as I looked at the row of plastic-wrapped boxes lined up inside the box.

"Why is Talia sending my brother a box full of sex toys?"

"It wouldn't be the first time she'd sent someone sex toys. Gifting is her love language, and she loves to gift her friends with new toys to play with." Nathan's voice was more amused than annoyed, but knowing another woman was sending him this kind of stuff made a tiny flare of jealousy flame to life.

"She sends you sex toys? Why?"

"It's her job, Kelly," he laughed. "She's a blogger who reviews sex toys."

Relaxing a little at his explanation, I wasn't quite ready to rip her head off yet. And if he was suggesting she be my possible mentor, he trusted her. "Can she be my friend too?" I joked, but the heated look Nathan gave me in return was unexpected.

"Or I can share mine..." he drawled out slowly, taking a step toward me.

"Holy, shit." My mouth dropped open as I looked at the last box. It was black with a sleek-looking purple vibrator pictured on the side, but it wasn't like any vibrator I'd seen before. "What is this for?"

"Maybe we should put the box back, Kelly."

"No fucking way. Tell me," I demanded as I pulled it free and turned it over, my eyes scanning the back label.

"It's for use with a partner."

"What's pegging?" I frowned as I squinted at the print on the box in the dim light.

"Something you don't need to worry about."

Turning toward him, I raised an eyebrow, but he was staring at the box in my hand. "I thought we were supposed to be honest with each other. You told me we'd have open and honest communication."

He paused for a moment, his quiet voice coming out much deeper. "It's a vibrator that is worn internally by a female to penetrate a male or another female, but this one with a tapered tip is designed for a male."

"Like I'd..." My brain was having a hard time wrapping around the concept of how this thing worked. It meant one end went inside me if it was worn internally and... "Oh."

"Put it back in the box." The commanding tone of his voice sent a shiver up my spine, but I was too curious to care as he advanced on me.

"No," I shook my head. "I want to look at it. Have you ever...?"

He shook his head, looking away from me, his posture suddenly tense. "No. Anal penetration is a soft limit for me."

"Oh." I paused, thinking about what that meant. He wasn't completely opposed to it, but he wasn't eager for it either. Was I?

"Why? Would doing something like that interest you?"

Turning the box over in my hand, I lifted open the magnetic clasp at the side and pulled the toy out, feeling the weight of it in my hand. "I have to admit, the thought of it is making me a little hot." More than a little hot, but this was something I'd never even considered. My research so far had been in other areas. I'd never considered dominating Nathan like this.

"Only a little?" he chuckled darkly as he took the box from my hand and placed it on the ground, stepping in close. The light from where my phone had fallen cast some ominous shadows across his face.

"Would you like it if I fucked you, Nathan?" I breathed, my chest heaving as he pinned me down with one of those intimidating Dom stares of his. He was a powerful man, and it intrigued me to see how he'd submit.

"There are a lot of things I think I'd let you do to me," he whispered as he cupped my hand, pressing the button on the base of the toy. It softly hummed to life in our clasped hands, and my breath caught as I looked up into his eyes. He stared down at me for one long moment, the fierce expression on his shadowy face making my heart pound.

"God, fucking, dammit," he growled before he dropped the toy to the ground and grasped my neck under my chin, crashing his mouth into mine.

It wasn't a gentle kiss, my lungs burning as he possessed my lips, his tongue thrusting into my mouth in a way that made my entire body ignite. He'd been so restrained the last few days, practically ignoring my flirting and calmly avoiding my unsubtle advances. Almost acting like I hadn't sucked him off on a gravel road in broad daylight on the way back from a shopping trip.

He had significantly more self-restraint than I had, but it appeared he'd reached his breaking point.

"You just have to fucking push me, don't you?" He groaned into my neck, his fingers roughly tilting my head to the side. My hands grasped his biceps, the muscles underneath flexing as he manipulated my body, forcing me backward until my back hit the wall next to the closet door.

Nathan was dropping to his knees before I could react, yanking my leggings down to my ankles and grasping my ass with both his strong hands. I could barely see his face, his damp hair tickling my thighs as he leaned in, inhaling deeply.

"I want to fucking devour you." His voice was low and rough, sending a shockwave of pure lust through my system as he made good on his threat — although it was looking more like a promise. "Tongue fuck you until your legs shake."

His fingertips grasped my hips tightly as his lips descended between my legs, his tongue doing something so deliciously obscene my knees started to quake in response, almost as if he'd willed it into fruition.

"Oh, fuck...keep going," I panted as he lifted one of my legs, pulling it over his shoulder as he used a single long finger to penetrate me while he growled against my skin.

Even after the wedding, he'd never been this unrestrained, this wild...and as my hand found its way into his hair and pulled, I realized that maybe he was exactly what I'd been looking for in my life.

"Don't stop," I moaned as his finger curled, making stars dance behind my closed eyelids. "Don't fucking stop. Make me cum."

Nathan groaned loudly against my clit. The vibration combined with the rasp of his beard against my skin was too much, the heel of my foot digging into the hard muscles of his back as I clenched on his finger, spasming against his mouth that hadn't stopped moving.

If anything, my orgasm had made him wilder, his finger going deeper and curling, his teeth dragging against my overstimulated clit and making me cry out as I tugged hard on the hair grasped in my fist. It was like he was making good on his promise to punish me. But this felt too good to be any real punishment.

"Oh, oh," I moaned, snapping my neck backward until my head hit the wall with a thump, but Nathan still didn't stop, adding another finger and making me writhe against his hand until my entire face was numb with intense pleasure.

"Give me another one," he growled as he looked up at me from between my legs. The dim light of the flashlight made his features look menacing, and I moaned as I pushed his face back into me. I was so desperate to cum I found myself pulling his hair harder as I ground myself against his mouth.

"Mmm," he moaned, spearing me with his tongue as the fingers on my hip tightened, angling my center toward his mouth.

I couldn't breathe as he plunged his thick fingers back in, rotating and pushing roughly until I couldn't hold it in any longer, and I screamed, my body detonating like a live grenade.

"That's it, fucking use me. Ride my hand, sunshine." His voice was low and gruff, encouraging me to continue grinding myself against his hand as I came...and came...and came...

Until I slumped back against the wall, my hand across my quivering lips as I tried to regain any sense of equilibrium.

"You alright?" Nathan asked as he gently pulled my leg from his shoulder, holding onto my hips to keep me from slumping to the floor in a post-orgasmic puddle.

"Give me a minute," I gasped, flailing my hand toward him.

He caught my fingers, kissing them before he stood in front of me, trailing one fingertip down my cheek and across my exposed shoulder. My loose sweatshirt had shifted during his relentless attack on me, my breast practically begging to escape.

He hadn't been wrong earlier, I *wasn't* wearing a bra, and as his finger trailed lower, my nipples strained against the thin material, dying for his touch.

"You going to listen to me next time I tell you something?" he asked, his nose trailing along the side of my face, his breath hot in my ear.

"No," I laughed, my voice breathy and rough. "If this is what I have to look forward to when I don't listen. Most definitely not."

"And here I thought my sunshine was a *good girl*," he breathed, his teeth scraping against my earlobe before he bit down and tugged.

"You make me want to be bad," I moaned, grasping his damp shirt in my fist and yanking his face toward me.

"You want me to kiss you?" His voice was low and teasing. I could feel him resisting. The muscles of his neck strained as his lips hovered near mine.

"You're going to make me beg, aren't you?"

"Not this time," he murmured before his lips crashed to mine.

As he kissed me roughly, sucking the oxygen from my lungs with his frantic pace, I found I wasn't scared at the thought of him making me beg. I was afraid that this would all fade away once the lights came   back   on.

TWENTY

Nathan

Connecticut

My head was spinning as I gasped, yanking my lips from Kelly's and taking a hesitant step away from her. She was driving me insane. Every little thing she did either infuriated me or made me so fucking horny I was almost worried I'd revert to my teen years walking around with a perpetual hard-on. Which for a male pushing forty without the aid of pharmaceuticals was kind of impressive.

Emory had bemoaned latent recovery time or decrease in firmness enough to know this wasn't normal. I knew he used cock rings to alleviate some of his issues, but apparently, all I needed was being secluded in the woods with Kelly to achieve raging wood in my pants.

"Do you want me to help with this?" Kelly whispered as her hand wandered down my shirt and grasped me through the damp denim of my jeans.

Despite wearing a coat, I'd gotten soaked when the wind picked up again as I ran to and from the garage, bringing in the light and batteries, my small generator, a space heater, propane stove, and some dry firewood. The temperature was still brutally cold outside, and with the storm knocking out the power, we would both have to stay close to the fireplace tonight to stay warm.

Kelly shivered against my chest, and as much as I wanted to see how she planned on taking care of the situation in my pants — the vivid memory of her mouth wrapped around my cock as she leaned over my lap in the Jeep running through my consciousness like a movie — we were on a time crunch. We needed to get changed into warm clothes, gather all the blankets we could find, and get the fire going before the temperature inside the house dropped any further.

The storm was starting to shift fully to sleet, and I knew that we'd likely get a coating of ice and several inches of snow if the predictions of the radar map on my phone held true.

We'd be fine without the power overnight, but if the temperatures continued to stay low, we needed to keep each other and the house warm to prevent some costly outcomes.

I highly doubted that Evan and Chase wanted to come home from their honeymoon to a flooded house because one of their pipes burst. And I knew he'd kill me if I let his sister get hypothermia.

Grasping her hand, I pulled it to my lips, leaving a kiss on her palm, before I tilted her face up with my fingers on her chin.

"As much as I'm sure we'd both enjoy it, you're cold, I'm wet, and we need to get a fire started. And we need to hurry before it gets much colder in here. I can already feel the temperature dropping with the furnace off."

"Ugh. Adulting is such a cockblock," she groaned, and I tried to stifle a laugh, but she wasn't wrong. Adulting *was* a cockblock.

"It is. But we must do it anyway. Come on, sunshine."

"Fine," she muttered as she reached down to pull her leggings back up. I retrieved her phone from the floor, handing it to her before I put the vibrator back into the box and tucked it on the shelf again.

As I turned to leave the closet, she called my name.

"Hey, Nathan?"

"Yes?"

"You're not the only one who's wet," she giggled.

Shaking my head, I turned away from her and adjusted my pants, trying not to engage in the flirting — or recall the events that had gotten her that wet. At least for the moment.

"And my list is done…"

Well, our night was about to get a lot more interesting. I stopped in the doorway, watching as she tried to tame her messy hair. She looked freshly fucked, and while my tongue and fingers had gotten the rights to make her look like that, my cock was aching at the possibility of taking things further. "Meet me in the living room. I need to go back out to the garage for a few minutes."

"I'll keep looking for candles or something," she offered, nodding toward the bathroom.

Quickly crossing the room and wrapping my arm around her waist, I pulled her toward me, kissing her roughly before I stepped away. "Be right back."

Jogging down the hallway to the front door, adjusting the uncomfortable rod in my pants, I grabbed my coat from the hook and braced myself for the cold. It was rare for the temperature to plummet this late into the spring, but it wasn't unheard of.

At least we'd been able to make the trip into town to get a few more days' worth of food. Depending on how much ice accumulated, we might not be going back into town for a while.

The wind whipped my hair as the sleet pelted the back of my head. I stuck to the gravel at the side of the driveway, not wanting to risk hitting a patch of ice. The last thing we needed was me breaking a limb out here.

"Fuck." I shivered as I ducked inside the side door of the garage, shaking my arms before I pulled open the trailer door. I grabbed the envelope I'd shoved my printed-out list inside, as well as something I'd snuck out here to prepare after Talia had emailed it to me yesterday.

Placing the cards and envelope inside the bottom of my duffel bag, I grabbed dry clothes, a few extra pairs of socks, the rope I'd bought at the hardware store, and the contents of the package Talia had express shipped to me. Now that Kelly had finished her list, the real fun could begin.

I had the perfect way to fill our time as we waited out the storm.

…

When I entered the house, securely locking the door and ensuring the front windows were sealed tightly, Kelly was standing in the kitchen humming. I had a feeling she had a fantastic singing voice, but I had to admit, the only music I wanted to escape those lips was the sound of her moaning her way through another orgasm.

I wasn't typically this sex-obsessed, reserving playtime for the weekends or carefully scheduled weekday outings. Living the lifestyle 24/7 had never appealed to me. Still, Kelly had flipped a switch in my libido, and I was now likely giving a twenty-year-old a run for his money in the sexual appetite category. It was simultaneously addicting and terrifying. I hadn't gotten this hard, this often, in years.

"What are you up to?" She'd scattered battery-powered candles across the island, giving the room a soft glow, despite the raging storm that continued to shake the windows. "Setting the ambiance for something?" I asked as I wiped my cold hands on my thighs, fruitlessly trying to warm them up before I touched her. Because I was going to touch her, it was inevitable. I'd largely kept my hands to myself until she was ready, but my restraint was wearing thin.

"I found these in the bathroom and some batteries in a drawer in the island," she said over her shoulder as she resumed stirring something in a mug on the counter. "I'm not sure how long they'll last, but they're a little less jarring than your crime scene lights over there." She gestured to the work light I'd aimed toward a corner, but she was right. The bright white light was a little much. I'd have to try to drape something over it to lessen the harshness of it.

"Smells good in here," I hummed, bracing my hands against the counter on either side of her hips.

"Hot cocoa. There's plenty for you too," she smiled as she leaned back against my shoulder. "I think the water heater might be gas. I managed to fill some thermos' I found in the pantry with super hot water. Figured this would be the easiest way to warm us up until you get the fire going."

"Hmm," I hummed, placing a soft kiss on the back of her neck, enjoying the way she visibly shuddered and sagged back into my chest. I was likely getting her sweater all wet, but I didn't intend to let her keep it on all night. It'd have plenty of time to dry draped over the arm of the couch. "I bet that cocoa doesn't taste nearly as good as you did. I can still taste you on my lips."

"What happened to restrained Nathan?" she chuckled, tilting her mouth toward mine, her warm chocolate scented breath fanning over my lips.

"You finished your checklist. He's not here anymore. It's time to play, sunshine. Are you ready for me?"

"Are you finally going to show me yours?" she whispered, ghosting her lips over mine softly.

"I'm going to show you all kinds of things, gorgeous. Let's get that fire going, and we can lay it all on the table."

"You can lay me on the table," she giggled, nipping at my bottom lip.

"I'm going to lay you everywhere you'll let me, as often as you want," I growled as I spun her around and grasped her hips tightly, no longer caring if I was getting her clothing wet as I kissed her with all the pent-up energy I'd been repressing for days.

"We don't need the lists right now, do we?" she gasped as I lifted her, her legs wrapping around my waist as I stumbled toward the living room.

"Fuck," I grunted as she yanked at the hair on the back of my head, biting at my neck. "I had plans for us tonight."

"I have better plans," she growled into my skin. "Fuck me. Right here. Right now. I can't take it anymore."

"Such a naughty girl, sunshine," I groaned as my fingers dug into her ass. Nearly stumbling over the rug under the couch, I perched her on the back of it, gripping her cheeks and kissing her like I'd wanted to for days. It was rough and messy, lips fighting for dominance as she ripped at the buttons on my shirt, her fingers digging into my pecs as she yanked the sides apart.

My fingers crept beneath the hem of her sweater, tracing a line across her lower back.

"Fuck," she shrieked as she pulled away from me, flailing for a moment before she fell backward against the couch cushions.

"Oh fuck," I chuckled as I looked down at her shocked face. Well, just like everything else between us, that hadn't gone to plan. "Are you alright?"

"Your fingers are fucking freezing," she giggled as she poked one of her sock-covered toes into the center of my chest.

"It's fucking cold outside. What were you expecting?"

Shaking my head, I left her lying there upside down on the couch as I moved to the fireplace, getting started on what I should have done before she distracted me in the closet.

"Where do you think you're going?" she asked as she swung her legs around and joined me in front of the fireplace.

"You said I was freezing, so I'm making a fire to warm up," I smirked as she sat back on her heels, watching as I opened the heat-resistant glass doors of the fireplace, a cold wind spiraling into the room.

"We were in the middle of something. Your fingers would have warmed up," she pouted as she watched me arrange the pieces of wood in the grate carefully around some pieces of tinder.

"Or you can be patient and wait until I ensure we don't freeze tonight."

An adorable little growl built in her chest as she watched me work, but she didn't say anything further until I'd stoked the flame and closed the doors once the fire had caught the pieces of firewood.

"Are you finished now?"

Dusting my hands off on my thighs, I sat back, watching her squirm across from me. She was such an impatient little thing sometimes. Maybe it was time to teach her a lesson in restraint.

"Actually," I started, sadistically enjoying the little thrill I got from the flare of defiance I saw cross her features. "I'd like to change into something dry, and then we're going to play a little game."

Her mouth opened, and I smiled, waiting for whatever little verbal barb she was about to throw at me. Surprisingly, she snapped her mouth shut, her jaw clenching as she gave me a jerky nod.

"No comment?" I smirked. It was easy to tell from her body language she was holding in something.

She shook her head as her jaw flexed.

"Oh, come on, sunshine. Say it. I dare you."

Her eyes flared wide as she arched one brow. "Fine," she sighed, looking me straight in the eye. "Is this game called let's continue to cockblock Kelly?"

Surprised laughter bubbled out of me as she smiled. I loved her sarcastic mouth. It'd likely get her into all kinds of trouble, but I still loved it.

"I'm sure you can restrain yourself a little longer."

"I'd prefer it if *you* restrained me," she quipped and joined me as I laughed loudly.

"All in good time." We were just getting started. There was plenty of time for me to tie her up in knots as she'd already done to my heart.

Disappearing into Kelly's bathroom, I changed quickly, donning a pair of tapered gray sweatpants and a black long-sleeved thermal Henley. In my hurry to pack my things in the trailer, I'd forgotten my boxers, but judging from the way Kelly's mouth dropped as I emerged from the bathroom, rubbing a towel over my damp hair, she didn't have a problem with my attire.

"You look comfy," she smiled as she lay sideways against her comforter with her head propped on her palm. "Nice sweats."

"Nice sweater," I smirked, motioning down with my finger as I stepped closer to the bed. "If you lean forward a little more, I can see your nipples. You cold?"

Holding in a laugh at the way her eyes narrowed at my teasing tone, I watched as she reached up and cupped one breast, squeezing the swell. "They're not that cold."

"Am I interrupting? Should I leave you alone with those?" I chuckled, sitting on the bed beside her. She was starting to get a little feisty today.

"No, you should help me out of this wet sweater and into something warmer. Or maybe you could help me generate some body heat."

"Hmmm. Wish I could, sunshine, but I'm afraid you're on your own for now."

The minx slowly drew one hand down her stomach, dipping it below the waistband of her leggings. "I can handle that. I really should take off these wet panties too. Wouldn't want to catch a chill."

"You do that," I nodded as I stood from the bed, not rising to the bait before heading for the door. "Join me in the living room once you're done."

Holding in a laugh, I left the bedroom, shaking my head as I heard her let out a little growl of frustration. She didn't realize who she was playing with.

This kind of relationship was all new to her, and I could tell she was impatient to get started. We'd all been the new person in the community at one time or another, eager to learn and jump right into things, but she wasn't ready yet.

Being out here in the woods, isolated from reality, was making it easier to get to know each other, but it didn't even come close to giving her a *real* introduction to kink. I'd found out quickly through attending munches, instructional classes, and play parties, that this lifestyle was nothing like you'd ever experience anywhere else. It was intense and a little intimidating at times, but it was all about exploring what you wanted. No one did kink like anyone else. Even if you moved in the same circles within the community, you didn't necessarily play the same way.

Emory and I were both experienced riggers, but he hadn't submitted to Talia in years. I couldn't go a few months without switching. I'd tried to be solely a Dom, but it didn't feel right for me. And I'd tried to sub without switching, but I struggled to tamp down my need for control long term.

We had friends who practiced the lifestyle 24/7. We had friends who were polyamorous. It was all different, and even when I'd tried to play with multiple partners simultaneously when I was younger, each dynamic set-up was vastly different.

Kelly had no clue what it was truly like. There wasn't any way for me to show her while we were here, either, but I hoped getting her to open herself to it and relax would help. Remembering the startled look her brother had worn when we took him to his first Dom showcase made me wonder how she'd react to something like that. My email was constantly filled with invitations to one gathering or another. I rarely attended more than one per month, but the option was always there.

While Kelly got changed, I quickly rushed around, setting a more calming scene for this to happen. The fire was finally putting out some heat, and with the howling outside as the storm beat down on the house, it felt like we were the only people in the world. It wasn't the ideal situation by any means, but being stuck inside made it easier to get things started.

Right now, she was the only person in my world who mattered. It was hard for me to pinpoint why I needed this to go well with her, but I could sense that she was important. It'd never been this easy for me to form an attachment to someone. I'd dated a lot over the last twenty years, both in and out of the scene, but I'd never found myself wanting to divulge all my secrets to someone like I did with her.

Her checklist was sitting on the corner of the coffee table as I rearranged the furniture, but I didn't even let myself look at it. That was her list to share with me whenever and however she wanted. It'd been a true test to wait until she was ready, but when she'd called out earlier that it was done, I'd felt a tremendous sense of relief. She'd done her research and filled it out without my influence, and that was the first important step in this process.

That didn't mean I wouldn't start moving her along, though. It was time to quit avoiding the elephants in the room. She needed to hurry her cute butt and get changed already.

TWENTY-ONE

Kelly

Connecticut

"If I have to come get you and carry you out here, you'll be getting a spanking demonstration as your first lesson," Nathan shouted from the other room, and my eyes widened as I rolled off the side of the bed.

"Does that mean I get to spank you?" I hollered back, giggling at the loud growling sound he emitted. It was fun pushing his buttons.

Quickly pulling down my leggings, I tossed my ruined panties in the hamper, opting not to replace them before I put my leggings back on. I debated putting on a bra but decided two could play this game, discarding my damp sweater and pulling a long-sleeved shirt out of my suitcase.

Grabbing the comforter from my bed, I wrapped it around my shoulders and snagged both pillows, heading back into the living room.

My completed checklist sat on the coffee table, just waiting for him, but I knew he'd never peek without my permission. His respect for my boundaries was admirable, and I found it hard not to walk in there and demand a copy of his list in my eagerness to get started.

Nathan had moved his work light into the kitchen nook, covering it with a lampshade he'd scavenged from the living room. The candles I'd found were arranged in the center of the coffee table, and all the cushions from the couch and armchairs had been laid out in front of the fireplace. It still wasn't as warm as it would be with the power on, but the temperature in the living room had a cozy feel to it.

"You've been busy," I commented as he stared at me impassively.

Nathan was sitting with his back against the couch, his long legs stretched out beneath the coffee table.

"Forget something?" he asked as he nodded at my chest. The man seemed to have a radar for my nipples, ogling how the hard nubs stood out in my thin shirt.

"Nope," I smiled as I sat across from him, cross-legged on the other side of the square table. "If you don't need to wear underwear in those sweats, then I surely don't need a bra," I paused as his eyes widened, "or the matching panties." He had to know I could see the outline of his dick in those, but maybe that was part of his game. I had to admit, despite the orgasms earlier, I was rocking a solid set of blue lady balls.

"You're not going to make this easy, are you, sunshine?"

My smile widened, enjoying the return of the playful banter. "Who gave you that idea? It certainly wasn't me," I giggled, my eyes scanning the new additions to the table. A duffel bag was sitting open on top, a bundle of red rope visible through the open zipper, and a stack of paper cards with a single six-sided die on top were sitting in front of Nathan. It appeared he did want to play a game, but something told me it wasn't any game I'd seen before.

"Oh, Kelly. You're just letting your bratty flag fly tonight, aren't you?"

I shrugged, enjoying the way his gaze on me shifted, his eyes scanning my face in another one of those intimidating Dom stares. I was getting used to not squirming under his scrutiny, but damn, he could flip the switch from playful to Dominant in a few seconds. It made me unbelievably hot.

"Did you think earning my submission was going to be easy for you?" I challenged, and his eyebrows rose almost comically into his forehead.

"I have to admit, this side of you is infuriatingly sexy."

"Such a sweet-talker," I laughed as I craned my neck to peer at the plain manila envelope he had placed on my side of the table. "Is this for me?"

"In a way," he grinned, gesturing to my checklist in the corner closest to him. "May I?"

"Nope," I teased, and he growled, using one of his feet to nudge my knee underneath the table.

"You're right on the edge of pushing your luck, Kelly," he warned, and I felt my face warm with more than just the ambient heat of the fireplace behind me.

"Go on, tell me more," I encouraged, picking up the envelope from the table and pulling the flap open as I peered at him over the top.

"No more idle threats after tonight, sunshine. I hope you're ready for this." His intense stare should have made me squirm, but I felt a rush of adrenaline hit my system as I started scanning the first page of his checklist. Without knowing it, our limits — at least on the first page — seemed to align quite well with each other. I scanned down to the one that'd been the hardest for me to fill in without any experience.

X Impact play – *yes*
Implements –
Hand – *yes*
Paddles – *yes*
Canes – *no*
Whips soft – *yes*
Whips hard – *no*
Floggers – *yes*

The list continued, but what struck me was his answers were identical to mine, in both the column for giving and receiving. I had no idea how to use a flogger, but I had a feeling he'd teach me. After watching a few videos of erotic floggings, I was down to try it.

"You can look," I finally sighed, taking pity on him.

"Hmm," he hummed as he flipped over the first page, and his eyes scanned it thoughtfully.

"What?" I asked self-consciously. "Is there something wrong?"

"No." He didn't look up from the paper in his hands, but he was smiling. "Quite the opposite. Seems we're very well suited to each other, sunshine. I'm kind of surprised at how open you are to trying some new things." Suddenly feeling a little vulnerable, I cleared my throat, and he looked up toward me. "What's wrong?"

"I can always change things if there is something I don't like, right?" I whispered, my heart starting to pound.

"Of course," he said with a smile. "As I told you before, this isn't anything legally binding. Things are always subject to change and negotiation. That's why we're doing this. The checklist isn't written in stone, but it gives me a guide to what you think you'll like. If we discover you're not into something, you can adjust your list accordingly."

Nodding, I flipped the page on his, my eyes stopping when I got to the section on anal play. I scanned down the list, pausing when I got to the note scrawled in red pen in the margin.

Soft limit of pegging is up for negotiation with Kelly. Only if she is open to anal play as a submissive partner.

"What's that smile for?" Nathan asked as he leaned into the couch behind him, his arms stretched wide. "You look quite thrilled with something over there."

"Just perusing the section on butt stuff," I shrugged, enjoying the almost predatory shift to the way he was gazing at me.

"And? What's the verdict?" he asked, his eyes never leaving my face.

Anal hadn't been something I'd experienced before. I mean, I knew some guys liked it, and I'd had one brave college boyfriend try to put a finger up there once, but that was the extent of my knowledge.

"I'm taking it that you have experience in providing it given your answers," I guessed.

"Yes," he nodded. "But we're not talking about me. What are your thoughts? You put maybe on your list. That makes it a soft limit. Are you interested in trying it, or would you rather take that off the table entirely?"

Holding that pegging vibrator in my hand earlier with him had excited me. There wasn't any doubt about that, but to put his...in my... "Can we try first and stop if I don't like it?"

"Definitely," he smiled, using his foot to stroke my shin. "But I have a feeling you'll enjoy it. Should I be getting ready for you to try something too?"

My face flamed as I blew out a shaky breath. "Let's revisit that one later."

"Calm down, sunshine. This isn't supposed to be stressful." Easy for him to say. He wasn't the one having to think about putting things in his...well, yeah. Maybe he was. "There's that pretty smile of yours. Why don't you scan my list, and we can get our game started? It'll help with all this."

Nodding, I slowly studied the next few pages, widening my eyes on the rope bondage and suspension section. It was clear from the older handwritten notes in the margin that Nathan was quite experienced in that aspect.

"I've got a few questions for you," Nathan prompted, and I looked up where he was holding the second page of my checklist.

"Yes?"

"It says here you're into light degradation. What would that mean for you?"

"Um," I paused, not exactly sure what it meant. I knew what degradation was, but the subject was so vast. I didn't think I'd be into open humiliation, but some name-calling sounded intriguing.

"I need to know what you'd like so I can provide it for you, sunshine. Which means you need to use your words. What kinds of degrading things are you interested in trying? Name-calling? Taunting? Open criticism? Using you as furniture?"

"Name-calling sounds like something I'd want to explore," I answered quietly, and he nodded, deliberately waiting for me to make eye contact.

"What kinds of names?"

"I, uh…"

"Slut? Whore? Skank? Cum receptacle?" He smirked on the last one, a smile breaking through. Although with the deep Dom voice he adopted while in the moment, I might not mind him calling me all kinds of filthy things.

"Slut and whore sound OK." This was not a conversation I ever expected to have with a partner. I'd clearly been missing out.

"As long as you know I'm calling you those because you want me to. Women who own their sexuality and aren't ashamed of it are the goal, not something to be ashamed of. I think it's sexy as fuck you are taking charge of what you want. It's a turn on to see you blossom in front of my eyes, sunshine." He paused, watching my reaction to his words. "But alright." He nodded, gesturing back to the paper in my hands. "Keep reading, and I'll take those under advisement."

A tense silence seemed to take up space in the room while he continued working on the deck of cards, and I kept reading his checklist. I wasn't surprised at the contents, but I was intrigued by some of his penciled notes.

"Alright, done." I nodded as I closed the folder, pushing it back into the middle of the table. Several smaller piles of cards sat on the table in front of him as he'd been sorting through the larger stack while he waited for me to finish reading. "Did you even look at mine?"

"Yes, Kelly. I looked at it. I've been adjusting our playing deck to fit accordingly." He passed a small stack of cards across the table, and I took it, my eyes widening as I read the first line. Um… "That would be the hard limit stack. Make sure there isn't anything in there you'd like to try as the Dominant or the submissive. If there aren't any cards you'd like returned to the deck, you can put them over on the end table. We won't play with those. I took out the cards with supplies we don't have either. You can look at those next time."

As I sifted through the stack of cards, my assessment that this wasn't a game I'd played before was confirmed. Every card had something that made my eyes widen or my blush deepen. While I didn't want to try any of them, it still set my imagination racing.

"How does this game work?" He had a sheet of rules I couldn't make out in front of him, but this was his show.

"Stoplight system cards for game play." He slid a set of three cards toward me. "Red for something you don't want to do, and it'll go in the hard limits stack. Yellow for something you'd try, but not right now. Those go in the soft limits pile, and we can revisit them later in the game. Green for go. That means we follow the directions on the card."

"Alright, sounds simple enough." I nodded.

"Since neither of us is the established Dominant, we'll both be switches and take turns drawing. When I draw a card, I'm the Dom. When you draw a card, you're the Domme."

Nodding again, I sat up on my knees so I could reach the cards he'd placed in the center of the table.

"You go first, sunshine. Are you alright if we don't keep score this time? We can just play until one of us decides we're done or until the cards run out."

"That's OK." I knew if I wanted to stop, he'd listen, and I was intrigued to see where this would lead us.

"Go ahead," he nodded at the cards.

My trembling fingers pulled the first one from the stack, sitting back to read it. "And I'm the dominant?"

He nodded, and I took a deep breath before I read the card aloud.

*"**Striptease** - Dominant chooses a song. Submissive must dance for the duration of the song Submissive may remove clothing as desired. Song must be less than 5 minutes."*

Nathan sat up, rubbing his hands together as he nodded toward my phone. "Go ahead and pick a song, sweetheart." He stood from the table, walked toward the kitchen table, and grabbed one of the chairs, placing it next to the coffee table facing the fireplace.

Swiping the screen to unlock my phone, I pulled up the music app and typed in the song I had in mind. It was super cheesy and likely predictable, but I still wanted to see Nathan strip to it.

"Take a seat." He nodded to the chair, and I stood, turning to sit down and enjoy the show. Nathan stretched his arms across his chest, unbuttoning the top two buttons on his shirt before he kicked a few pillows out of his way. He gestured toward my phone with a nod. "Go for it."

Selecting the track, I turned on the speaker phone, pressing play before lying it on the coffee table.

Nathan shook his head as the music started, laughing as he began to playfully roll his hips to the heavy bass beats of Ginuwine's *Pony*.

When the lyrics began, I was the one left surprised as he seemed to know every single one — not missing a beat with either the words or his fluid movements.

With wide eyes, I watched as he completely owned the song, rolling his hips, shaking his ass, teasing me with lifting the hem of his shirt, and then pulling it back down with a wink. I knew this song was meant to be enticing to a woman, but damn. Nathan's delivery made it something that had me panting and squirming in my chair.

He got into it, backing me into the chair and giving me a lap dance, smacking my hand when I tried to touch him. But that didn't stop him from tracing his hands all over me. It was clear from the way things shifted in the front of his tight gray sweats that he was enjoying himself. The distinct outline of his hard cock bounced with each of his fluid movements.

At one point, he whipped his shirt off over his head, and when a certain lyric about showing and telling sounded, he slung it around my neck, yanking me forward. Nathan's hand pulled my hair into a ponytail and gripped it tightly in his fist, tugging my head backward as he teasingly ran his tongue up my cheek.

My heart was racing as the last chorus played, my brain on overload as he continued the sensual hip movements and grinding while he held onto the back of my chair.

If construction management didn't work out for him, he could easily make some serious money as a male stripper.

As soon as the music cut off, I slumped back, a turned-on horny mess as he calmly stood and reached down to grab his discarded shirt, pulling it back on over his head. He leaned in and kissed me on the cheek. "My turn, sunshine. Sit your ass down and get ready for it."

Fuck. This game was gonna kill me. But what a way to go.

We took turns drawing cards, performing different acts, or answering questions. Nathan laughed and smiled at my reactions to some things. I knew I was a novice, and this was literally playing a game with kink as the underlying theme, but it helped me understand this lifestyle better. We both shared more than just the contents of the cards with each other, and several times our conversations drifted to topics I'd never expected to discuss with him. Every word out of his mouth had me drawn in more by him, our personalities similar, but also complementary.

He'd said it before, multiple times, but being involved with kink truly was like building a custom relationship. If I yellow-carded a drawn card, he simply put it in the soft limits pile and moved on. He didn't judge me or try to convince me why I should try or like something. Everything was *my* choice about what *I* wanted.

Negotiation as a word didn't scream seduction, but as he talked to me about his limits and encouraged me to be open about mine, I found myself even more attracted to him. Consent *was* sexy.

One by one, the candles on the table started to flicker off, the batteries dying. We quickly changed them out and kept going, both of us eager to continue.

Nathan gave me a taste of what it was like to be bound by him — creating an elaborate criss-crossing vest around my torso with the red rope in the top of his bag. While he'd released me from the tie after a few cards, I had to admit something was alluring about the feeling it gave me and that he was the one to do it. My fingers traced the marks it'd left on my skin and the rush of adrenaline that followed confirmed that I might like bondage.

I wasn't sure how long we'd been playing, but I hardly remembered there was a storm going on outside. I'd been so consumed by navigating this game with Nathan that the weather hadn't even been an afterthought.

Every so often, he would get up and check the fireplace, stoking the logs or adding another one into the grate before sitting back down to resume play. We quickly ate a dinner of cheese and crackers as we asked each other questions, the conversation never stopping or becoming stilted. If we were in the real world, I would've found myself falling for Nathan fast.

But I still felt the ax of time hanging over our heads, waiting to destroy everything between us. I wasn't naïve; I knew most long-distance relationships were doomed to fail, but I held out hope that things would be different this time when I returned home. *If* I returned home. With the whirlwind this trip had morphed into, I hadn't focused on the distant future. What would happen once my name was cleared, and I returned to Chicago to resume my real life?

"You still doing alright?" Nathan asked as he closed the heat-resistant glass door to the fireplace, sitting down on the cushion behind me instead of returning to his side of the table. There were only a few cards left, signaling the end of playtime, and I found myself wanting to slow down time.

"Mmmhmm," I hummed as I leaned back into his broad chest. His fingers carefully shifted my hair over one shoulder, his lips softly brushing the back of my neck as he wrapped his arms around me.

"Feeling less intimidated by everything?" he asked quietly, resting his chin on my shoulder, seemingly in no hurry to have me take my next turn.

"I think so," I replied, closing my eyes as I leaned into his embrace. "This hasn't been as scary as I thought it'd be. While a few things stalled me for a moment, this has been fun."

"Want to keep going? Or are you ready for bed? You seem a little tired, sunshine."

Shaking my head, I turned toward him, softly kissing the underside of his neck, his beard tickling my cheek. "I want to finish. There are only a few cards left." While I'd initially been a little surprised by the heavy scruff and the longer hair, the rugged look had grown on me. I reached up, scratching my fingers through his beard as he kissed my forehead.

"I know, I need to tame this thing. Maybe once we get back to Boston, I'll make an appointment with my barber."

A loud ding from the table drew my attention away from his face, and I frowned as I saw a text message scroll across the screen. But the message was quickly forgotten when Nathan chuckled behind me, his hands falling to my waist. "You know what that means."

Earlier in the game, he'd drawn a card that, any time my phone rang or I received a text message I'd get two strikes, but it hadn't done so before now. Service had been spotty since I arrived, and with the power outage taking out the internet, it was surprising that a message had come through.

My heart started to race as I pushed up to my knees, Nathan bending me forward as he rose to his knees behind me. As I hurried to get into position, his voice was a harsh whisper in my ear, my hands hovering, ready to brace myself against the coffee table.

"Hands against the edge, arch your back, ass out toward me, and hold perfectly still. Don't forget you need to count, or you get another two."

Another card that'd been sitting on the table from earlier in the game. Any time the submissive neglects to count out strikes, they earn two more.

With my fingers gripping the edge of the table, I let my head fall forward as Nathan pulled on my hips until I was in the position he desired. After the first few cards, I'd become accustomed to him manipulating my body where he wanted, relaxing as he coached me with soft commands.

"Breathe, sunshine," he cooed before he leaned back, slowly running his palm down my back. His touches tonight had been reverent and lingering, just further adding to how aroused I became around him. He treated me like I was something precious while simultaneously using my body for his enjoyment. It was a heady feeling to be with him like this.

My breath caught at the first impact of his palm against my covered ass, a low moan escaping my lips. "One."

With my eyes closed, I exhaled a heavy breath as I waited for his second strike, but he was teasing me, prolonging the torture. The only sound in the room was my harsh breathing mixed with the low crackle of the logs on the fire as they burned. I'd almost started to relax when he struck again, the impact causing me to pitch forward, barely catching myself before my hips hit the table.

"Careful there," Nathan cooed as he pressed himself into my back, kissing my neck as I panted. "You forgot to count."

A flash of heat ran through me at his words, anticipation building as he backed away, smacking the fleshy part of my outer thigh on one side before quickly swatting the other. This felt vastly different than him spanking me while he was inside me. For one, I wasn't seconds from orgasm, and two, I could tell he was putting a little more force behind it. It still managed to get my pulse racing regardless.

"Still not counting, sunshine," he taunted before he struck again, but I'd lost count.

"Five," I moaned, immediately regretting it, knowing the fifth strike hadn't come yet. He quickly smacked the fleshy part of my ass, and I whimpered as Nathan leaned in toward me again.

"Six," he grunted as he massaged the sting out of my skin, his breath hot against my ear. "This next one is six."

Nodding, I braced myself once more, panting hard as his hand connected toward the inside of my thigh, the sting causing the wetness building between my legs to be almost unbearable.

"Six," I whispered as my legs started shaking, waiting for the last strike.

His breathing was hard behind me as he slowly kneaded the skin along my thigh, his fingers brushing the crease between my legs and making me gasp as his fingertips brushed my clit.

"One more," he whispered against my ear, biting the lobe before he disappeared again.

"Seven," I cried out hoarsely at his last strike, my back bowing as my head dropped forward.

Nathan was immediately there, curling himself around me as his fingers pried mine off the edge of the coffee table. "Such a good girl," he whispered as one hand cupped my neck loosely, forcing my head backward. The other slowly traced across my stomach, his fingertips dipping beneath my waistband. When he discovered I hadn't put panties back on, he groaned, his hand moving lower. "Or should I say, naughty girl? Feel how wet you are."

My moan was almost obscenely loud as his fingers parted my folds, the tip of his finger slowly circling my overstimulated clit. "Are you ready for that one?" he asked as he nodded toward the table.

I knew Nathan had removed most of the purely sexual cards from the deck, wanting to ease me into this experience, but there was one card off to the side of the table lying face down that hadn't been played. He'd quickly turned it over, pushed it to the side, and redrawn another card when he'd chosen it before.

"Yes," I panted as he leaned me forward, reaching over to grab the card.

"Read it to me," he commanded as he pressed it into my hand, the movements of the fingers on his other hand not stopping.

"Fuck," I exhaled in a harsh whisper as the pressure increased, stars dancing in my vision as the pleasure started to build. This entire game had been one extended game of foreplay, and I wasn't going to last long.

"That's not what it says," he chuckled, his teeth scraping my shoulder. "Although that is what I'm going to do to you."

"Oh God," I whimpered as I tried to process the words on the paper.

"Not my name either," he laughed, pressing firmly on my clit, and rubbing circles that made my eyes cross. "Read the card, sunshine, or I'm not going to let you cum."

"*DTF*," I read, my voice almost a whimper. "*Halt gameplay and engage in a mutually agreeable sex act.*"

"Hmmm," Nathan hummed, increasing the pressure of his hand on my throat. "Do you think this counts as a mutually agreeable sex act, or should we take this further?"

"Fuck, oh my God," I moaned as he thrust two fingers inside me, slowly curling them and pressing against a place that had me arching my back.

"Yes or no, sunshine," he whispered, the movement of his hand stopping. "Am I making you cum like this? Or with my cock? Or both?"

"Oh," I panted, neediness laced in my voice. "Make me cum with..." My voice trailed off as he pressed his curled fingers firmly, making me jolt in his arms at the sensation.

"Hmm..." he hummed again, softly pressing his fingers against my G-spot and circling them so slowly it just drove me insane instead of getting me closer to cumming. "That wasn't an answer, and while you are sexy as fuck like this — I'm not sure my cock thinks that this is mutually agreeable."

"Then fuck me," I moaned as I rotated my hips, pressing back into the hardness that was lodged against my ass.

"Are you sure?" he taunted as he nipped at the curve of my shoulder with his teeth. "Maybe you need to think about this some more. I'm not sure this would qualify as satisfying the conditions of the card. I need you to tell me exactly what you want. In detail."

"I...I..." My voice was a needy whimper as his fingers pulled out and circled my clit slowly. The pressure of his touch wasn't enough to get me close but made it hard to concentrate as the pleasurable sensations flooded my body. I had a feeling I was getting a demonstration of what edging felt like with a dash of orgasm denial.

"You must not want it very badly if you won't tell me," he taunted, chuckling against my neck. "Use your words."

Closing my eyes, I leaned back into his embrace and tried to sort my thoughts. While we'd been in several positions in the past — there was one we hadn't done yet, surprisingly, and I wanted it.

"I want," I panted as he pressed down, sucking hard on the side of my neck as I tried to get the words out. He was surely leaving a mark, but I wanted it. I wanted him to brand me with the shape of his mouth. "In front of the fire, bare, you on top of me."

"Hmm," he hummed, rubbing his lips softly over my neck to soothe the sting. "Hard and slow or rough and fast."

My chest heaved as the hand on my neck slowly trailed down my stomach, dipping underneath my shirt and dragging it up as he cupped my breast. He pinched the bare skin just hard enough to send a bolt of pain through me, immediately followed by pleasure as he released his fingers. While I knew it wasn't the same, it made thoughts of him using nipple clamps on me race through my brain.

"How do you want me to fuck you?" He repeated, his voice low while his hot breath washed over my nape. His fingers continued their slow assault on my clit, and I pressed my hips back into his. He was so hard.

"Hard," I exhaled, my arching backward as his teeth clenched down on the back of my neck. I'd never been bitten before, but I liked how it made me feel. Wild and a little out of control.

"Take off your clothes," he commanded as he slowly dragged his hands away from my needy flesh.

I slowly pulled my shirt over my head in a daze, looking over my shoulder at Nathan. He was pushing the cushions from the couch together, laying my comforter over the top and tucking it under the sides.

Shimmying my leggings down, I held onto the edge of the table to pull them free, turning to face him.

"So fucking sexy," he growled as he looked over at me, his eyes greedily taking their fill of my bare body. He tilted his head toward the floor, raising an eyebrow. "Crawl."

My breath caught at the simple command, somehow knowing this is what he'd be like in a scene. Commanding stares, arched brows, deep voice that made me want to do whatever he asked.

Dropping to my hands and knees, I started to crawl in his direction, arching my back like he'd done when he was forced to crawl during one of my turns earlier in the evening. Unknowingly, this entire evening had been training me for this moment.

"Lie down." He nodded toward the makeshift bed, his hands falling to the hem of his shirt. As I reclined back against the warm comforter, I watched the shadows dance across his lean torso as the skin was revealed, my eyes lingering on the way his neck was flushed.

They didn't stay there for long as he began to push his sweats down his hips, his hard cock springing free. His movements were predatory as he finished disrobing and slowly climbed over the top of me. He grasped my fingers in his hands and raised them above my head as one muscular thigh settled between mine.

"You're gorgeous, sunshine," he whispered as he kissed my jaw, barely touching me. But the feeling of his coarse chest hair slowly scraping against my sensitive breasts had me arching toward him. "So responsive to my touch."

"Yes," I exhaled as the kisses trailed south, his mouth floating down my skin before he captured one nipple, his large hand cupping my breast as he sucked it into his mouth, biting down hard enough that I cried out.

"That's right, let me hear you," he growled as he freed his other hand from mine, leaving me arching into his rough touches as he kneaded my flesh and drove me into a frenzy. "Show me who owns this body. It's mine now. You're fucking mine, sunshine."

Gasping, I cried out, my voice hoarse when his lips trailed down my stomach, teasing the skin along my hips before he zeroed in on where I was aching for him. His teeth nipped at my clit as his fingertips played in the moisture at my entrance. I never needed to worry about it not being enough with him because he had me practically dripping.

218

"So needy," he cooed as I ground my hips against his fingers. "Does my sunshine need something more?"

"Yes," I hissed as he teased me with his barely-there touches. He was getting me so wound up I had a hard time concentrating on anything other than the need to cum.

"Tell me," he commanded. "Tell me what you want, what you need. What you *crave*."

"Fuck," I cried out as he roughly thrust a single finger inside of me, massaging my G-spot firmly as his other hand pressed on my stomach from the outside.

"Not yet," he chuckled, and my eyes blinked open, hazily focusing on the naughty grin that was pulled across his shadowy features. "Use your words."

"I…" I panted. "I need you inside me. Please."

"Keep going," he nodded, increasing the pressure of his hands. Pushing me closer to exploding, but it wasn't quite enough. My clit throbbed, desperate for more of his attention.

"Fuck me," I moaned, my hips squirming in his hold, trying to find some other kind of stimulation to get me closer.

"Hold still." His voice was harsh as he narrowed his eyes at me. "Or I stop and leave you here."

I whimpered, gasping as I tried to find the words in my muddled brain. "I want you so deep inside me I can't breathe. Please make me cum. Fuck me hard. Oh God, I'm so close."

His smile widened as the pressure of his finger increased, the tip of it rubbing maddening patterns against a spot so deep inside of me. My back bowed up from the covers as the thumb of his other hand pressed against my clit, circling until I couldn't hold back anymore.

"Oh, fuck," I cried out hoarsely as I came, his fingers increasing their pace as I thrashed against the bedding, my hands tightly clenching the material.

"More," he growled. "Look at me."

My eyes snapped open as he hovered over me, my eyes drawn to his as he continued to work his hands on my needy flesh.

"Breathe," he nodded, "I need more. One more. Watch me. Relax your breathing."

I tried to catch my breath, nodding as his eyes held mine captive. He kept me there for one torturous moment before my body detonated again, a gush of wetness covering his hand as my eyes drifted down, mesmerized by the sight.

"Fuck, yes," he growled as he leaned over me, slowly withdrawing his fingers.

His lips trailed up my body, his warm skin covering mine as he cupped my cheeks with his hands. Strong hips settled between mine, and I could feel him hard against me.

"That was gorgeous. You're so gorgeous, Kelly. My good, naughty little slut, soaking my hand." My eyes widened at the word he'd never used before, but a thrill ran through me as his grin widened. "You're my greedy little slut now, aren't you?"

Feeling suddenly shy, I averted my eyes, but he held my face immobile between his palms.

"Look at me." My eyes connected with his, and I relaxed, knowing I didn't need to feel shame and embarrassment with him. "Tell me what you are."

"A…" I stuttered, moaning when he ground his hips against mine, his cock sliding in the wetness pooling between my thighs. "Greedy…"

"Yes, you are," he chuckled, flexing his hips again. "So greedy. What are you?"

"A…slut," I whispered, watching as his pupils dilated at my words.

"And who do you belong to now?" His voice was softer as his fingers combed through my hair. "Who does your body belong to? Who is it greedy for?"

"You," I gasped, arching my head back as he shifted and lodged himself firmly inside me. And I never wanted to belong to anyone else.

TWENTY-TWO

Nathan

Connecticut

Kelly gasped and moaned beneath me as I drove into her, unable to keep myself under control after she said she belonged to me. I'd never been jealous or this possessive with a woman before, but the thought of her with another man, even one who she hadn't met yet, made me feel frantic. She was made for me and me alone.

"Your pussy is only a greedy little slut for me, isn't it? You want me to fuck it hard because it's mine, don't you?"

Her hips met me thrust for thrust as I rained kisses on every inch of exposed skin I could reach. I adored her. Kelly was everything I'd wanted in a woman for so long, and it killed me that she might be leaving soon, and I couldn't go with her.

"Fuck," she whimpered as I sucked on her neck, leaving another mark next to where I'd bitten her before. She was mine. Her body — and hopefully her heart — was mine, and I was desperate to possess her.

"You're so wet. Fuck. I love being inside you," I groaned as I thrust into her easily, reveling in the volume of her hoarse cries increasing. Her fingers clung to my shoulders, one moving up to grasp the hair at the back of my head, pulling me toward her mouth.

"Kiss me, please," she begged against my lips as I hovered over her, my hard thrusts slowing into a grinding rhythm that had her squirming against me.

"These belong to me," I whispered before I sucked her bottom lip into my mouth, laughing as she tugged at my hair, the nails of her other hand scratching down my back.

"You belong to me too," she moaned as her head fell back, breaking the kiss, her gasping cries almost desperate in their intensity.

"All yours," I agreed as I tucked my face into her neck, snapping my hips forward hard enough to shift her up the cushions. While I wanted to draw this out, tease her some more, she'd been almost

221

wild when I edged her before. I felt myself tightening, my release begging to fill her. "I'm yours as long as you want me."

I'd had sex without a condom before Kelly, but everything with her felt different. Maybe it was because my emotions were more deeply involved this time. Unbidden fantasies of cumming inside her and creating the spark of life had me growling against her neck. It'd never happen outside of my imagination, but claiming more of her body like that made me crave it. I wanted to own her — her heart, her mind, and her body.

"Are you close?" I whispered in her ear, my hands caressing her sides, pulling one hip further around me and changing the angle of my thrusts. "I want to feel you come apart around me before I fill you."

"So close," she panted as I leaned back on my knees, pulling her onto my thighs as I snapped my hips forward. The angle seemed to help, her cries becoming desperate. My thumb pressed down on her clit, and I rocked it from side to side with every push of my hips. "Almost there."

"Yes, I can feel you," I groaned as I watched a flush form on her chest, moving slowly between her breasts as she closed her eyes. As my pace increased, she moaned louder, her back arching as the telltale flutters of her inner muscles started to contract around me. Grunting, I tried to prolong her orgasm, holding off until I couldn't anymore, roughly grasping the sides of her hips as I poured myself into her.

Neither one of us moved, the sound of the wind shaking the windows at the front of the house and the fire the only things I could hear as I threw my head back and took a deep breath.

"Dayum, stud," Kelly giggled, and I came back to myself, looking down at the broad smile spread across her lips as she stretched her arms above her head.

Never one to pass up a golden opportunity, I leaned forward, cupping her breasts and pinching her nipples as she giggled in response. I'd taken the erotic tickling card out of the deck, not wanting to push her too hard too soon, but I couldn't stop thinking about revisiting this game with her in the future.

"Are we going to keep playing?" she asked as I leaned over her, slowly pushing a few strands of loose hair behind her ear, my fingers lingering on her cheek. She was blossoming before my eyes, and I was having a hard time refocusing.

"One more card," I nodded, pulling the edge of her comforter around her body, kissing her lightly on the forehead before I reached toward the small stack of remaining cards.

The rules said to choose the next one, but I wasn't known for my desire to follow directions. Quickly scanning the text, I decided on the card at the bottom of the pile, lying down beside Kelly and tucking her into my side as I held it up for both of us to read. It wasn't a standard card from the deck, Talia's sloping script filling the lines on the card:

"Requesting Aftercare," I read slowly, combing my fingers through her hair. *"Submissive partner may request a preferred aftercare position from Dominant partner. Then share one hidden truth about self and let Dominant partner provide aftercare."*

"Pro Tip:" Kelly's voice carried on. *"Reciprocation in communication helps build emotional intimacy in a dynamic. If comfortable, the Dominant partner can request the same."*

Neither of us said a word as she burrowed deeper into my embrace, kissing the skin on my chest a few times before reaching up to cup my cheek. "Hold me," she requested quietly, rolling in my arms until she was facing the fireplace. I shifted closer, wrapping my arm around her waist, and propping my head up on my hand as she pressed herself back into me. "Can you play with my hair? I like it when you do that."

Completely in awe of the way she was simultaneously submitting to me without any discussion and revealing another layer of vulnerability, I carefully drew her hair over her shoulder. I softly combed my fingers through the strands as she sighed and placed her hand beneath her cheek. She was so beautifully adorable as I gazed down at her profile, enamored with how much trust she continued to put in me.

"About a year and a half ago, I met a man named Tyler." I tried to keep myself from tensing up at the mention of a man she was no longer with. "We'd been dating for about eight weeks when I developed a sinus infection. Somehow, in the heat of the moment — while I was still on antibiotics — I thought it'd be a good idea to have sex with him without a condom."

Clenching my jaw, I let her continue, knowing this was a vulnerable moment for her. I had a feeling this wasn't something she shared freely with people. It worried me that she didn't protect herself, but it wasn't like he was a one-night stand. She'd been open with me about being safe with testing earlier, so I had to assume she'd had the same conversations with him.

"A few weeks and one positive pregnancy test later, we were talking about moving in together." She paused, sighing heavily. "I know now that I wasn't in love with him, but I did like him a lot.

"As we started looking at places to live." An irrational flare of jealousy tore through me at her words, and my fingers paused. If things had gone differently, she could be living with another man and have had a baby by now.

She reached up to grasp my hand, kissing my palm before she nested our fingers together. "I realized that maybe we were jumping the gun. My first appointment at eight weeks was normal, the doctor finding a heartbeat..." Her voice trailed off, and I watched as a single tear escaped the corner of her eye.

"You don't have to tell me if it hurts you," I whispered, pulling her closer.

"I need to," she said quietly, her chest rising as she took a deep breath. Kelly was quiet for a few moments, her eyes staring at the fireplace. "Three weeks later, I started bleeding at work."

"Oh, sunshine," I sighed sadly, shifting her so she faced me. "I'm so sorry." Her face crumpled as my lips lingered on her forehead. A few tears leaked from her eyes as I loosely held her waist. She curled against my chest, burrowing her face into me as my arms tightened behind her back.

"They ran some tests, but it was too late — the baby was gone. But there was something else. My OB said the tilt of my uterus was abnormal, one of my ovaries wasn't functioning at all, and that she was surprised I'd even gotten pregnant."

My fingers idly played with her hair as she talked.

"At first, Tyler was amazing, supporting me through everything, but after the second specialist told me it was unlikely I'd conceive again, he started making excuses not to see me. I spent my adult life protecting myself against unwanted pregnancy, but as soon as I thought I might want it, or at least was open to the possibility of it, it was over."

It was hard not to comment on what an asswipe this Tyler guy was for abandoning her, but I didn't want to interrupt.

"He finally told me that if I couldn't give him a family, he felt like we needed to cut our losses. Even thought we'd been dating for less than six months, I'd fooled myself into thinking we could make something work long term. In reality, we hadn't even met each other's families." She shook her head, her fingers creeping up my chest, playing in the ends of my hair. "You probably think I'm an impulsive idiot."

"Hardly," I laughed, tilting my head to kiss the side of her palm. "I think Tyler is a dumbass, but you're not an idiot. You just got caught up in things. It's easy to do when you're infatuated."

"I don't even think I wanted kids before that," she confessed quietly, shaking her head. "It'd never seemed important to me to start a family. I perhaps thought I might if I met the right man, but I knew my career would take a hit. I always felt selfish thinking that, but…"

"Do you want them now?" I asked after she was quiet for a few moments, my heart pounding. If she did, then I'd have to let her go. I couldn't do that to her, dash her hopes for a family. I didn't even know if she wanted a future with me past the next several weeks.

She was quiet, turning her face into my chest as she wrapped her calf around mine.

"No," she sighed softly, and I felt the weight of expectations lift from between us. "Do you?"

"I don't. I don't plan on ever having kids." My voice was quiet as I answered, and she didn't respond right away, flattening her palm over my heart.

"Can my turn be over now?" she asked with a little laugh, reaching up to wipe the corner of her eye.

Part of me felt like she was still holding back, but I had to trust that she'd shared the important details with me.

"Of course. I'm so proud of you for sharing that with me. Thank you for confiding in me. My turn now?"

She looked up, cupping my cheek, rubbing her thumb through my beard. "Only if you want."

As I stared into her eyes, I realized that for the first time, I might be comfortable entrusting all my secrets to someone other than myself.

TWENTY-THREE

Kelly

Connecticut

It almost felt like I could breathe freely again as I looked up at Nathan. My parents didn't even know what happened with Tyler. I hadn't wanted to tell them about the baby before twelve weeks, and it was weird to introduce a guy you'd sort of casually been dating and accidentally gotten pregnant with to your family. My mom knew I was dating someone, but since I hadn't told her about the pregnancy, it was just easier to forget he existed and tell her we broke up once everything fell apart.

"Can we stay like this?" he asked while his palm trailed down my back, cupping my butt as he pulled me even closer.

"With your hand on my ass?" I giggled, loving the way he nodded his head, and his hand squeezed as his legs wrapped around mine.

"Yes. I think we need to stay like this from now on, with my hand glued to your ass."

"Might make things awkward if we want to go out in public," I laughed, kissing his chin.

"Hmmm..." his deep voice rumbled. "Guess we can detach to work, but I want you naked like this as much as possible."

"Might be hard when I..." My voice trailed off as I ducked my face into his chest, not wanting to ruin the moment. His palm cupped the back of my head, pulling me in closer as he kissed the crown of my head.

"My turn now?" he asked again as his fingers trailed across my shoulders.

Nodding, I laid my cheek flat against his chest, listening to the low rumble of his voice as he started talking.

"My parents were happily married for twenty-one years," he started, his voice sounding strangely bitter. "Or at least that was what they wanted everyone to think, their children included."

A shiver ran up my spine as I heard his heart start to beat faster. "My father died in a car accident the week after my sixteenth birthday, driving the car my parents had bought for me as a belated birthday present." He paused, exhaling roughly. "With his mistress in the passenger seat who he'd been keeping a secret for almost two years and a sitter back at her apartment watching my little brother."

My eyes widened, my breath catching as he squeezed me closer to him.

"My mother had always been a little emotionally fragile," he murmured into my hair. "But when everyone we knew learned of his dirty little secrets, she fell apart before my eyes. He killed a part of her too when he left my half-brother an orphan because he'd had one too many drinks at dinner. When we all thought he was working extra hours on a new job to help pay for my car."

Oh my God. When Nathan had told me he had daddy issues, I hadn't thought that this was what he was hiding. I couldn't even imagine what he'd gone through.

"My grandfather took my half-brother in when my mother refused to take him, and my older brother and sister returned to college shortly after the funeral, leaving me to pick up the pieces. She wouldn't get out of bed most days. I had to practically force-feed her every day after I got home from school. The life insurance money was delayed because he'd changed my little brother to his beneficiary on all but one policy instead of my mother. And since he caused the accident, there was an investigation."

His voice was choked up as he continued. "The house was paid for, but I went to work for my grandfather's construction company to make enough money to pay the utilities when my mother lost her job because she wouldn't get out of bed."

"My brother and sister had to get jobs while they were at school too, so I was left by myself a lot, trying to keep things together. My grandfather helped as much as he could, but he had a traumatized toddler whose parents were both dead to deal with."

My lip quivered as I thought of what he'd gone through, trying to help his mother but only being a teenager left to deal with the fallout of his father's betrayal.

"As she started to come out of the depression, she was able to get a job again, but I found myself working longer hours when I wasn't in school, using the excuse of building skills necessary to my future profession as an excuse."

"The truth was, she cried most days when she saw me come home, covered in sawdust or dry wall, wearing the younger version of the face of the man who betrayed her."

"When I was offered a scholarship to go to school in Boston," he paused as he took a deep breath. "I'm ashamed to admit I accepted it and moved out of that house as soon as I could, my desperation to get away from the situation clouding my judgment."

He shook his head, his voice hoarse. I looked up and saw tears building in his eyes as his jaw clenched.

"It's alright if you need to stop," I whispered as I combed my hand through his hair. He could tell me the rest when he was ready.

He clenched his eyes closed, a tear leaking out. "She tried to kill herself while I was out at my first college party, and I didn't even know about it until my brother showed up in my dorm the next day while I was hung over. I know it wasn't my fault, but I carried that guilt around for years."

"Oh, baby," I whispered, pulling his head down to my chest and kissing his forehead. "You're so strong. I…" My voice cut off before I told him something I shouldn't, clamping my lips shut, so the words didn't escape.

"I'm not," he shook his head. "I'm not. I left her. Like he did."

He was quiet for a moment before he continued, his voice a little stronger.

"She was fine for a long time, taking her medications, going to all her appointments, but when my nephew was born, she relapsed, swallowing half a bottle of pills and ending up in a facility for months. She's alright now, but…"

I couldn't even imagine going through something like that. My parents were still happily married after nearly forty years. My childhood was idyllic and downright boring in comparison.

"I can't have kids either," he whispered, his lips ghosting against my shoulder. "I got a vasectomy a few months after he was born. I never wanted to put a child through what my father did to me."

"Nathan," I choked out, reaching down to cup his cheeks and pull his face toward mine. "You're not him." His eyes were sad when they opened, his gaze intensely broken as he looked at me. "You are *not* him."

"I know," he sighed, leaning forward to kiss my lips softly, his lingering as he exhaled a shaky breath.

"You can run now," he smiled sadly, cupping the back of my head. "I wouldn't blame you."

"If you think something that happened *to* you in your past is going to scare me away, you're sadly mistaken." Just because his life had been difficult didn't mean I'd run in the other direction. "What happened to your brother?"

"Honestly, I don't know anymore. Brad stopped talking to everyone back home once my grandfather died. He took his portion of the inheritance, went to college somewhere in Iowa and never came back. I know my sister tried to find him at one point, but he didn't have any social media accounts."

"Sounds like things were rough for all four of you."

He nodded sadly, leaning his forehead against mine. "I didn't want to unload this on you, but I didn't want to start this by keeping secrets."

"Anything else hiding in there?" I joked, but his face sobered. When he didn't say anything, nervous tension ran up my spine. "I was just kidding."

"My ex is pregnant," he whispered, his gaze suddenly very serious. My eyes widened as I stopped breathing for a moment. "It's not mine," he quickly rushed out, shifting back slightly as he laid his head on the cushion next to mine. "But that's why I'm here. She told my..." He shook his head, sighing. "She told my *former* Domme that it was mine."

"Holy shit, stud. It's like your life is a telenovela," I exhaled, and he finally smiled, reaching up to comb his fingers through my hair.

"I needed you to know everything. I don't want to keep things from you if this ends up progressing past a temporary dynamic. I'm tired of only letting people see parts of me."

"Thank you," I whispered, placing my hand over his. "For being honest with me. For trusting me enough to share all that with me. I see you."

"Thank you as well, for trusting me with what you went through. I know that wasn't easy for you to talk about," Nathan replied.

As he pulled me back toward his chest, kissing my forehead, I wrapped my arms around his back. Snuggling deeper into his embrace, I sighed as he reached over to pull the extra blankets around us.

"I'm trusting you with my heart too, sunshine."

Those words, whispered into my hair as I drifted to sleep, should have scared me, but they just pulled the bonds attaching my heart to his even tighter. I had to have faith I could trust him to know how to get us through this when we were inevitably separated.

The room was colder as I stirred awake, shifting closer to Nathan as I tried to absorb some of his body heat. He didn't move as I pressed my cold toes to his calf, kissing his chest. I wasn't sure how to act around him now that it was daylight.

Being trapped indoors last night with the power out had almost made it seem like we were in a different world. I didn't know how that would translate outside of this place, out of being confined together. While it was a big house, and we could have easily spent the night apart — not that either of us had wanted to — we'd spent our time getting closer to each other. Not just with the hot sex and spankings, but with the words and the laughs and the big truths about our lives we'd shared.

This couldn't be real. People didn't fall for each other this fast. Was I crazy to consider that we'd survive this without breaking each other?

"Stop thinking, sunshine," Nathan whispered as he leaned forward to kiss my shoulder. My skin felt sticky where we'd been pressed against each other all night, but I had zero desire to move. That panic that sometimes built inside my chest when I woke up with a man was conspicuously absent, replaced with the butterflies I often felt when he looked at me. "It's too early. And it's too cold to get up."

"I think the fire went out," I whispered, reaching down to pull the blanket that'd drifted to my waist up over my shoulder.

He laughed, pulling it up over our heads, leaving our legs exposed, but I didn't care as he kissed the tip of my nose, a tired smile on his face. "We can stay in here all day," he murmured, his fingers skating along my spine. His stomach growled, interrupting the moment, and I giggled, pressing my hand against him.

"I thought we were supposed to be taking care of ourselves," I teased, my hand drifting lower.

He hissed as I gripped him, his forehead pressing against mine as he stilled my hand. "Behave."

"What if I don't want to?"

"Kelly," he sighed, leaning forward to kiss me, his lips lightly pressing into mine.

"Call me sunshine," I whispered against his lips as his eyes locked with mine. "Stay with me in this fantasy for just a little longer."

"Sunshine," he murmured as he reached forward to cup my cheeks, driving his thigh between mine as he rolled me back into the cushions. "This doesn't have to be only a fantasy."

As he pressed inside of me, I clung to him, meeting each of his driving movements with one of my own. I couldn't get enough of his taste, of the feel of his skin on mine, of the way he made me feel as he clung to me just as desperately.

The dirty talking was gone, replaced with harsh pants against my ear or neck and soft sighs as his fingertips dug into my hips. Everything fell away as our bodies said all the things our mouths were too afraid to say.

Nathan owned me, and I hoped that I wasn't the only one feeling this vulnerability. I wanted to protect him, *love* him, show him that it didn't have to hurt.

"Kelly," he whispered into my cheek as he held me close once we'd fallen off the edge together, our bodies pressed tightly against each other. "Stay with me. Please come home with me when I leave."

"I…" My voice cracked as I tucked my face into his chest. Eventually, he would break my heart, and I was powerless to stop it.

"Please."

Despite my self-preservation instinct flaring, I nodded, whispering my answer into his chest. "Yes."

When we woke up later, it was to *my* stomach growling, the noise causing a deep chuckle to emanate from Nathan as he pulled the blanket from my shoulders.

"Hey," I shrieked as he stood, taking the comforter with him as he walked to where our discarded clothing lay from the night before.

"Get dressed, sunshine," he laughed as I pouted, trying to grab the blanket back. He tossed my clothes at me before he reached down to pull up his sweatpants. "I'll make you breakfast."

"Is the power still off?" I asked as I looked toward the kitchen. The usual hum of the appliances was still absent, the LED clock panels dark. "Let me guess. You're going to work some scouting magic trick."

"Hardly," he laughed, crossing the room, picking up a large metal box, and placing it in the middle of the kitchen island. "Propane stove top."

"Aren't you fancy?" I teased as I pulled my shirt back on, shivering while I tried to turn my pants right side out.

"Not really. It's from the forty-year-old trailer in the garage. This baby might be as old as I am." He moved around the kitchen, pulling out a small frying pan and rummaging around in the cooler we'd left on the floor next to the island. "Can you bring my phone when you come over?"

Nodding, I wiggled into my pants, standing up to grab both of our phones from the coffee table. The battery was dangerously low on mine, but I saw I had a list of text notifications, most of them from Chase or Evan. I was guessing word had gotten to them about the snowstorm.

"What are you making?" I asked as I sat down on a barstool, pulling my legs up and wrapping my arms around them. It was cold in the house this morning, but not as brutal as it looked outside as I spied the almost foot of snow that'd accumulated on the patio table.

"How do you like your eggs fried?" he asked as he rubbed a stick of butter around the inside of the pan.

"Sunny side up," I smiled, resting my chin on my knees as I watched him work.

"That's fitting," he chuckled as he cracked open the first egg.

While he didn't have the body of a male supermodel, he was also more built than I assumed most thirty-nine-year-old men were, with thick biceps and defined shoulders. With how full his beard had gotten, it was surprising how sparsely covered his chest was, a smattering of dark hair with a few tinges of gray trailing across his pecs and down his stomach, into the waistband of his low-slung gray sweats. He looked soft and cuddly as I watched him move, and I felt a rush of affection for him.

"You enjoying the show?" he teased as he looked up at me, bracing his hands on the island, the muscles in his biceps popping as the ones in his shoulders flexed.

"Yes," I responded, unashamed at my ogling. He'd seen the checklist. He knew I was curious about both exhibitionism and voyeurism, so my behavior shouldn't surprise him.

"Keep it in your pants, sunshine," he laughed as he turned around and grabbed two plates from one of the upper cabinets. He slid the eggs from the pan onto one of them, pulling out a fork before he pushed it in my direction. "The bacon is in the fridge, and I didn't want to break the seal on the door since we don't know when the power is going to come back on."

"I already had my fill of meat this morning," I giggled as he cracked another egg against the edge of the counter.

"You're going to make me think you're just using me for my sausage, Kelly," he chuckled as he worked on making his eggs.

"Hmm," I hummed, taking a bite of gooey egg, wishing I had a piece of toast to go along with it. "There are other parts of you I like just as much. I think I'm discovering I may have a bit of a voice kink as well, Mister Dirty Talker."

My phone chimed again, pausing the flirting, Nathan frowning at where I'd laid our phones. "Too bad the game is over," he taunted, smacking the spatula against the base of his palm.

"Hold that thought, stud," I mumbled with my mouth full, reaching for my phone. "And you're not touching me with anything from this kitchen. I found a spanking spoon in that drawer last night."

Nathan laughed as he rummaged in the drawer at his waist, pulling out the wooden spoon I'd discovered when looking for flashlights. I'd thrown it back in the drawer when I was searching for batteries for the candles. "Wonder if Chase has any more of these," he mused as he turned it over in his hand.

"No!" I pointed at him, narrowing my eyes. He continued to chuckle to himself as he finished making his breakfast, sliding it onto a plate.

As I unlocked my phone, I frowned when I saw a number I didn't recognize with a Chicago area code about halfway down the list.

The messages from my brother and Chase were first.

Evan: Are you alright? Heard there was a weather front coming through the area.

233

Evan: I can't get ahold of Nathan either. Can you please text Chase to let her know you're alright? She's freaking out since the alert for the security system indicated a power outage.

Chase: Are you alive? Is Nathan still there with you? Liz from the grocery store texted me that you got a foot of snow.

Chase: And that she thought he was hot.

Chase: And that you were a lucky bitch. Heard you've been listening to one of my books in public, you freak.

Freak?

She was the one who wrote it!

Chase: You better not be dead in my house since you're not replying. You can't ever get rid of that smell...or the stench of raunchy sex.

I laughed, shaking my head at my ridiculous sister-in-law until I read the next one.

Chase: If you're doing it in my bed, just burn the mattress.

Nope, just on your couch cushions. And the comforter from your guest bedroom.

There were also a few from Christine, checking in since she hadn't heard from me in a few days.

Christine: How are you holding up? The offer for Sam to pay a visit to Trent still stands. I've heard a lacrosse stick to the knee caps hurts like a bitch.

Christine: Heard you're snowed in with a hunky lumberjack. How's that going?

Christine: Tal told me she shipped a very interesting package to Evan's house a few days ago.

Geez, my friends were nosy. Although it appeared that everyone knew we were stuck here and likely enjoying our time together — a lot. Nathan still hadn't shown me all of what Talia had sent him, but I trusted he would when I was ready.

"Anything interesting?" Nathan asked as he wrapped his arm around my shoulder, kissing the side of my neck.

"Just my nosy sister-in-law and her equally nosy friends. They've been passing information about us."

"Oh, I know they have," he laughed, holding up his phone with a few text messages from Talia.

Talia: How's the sex nest going?

Talia: Did you guys get hit by the weather? Did the package get there alright?

Talia: Did you play the game yet? Let me know how it goes. My followers want a review in my next blog post.

Talia: Em wants to have dinner with you once you return to town. Are you coming home when they get back next week? Is she coming with you?

The last message made me pause, wondering what would happen once my brother and Chase returned. I'd agreed to go back to Boston with Nathan, but when and for how long?

He rested his chin on my shoulder as I typed back a few responses, my finger hovering over the last message from the unknown number.

"Who the fuck is that?" Nathan growled as he read the message, his hold on me tightening.

???: You can run to your brother's house, but you can't hide. I'll be waiting for you to return to Chicago to give you what you deserve.

TWENTY-FOUR

Nathan

Connecticut

Thankfully the snow didn't stick around long, the temperature climbing into the fifties the following few days, causing it to melt off fairly quickly. The power came back in the evening after the storm, and Kelly had been able to get back to work once the Wi-Fi was reset.

Once the snow and ice melted completely, we finally emerged from the house, making a quick run into town to replace all the food that'd spoiled in the fridge. Elizabeth smiled brightly at us as we shopped, Kelly holding tightly onto my hand the entire time.

After we returned, I pumped the water off the foundation, giving it a day to dry off before my lumber order arrived. My motivation to get the house framed and get Kelly back to Boston with me multiplied each day.

That text message worried me. We didn't know for sure that it was Trent, although he was obviously the prime suspect. The number wasn't showing up in online searches. There weren't any other messages from that number since then, but the damage had been done.

Kelly had been visibly shaken, spending most of the day we were snowed in clinging to me and seeking affection. I was happy to provide her with as many snuggles as she wanted, but my desire to protect her needed Kelly to be somewhere he didn't know about sooner rather than later. She'd gradually relaxed as the days passed, but she'd been keeping her phone off for long periods.

"How's it going, stud?" She asked as she joined me in the side yard, surveying the progress I'd made in the last few days.

"Might need your help with a few things later on," I sighed as I put my power drill down, taking a break momentarily. "How's work going?"

"Meh, it's OK," she responded with a shrug. "Still anxious to check in on my clients, if they even are still my clients, but Deacon keeps sending me busy work."

"Any word on…?" I trailed off, not knowing how to ask her if things had changed in her case.

"No, but Deacon hasn't fired me, so I'm taking that as a positive. He even sent me an email thanking me for helping with one of his clients."

I hated that she had to go through this uncertainty about her place in her company. If a partner was having her help him with his work, she was a necessary employee.

"Any word from Tom?" She'd also been worried about her friend, but I knew she was trying not to push things since he was technically her supervisor as well as being the boss' son-in-law.

"Actually." She smiled widely as she reached into her back pocket, pulling out her phone. "I got a video this morning."

The video began with a loud baby's wail and a woman's amused voice narrating. "Say Hi to auntie Kelly, little man," she laughed.

A not-so-little man with light brown hair was leaning over the angry child, frantically trying to wipe something disgusting off the infant's leg while gagging.

"As you can see, Tom is totally killing this parenthood thing." The woman laughed again before the video screen flipped around. An exhausted-looking blonde was sitting in a hospital bed, an IV pole in the background.

"Sorry we haven't called you. I was admitted last week with high blood pressure and some liver enzyme issues. They gave me all kinds of shots and then finally induced me, but Porter's heart rate kept dropping, so they ended up performing an emergency C."

Kelly's smile was wistful as she watched her friend talk.

The man joined the woman on the bed; a little blue bundle tucked in his arms. Carefully transferring the now calmer baby to his mother, Tom took hold of the phone, jostling the camera slightly.

"I wish you were here, Kell," he said. The woman shouted "Me too." in the background. "I haven't been in, but Deacon said things are a mess at the office. I know why you left town, but let us know when you get back to the city. We want you to meet Porter."

The man stood, the camera bouncing slightly as he sat on a couch across the room. "He's out on sabbatical too, but Deacon confiscated his computers and his work phone. He won't tell me what's going on, but I don't think Trent will be around when you get back."

The baby started crying again in the background, and Tom groaned. "Again? He literally just crapped all over the place. How did he have anything left in there?" Kelly giggled at the look of disgust on her friend's face. "Back to the glamorous duties of poop patrol. Aren't you jealous?"

I looked down at Kelly, squeezing her a little tighter at the bittersweet smile on her face.

"I'll try to call soon. Please text me to let me know you got this. I miss you, Kell," Tom finished.

The video cut off, and she sighed heavily, leaning in to wrap her arms around my waist.

"You alright?" I asked, kissing her temple.

"Yeah, I'm good. Just sad I wasn't there to meet him," she sighed. "Not sad that I missed the newborn blowouts, though. Nasty."

I stayed quiet, unsure of what to say. Kelly meeting Tom's new baby meant her returning home to Chicago, and I didn't want that happening so soon. I still needed more time with her, although I worried it would never be enough as my attachment grew more each day.

"You coming inside for lunch?" she asked quietly as she leaned back, smiling up at me. I'd never get tired of the way she looked at me.

"I can come inside something," I teased, leaning down to nip at her neck.

She giggled, trying to push against my chest as I started tickling her. "Behave, or I'll get out that bondage tape," she laughed loudly, grabbing one of my wrists to keep me from continuing my attack.

"I thought I was supposed to be behaving," I grinned. "Tying me up sounds like playtime, sunshine."

"Fine," she sighed dramatically, leaning her forehead against my shoulder. "You go back to work out here, and I'll finish up what I need to on my laptop. Any requests for your sandwich?"

"Nope, you know what I like. Thank you." I leaned in, stealing a quick kiss before she headed back toward the house.

The chime of a text message drew my attention, and I watched as she pulled her phone out of her pocket, immediately stopping as she read what it said. A sense of urgency propelled my movements, my feet striding quickly to where she was standing by the front door, taking the phone from her hand seconds before it slipped from her grasp.

???: I hope you're happy, whore. Don't think I can't find you. Now that I have time on my hands, I don't need to wait for you to return to Chicago. Good luck hiding. You're going to need it.

A red haze clouded my vision as my jaw clenched. That fucker would regret threatening her.

Kelly was shaking as I pulled her into my chest, tucking her head under my chin and squeezing her tightly. "You're safe, sunshine. I've got you."

My chest tightened at her first quiet sniffle, and then my heart cracked wide open at the sob she tried to muffle into my shirt.

"We're leaving in the morning. You need to go pack," I whispered as I grasped her shoulders, pulling her back to look at me. "He's not going to hurt you, but we need to leave. I don't feel comfortable staying here anymore."

"But the house," she sputtered, waving her hand at the unfinished framing behind me.

"Fuck the guest house, Kelly. I'm not risking it. We're going back to Boston tomorrow. I'll finish up as much as I can today, but you need to be ready to drive back in the morning."

With a shaky nod, she pitched forward, her forehead resting on my chest as her fingers clenched the material of my shirt.

Throwing off my work gloves, I combed my fingers through her hair, hating that she was becoming the target for this psychopath. At least I was here to support her through this, to protect her. Images of what could have happened if she was here by herself made my pulse race, and the urgency I'd been feeling a few minutes ago intensified.

Cupping her cheeks, I lifted her face toward me. "Please go get ready. I'd feel safer if we weren't here tonight. We can take the trailer to my property and spend the night there before we go home tomorrow."

I knew I was probably being paranoid. Even if he did know Evan's address, it'd take him a day to get here, maybe more, so we were probably safe for now, but he was clearly unstable and targeting Kelly for what was happening.

Kelly's lips quivered as I leaned forward to kiss her, lingering for a moment before I pulled back. "I'll keep you safe," I vowed, staring into her eyes. "I promise. You're safe with me."

She nodded, her hands grasping my wrists as her eyes darted between mine. "Take me home."

For a moment, I thought maybe she meant Chicago, but then I realized she was asking me to take her to *my* home. I found myself desperately wishing that someday it could be our home, but I'd stopped trying to put expectations on this. Unfulfilled expectations only led to heartbreak.

"I will. You'll be safe there."

This piece of shit, Trent, had no idea who I was, so once she left here, she was untraceable. I doubted he was smart enough to know how to track her phone. Just send bullshit text messages from a burner phone like a coward to terrify a woman who had embarrassed him by being a better employee and a better human being.

Kelly reluctantly let go of me, glancing back over her shoulder before disappearing inside the house.

"Fuck," I exhaled, reaching down to pick up my gloves. I tucked them under my arm before I pulled my phone from my pocket, quickly selecting Tal's number from the speed dial menu and waiting for it to connect.

"Hey!" she greeted, her voice chipper. "You *are* alive. I was beginning to wonder since you were only responding to me in three-word texts. Kelly finally let you up for air? One more week, right?"

"Not exactly," I responded, hating that this was going to ruin her good mood, but I needed her help.

"I just got some fun stuff in yesterday," she continued, missing the tone of my voice. "I know you don't like it when I meddle, but this lingerie company sent some things you'd probably like to see on Kelly. Lots of lace with leather accents. It's hot stuff. Emory loves it. He's already shot like a hundred pictures of me modeling it."

"Tal," I interrupted.

She paused for a moment, sensing the shift in the conversation. "What's wrong?"

"We're going to come back to Boston in the morning. I need your help with something."

"Yeah, of course," she responded quickly. "Just tell me what you need."

"Kelly has been getting some threats from a man in her office. I think she needs someone to confide in that isn't me. I'm helping her through it as much as possible, but maybe you can come to talk to her once we get resettled. I know your situation was different, but I...." I trailed off, my voice raspy. The thought of Trent hurting her like Miles had hurt Talia was not something I wanted to contemplate.

"I can do that," Tal responded immediately. "Em and I can bring dinner over. You can introduce her to us. I'll do what I can to help."

"Thank you. I'm just worried this will make her withdraw from me. She's been anxious and seeking more affection over the last few days. I'm doing what I can to keep her mind occupied, but you know how quickly things can change."

"Let us know if there is anything else we can do for you guys," Tal responded quietly, her voice more subdued than before.

"I will. I'll text once we're back at my place. I need to ask if she's alright meeting you guys once we get back. I don't want to overwhelm her."

The remainder of my afternoon was spent finishing the framing on the first floor, and the rest would have to wait. I knew a few contractors who owed me a favor who could come in and finish the rest. I was sure Evan would understand that Kelly's safety was my first priority.

I debated sending him a text to let him know we were leaving, finally settling for something innocuous. If Kelly wanted to tell him what was going on, that was her business. I felt bad enough telling Talia, but I knew she could help her navigate this.

Nathan: I need to return to Boston tomorrow, and Kelly is coming with me. The first floor is framed, but I'll make some calls to have someone finish the rest. I left the plans on the workbench in the garage.

He responded within a few minutes.

Evan: Be careful with my sister. She's crazy. Don't let her convince you to do anything reckless.

I laughed as I texted back. The only reckless thing Kelly had convinced me to do was fall in love with her, but she didn't know that yet. Confessing my changing feelings had been pushed to the back burner, partially because I was terrified of telling her that I loved her and then watching her go back to Chicago, but mostly

241

because she was under a lot of stress right now, and I didn't want to add to that.

Nathan: She's safe with me, I promise. No crazy stuff. I'll let you know when we get back to my place.

Evan: She knows the security code to the house. Just lock up when you leave.

I returned to the task at hand and packed up the rest of my tools, loading the equipment trailer. I needed to take it back to the barn, but I wasn't leaving Kelly here by herself.

She was watching from the front windows as I hitched the Jeep and pulled the Airstream out into the driveway, moving it into the access road so I could put my work trailer inside the garage.

I debated moving Evan's car into the garage, but I knew Kelly would never agree to leave the car here. She'd planned on driving it back to their condo before they got back from their honeymoon, but it didn't mean that I'd like it. She'd just have to follow me back to the city tomorrow. I could survive a few hours without her company, although I'd become quite addicted to her presence.

By the time I had packed the Airstream and re-hitched it to the Jeep, the sun was starting to set. Kelly wasn't in the living room when I entered the house. I spied two suitcases sitting in the front entryway, ready to go. The kitchen and the living room had been straightened, the dirty dishes from breakfast were gone from the drying rack, and the counter had been wiped down.

"Sunshine?" I asked as I moved toward the guest bedroom, hearing the shower. Part of me was sad that she hadn't come to find me before she took one, but as I heard a soft moan carry across the room, I realized why she hadn't.

I started unbuttoning my shirt as I pushed the door open, listening carefully for the sounds of her soft cries underneath the spray of the shower.

Not wanting to startle her, I quietly removed the rest of my dirty clothing, leaving it on the floor in the bedroom before I pulled open the glass door. Her head was leaned against the forearm she had propped in the corner of the shower, one leg on the shower bench as her other hand moved between her legs.

She paused, taking a deep breath as my finger traced down the center of her back, with me watching the way the water droplets tracked down her soft skin before disappearing.

242

"Why didn't you wait for me?" I whispered as I stepped in closer, melding my chest to her back. She shuddered in my arms as I pulled her into me, tracing my palm down her stomach and pulling her hand away.

She shook her head, softly moaning as my fingers continued what she'd started, sliding between her legs. My other hand cupped her throat, stretching her back against me, using my fingers to make her quake in my arms. Her clit throbbed under my fingers, and I twitched against her back, desperate to be inside her again but knowing that wasn't what she needed.

"You're going to come for me, aren't you, sunshine?" I asked, loving the way her back arched, and she moaned as I slipped my fingers inside, finding that place I knew could push her over the edge quickly. Her hips squirmed against me as her cries increased in volume, echoing around us in the steamy room.

"Fuck, yes," I groaned into the side of her neck as I felt her pulse against me, sagging in my arms. "That was beautiful. Next time find me. You know I'm happy to lend a helping hand," I chuckled as she panted, slowly disentangling herself and turning in my arms.

"I just needed to..." she whispered, ducking her face and pressing her forehead into my chest.

"Don't feel ashamed for making yourself feel good, sunshine. Unless I've told you otherwise, you can make yourself cum whenever you need to. I'll always want to help, but I know there are times I won't be able to."

"I know," she sighed, not looking at me, but I could tell she was still a little embarrassed. "But you were busy, and I just needed to do something after I finished packing. I didn't come in here intending to start touching myself, but it felt good, and then I was desperate to cum."

"You made me so hard when I heard and saw what you were doing. Those little moans kill me," I murmured, combing my fingers through her wet hair. After a few moments, I reached forward to grab the shampoo, squirting some into my palm before I worked it into her hair. By the time I got to her scalp, softly scratching, Kelly was practically purring against my chest, prolonging my torture.

Her slippery fingers traced down my stomach, grasping me firmly in her palm. I rinsed my hands, halting her movements, even though it felt fucking amazing. "That's not why I came in here," I whispered.

"I want to make you feel good too," she replied, her slick fist squeezing slightly, causing my hand to shoot out to the tile against the side of the shower to hold myself up. "I was thinking about you when I was touching myself. Imagining what it'd feel like when you tie me up again. I can't stop thinking about it."

"Kell," I protested, groaning as her other hand cupped my balls. "I don't want you to feel obligated to play with me. You've got a lot going on right now. Maybe we need to ease off...."

She cut me off quickly, her hand roughly pulling on my flesh. "No. He doesn't get to take this from me too. The only thing we're backing off from is talking about this. You're going to tie me to that spanking bench you told me about and make me forget anyone but you exists."

"Fuck, sunshine," I panted, feeling the urge to cum rising through my body.

"Later," she giggled, rubbing the place behind my balls that had me shaking.

As the pleasure grew with her insistent touches, I grasped the side of her neck, kissing her roughly as she pushed me closer and closer. Her tongue pressing back against mine with almost equal desperation tipped me over the edge, and I groaned into her mouth as I spurted against the creamy flesh of her stomach and chest.

"Feel better?" she sighed as she reached up to comb her fingers through my hair, scratching at my scalp. When we'd first spent the night together, she was hesitant to touch me. Now, she was touching me in all the ways I craved without having to tell her. She just instinctively got me, and I was still having a hard time believing she was real.

"Let's get dressed and get out of here," I whispered as I gently turned her, squirting some body wash on my hands before I cleaned her chest.

"Yes, sir," she giggled playfully, wiggling her ass against my spent cock. Reflexively, I smacked her ass, loving the way she yelped, and then turned around, giving me a seductive look. "You can do that later too."

TWENTY-FIVE

Kelly

Boston

Following Nathan's Jeep along the highway kept my mind from wandering once we started to get into the traffic outside of Boston. He'd been extra sweet, keeping his affection from drifting into anything possibly kinky over the last few days — and I hated it. I didn't want him to treat me like I was made of glass, but I understood he didn't want to push me into anything.

Before those text messages, I'd been excited for things to change between us, but other than letting me use the bondage tape on him — non-sexually, of course — and going through a few basic rope ties, he'd taken the spicy stuff off the table.

Last night, he'd been borderline desperate, covering his body with mine on the small trailer mattress, making love to me slowly as he continually whispered sweet things to me. I'd felt completely and utterly adored by him, shaking as I finally fell apart with his steady motions, but sometimes you needed to be fucked and called a dirty little cum slut.

Part of me felt guilty for thinking it, but the greater part of me didn't want him to handle me carefully anymore.

My phone chimed as he pulled into the parking garage of Chase's building, heading to the level I'd told him the parking space was located on.

Chase: If you fucked in my bed, change the sheets.

Kelly: Oh crap, I knew we forgot to do something before leaving the house. Hope the cum stains wash out.

I could just picture the hysterical laughter she'd let out at my response, and I knew once she showed Evan, his face would turn bright red, but it was worth it.

Chase: Dirty! I like it, but you didn't really fuck in our bed, did you?

245

Nathan knocked on the window and I responded with a laugh. I unlocked the car door, and he pulled it open, leaning against the frame as he smiled at me. "What's so funny?"

I pressed send and then handed him my phone.

Kelly: No. But we did on your couch, and your rug, and in your closet, and in your guest shower...and the kitchen island.

Technically the last one wasn't true; we'd only made out on the kitchen island, but I was enjoying the shock factor.

"Such a naughty girl," Nathan laughed as he pocketed my phone, reaching down to help me out of the driver's seat. "But you shouldn't lie to people. Even if it is funny."

"Well, in my imagination, you pushed me up against the island with a knife and fucked the life out of me during that storm, so it wasn't completely a lie. It was just a blurring of the lines between fiction and reality."

His eyes widened as he pulled me in closer, growling in my ear. "Why the fuck didn't you tell me about this fantasy of yours while we were there?"

I pushed back with my hand in the center of his chest. "Because the box of *supplies* distracted me, then you made me cum so hard I forgot until now."

"Fuck," he sighed, rubbing his hand down his face before he leaned forward, kissing me firmly, one hand pressing into the center of my back.

"That's the idea," I whispered as I pushed up to my toes once he broke the kiss, nipping at his earlobe. He groaned, spinning me away from the car and slamming the door, picking me up and carrying me to the back of the vehicle, and setting me on the trunk.

"What are you doing?" I giggled, running my hands through his hair as his palms settled on either side of my thighs.

"Fighting the urge to bend you over this car and rip off those pink panties I saw you wiggle into this morning."

He kissed me again, plunging his tongue into my mouth.

"Take me home," I whispered against his lips as I pushed him back, hopping off the back of the car.

He helped me transfer my bags to the Jeep, double parking behind Evan's car while he insisted on escorting me up to the condo to return the extra key. I wasn't sure I'd see my brother before I left

Boston, so I didn't want him to freak out thinking I lost his precious car key.

Nathan was quiet as he drove across the city, pulling into a parking garage attached to what looked like an old refurbished brick factory. The architecture was similar to what I was surrounded with in Chicago, tall skyscrapers mixed with older industrial buildings, but there was something palpably different about it. The buildings here were older, the history ran deeper, and I felt a little melancholy that I'd be leaving in a few weeks.

"You ready?" he asked as he shouldered his duffel bag, pulling the larger of my suitcases behind him into the old industrial elevator in the building next to the parking structure. He pulled down the metal cage, pushed a few buttons on the vintage control panel, and the pulley system engaged. We started ascending and I kissed his shoulder as he grasped my hand, squeezing tightly before the elevator stopped.

Somehow I'd pictured him in a place like this. Old architecture, rustic building. It just fit him. I couldn't see him in a modern high-rise or a condo like mine. As his arms flexed while he was pulling up the gate, leaning backward to yank the heavy metal door to the hallway open, I watched him, noting the relaxed set of his shoulders.

"Thank you for showing me your home," I murmured as he led me into the hallway, stopping at a large wooden door.

"You'll always be welcome here," he responded, kissing my cheek as he reached into his pocket for his keys.

My nerves resurfaced as he unlocked the door, pushing it open and wheeling my suitcase inside. He dropped his duffel on the floor next to it and extended his hand back toward where I was frozen in the doorway.

This moment felt significant, somehow, like he was inviting me inside his world, and my fingers shook as I reached for him, clasping his hand tightly. How could I ever think about leaving him to return to my real life? Being with him felt more real than going home to an empty condo and a career in shambles.

"Would you like something to drink?" he asked as he led me into the open plan apartment, the walls a dark red rustic brick mixed with wood elements I somehow instinctively knew he'd put in place himself.

A small U-shaped kitchen with a tiny island was off to the right, and a single barstool was pushed beneath the countertop's overhang.

"Yeah," I cleared my throat.

"You nervous, sunshine?" he grinned as he walked toward me, leaning down to kiss the side of my neck as the sound of metal scraping against concrete sounded from behind him. "Take a seat. I can make you a snack if you're hungry."

I perched myself on the stool, tapping my fingers on the repurposed wood countertop on the island, watching him move around his kitchen with ease. He pulled down a bottle of wine from a rack mounted above the long wooden shelves that served as his non-traditional cabinet space.

Shaking my head, I responded. "No. I'm good, but you go ahead if you want to." The week we'd spent in Connecticut had halted my stress drinking habit, and I didn't want to revert to old vices. Despite how scared I was with the threats hanging over my head, I wanted to enjoy my time with Nathan. Going back to Chicago and facing things was pushed to the back of my mind, along with Trent's volatile behavior. Nathan made me feel safe, so I would focus on that instead.

Drinking would diminish my senses, and I wanted to remember my time here with vivid clarity. Commit every little detail to memory so I could picture him here when we were apart.

"Water? Sports drink?" he asked as he opened the refrigerator. "You need to rehydrate after all that coffee you drank this morning."

"Coffee has water in it," I laughed, watching as he turned his head and scowled at me.

"Don't start with me on that bullshit," he growled. "If you want me to give you orgasms, you need to stay hydrated."

"You'll withhold orgasms if I don't drink water?" I laughed as he thrust a bottle in my direction.

"No," he chuckled as he leaned against the counter in front of me. "But playtime will dehydrate you, and sometimes, if you're dehydrated, it can be hard to achieve maximum intensity. So if you want your body to keep giving you orgasms, you'll drink the water."

"I did not know that," I responded, unscrewing the cap on my bottle and chugging down a third of it before I exhaled and put the bottle down on the island.

248

He leaned in, his lips grazing my ear. "You'll get wetter if you're hydrated. And it can help me stay hard too."

"Then drink up," I giggled as I grabbed his hand and pushed his bottle toward his face.

He uncapped his bottle, downing the rest of it. I watched with rapt interest as the muscles in his throat flexed as he swallowed.

"Are you OK if we have some guests tonight?" he asked as he tossed his bottle toward a recycling bin tucked under the counter. Nathan turned, coming around behind me and placing his hands on the island, resting his scruffy chin on my shoulder. "Talia and Emory want to meet you." My nerves resurfaced as he leaned in, softly humming into the skin of my neck. "It's alright if it's just us tonight."

"It's OK," I answered quietly. Despite my initial reaction being to hide, I wanted to meet Talia. Emory had been dark and mysterious looking at the wedding, but if Chase loved him, I was sure I would as well. "I want to meet them too."

"Let me text Tal, and then we'll get you settled. I would offer you the guest bedroom, but it's my playroom, so I guess you'll have to sleep in my bed. That alright with you?"

Shifting in his arms to face him, I cupped his cheek, gazing at him seriously. "I hope the couch is comfortable enough for you."

He growled, his fingers digging into my sides, eliciting a startled laugh from me as he rubbed his beard into my neck. "You're not funny, sunshine."

"I am a little funny," I giggled as he leaned away from me. He cupped my cheeks and placed a firm kiss on my lips.

"You keep thinking that," he tossed out casually as he stepped back, turning toward the small hallway off the living area. "I'm going to go try to tame this wild thing," he laughed as he combed his fingers through his beard. I'd gotten used to the longer hair on the top of his head, and the fluffy beard, but recalling how handsome he'd been clean shaven with slightly shorter hair at the wedding had my pulse racing.

He pulled me to stand, leading me down the hallway. The rough brick walls continued, and I briefly studied the black and white architectural prints he had mounted, wondering who had been the one to shoot them. "Are these Emory's?" I asked as he slid open a heavy wooden door mounted on a barn door bracket, motioning for me to follow him.

"No, they're mine," he smiled as he led me into his bedroom. I don't know if I was subconsciously expecting something out of *Fifty Shades*, but I was pleasantly surprised by all the warm colors and the beautifully designed wooden furniture. "I'm a man of many talents," he joked, but as I admired the clean lines of a beautifully crafted armoire that was across from the bed, I knew he truly was.

"This is yours too, isn't it?" I questioned as I traced my palm down the smooth finish, admiring the depth of the color in the stain.

"It is," he smiled, leaning against the wall next to another sliding barn door. He'd shown me a few of the things he had in his workshop back in Connecticut, and I'd been impressed at the quality of his craftsmanship. It was easy to tell that Nathan took a lot of pride in his work, showcasing his talents. When I finished a project, I was the same way, often sending my mom links to the sites I'd helped develop for some of my clients.

"It's all beautiful."

"It is," he answered again, observing me move around his space. I had a feeling he wasn't talking about the furniture as he watched me take everything in, a soft smile on his face. "You can make yourself at home while I'm in here," he gestured to the door, slowly pulling it to the side.

My mouth dropped open as the huge lighted mirror above the double sinks came into view. An elaborate tile pattern covered the walls from waist height to the stone floors. Nathan grasped my hand again, guiding me into the small room and turning me toward the floor-to-ceiling glass enclosure that was his impressive walk-in shower.

"Um. Can I move in here?" I laughed as I leaned back into his chest while he wrapped his arms around my waist.

"I can make some space," he chuckled.

"No. I think you misunderstood me. I want to live in this bathroom."

"You haven't seen the tub yet," he chuckled, pointing to another sliding door.

"I don't want to go home," I pouted, turning to face him, suddenly feeling a little out of sorts.

"Aw, sunshine," he murmured as he cupped the back of my head and pulled me into his chest. "I don't want you to go either. But let's enjoy the time we have together, don't focus on the end."

"I don't want it to be the end," I whispered into his shirt, tears forming in my eyes.

"It won't be," he murmured as he combed his fingers through my hair. "I don't believe that. Not for a second. It might be the end of this trip, but you can't get rid of me that easily."

"Promise me?" The needy quality of my voice worried me but leaving the bubble of the farmhouse had thrust us back into reality.

It was time to let other people around this developing relationship, which scared me. What if his friends didn't like me? What if he thought I was annoying now that the suspense had worn off?

What if the biggest threat of returning to Chicago wasn't Trent but my feelings for Nathan pulling me apart?

"Why don't you go lie down?" Nathan suggested as he steered me back toward his large bed. He leaned around me, discarding the few decorative pillows and pulling down the comforter. "I can tell you're tired."

I yelped as he reached down to sweep me into his arms, gently laying me on the bed. My fingers gripped the front of his shirt, pulling his mouth to mine as he tried to back away.

"Mmm, quit distracting me," he hummed against my lips before he quickly kissed my forehead and stepped back. "Take some time to rest, and then I'll help you unpack. Any requests for dinner?"

"No," I murmured, suddenly feeling drowsy as I burrowed my head into a pillow that smelled like Nathan. Warm and woodsy with a hint of spice. Placing my hand over my mouth, I let out a loud yawn.

"Rest, sunshine," he encouraged, leaning in to kiss me again as his palm trailed down where my hair had spread across his soft sheets.

...

Gasping, my head shot up from the pillow, momentarily disoriented. I looked around the dim room, my heart pounding as I tried to remember where I was. Vague images of being chased by something faded away as I stared at the familiar armoire in front of the bed.

"Relax, sunshine," Nathan cooed as he wrapped his arms around my waist and pulled me back into the nest of covers. "It was just a bad dream, sweet girl. Breathe."

Taking in a few shaky breaths, I let myself relax back into his hold. His fingers traced softly over the sliver of skin exposed on my stomach, and I took another deep breath.

"How long was I asleep?" I asked quietly.

Nathan held his forearm out, studying his watch. "Just a few hours. Do you feel better now? We can go back to sleep for another hour or so before they get here if you need some more rest."

"No," I sighed, snuggling back into his embrace. "If I sleep anymore, I won't sleep tonight."

"Who said I was going to let you sleep tonight?" he hummed into my shoulder, his voice rough.

Reaching my hand back, I ran it through his hair, pausing when it didn't encounter the bushy beard I'd gotten used to. Quickly rolling over, my eyes widened as I took in his new look.

Nathan was smiling widely, his hair rumpled and his eyes soft as his head laid against the pillow. "Better?"

"Just different," I whispered, reaching forward to trail my fingers over his much shorter facial hair and across his lips. They looked fuller without all that hair surrounding them. "You look handsome."

His fingers crept beneath the hem of my shirt, tracing the skin on my lower back as I cupped his cheeks, rubbing my thumbs along his cheekbones. I'd almost forgotten how chiseled his jawline was, and he looked younger without the extra facial hair. I could see the hint of gray in his sideburns more clearly, but it just added to his masculine beauty.

"You keep looking at me like that," he warned, scooting forward and deliberately scraping the light layer of scruff on his jaw across my neck, "and I won't be responsible for ripping off your panties."

"That wasn't really much of a threat," I teased, grabbing a fistful of hair on the back of his head into my palm. "Maybe I put these on this morning knowing you'd want to rip them off." He'd confessed that he found understated undergarments enticing during our game.

He growled, nipping at my throat as he rolled me onto my back, the weight of his hips pinning me to the bed. "Having you in my bed and knowing I can't have you yet is torture."

"Then have me," I whispered. "You said we have an hour."

He studied my face as I lay beneath him, his eyes soft. Pushing up onto his forearms, he cradled my head between his palms.

"Later. I want to take my time with you. But I do have a present for you," he whispered before he sat up, throwing the covers off as he climbed from the bed.

I watched as he walked over to the armoire, pushing it to the side until a set of two sliding doors came into view. He pulled one open, slipping into the dimly lit room on the other side.

Sitting up, I tried to peer through the opening, but all I could make out were the vague shapes of the furniture in the room.

He returned quickly, with a small black box in his palm.

"Should I be worried?" I asked as he peeled off the plastic outer layer, slowly pulling open the side flap of the package.

"Maybe a little," he teased, arching his brow playfully. He tilted the box to the side, and a small curved purple disc landed in his open palm.

"What is that?" I asked wide-eyed. Judging by the grin on his face, it was something naughty, but I didn't know why.

"You'll see."

He grabbed my hand, placing it in my palm as he pulled his phone out of his pocket. He completely ignored me as he typed something and then flipped the box in his hand over to study the back.

Turning my attention to the little piece of equipment in my hand, I turned it over, looking for something that might give me a hint as to what it was. It was completely smooth. Only a small ribbed indentation was visible at one end. There weren't any controls or buttons, and it didn't look like any sex toy I'd seen before — not that there had been a lot.

"Don't drop it," he warned ominously, and then it hummed to life in my palm, a low vibration making it shake.

"Oh." My eyes widened as I watched it dance across my skin, the gentle vibration carrying up my arm. "This is the present?" I asked as I closed my fingers around the toy, Nathan grinned, and the pulsing picked up after a few swipes on his phone. "Am I supposed to know what this is for? Does it go inside me?"

"No, sunshine," he chuckled as he stopped the toy. He reached into his pocket, pulling out something lacy. "It goes inside these."

My eyes widened as he held up a black satin and lace thong, my heart starting to pound.

"And you just had these lying around?" I asked, a little leery of something he may have bought to use with someone else.

"Are you jealous?" His eyes narrowed as he uncurled my fingers, taking the little vibrator and slipping it into a concealed pocket in the panties he held.

"No," I pouted. *Yes*

"By the time I finished taming the lumberjack beard, you were fast asleep, so I slipped out to run a few errands. Then when I got back, you looked so inviting. I climbed in with you and fell asleep myself."

"You bought this for me?" I asked, simultaneously flattered and a little embarrassed that I'd assumed incorrectly.

"While I was in the bathroom, I was thinking..."

"That's dangerous," I giggled, and he frowned at me.

"Behave," he warned. Remembering his comment about no further idle threats, I closed my mouth, trying not to provoke him. I could sense that now wasn't the time to push things.

"Talia and Emory are into voyeurism, and you were curious about exhibitionism, so..." he trailed off as he saw me shift my hips against the mattress, suddenly feeling a little turned on by what he was suggesting. "And I thought this might be a chance for you to practice your breathing. I want to tease you with this and see how long you can hold off and how quiet you can be."

"Are you going to tell them that I'm wearing those?" I nodded toward the panties hooked around his finger, and he grinned, shaking his head.

"That's up to you, sunshine. If you can manage to keep it a secret, it stays between us, but if you cum loudly in front of my friends like you did last night, then they'll likely figure it out. Are you interested in trying?"

Licking my suddenly dry lips, I swallowed, thinking about his proposition. Could I spend the entire evening with this little toy pressed against me, humming at his command, and manage to either cum quietly or hold off without alerting his friends?

I wasn't sure what the outcome would be, but as I shifted again, I could tell the possibility of either aroused me. I'd never orgasmed in front of anyone but my partner before, and I'd never tried to hold back either once I was close.

Nodding, I stepped off the bed, pushing down my leggings as I held my hand out. Nathan shook his head again, stepping forward. He laid the panties down on the bed while he reached for me, pulling my shirt over my head and dropping it to the floor. His palms trailed down my sides as he toyed with the sides of my unassuming pink panties, pulling them down a few inches before he grasped them in his fists and yanked suddenly. The material tore with a loud rip, and he dropped them to the floor, the fingers of one hand slipping between my legs and across my folds.

"You're drenched, sunshine," he murmured as he stepped forward, leaning down to whisper in my ear. "So slick against my fingers. Does the thought of cumming while someone watches make you this wet?"

"Yes," I moaned as my head fell backward, suddenly anxious for his friends to arrive.

TWENTY-SIX

Nathan

Boston

Kelly disappeared into the bathroom wearing the sexy little thong I'd given her after I'd moved her luggage into my room. Watching her walk around my space mostly naked almost pushed my control past its limits, but I held back from seducing her, despite her teasing.

Emory: Just picked up the food. We should be there in twenty.

Talia: How much does she know about us?

I laughed, knowing that Talia was trying to gauge how much she could say. Being discreet was easy for her, but it was hard to predict what she'd say to get a reaction out of people if she was comfortable with you. I texted her back quickly, making sure she read the message before they arrived.

Nathan: Enough to know you're both in the scene. Emory is a Dominant rigger. You don't play 24/7, and you like to watch.

Talia: Does she know you like to watch too?

Nathan: She's seen my checklist. Full disclosure: she's excited by the idea of someone watching her finish. If you and Em are into it, she's game. I told her if she had questions about the lifestyle to feel free to ask you.

Talia: You must be serious about this. You never let me this close to your subs without hovering. And you know we'll never pass up the opportunity to watch as long as she's alright with it.

Nathan: Then behave, and I won't have to worry about you embarrassing me.

Talia: But it's such fun.

Kelly still hadn't emerged from the bedroom, so I quickly converted the coffee table into a dining table by adding in a leaf, and I pulled the wooden folding chairs out of the hall closet. I knew I needed to check on her by the time I was done, but I wanted to try something first.

Pulling my phone from my pocket, I unlocked it and opened the app that controlled the toy. It was better to test it out now than surprise her when Talia and Emory were watching. I was honest with Kelly, and if she could manage to keep it a secret, I wouldn't say a word to my friends about the vibe in her panties. I'd given Talia enough information to obtain their consent, and that was enough. If they figured it out on their own — which they likely would — that was just an added bonus. The selfish part of me wanted to keep all of Kelly's pleasure for me alone, but if she wanted people to watch, I would let them if it excited her.

Slowly pushing the control bar for the vibrations up, I stopped just outside the door to the bathroom. She was leaning forward, an eye shadow brush sweeping across her closed eyelid. I could tell she couldn't see me in the mirror, concentrating on applying her makeup. I'd gotten used to seeing her fresh-faced but recalling the sultry makeup she'd worn during the wedding had me anxious to see her all done up for my friends.

She ignored the sensation at first, but as she straightened up, I pushed the bar up to the next level, and she grasped the edge of the countertop, her head falling backward. A waterfall of dark curls swept down her back, and her knuckles turned white.

Pushing the control bar back down, I watched as her eyes snapped open, meeting mine in the mirror.

"That was mean," she laughed.

"Just testing it out before we have company. They should be here soon. If you react like that later, they'll know what a dirty girl you are." Her nostrils flared as she turned toward me, her black dress coming into view. It hugged all her curves, and although it was a conservative cut with a high neckline and a hem that fell to her knees, it still sent my pulse racing.

"Isn't that the objective?" she laughed, and I couldn't resist her any longer.

Taking a step forward, I pinned her facing the counter with my hips. "Grip the edge of the counter."

Her eyes flashed with surprise, her fingers clasping the edge of the stone countertop as she looked at me over her shoulder.

"Face forward. Watch yourself in the mirror."

She turned back toward her reflection, our eyes connecting in the glass as my fingers slowly bunched up the hem of her dress. With one hand, I reopened the app for the vibrator, set it on medium, and placed my phone back into my pocket as I pressed my hand into where it was nestled against her clit.

"Oh, god," she panted as I slowly circled the tiny humming toy against her, her neck starting to flush as she pressed her hips back into me.

"Good girl, sunshine," I hummed, kissing her neck as she gasped and moaned with the vibrations of the toy. I slipped a finger beneath her soaked panties, pressing it inside her and slowly rubbing my fingertip against a place I knew would make her squirm.

"Fuck," she moaned as her head dropped forward, her knuckles turning white with her grip on the counter.

Chuckling, I reached into my pocket, still rubbing maddening circles inside her while she panted loudly. "Think you can take some more?"

"Yes," she gasped as I increased the toy's speed, setting my phone on the counter and pressing it against her again.

"I want you," she moaned as she reached back with one hand, gripping the side of my leg.

As her fingernails bit into my thigh through the material of my pants, I laughed, placing my lips against her ear. "You can't have my cock inside you until you cum for me. I want to feel you throb against my fingers, and after our guests leave tonight, I might give you what you want."

"Oh," she moaned loudly as I increased the movements of my hands, watching her reactions in the mirror. Her tightly closed eyes, swollen lips, and the pink flush across her chest all painted an alluring picture of how aroused she was. "Please."

"You've got to earn it, sunshine. Cum and give me what I want."

Her fingers tightened as she arched backward, her head pressing against my shoulder. "Oh God, I'm coming."

"That's it, just like that," I cooed in her ear as I felt her spasm against my fingers.

"Fuck, stop," she gasped as I held the vibrator against her.

"You can take it. Give me another one." Pressing another finger inside her, my cock ached as she moaned louder, the sound of myself fucking her with my fingers only drowned out by her almost desperate wails.

Clenching her eyes tightly closed, she gasped and then groaned, pulsing around my fingers.

"Oh God, turn it off," she panted as I removed my hands, pulling the skirt of her dress back into place before I reached forward and turned off the toy.

"Touch up your makeup. They should be here any minute," I told her as I reached down to adjust myself. It was going to be a long night.

"Is this alright?" she asked, ducking her head to the side. "It was the only dress I had in my suitcase."

I tucked my phone into my pocket, reaching up to grasp her jaw, tilting her face up so she'd look at me. "You're sexy as fuck, sunshine. Own it."

She nodded, taking a deep breath.

I couldn't help myself as I lowered my hand, grasping her throat and stepping in to crowd her against the vanity. Now that things were changing between us, I didn't need to worry about scaring her. Neck grabbing had been in all caps as a yes on her checklist. Her hands reached back to grab the countertop, her fingers clenching the edge as she bowed backward.

"You're mine. Don't forget that. If you cum. It's because I wanted you to," I whispered roughly, tightening my fingers slightly. She gasped, a moan echoing around us in the bathroom, but as one long leg rose from the floor and wrapped around my calf, I knew it was from arousal, not fear. "If you're quiet later, I'll let you do whatever you want to me."

"Anything?" she whispered, arching further back over the counter.

Pressing my cock into her stomach, I whispered harshly in her ear. "Anything."

"And if I want you to do something to me instead?" she asked, her voice breathy.

"Whatever my little slut wants," I chuckled, leaning in to kiss her cheek before releasing her, stepping back.

She had a naughty little grin as she straightened her dress, turning around to inspect herself in the mirror. There was a faint pink mark across her throat where I'd held her, but other than how her eyes were slightly dilated and the flush in her cheeks and across the tops of her breasts, you couldn't tell what I had done.

As the buzzer for the front entrance sounded from the entryway, I extended a hand toward her. "Time to go, sunshine."

259

She grasped my hand, smiling softly as her thumb rubbed the back of my fingers affectionately.

"Wait? You took my brother where?" Kelly laughed as she leaned against my shoulder, looking up at me briefly before pushing another bite of the garlic naan past her lips.

"To a Dominant showcase," Emory answered, leaning back in his chair and draping his arm casually behind Talia.

Talia and Emory had brought take-out from one of our favorite Indian fusion restaurants. Kelly had been a tempting distraction the entire meal, using her fingers to eat and moaning indulgently as she closed her eyes with each bite. A few times, I'd turned the controls for the toy to the lowest setting, watching a flush settle in her cheeks before turning it back off again, but she'd played the pink in her cheeks and down her throat off as a response to the spicier dishes that Talia enjoyed.

Watching Kelly was addictive, but Talia had been watching me too all night. I could tell she was trying to decipher our dynamic, but she hadn't been obvious about it. I knew Kelly wasn't the type of woman I'd previously pursued, but that was what I loved about her. She didn't fit the submissive mold; she was a little wild and unpredictable, but not in a bratty way. At least not intentionally — she did have her moments where she tried to push my buttons.

"Like a play party?" Kelly asked excitedly. She was still full of surprises.

"Not exactly," Talia laughed. "It's more like a performance night where the big bad Doms show off all their skills for others to admire. There isn't any group sex or anything, just scheduled shows."

"Tal," Emory warned, but I could tell he wasn't upset. He knew she liked to tease him about being a big scary Dom because of his more serious demeanor.

"Talia likes them because she can watch without having to be sneaky about it," I teased, watching as my friend shrugged. Emory didn't like to go to hardcore play parties much anymore. The hedonistic aspect of it all made his protective instincts flare.

"Well, since you hadn't been going to them, I couldn't convince grumpy bear to let me go either," Talia laughed.

Kelly glanced over at me briefly, squeezing my thigh underneath the table. "Tell me more about Evan. I'm sure he was freaking out."

260

"He was actually a good sport about it all," Tal laughed. "Kept mumbling about Barbies, but Grace's demos are usually a little over the top, so I couldn't blame him for being startled by watching her peg a guy wearing a ball gag while he was chained to a pedestal."

Kelly's eyes widened comically, a startled laugh escaping her. "Oh my God, I would have paid to see that."

"It wasn't as entertaining as when I asked if I could watch him get spanked, but Em wouldn't let me," Tal pouted dramatically.

"He was barely keeping calm with me in there. He didn't need an audience," Em chuckled.

"I'm sure Chase loved it. That girl is fearless," Kelly giggled. "I knew any woman who could get my brother to wear leather pants must have some kind of magical powers."

"I still remember when Grace started eyeing him. I thought he was going to bolt out of that building before he saw anything," Tal giggled but abruptly stopped with a shake of Emory's head.

"Is Grace a friend of yours?" Kelly asked, sensing the tension in the room.

I hadn't given her names, but she knew the gist of what had happened before I ended up in Connecticut with her. "No," I answered calmly, turning her palm over to trace it with my finger as I glanced down at her. "I wouldn't call her a close friend. But she was my Domme for a while."

"Sorry," Talia apologized, looking a little guilty for the turn in the conversation, but I wasn't going to hide anything.

"Don't worry about it," I waved away her concern, turning to face Kelly. Reaching up to push a lock of Kelly's hair behind her ear, I took a deep breath and told her the truth. "She's a rope top, but she's into humiliation and degradation. She's polyamorous and has quite a few pain and pleasure subs. So when she does a showcase, she puts on a show."

Kelly's eyes widened at my admission, her mouth falling open softly. "And you had a relationship with her?"

"I had an arranged play only agreement with her. We weren't romantic."

"Is she the one who...?" Kelly trailed off as she looked over at Emory and Talia and then back to me.

I nodded once, squeezing her hand. I appreciated that she was protecting my privacy.

"So you told her but not me?" Emory asked, leaning back into his chair and crossing his arms. He narrowed his eyes, trying to look intimidating, and I heard Kelly inhale a nervous breath next to me.

"Well. *She* keeps my secrets," I teased, "and I just hadn't had the chance to tell you before I left. Kind of awkward to talk about in a text message."

"Are you going to tell us now?" Talia smiled, probably getting worked up as I faced off against her partner. She loved it when Doms got all alpha male in front of her.

Looking over at Kelly, she gave me an encouraging nod, silently supporting me.

"Marisa is pregnant," I told them, watching as Talia's eyes widened. She opened her mouth to respond, but I held my hand up.

"She convinced Grace it was mine, and Marisa gave her some questionable audio recordings. Grace made me listen to Marisa with some guy while I was suspended. The man was growling in my earbud about how he was enjoying having her while she was pregnant with another man's baby. Then another one of her crying and pleading with Grace to help her since I was abandoning her with my baby."

"What the fuck? That chick is full-on psycho," Tal blurted out, and Em frowned at her. Kelly didn't seem fazed by her comment.

"I safeworded and broke things off with Grace. Walked out and left for Evan's the next day."

Talia smiled, raising her eyebrows as she gave Kelly an appraising look. "Where you ran into the woman you've secretly been obsessed with for months."

Kelly smiled nervously, leaning into my side again, laughing a little at Tal's comment.

"Talia," Emory sighed, shaking his head.

"Well, he has," she defended, bouncing in her seat a little. "And now she's here to play." Talia clapped her hands together, and I looked down at Kelly. She was biting her lip, looking a little nervous as her cheeks tinged pink. I knew it wasn't from the wine because she hadn't touched hers the entire meal, opting to drink her full glass of water, smirking at me every time she returned the glass to the table.

"Don't scare her," Em laughed, his serious demeanor finally cracking a little.

"But it's perfect," Talia said, looking at him expectantly. "Now she can come with us on Friday."

"What's Friday?" I frowned, looking over to Em.

"Don't worry, G isn't invited," Talia started, smiling widely. "We've been invited to a party out in the burbs. A Dom Emory knows is looking to show off his new house and his new fiancée. He extended the invitation to you also."

"Do we know this guy?" I asked Em. He nodded, signaling to Talia to calm down by tapping on the back of her hand where it rested on the table. If you didn't know them, it just looked like he was touching her hand, but as she took a deep breath and straightened her posture, looking down at the table, I watched as she responded to his non-verbal command. Kelly was oblivious, her face impassive as she looked up at me briefly before nervously pulling apart the remaining piece of naan bread on her plate.

"Yeah. He just relocated from upstate New York. He had me do some headshots for his real estate business."

"Didn't think you did those anymore," I frowned. "Are you sure he doesn't know Grace?"

"He found me through some mutual connections from my time at school in Rhode Island. He's not the type to put up with Grace's antics. I asked around. He's a solid guy."

"Can we go to the party, please?" Talia asked, her gaze still in her lap and her voice calmer.

Kelly's eyes narrowed at her suddenly subdued behavior, and I could tell she was analyzing the sudden changes. Emory hadn't tapped another warning on her hand, but it was clear something had shifted.

I found myself wondering how Kelly would react if we developed our own form of non-verbal communication. For Talia and Emory, it was something they'd adopted early on, and it was an instinctual part of their behavior now, but they also lived and worked together full time. While they weren't a 24/7 couple, they still respected each other's signals.

"It's up to Kelly." Emory nodded, waiting for Kelly to look at him to make eye contact.

She stared at him for a long moment before she glanced over at me. I raised an eyebrow, giving her a subtle nod. This was her decision. I couldn't tell her if she was ready or not. This was a choice she needed to make on her own.

"I'd like to go if Nathan is alright with it," she answered quietly, and Em smiled at her before giving me a subtle nod. He was seeing the same parts of her natural behavior that had drawn me to her.

"Are you finished?" I asked her quietly, nodding at her plate.

Kelly narrowed her eyes at my sudden change in subject. "Yes, thank you." She turned toward our guests. "I loved that. Thank you for bringing dinner."

Talia smiled widely as Emory removed his hand from the back of her hand. He reached down to grab their plates, following me into the kitchen. I glanced back, watching Tal tug Kelly toward the couch.

"You love her." Emory's voice was low as he followed me toward the sink.

I nodded. There was no denying how I felt.

"How's that going to work?" he asked, leaning back against the small island.

"I have no idea," I sighed, rubbing my hand down my face. "She's here for at least the next few weeks. Some things are going on at work she needed to get away from."

"She's got a stalker?" he guessed. I was sure Talia had told him what I asked of her.

"Not exactly. More like a jealous co-worker who she shot down. He's been harassing her for years and finally pushed things too far. Accused her of sexual harassment to HR."

"Her?" he asked, nodding toward where Kelly and Tal were seated closely on the couch.

"Yeah, I know, right?" I laughed. "Like she'd ever be capable of that. She's got a smart mouth sometimes, but she's not the type to disregard boundaries."

"Have you told her?" he asked suddenly, looking past me to the living room.

"No. I don't know if I should yet. She's been through a lot in the last few weeks. I'm trying not to pressure her."

He nodded, likely remembering how carefully he'd had to tread with Talia at the beginning of their relationship. It'd been hard to watch the two of them resist each other. I couldn't even imagine what it'd been like to be in the middle of it.

His phone rang, and he frowned, shaking his head with a sigh. "I've got to take this, but you should think about telling her you love her. If you feel it, it's not too soon to tell her. And she probably feels the same way, judging by the way she looks at you."

Emory escaped into the hallway, and my attention was drawn to Talia sitting with Kelly in the living room. Checking to make sure they weren't looking, I discreetly pulled my phone from my pocket.

As I slid the bar upward on the screen with my thumb, I watched Kelly's hand reach out to grab the arm of the couch. Talia didn't notice as Kelly shifted, crossing and un-crossing her legs slowly before she sat forward a little. I could see the flush working its way up her neck and lowered the speed, enjoying the way she took in slow deep breaths to calm down.

My friend kept talking in her usual animated way. I was sure she was likely telling stories about me and the dumb things I'd done in her presence over the last eight years, but I didn't care. Kelly could know all my secrets. After a few moments, I slid the bar up again, going a little further than I had the last time.

Kelly reached for her glass of water from the nearby table, her hand shaking a little as she tilted the glass toward her mouth. I saw the front door opening out of my peripheral vision, so I turned it down to the lowest setting, slipping my phone back into my pocket with the app open.

As Emory joined me, Kelly looked up toward the kitchen, holding my gaze before turning her attention back to Talia.

"She watches you too," Emory observed as he glanced toward the living room and then leaned against the opposite side of the island, his elbows resting on the surface as he gave me a smug look. "Her eyes have followed you all night."

"I like her eyes on me," I murmured, watching her trying not to squirm. I knew the vibrations were probably too low to make her cum, but as she subtly began to rock her hips from side to side, I quickly reached into my pocket, glancing down to turn the vibe off.

"Do I even want to know what has you distracted?" he laughed as he turned to face the living room. He glanced back at me with a calculating smile before returning his eyes to the women seated on the couch.

Deciding to give him a show, I pulled my phone out, pushing the bar up to the medium setting, watching as Kelly's eyes shot up

265

toward where we were standing. She looked up at me first, and then her eyes slowly glanced to where Emory was watching her. Her eyes darted away as she shifted her hips, her grip on the arm of the couch tightening.

"She's lovely," he murmured as he watched her. I knew it wasn't in a way that should make me feel threatened. I trusted my friends implicitly. But the possessive part of me flared angrily as I turned the setting up a little more, staring at her face. She was still trying to concentrate on keeping quiet, reaching forward to take a drink again. As the glass left her lips, I pushed it to the highest setting, watching as she coughed, spilling a little water over the edge of her drink and onto the skirt of her dress.

Talia reached over to help her brush it off, and I watched as Kelly gasped, her mouth falling open. It was clear from where I was standing that she was overstimulated. I watched as she tried to shift away from Talia but moving must have put the toy in a position that finally pushed her over the edge.

Kelly's head shot up, her eyes connecting with mine as I stared straight at her. I watched as her mouth opened softly, her eyes widening. Her teeth suddenly clamped down on her bottom lip as she tried to hold it in, but I heard the faint noise she made as her climax rolled through her. One hand was still clenching the arm of the couch as the other held tightly onto the cushion beside her. She was almost still, but a shudder ran through her as her eyes closed briefly.

Talia had gone still beside her, watching with rapt attention as Kelly almost silently came next to her.

I slid my thumb down the screen, turning the toy off as I tucked my phone into my pocket, discreetly adjusting myself before my friend noticed the effect that making Kelly cum in front of him had caused.

Talia glanced up at me, shaking her head as she briefly looked between Emory and me. She started talking again like nothing had happened, but I knew she had figured it out. Kelly hadn't noticed the exchange, but I could see the crease in her brow as she tried to gauge if Talia had seen what she did.

Emory turned around, laughing at me for a moment before he started telling me about the details for the party on Friday.

"I'm not sure how things will turn as the night goes on, but I'd make sure she's marked before you go. Our host is poly and so is a lot of his circle, so if you don't want them to approach her, I'd at least get her a red cuff."

"And if I want her to be able to play?" I asked, already knowing his answer. If she had a red cuff, she wouldn't be allowed to touch me. No one would touch her without her consent, but I knew that people would approach her if they thought she was available to play.

"Then I'd start looking at collars." He didn't know that I'd already found one on my shopping trip earlier and was picking it up in the morning. There was no way Kelly was going back to Chicago without me staking an official claim on her. She hadn't asked many questions about official collaring practices when she was researching, but I'd also told her our dynamic was likely temporary. It'd come up briefly during the card game, but we'd only spoken in hypotheticals. I intended to change that; this party had just moved my timeline forward. She could always tell me 'no' to accepting it, but I hoped she wouldn't.

Kelly joined us in the kitchen just then, yawning as she walked in front of me to fill her glass at the sink.

"Ready for bed, sunshine?"

"Aw, that's adorable," Talia cooed as she heard my nickname, causing Kelly to blush and press her forehead into my arm. "Why don't I have a cute nickname like that?"

Emory leaned down to whisper something — likely extremely suggestive — in her ear, and she grinned.

"Is it alright if we take off?" he asked as Talia headed toward the front door, grabbing their coats. She handed Em his jacket, and they quickly started to say their goodbyes.

Talia hugged Kelly, whispering something in her ear. I watched as sunshine's eyes widened, her cheeks flushing adorably.

"Want to take the car service on Friday?" Emory asked as he reached up to squeeze my shoulder before turning toward Kelly.

"Yeah, sounds good. We can meet at the studio if that's easier," I responded, watching as Kelly extended her hand toward him. He surprised us both by pulling her into a brief hug. Turning to nod at me as he opened the door for Talia, I knew my friend approved.

Once they'd disappeared, Kelly sighed, taking a deep breath before she turned toward me, wrapping her arms around my waist and laying her head against my chest.

I couldn't resist as I leaned down, asking her a question I likely already knew the answer to. "What did Talia tell you as they left?"

Kelly giggled nervously, gripping the back of my shirt as she shook her head against my chest.

"Sunshine?" I asked again, a little bit of warning in my tone.

She took in a heavy breath, tilting her head up to look at me. "She told me I was gorgeous when I came. I'm so embarrassed." She tried to duck her head again, hiding her eyes from me.

"Ah, ah. Look at me," I urged, as I used my fingers to turn her head back toward me. She closed her eyes, cringing. "Now, Kelly."

Her eyes opened, her face relaxing despite my authoritative tone.

"She was right. You *were* gorgeous as you came. But that shouldn't be embarrassing. And now you get to do whatever you want to me because you lasted so long, and you were quiet while you did it."

Excitement flashed through her eyes before she pushed to her toes, kissing me enthusiastically. As her tongue slipped past my lips, I wasn't even worried about what she was going to do because I was thrilled simply to be along for the ride.

TWENTY-SEVEN

Kelly

Boston

Waking up for the second time the morning after meeting Talia and Emory was surprisingly pleasant. I stretched, enjoying the ache that'd taken root in my abdominal muscles because of trying to breathe through his teasing last night. The covers on Nathan's side of the bed were rumpled, but he was long gone, his side of the mattress cool to the touch. He was good at sneaking around when I was passed out, or maybe he'd just tired me out that much before we'd gone to bed.

Spending a quiet evening with friends where someone else was the one who initiated the conversation was nice. Admittedly, none of my friends had seen me cum during a dinner party — like Nathan's now had — but they'd also likely never had as much fun in a new relationship as I was having.

I knew that there were things Nathan was likely not to expose me to that he'd done in the past when he was new to the scene, but I was excited to experience this with him.

When he'd found me at the wedding, I'd been wallowing in self-pity, struggling to come to terms with where my life was headed. Now, I felt like while I had no idea what was going on with my career and didn't want to get on the plane to go back to my empty condo in Chicago, Nathan was here to support me and be the solid backbone that helped me through it.

Last night, he'd let me play with his underbed cuffs, restraining his arms while I gave him a teasing blow job. It'd ended with me climbing on top of him and riding him until I exploded, finally giving him permission to cum with my hand sealed over his mouth to hold in his loud groans. I wasn't worried about anyone hearing him, but it'd been fun to be the one who led things. I knew I wasn't a pain Domme who liked to humiliate people, but I was trying to figure out if I could be what he needed. His checklist hadn't indicated he needed any of that, but I was still a little insecure after the mentions of his last Domme, Grace.

"Ah, you're awake." Nathan leaned against the door frame to the hallway wearing low-slung plaid pajama pants and nothing else. My eyes traced the long, faint outline of the inguinal crease that sloped beneath the soft flannel, my mouth watering at the sudden need to lick him there. I had last night and discovered he was ticklish. I knew I needed to stop staring, but he'd activated a switch inside me or something — I was now constantly horny. And wet. I wasn't sure if it was the increased water intake or just him — probably both.

"Quit looking at me like that," he scolded, narrowing his eyes. "We need to talk and prepare some things before Friday."

"Then don't stand around wearing those," I responded, laughing lightly at the way he shook his head at me.

The mention of Friday caused a shiver to run through me, part excitement, part sheer nerves. When we stepped into that party, it'd be something I'd never experienced before. I knew that there would be things happening as the night went on that'd likely scare the shit out of me, but the part of me that loved submitting to Nathan and the way he made me feel was beyond excited.

"I have breakfast ready in the living room. Get dressed and join me."

Nodding, I pulled back the covers, enjoying the way he didn't even bother to hide the fact he was observing me climb out of his bed naked. He watched as I purposefully bent down with my ass aimed right in his direction to gather my underwear from the foot of the bed. My dress had been placed on a hanger on a hook beside his closet door, and I smiled at the little ways he continued to look after me without having to be asked or seeking acknowledgment for it.

Nathan took care of me because he wanted to, and it gave him pleasure, not because it was expected. It made me want to find ways to do the same for him, but I wasn't sure how. He seemed to beat me to everything, like making me breakfast.

"If you hurry, I'll let you have two cups of coffee," he teased as I pulled open the drawer in his long dresser that I'd packed my clean clothes inside yesterday. I needed to ask him where I could do laundry, not having had time before we left Evan's house to take care of it.

270

"Hmm," he hummed as I pulled out a pair of black joggers, another slouchy sweater and some fuzzy socks. The concrete floors were nice in his apartment, but they held a little bit of a chill. "You know those will be off in an hour, right?"

Looking back in his direction, I rolled my eyes and scoffed playfully, shaking my head as I took a step toward the bathroom door. Nathan's usual tolerance of my behavior had shifted since we were back in his space, and my breath caught as he tilted his head down, pinning me with an intimidating eyebrow raise.

"What?" I asked innocently as I turned around in the doorway, the clothes in my hands the only thing poorly concealing my nudity from him.

"Change of plans," he said, pointing to the floor. "Put the clothes down and crawl to the playroom."

"What?" I asked, my heart pounding.

"You heard me. If I have to ask again, I'm not letting you cum today."

"Uh." I knew my mouth was hanging open a little, waiting for him to smile or indicate he was joking. He continued to stare me down with his jaw clenched as he waited. Shit. He was serious.

"Would you like to add tomorrow too?" he asked when I didn't move.

"No, sir," I responded quietly, turning to place my clothes on the bathroom counter quickly.

When I walked back into the bedroom, he'd moved the armoire to the side again and used his hands to push the double sliding doors open. Without turning around, he issued another command. "I said crawl. On your knees, sunshine."

Dropping to my knees on the rug next to the bed, I looked down to the floor, trying to figure out which submissive pose he would want to see.

We hadn't discussed that specifically earlier this morning when we'd talked about trying my first scene, but I found myself sitting back on my heels, placing my wrists against my thighs with my palms up and finding a spot to stare at on the floor a few feet away.

Nathan left me sitting there, stepping into the adjoining room and turning on the light. I couldn't see what he was doing, but I could hear him moving things around, grumbling under his breath.

"Follow me," he instructed after he'd returned to the bedroom, stopping right in front of me. I didn't dare look up, afraid he would follow through on his threats from earlier. He'd asked if I wanted to start anal training today when we'd woken up earlier, but we'd stayed in bed snuggling and talking, and I'd fallen asleep again. "Hands and knees. Slowly."

His feet disappeared, and I leaned forward, flattening my palms against the cool floor. Goosebumps rippled across my back as I followed him, but they weren't from being cold. For once, I wasn't sure what he was going to do to me. He'd explained training and what he was planning to introduce me to, so I knew what to expect in that aspect, but I knew my eye-rolling had changed the script he'd proposed.

My mind raced through what I'd checked and filled in on the section on punishments. Crawling across the floor naked would likely not end in doing meditation or writing lines of self-affirmation, so I tried to remain calm as I followed him into his playroom.

I'd been tempted to peek into the room last night, but Nathan hadn't shown me his space yet, and I didn't ask out of respect for his privacy.

A plush cream-colored rug covered the floor as I crossed the threshold, the fibers soft on my knees.

"Stop." His voice was low as his bare feet and plaid-covered legs entered my limited field of vision.

Before I could stop myself, a tiny giggle escaped my mouth. There was something endlessly amusing about Nathan channeling this intimidating Dom leading me into his playroom while I was naked but he was wearing loose plaid pajama pants. Wasn't it in their handbook to play in ripped denim or leather pants? I doubted Michael in Chase's book ever played in his PJs.

"Something funny, sunshine?" he asked as he reached down, gathering my loose hair at the nape of my neck and pulling my head back. My eyes closed as he pulled hard enough for my back to arch.

"Eyes on mine," he commanded, his voice lower than it typically sounded.

As my eyes slowly opened, I looked up toward him, expecting at least a little smirk, but his face was entirely sober as he looked down at me, his posture rigid. The muscles in his chest flexed as he leaned

272

down, his hand moving backward as he steered me with my hair still held tightly in his fist.

"On your knees."

Pushing my hands against the floor, I leaned back on my knees, my eyes locked with his.

"What was so funny, sunshine?"

Unsure of what to say, I remained quiet, just staring up at him as the slight pain in my scalp radiated through my body. Wetness pooled between my legs, and a tremor raced through my thighs as I fought the urge to seek friction.

"That's fine," he said ominously after a few moments of loaded silence. "Don't tell me. That will just make this more fun for me."

My mouth opened, ready to speak, but he tilted his head to the side, shaking slightly. "I gave you a chance, and you didn't say a word. Now, I want you to remain quiet while I give you five strikes. The only thing I should hear is counting." My pulse was pounding when he straightened, tugging lightly as he stood. "On the bench. Up you go."

Nathan grasped my elbow as I stood, steadying me as he rotated his hand, changing the hold on my hair but not letting go. He turned me toward a wooden bench that was taller than waist height, the top covered in padded black leather. It had two L-shaped padded brackets mounted on the legs closest to me, and I could see two platforms attached to the sides of the far legs, a black leather buckle attached to each side. I didn't even need to ask if he'd made it because the deep mahogany stain matched the furniture in his bedroom.

"Lie across the bench, knees on the holsters," he instructed his lips only a few inches from my ear.

He followed closely, offering a hand as I tried to get into position, the leather cool against the fronts of my thighs as I leaned down.

"Arms out in front of you."

My hands were shaking as I reached forward, my breasts flattening against the soft leather as I stretched my arms out in front of me.

Nathan released my hair, grasping my hips and pushing me forward slightly before I felt the leather strap wrap around the back of my thigh. He repeated it on the other side as I tried to keep from trembling, my breath coming out in pants.

When he appeared in my line of sight, bending down and placing a finger underneath my chin, I finally got a glimpse of playful Nathan; his lips pulled into a wry smile.

"Did you ever settle on a safeword, sunshine?" he asked as he crouched down in front of me.

I nodded, exhaling as his thumb caressed the side of my jaw softly. "Matrix."

"Like the movie?" He chuckled, his serious demeanor softening momentarily.

"No, like in computer science."

"Hmm…interesting," he hummed.

"You'd be surprised at how dirty most computer programming terms sound."

"But I'm not surprised that you interpreted them as dirty," he laughed, leaning forward to kiss me softly. "You ready for me to rearrange your back end code now?"

Biting my lip to hold in the laugh that wanted to escape, I nodded.

"My brave little sunshine," he cooed as he kissed my cheek, his facial hair scraping my skin. "Don't worry. We'll work up to my one sliding into your trailing zero."

My stomach clenched as I laughed quietly, my lips pressed together. He'd turned a punishment for being disrespectful into something fun. I knew his use of programmer humor was likely designed to relax me, but it was working.

"Hand or paddle?" he asked after a few moments once my laughter stopped.

"What kind of paddle?" I hadn't realized I'd have so much input in my punishment.

"What kind would you like?" he asked with a low laugh.

"Leather?"

Nathan nodded, stepping back. He hadn't bound my hands, so I tilted my head, my eyes following as he walked toward a tall wooden cabinet in the corner of the room. He pulled open one door, taking an item from a hook inside and turning back toward me.

The sound of leather slapping against his palm made me jump a little, and I immediately dropped my gaze to the rug beneath the bench. I expected him to come right back, but I heard a drawer closing, and my heart raced as I waited for him.

"Would you like a little pleasure with your pain, sunshine?" he chuckled, but the usual warmth was missing from his voice, a dark edge to it.

Again, I remained silent, not knowing if he expected a response from me.

"Ah," I jumped slightly, my body jolting forward as Nathan's hand slowly caressed my bare ass, his warm palm tracing from one hip to the other.

"Breathe," he whispered, his hand slipping between my legs. A quiet groan sounded as he briefly caressed my lips, spreading out the slick moisture he'd inspired. "I'm going to put in the plug before I spank you. Is that alright?"

My breath was shaky as I inhaled, nodding. "Yes." When he'd requested consent in the past, he always wanted me to respond verbally, and I understood why as my body started to shake with nervous tension.

"Are you cold, sunshine?" he asked as his hands caressed my bare back, his warm palms gently kneading my muscles.

"No," I whispered, my voice shaky. "Just nervous…and excited."

"Close your eyes and just enjoy my touch," he whispered as his strong hands continued to slowly roam my body, occasionally dipping between my legs to play softly against my folds.

My body relaxed at my growing arousal, my thighs shaking a little as I became more excited at what was to come.

The sound of a plastic cap flipping open startled me, but his warm hand was there, rubbing against my lower back. "It's just the lube. I'll warm it up a little first. Breathe."

Closing my eyes again, I tried to breathe deeply, letting myself relax as I listened to the faint sound of the lube against Nathan's fingers.

He braced his hand on my lower back, his thumb rubbing slowly for a moment. "Exhale, inhale," he whispered, and I tried to sync my breathing to his words, feeling myself relax and my mind starting to drift.

"Just a finger to start." My thighs tensed as he touched me, the warm lube on his fingertip pressing against the tiny pucker. "Breathe."

Trying to remember what he'd told me, I forced myself to let out a breath, focusing on how good the hand on my back felt. As his finger started to press more firmly, a small involuntary moan escaped. It wasn't that it felt good yet, but I was so aroused at the thought of what was to come the discomfort didn't matter.

"Slowly." His voice was low as he penetrated me, pausing to let me get used to the feeling, twisting his finger slightly and trailing his other hand down the back of my thigh. "Good girl."

My breath was choppy as he slipped it in a little further, but I moaned again as he reached down to caress my clit with his fingertips.

"Ah, there we go," he chuckled as his finger slid in with less resistance, my hips squirming as much as they could without the capability to move my thighs. "Just breathe. I'm all the way in. Does that feel good, sunshine?"

"Yes," I gasped as the pressure on my clit increased, and he began to thrust his finger in my ass slowly.

He let out a satisfied hum as I started pressing back into his motions. "Fuck, yes. So damn sexy. Are you ready for more?"

Exhaling a hard breath at his question, I nodded, gasping out a yes as he slipped a finger inside my pussy, slowly pressing forward until I was moaning.

"You like it when I fill both holes, don't you?" He chuckled as he leaned over me, kissing the back of my neck as he paused, fingers pressed all the way inside. "I'm going to fuck you later and let you pretend it's me and someone else. Would having another man's cock inside you while I fucked your ass turn you on?"

"Oh God," I moaned, pressing back into him. The soft flannel of his pants rested on my hip, but it was in stark contrast to the hard bar I could feel beneath the material as he flexed his covered cock against me.

"That wasn't a no," he laughed, trailing kisses down my back as he slowly removed both his hands. "Don't worry, I won't tell anyone about your filthy fantasies about being filled by two men."

I felt strangely empty as he left me, but it was only a moment before something else was nudging against my back entrance, causing me to clench in surprise.

"It's just the plug. Breathe."

Letting out a shaky breath, I tried to relax as he pressed the plug inside just a little, twisting it as he waited. When my hips moved back slightly, he chuckled, giving me a little more.

"I told you it'd feel good." He was right; it did feel good. Different — definitely not the same as him sliding inside my pussy — but still in a way that felt oddly pleasurable. I felt stretched as he slipped it in a little further.

His large palm covered my bare ass, caressing and squeezing as he started to slowly thrust the plug inside, pausing to let me adjust and then pulling it out slightly before he pushed in again.

"Next time, I'm going to record this," he said lowly, twisting the plug. "So you can see how fucking hot it is to watch. You're going to love it when I take you like this. Fuck…"

His satisfied groan was almost my undoing, a moan escaping as he finally pressed the plug in fully, my hips jumping a little as it settled into place.

Both his hands rubbed up and down the outsides of my thighs, pausing to grab my cheeks and massaging them slowly in his big palms before he stepped back.

My eyes drifted open as a fingertip traced along my hairline. Nathan was crouched in front of me, his eyes shining with pride as he softly combed my hair out of my face, cupping the back of my head.

"That was…" he exhaled, shaking his head. "So fucking hot. You did so well, sweetheart."

He kissed the tip of my nose, causing me to let out a little chuckle, followed almost immediately by a moan as my eyes widened.

"Felt that, huh?" He grinned as a smirk tugged at his mouth briefly before his face settled into a more somber expression. "I know it's part of your personality, but you're not going to roll your eyes when I'm trying to have a serious conversation with you again, are you?"

"No," I whispered as I shook my head. I knew from our previous discussions that the eye-rolling wasn't a behavior he would tolerate. "I'm sorry."

"Hmm," he hummed as he nodded his head. "You still ready for the paddle?"

Blowing out a breath, I nodded.

"Don't forget to count, or I start over. Alright, sunshine?"

"Yes, sir," I whispered, a thrill running through me as he smiled, tracing his knuckle against my cheekbone.

"Good girl."

With one last soft kiss against my forehead, he disappeared again.

Nathan didn't waste any time, the sound of the leather smacking against my skin loud with his first strike moments later.

While I'd intended my voice to be strong as I counted, I hadn't anticipated what it'd feel like for him to paddle me with the plug in place.

"One," immediately turned into a moan as I shifted my hips.

"Two," had me groaning against the bench.

"Three," and I was gasping as his large hand massaged out the sting in my skin slowly, teasing along the crease of my thigh but not touching me.

By the time I counted "four", I was close, both holes clenching as I tried to relax.

"Five. Oh, fuck," I groaned as Nathan dropped the paddle to the floor, his fingers slipping inside of me as I practically vibrated with need.

"Does my sunshine need something?" he asked, his tone taunting. "You're so wet. Do you want me to fuck you?"

When I didn't answer, he hummed, withdrawing his fingers. I clenched my eyes closed, panting as I tried to keep still. When he'd said he'd make me beg, he wasn't kidding.

"Open your eyes," he ordered in a gruff voice, and I instinctively obeyed, my gaze rising to the man standing in front of me. The flannel pajamas were gone, leaving Nathan bare, his hand slowly working his rigid cock as he stood a few feet in front of me.

"Which hole do you want me to fill with this?"

My eyes widened as I watched him move, his forearm flexing, and I felt myself clenching whenever he twisted his wrist, squeezing as he reached the crown.

"Or I can make you watch while I take care of this myself," he taunted, waiting for an answer.

Shaking my head, I closed my eyes. I hadn't anticipated feeling this out of control when this happened. He'd turned me into a desperate panting mess. My thoughts raced, my chest heaving as I tried to catch my breath.

"Sunshine," Nathan cooed, his voice close to my head and his fingers tracing the skin between my shoulder blades. "Do you need me to stop?"

Shaking my head, I opened my eyes, trying to focus. He was standing right in front of me, still gloriously hard, but he was no longer touching himself. His focus was on me as he softly trailed his fingers through my hair.

"Good girl, focus on me," he whispered as his fingers traced my lips, his thumb lingering on the bottom one as he crouched down again. "I want you to breathe and tell me what you want."

"You," I whispered, clenching his fingers as he grasped my hand.

"Good girl. What else?"

"Inside me," I whispered as I felt myself relax a little more.

Nathan cupped my cheek and then squeezed my hand, his eyes never leaving mine. "How? How do you want me inside you?" He waited a few moments as my breathing evened out. "Do you want me to keep the plug in?"

"No," I shook my head, and he smiled.

"OK, sunshine, we can take it out. I think you've had enough today."

"No," I shook my head again, clearing my throat. "I want you in my ass instead."

His eyes widened as he sat back on his heels. "Are you sure? We can work our way up to that. There's no rush."

"Please. I don't want to wait." I'd thought about Nathan's promise that he'd do or let me do anything, and I knew this was a step we needed to take to make that happen. He'd made the whole experience pleasurable so far, I wanted to feel all of him. I knew I was pushing things quickly, but I wanted him.

"You're sure you want me in your ass?" he asked, his brow furrowed. "This isn't what we talked about this morning. I don't want you to feel pressured to do this."

"Yes, I want it."

"You might not cum. I mean, I can get out a toy to help keep you relaxed, but it might take a little adjusting for you to enjoy it the first time. It'll be tight, and not what you're used to feeling."

I nodded, licking my dry lips. I could see why Nathan was so insistent on me staying hydrated. "I want to try."

He nodded slowly, squeezing my hand one last time before he stood.

"Tell me to stop, and I will." His hand slowly traced my side as he stepped around me. The quiet click of the cap of the lube bottle made my pulse race, and I closed my eyes, trying to take in deep breaths as I waited. I could do this. He wouldn't hurt me. I was ready to push things a little further.

The slick sound of him rubbing the lube on himself made me squirm, and when I heard the quiet hum of something, my thighs tensed in anticipation. I moaned softly, the feeling of my muscles clenching against the plug intense.

"Almost ready. You're being so patient," Nathan praised as I felt his fingers cup around mine. He leaned over me, pulling my hair over my shoulders to run down the center of my back. "I am going to put this on your finger, and I want you to hold it against your clit."

Nathan slipped something on my middle finger, and it buzzed slightly, the tiny vibrations traveling up my arm. His hands grasped my hips, urging them backward slightly as one of his hands reached forward to grab my upper arm. He traced his palm up to my hand, intertwining our fingers as he coaxed my arm backward and underneath my body, pressing my hand in between my legs.

"I'm going to use the plug to loosen you up a bit, but I want to make you cum first. Fingers…tongue…or my cock?"

Gasping as he pulled slightly on the end of the plug before pressing it back in, I moaned, trying to remember the question.

"Guess I get to decide then," he chuckled, and I felt my pulse race with   anticipation.   I   was   ready.

TWENTY-EIGHT

Nathan

Boston

Kelly gasped as I pressed my thumb into the plug, rotating it against the flat end at the base. She'd done so beautifully as I built her up, but I hadn't been expecting her to ask me to fuck her ass today. She'd been open to the idea when we talked about it early this morning, but I thought today would be the warm-up. Once again, my sunshine had proved me wrong — jumping into her first scene with both feet.

"Say 'red' or 'matrix' and I stop immediately," I whispered as I dipped my hand beneath her, slowly pressing two fingers inside. She gasped again as I pulled slightly on the end of the plug with my other hand, but her hips rocked back into the movement.

She was wetter than I'd anticipated, her pussy almost dripping as I pressed my fingers down on the inner wall, loving the moan that came out of her mouth, her neck arching backward.

I could feel the subtle vibrations of the finger vibe I'd slid onto her hand, but I could tell she was having trouble concentrating enough to play with herself.

"Just relax," I breathed as I removed my fingers, slowly replacing them with my cock as I slipped inside of her pussy. She was tight, the plug narrowing her slightly, but not enough that I could feel it. The next time I wanted to try the vibrating one I'd gotten her, knowing that it'd be intense for both of us.

"That's it, such a brave girl," I praised as I rubbed my hands over her hips, slowly rocking forward. Kelly tried to push back into my movements, but there was only so much leverage she could get with her legs buckled to the back of the bench.

"Oh God," she gasped as I rocked in, then slowly pulled the plug halfway out as I retreated, only to slip it back in while I did. The muscles in Kelly's back trembled as I fucked her gently with both my cock and the plug.

Leaning forward, I braced my palm on the edge of the bench next to her head. "Relax and breathe," I coached as her legs started to shake against the front of my thighs with each slow thrust. "Touch yourself. I want to feel you squeeze me."

"Fuck," she whined as she listened to my instructions, her moans getting louder as I moved faster. My thumb pressed firmly on the plug, and she cried out loudly as I rotated it slowly.

"That's it, sunshine. I can tell you're getting close," I panted as I felt her spasm around me. It felt fucking amazing, but I was trying not to cum yet because I knew it might take me a while to recover. "I need you to press harder and make yourself cum."

"I feel so full," she gasped as she started pressing back into my movements, rocking her hips as I kept a steady rhythm — gritting my teeth as she worked herself up.

"That's because you are."

"Oh, fuck. Oh, God." Her moans got louder as she got closer, until finally, her back arched, a loud moan escaping her mouth as she began to clench around me.

I pulled out, holding the base of my cock firmly and grasping it under the head with my other hand as I tried not to cum.

Kelly was gasping as she reached over and grabbed my wrist, squeezing as her climax continued to roll through her body. As her shoulders began to soften, I watched her body relax as she fell into what I knew was likely sub-space, her face pressed into the leather and a soft smile on her face. For a moment, I thought she'd passed out, but the loud moan that tore out of her as I slowly removed the plug indicated otherwise.

"Fucking hell, sunshine," I groaned as I placed the plug on the chest of drawers nearby, picking up the bottle of lube. I opened it, enjoying the way her body jolted at the sound. She knew what was going to happen next. "I don't think I'm going to last much longer," I confessed. I was too worked up.

Squirting a generous amount of lube on my cock, I stroked it slowly before I stepped forward, pressing the head into her puckered hole.

"Oh, God," she panted as I began to press inside, her hands seeking purchase on the front of the leather bench. Pausing for a moment, I reached forward for her hands, slowly rotating her arms and placing her hands on the backs of her thighs.

"Hold yourself open for me, sunshine," I instructed as I reached down to pull the finger vibe off, pushing the button to silence it and dropping it to the floor. I'd need to show her proper toy care later, but right now, I was going to show her how good it could feel for me to fuck her ass.

Her hips tensed as I pressed the head in again, but I used my free hand to caress her back, whispering encouragement as I felt her relax. It took several slow, shallow thrusts to get her to open for me finally, but once I slipped inside completely the first time, I stilled, my head thrown back as I tried to calm down with deep breaths.

"So fucking tight," I groaned as I rocked forward.

Kelly's soft moans combined with the way she was tilting her hips back to take the impact of my thrusts had me slowly increasing my pace, enjoying the way her fingers clenched against her flesh as I drove inside her.

"Fuck," she panted, her mouth slack as she lay with her cheek pressed to the leather beneath her. I could see the sweat building along her hairline and across her shoulders. Slowing my thrusts, I gathered her hair into a ponytail, wrapping the long strands around my wrist once as I loomed over her, watching her react to each slow flex of my hips.

"You have no idea how fucking sexy it is to watch you submit to me, sunshine. You look so pretty, holding your ass open for me. Fuck," I exhaled sharply as my balls started to tense, my impending orgasm beginning to wash over me. "I'm going to cum soon. Do you want it inside you, or do you want me to paint your back with it?"

"I..." she panted, her thighs tensing as she pushed back against me. Leaning down, I rested my head next to where I was holding her hair, reaching beneath her hips to press on her clit.

"Fuck, this is fucking intense," I panted into her skin as she moaned again, her cries intensifying as I snapped my hips forward. She was going to feel all this later today and tomorrow, but I felt a sick sense of pleasure roll through me at the fact every time she sat down, she'd remember what this moment felt like. "I wanna feel you cum again," I moaned, speeding my fingers as her hips rocked into my movements.

"Cum inside me," she gasped as I felt her clit start to throb.

"Oh fuck, Kelly, yes," I groaned as I pushed inside completely after a few jerky thrusts, emptying myself inside her ass as she clenched around me tightly.

After I caught my breath, I slowly rose, slipping out of her as gently as I could. She hissed, and I rubbed her back, petting her hair as she trembled against the bench.

My fingers dug into her shoulders, massaging the tight muscles as she tried to calm her breathing. That was fucking crazy. I didn't expect her to want me inside her, and it'd been a good thing she was already close when she whispered for me to cum inside her because it'd pushed me right over the edge.

"Oh, sweetheart," I whispered, an intense sense of pride swelling in my chest. "You did so good. That was more than I ever expected. Thank you for letting me share that with you. You looked so fucking gorgeous."

I could see the corner of her mouth turn up into a smile at my praise, but I needed to free her legs so I could get her tucked into bed and warm. I didn't want her to catch a chill as she came down, and I knew with this being her first real scene that she needed me to be there.

Her checklist had some solid suggestions on aftercare, but she hadn't been through this before, so we needed to figure this out together.

My fingers quickly released the buckles on her thighs, rubbing the skin with an aftercare oil that prevented bruising until her muscles felt relaxed.

Walking to the bathroom, I wet a washcloth with warm water, returning to my beautiful partner.

Kelly was still trembling; her jaw slack as she lay with her eyes closed. I could tell she'd fallen into sub-space fully as she lay completely still against the bench. She'd given me a few solid orgasms, and the build-up was more intense than she was used to. But she'd been so receptive and bravely trusted me to take care of her.

"Let's get you tucked into bed," I whispered as I slowly washed between her legs. Gently rolling her to the side, I gathered her into my arms and carried her to my bed. Pulling back the covers, I laid her down with her head on the pillow before pulling them up to her chin.

She was still shaking a little, but I didn't think it was from the slight chill in the room. I'd nonetheless have to remember to turn on the space heater in the playroom the next time, just in case. I paused, looking down at her tiny form tucked into my king-sized bed, hoping that there would be a next time.

We still didn't know when she was leaving, and I felt a sense of panic sweep through me when I thought of being separated from her. I'd become so addicted to her presence over the last few weeks and I wasn't sure what would happen when I didn't wake up next to her every day. We'd crammed the first few months of a typical relationship into just days. I felt closer to her than any previous dynamic I'd been a part of.

Exiting the room quickly, I yanked open the fridge and pulled out a few bottles of water, grabbing the bowl of fruit I'd prepared and a few protein bars off the coffee table on the way back into my room. I didn't want to have to leave her again, wanting to be there to reassure her as her endorphins wore off. The last thing she needed was to drop after her first scene because her blood sugar was low.

Depositing my supplies on the nightstand, I climbed under the covers, pulling Kelly tightly into my chest, my hands cupping the back of her head as she slowly uncurled from the fetal position she'd tucked herself into while I was gone.

"You're so beautiful," I whispered against her forehead, slowly trailing my fingers over every inch of exposed skin I could reach, combing my fingers through her hair and enjoying the way she sighed against me, her body relaxing. After a few moments, she untucked her legs, intertwining them with mine as her hand slipped up to the side of my neck, her fingers clinging to me. "I can't thank you enough for trusting me."

Aftercare was important after any scene, and I fully intended to give Kelly a massage once she was a little more coherent, kneading out the tension I still felt in the muscles of her back. But right now, *I* needed to hold her, to reassure myself that she wanted to be here with me. That she'd entrusted me to guide her through that experience, and she wanted me to keep her safe.

Emory's advice that I needed to tell her I loved her was on repeat in my subconscious, but I couldn't get my mouth to open — too afraid that her feelings for me weren't as strong as mine or that she'd regret what we'd done.

When I came in to get her for breakfast, I hadn't envisioned making her crawl into the playroom so I could paddle her for rolling her eyes at me. The anal training was supposed to be this afternoon after we'd talked about what the play party would be like. I hadn't intended to fuck her ass with a plug while I fucked her pussy until she came so hard she practically passed out, let alone follow up by cumming in her ass at her request.

I never wanted to lose myself so much I worried I might have gotten too rough with her. I certainly hadn't expected her to ask for all she had. That was...there were no words. The sheer amount of trust she placed in me was humbling, but I was proud of her for asking for what she wanted.

"Can I have a drink?" she whispered as her fingers idly traced the side of my neck, her other hand lying flat against the skin over my heart.

"Of course, gorgeous," I whispered, reaching over to uncap a bottle and helping her sit up a little to take some sips. She'd need to drink a lot more before we went to bed tonight, but this was a start.

Placing the bottle back on the nightstand, I grabbed a handful of grapes, shifting over and lying on my back so Kelly could rest her head on my chest.

"Open up." She looked up toward me, opening her mouth for me to pop a grape inside, smiling at me as she chewed.

"You take such good care of me," she whispered as her fingers traced over the tattoo on the side of my chest.

"I want to, sunshine. You're precious to me," I sighed, my jaw clenching as I tried to control the emotions welling up inside me. I'd felt vulnerable after a scene before, but not this early in a dynamic, and not like this. This woman was going to decimate me, and I'd willingly let her pull me to my destruction.

She was quiet as she traced my skin in an almost hypnotic pattern, my brain finally relaxing as our bodies came down from the endorphins. She'd stopped shaking, her body melting into my side as I curled a lock of her hair around my finger, my lips resting against her forehead.

My eyes closed, a deep sense of exhaustion catching up with me, the stress of the last few days finally taking its toll. The desire to protect Kelly — to *love* her — was consuming all my thoughts lately. I'd do anything for her.

As I felt myself starting to drift off to sleep, her motions slowed, becoming more intentional as she continued to trace my skin. The tip of her finger slowly traced a right angle over my heart, and it started pounding underneath. When she followed with a circle, and then the distinct shape of a V, I squeezed my eyes closed tighter, trying to hold still. My chest trembled a little as she slowly traced an uppercase E into my skin, marking me with the word I was afraid to say to her.

Swallowing hard, I held as still as I could as she traced the shape of a Y, followed by an oval and a slow, curving U. She was writing the letters into my skin like a tattoo, marking my heart in a way that physically ached.

When she finished, laying her palm against my skin and sighing, I held completely still, afraid of what I'd say if she spoke the words aloud. I'd never be able to let her go if she told me that was how she truly felt about me.

As she drifted off to sleep against my chest, I cupped my hand over the one she had covering my heart, trying to push away the inevitable pain I knew that'd tear me apart when she realized that maybe I wasn't worth her love. Because I desperately wanted her to abandon her life in Chicago and stay here with me forever, consequences be damned. And deep inside, I was terrified that she wouldn't   choose   me.

TWENTY-NINE

Kelly

Boston

Nathan let me sleep for several hours after our scene, and I woke up a little bit sore, but he laid a towel down in the middle of his big bed, using massage oil to relax all my muscles. We never got dressed as we cuddled in the bed afterward, talking. If this was aftercare, I was all in. We'd managed to fit months of a regular relationship into weeks, and I never got tired of the sound of his voice or the way he touched me. His hand was a constant presence on my skin, and not just on my ass.

He explained what would likely happen at the party on Friday, telling me to prepare for a cocktail party followed by a little time for conversation. Then things would start to change as the night went on, and people began to get comfortable with one another. In other words, there would be nudity and public sex acts — which was terrifying and exciting in equal measure. From what Emory had told him, I knew this party would be tamer than some they attended, but I felt like that might be good for me. Easing my way into the scene wouldn't be quite so terrifying that way.

Talia had texted him while we were cuddling, inviting me to spend the next day with her to find something appropriate to wear, and I was a little nervous despite him assuring me his friend had good intentions. And I was also a little embarrassed still that she'd been sitting next to me on the couch while I had an orgasm the other night. I knew that it hadn't bothered Nathan and his friends, but I was still struggling to push down the little voice in my brain telling me I was doing something dirty. The more time I spent with Nathan, the less I could hear it, but it was hard to break the ingrained stigma attached to enjoying what we were exploring.

He made me feel more comfortable with my body and expressing what I wanted, not only sexually, but in a partnership. I'd never had a man actually encourage me to use my words and tell him exactly what I wanted and thought. Twenty years of censoring myself for public consumption had conditioned me to shrink myself, and Nathan was encouraging me to break out of that box I'd stuffed myself inside and do what I wanted, purely because I wanted it.

As we shared more and more, I found myself addicted to the way he made me feel. I felt seen and heard in a way I'd never experienced, and it terrified me that it could all come to a screeching halt at any moment. But I wasn't going to dwell on that, because I knew what we were building was bigger than the thousand miles that could potentially separate us.

"She's going to be here in fifteen minutes," Nathan shouted from the bedroom while I tried to rinse the conditioner from my hair. He'd offered to do it for me if I showered with him earlier. I'd sadly turned him down because I knew we'd never be ready on time if he 'helped.' His idea of helping me shower involved his hands trying to impersonate a bra and bending me over and licking my pussy until my legs gave out. While I hadn't minded the day before, I was already running late.

"I'm coming," I shouted back as I turned off the spray from the rainfall showerhead. I hadn't been lying when I said I wanted to live in his bathroom. It wasn't that the one in my condo wasn't nice — it was high-end too — but his whole apartment felt warmer than my sterile shades of gray and pops of color.

Nathan, in general, brought warmth to my life, and I hated that there was the ax of time hanging over our heads. The sands were emptying into the bottom of the hourglass — whatever cheesy time metaphor I thought of, they described this sinking feeling of anxiety that had been building in my chest.

My phone had been silent, the text messages stopping after the second one, but I felt like it was lulling us into a false sense of security. I knew Trent couldn't trace me to Nathan's, but his volatile words had scared me more than I let on. When pushed into a corner, desperate people were dangerous, and if Tom said his computers had been confiscated, something major was happening. Deacon continued to throw busy work at me casually with little communication on my situation, but I still had remote access to the server, which gave me peace of mind.

"Sunshine, hurry," Nathan warned, and my head turned toward the bathroom door. He leaned against the frame with his arms crossed on his chest and a fitted blue dress shirt rolled up to his elbows. He looked yummy wearing a pair of fitted, neatly pressed, navy slacks and dark, shiny work boots. He'd spent twenty minutes carefully combing his long hair back, and he looked almost as good as he had at the wedding but in a hot construction manager type of way. I was sure he'd even make a hard hat look sexy. I was a goner for this man.

Talia's invitation had been serendipitous, but I had a feeling Nathan may have called in a favor when he told me he needed to go into the office for a meeting today.

He'd been up early, disappearing to the fitness center in his building's basement for an hour while I worked on my laptop. When he'd come back up, sweaty and the muscles in his biceps looking extra impressive, I'd only drooled a little. He teased me as he left a trail of clothing across his bedroom floor and into the bathroom, giving me a little wink as he disappeared behind the door, completely naked. If he'd thought that was revenge for me walking around naked the other day, I was all about revenge. He could punish me any day.

"Where's your hairdryer?" I asked as I reached out the glass shower door, grabbing the towel I'd left on the edge of the vanity.

"Come here," he instructed, patting the counter in front of him. I picked up my brush on the way, but before I could lift it to my head, he caught it, setting it down on the counter briefly before he spun me to face the mirror.

He carefully parted my hair, running the brush through my wet tangles with a serious look on his face. I wanted to lean back into his touch, but I didn't want to get his shirt wet, so I just watched him quietly take care of me.

"Thank you," I whispered, swallowing past the lump in my throat as he picked up a hand towel, slowly rubbing my hair.

"You're very welcome, sunshine," he smirked as he pointed at the bottom drawer of the cabinet bank. "Hairdryer is in there. I need to get going, but I'll wait to let Tal in before I leave."

I nodded, turning to face him. Nathan pushed my hair back over my shoulders, leaning in to kiss one softly, working his way up my neck, slowly taking possession of my mouth as he cupped my cheeks.

"Text me if you need anything. I'll send you Emory's contact information in case you need him. Please stay with Tal."

"I will, I promise," I confirmed, knowing he was anxious about letting me out of his sight. I was nervous too, but even if he was crazy enough to fly to the east coast, Trent thought I was in Connecticut. I just hoped he wasn't unhinged enough to do something to my brother's empty house.

"Buy whatever you want, my treat," he offered, but I had enough saved to take care of whatever I wanted to buy. I'd still been completing enough work to keep my normal salary while I wasn't in the office. Not having a life outside work wasn't very expensive.

"Alright." I nodded, not wanting to argue.

"I mean it," he insisted. "But I have a present to give you tonight when I get home."

"Hmm," I hummed, reaching to cup him through his slacks. He wasn't hard, but I loved how his face changed as he firmly grasped my wrist.

"That's not the present, but hold that thought until I come back home."

"Can I hold *it* when you come home?" I asked with a grin and giggled when he shook his head.

"Behave, and put some clothes on. Although, I think Tal might like the show if you walked around in a towel."

"Fine," I pouted, grabbing the bra and panties I'd left on the counter and pulling them on.

Nathan helped me secure the clasp before he kissed my shoulder again, blowing out a breath before he turned to leave. "Be good, sunshine. Don't let Tal talk you into anything you don't want."

As I zipped up my jeans, I heard him talking outside the bedroom, the door cracked open. I quickly tugged on a formfitting blouse and walked to the door.

Talia was sitting on the couch as I walked into the living room, a large handbag on her lap and her phone in her hand. "Do you have a skirt?" she asked without looking up.

"Um, not with me." My clothing options were limited. She was lucky I wasn't wearing plain black leggings as I had been for the last week.

"Here," she reached into her purse, tossing me a solid black maxi-length skirt. "Change into that."

"Are the jeans not alright for where we're going?"

"Not if you want to be comfortable after," she smiled, setting her phone down and shooing me toward the bedroom.

I disappeared back inside, leaving my jeans folded on top of the dresser as I pulled the skirt on. It was long and flowing, made out of soft cotton.

"What's the state of things downstairs?" Talia asked from the door, nodding toward my lower half.

"Um…" *What?*

"Oh, don't be shy. I've seen your O face. I think you can tell me when the last time you waxed was."

Cringing, I thought back to my last waxing — right before the wedding. It wasn't looking good down there, not that it'd slowed down Nathan any.

"That bad, huh? Don't worry. We'll get that remedied for Friday night," she nodded, turning toward the living room. "Dry your hair, and let's get going. Emory lent me his car today. Too bad we can't put the top down since it's raining again, but it's fun to drive."

Two hours and a seventy-dollar waxing that Talia insisted on paying for later, I felt a little bit sore and cold because I was walking around downtown Boston with my panties in my purse. The rain had stopped, but Talia hadn't, talking continuously as she led me in and out of clothing stores to get an idea of what I liked. We'd left Emory's sleek black Mercedes convertible in a parking garage, and she'd dragged me toward a clothing store before I could argue about my state of undress.

"Is this dinner going to be formal?" I asked as she held a dark blue mini dress up to my chest, tilting her head to the side.

"You'll see everything from latex bodysuits to cocktail dresses," she said in a conversational tone, oblivious to the people around us. "But I know Nathan will want to show you off, so let's get a conservative but sexy dress, and then we'll go find the fun stuff. Most people will have the kinky attire hidden until the play starts."

"Show me off?" I asked, and she giggled as she cupped my cheek.

"You'll be fine. He's not going to do anything to make you uncomfortable, but some people will notice he's got a new partner. Nathan refuses to play the politics in the scene, so there are always people curious about who's with him. I think that was part of why Marisa pursued him; she liked the attention."

"Is that a bad thing that he's got a new partner?" I wasn't sure if I wanted people to notice me at something like this. Observing it from the sidelines sounded like a better idea.

"No, but you're gorgeous, so they'll be curious. Most people in our circle know Nathan doesn't share, but I'm not sure about this Dom's friends. Don't worry though, Emory and Nathan will always make sure you feel safe."

"Who are they?" I asked with wide eyes.

"Relax, Kelly. I know it's a little scary, but you'll do great. You know the phrase 'fake it until you make it'? Just do that. If you walk in there like the confident badass I know you are, no one will question it."

Scary wasn't adequate to encompass what this was, but I was trying to relax because I knew Nathan would never take me somewhere that would make me feel uncomfortable. The fact that he'd been hesitant and left the decision up to me spoke volumes.

"Alright, I think this one will do," she told me as she headed toward the cash register with a dark blue cocktail dress that would hit just above my knees. The fabric was satiny and shimmered when I moved, but it was far from scandalous. "Then I'm taking you to find something that'll blow Nathan's mind to wear underneath."

My pulse pounded at the implications of her statement, but she knew more about this than I ever would, so I was following her lead.

"This one?" Talia asked as she held up another hanger with tiny leather straps hanging from it.

"I don't even know how to put that on," I laughed as she pushed my shoulder lightly to turn in the direction of the dressing rooms. "Is that supposed to cover me? It doesn't look like it's going to cover much."

"That's the point, and exactly why I'm here. I'll help you figure it out." She smiled, wiggling her eyebrows. "It's my duty as your new friend to encourage you to embrace your inner vixen. That starts with picking out lingerie that will bring Nathan to his knees."

"Uh…"

"Oh, relax, Kelly. I'm not into girls other than to admire their beautiful bodies." Her tone was dismissive, but my mind was racing about what that comment could be interpreted as. "I won't come in there if you don't want me to, but I'd like to help you."

"Uh...I..." I stuttered again, nodding. "Alright. Then let's try this on. I don't even know where to start."

She didn't look back as she pulled open a dark wooden door with heavy metal accents at the back of the high-end lingerie and fetish wear boutique she'd taken me to. It was in a nondescript brick building without signage, between a tax preparation office and a dog groomer. When she'd tugged me up the stairs to the second-floor loft after typing a passcode into the door, I never would have even known it was here just from passing by on the street.

"Strip, let's see that sexy body you've been hiding." She nodded as she settled into a plush chair in the corner. Three walls were covered with floor-to-ceiling mirrors, so no matter where I looked, I couldn't escape, but I was finding I didn't want to. Nathan had assured me that Talia was a safe person, and he'd been friends with her and her partner for years. If our relationship progressed like I hoped it would, Nathan had even suggested she might be a good mentor.

"Nathan warned me you liked to watch, but I didn't think that included dressing rooms," I chuckled nervously.

"Relax," she grinned, flashing me a naughty smile. "I'm here to help, I'm not interested in making you uncomfortable. If you want me to leave, kick me out, but then you'll have to figure out those straps on your own."

"Phew," I sighed, closing my eyes and flexing my fingers before I reached down to pull my blouse over my head. My skin tingled as the cool air caressed my skin, goosebumps covering my neck as my eyes rose to meet hers.

Talia simply sat back in the armchair, crossing one leg over her knee and nodding with an eyebrow raised.

Feeling short of breath with her right in front of me, I turned toward the mirror on the opposite wall, grasping the waistband of my borrowed skirt and lowering it to the floor. As I turned my gaze to the mirror in front of me, I could see her eyes roaming what I'd exposed to her view, lingering on my hips. I knew my body wasn't perfect, but that didn't seem to matter, judging from the soft smile on her face.

"How do I get into this thing?" I questioned as I grabbed the hanger holding the skimpy garment she'd selected for me. There were a few less intimidating things on the wall hook, with lots of lace and mesh, but this was the one that intrigued me, even if it also scared me.

"First, you need to lose that bra," she chuckled as she stood, crossing to where I was standing and releasing the clasp with a pinch of her fingers. I knew it was just a plain black cotton bra, but her cringe spoke volumes. "It needs to go. The girls deserve better."

My breath caught as she pushed one of the straps over the edge of my shoulder with her fingertip. I'd never been into women before, but the way she was watching me and her open admiration of my bare skin was a little arousing.

"Relax," she said on a soft sigh, reaching down to pull the hanger out of my hand. "Raise your arms above your head."

Talia and I were about the same height, but that didn't matter as she bunched up the leather straps and lifted them to my fingertips. I leaned forward slightly as she guided my hands through and began to pull the material down my arms. She paused as she reached my shoulders, gently moving my hair out of the way before continuing.

My nipples pebbled as her fingertips grazed the sides of my breasts on their way down, but she didn't linger, carefully straightening the straps that fell across my torso. "We need to find something to match your dress for underneath. Maybe a set in the same dark blue — do you want lace or satin?"

I thought about the small black satin and lace thong that Nathan had bought for me. I wondered if he'd want me to wear that out in public. The thought didn't frighten me. "Both?"

"We'll need some stockings too, these straps will clip into those," she commented as she held up the small black clips attached to the end of the leather strips that fell to my hips. I nodded, trusting she knew what she was doing. "How does the fit feel on this?"

"It's good, I think." Leather straps converged in the middle of my chest at a single gold O-ring centered on my breastbone. Another set crossed over my shoulders and behind my neck, crisscrossing at the back. A solid black band spanned my chest beneath my breasts, with several straps overlapping on my sides and connecting in the back.

As I gazed at myself in the mirror, I wasn't sure I recognized the woman staring back at me. Despite the nerves, my posture was impressive, my breasts jutting out slightly and my neck proud. The stark contrast of the leather against my fair skin was striking, and I imagined myself with a high curly ponytail and dark, dramatic makeup.

"I'll be back, but I think this one is it," Talia smiled as she slipped out the door, leaving me to face myself in the room of mirrors. "You already look hot."

Despite the lingering redness from my wax, I looked like something out of an erotic novel, and I found myself wondering if this was what Kayla felt like around Michael in Chase's book.

I shifted slightly, looking in the side mirrors at what the back looked like. What would Nathan think of this? Would he think I was sexy? Or would he think I was just trying to dress the part?

"Found the perfect set for you," Talia announced as she slipped back inside the room, holding up her find. "It'll look great against your skin and it'll soften the look of all this leather."

A dark blue satin bra with black lace sewn along the edges of the cups dangled from the wooden hanger, a small pair of matching satin panties clipped to the back. She was holding a little mesh bag in her other hand and tossed it to me as she began to pull the bra loose from its clips.

"Put those on," she instructed, nodding to the chair. I sat down on the edge of the velvet cushion, carefully bunching up the nude stockings until I could slip my toes into the end.

Talia waited until I had pulled up the stockings before she motioned for me to join her. "Without heels, we won't get quite the same effect, but try this."

She helped me slip the bra underneath the leather straps, fastening it in the back before I leaned over to pull on the tiny panties. I could tell from the satisfied look on her face that she approved, and I had to admit, it did make me feel insanely sexy. We'd left the dress in the car, but with how long it was — and since she'd insisted I needed to get it one size larger than I normally wore — I knew that it'd conceal all of this without a trace.

"He's gonna totally freak out when he sees this," she laughed as she stepped back, her hands on her hips as she appraised the whole set. "Should be interesting to see him flustered at one of these things for once."

I frowned, wondering what that meant.

296

"Oh." She grasped my shoulder, leaning her head against mine. "No, not that he's normally a total bastard or anything," she giggled, squeezing her hand before stepping back. "He's just always been a little bit reserved at events like these. He certainly never brought along a sub who he looks at like he does you. It's clear he adores you, and I'm sure he'd mess someone up if they touched you. I've honestly never seen him like he was with you before."

"Like what?"

"The other night when..." she trailed off with a naughty wink. "He watched your every move. Your facial expressions, everything. If he thought you were uncomfortable, I'm sure he would have kicked Emory and me out without blinking. And the way he deferred to you when we were all talking, that almost made me swoon. Nathan isn't one for lots of talking, but I can tell he's comfortable around you. He confided in you before Emory, that right there was sexy. Those two talk about everything."

"He's always respectful of me."

"But in the past, the way he checked in on his subs didn't seem as effortless as he does naturally with you. I've never seen him *in love* before. There was always a strong bond with his past submissives, but I never thought he was in love with one of them."

My breath caught, my eyes meeting hers in the mirror across the room.

"He...uh..." I nervously picked at the straps on my chest, avoiding eye contact.

"Hmmm. You too?" she grinned, bending forward to tilt my chin. "You should work on those communication skills. Take it from someone who played way too hard to get."

I laughed, suddenly feeling a little more comfortable.

"You weren't a fan of Emory in the beginning?"

"No, I was, but some fucked up shit happened when I joined this community, and I didn't have someone like Nathan to protect me. I hid from my feelings for Emory for a long time because of what another man did, and I hated myself when he finally told me how much it hurt him. We don't have any secrets now, but it took me a long time to trust myself enough to let him in."

Chills ran up my spine as I thought about everything going on with me. Predators were everywhere, it seemed, and someone in her past had targeted Talia.

"I know we're about the same age, but I was much younger than you are when I went diving right into the kink community with the naivety that only a twenty-five-year-old can. I get being worried. You should be a little cautious going in, but most of the people you'll meet are amazing. And I promise that dick harassing you back in Chicago won't touch you here. We won't let him. This community protects its own."

"He told you about…?" I asked as I started unclipping the garters, moving back to sit in the chair. Talia helped me get everything pulled off, talking as I got redressed.

"That fucker who threatened you? Yeah, but not because he wanted to abuse your trust or privacy. He knew I could relate, and he wanted you to have someone else to confide in. So, I'll tell you that myself. You can tell me anything, and I won't judge you. I won't tell Emory if you ask me not to, but don't let someone else's actions keep you from living your life and embracing love, because you can't get that time back."

"Do you think Nathan knows that I…?"

"That you love his heart as much as his dick?" she laughed, handing me the lingerie once it'd been returned to its hangers. "Yeah, I think he does, but he's scared, just like you. Give him the benefit of the doubt. His actions toward you speak much louder than his words ever will. He's a good one. And he deserves someone who loves him just as much. So please don't hurt him. Because I'd hate to choose between him and your family."

"Don't want to lose Chase?" I laughed, but she shook her head.

"No, strangely enough, I think I'd miss Evan. He's such a sweetheart. Still nervous as fuck around all of us, but he'll come around. And now we have you," she grinned. "But I will cut you."

"Noted," I chuckled nervously, pulling my borrowed skirt back on. It made me feel better knowing I had someone like Talia in my corner. And that she was just as willing to protect Nathan. Christine was probably my only friend that would ever threaten to physically harm someone if they hurt me.

We quickly made our purchases, things feeling a little calmer as I buckled myself into the passenger seat of the convertible.

"Let me know if there's anything else I can find you before Friday. I know Nathan told you what I do for a living. I'd be happy to guide you in the right direction with the fun stuff too. Nathan's got a pretty vast collection, but I'm always getting freebies."

I smiled, looking over at her as we idled at a stoplight. "Actually. There is something you can help me with. I want to surprise Nathan."

"Sounds fun. Tell me more," she grinned, and I knew that she could help me put together some of the pieces of my plan for after the party.

Nathan beat us back to his apartment and lounged on the couch as Talia helped me carry my purchases inside, along with the things she'd given me from her stash of new toys once I'd told her about my plans.

"Well, I'll leave you two to discuss tomorrow night. See you at the studio tomorrow, sexy." Talia winked in my direction as she walked into the kitchen. Nathan's eyebrows rose and I blushed as his eyes followed his friend and then came back to me. She laid my garment bag over the back of the barstool at the kitchen island, passing me on her way back toward the front door.

"Good luck," she whispered as she kissed me on the cheek, disappearing with a wave.

"You two seem to be getting along well," Nathan said with a smirk as he stood from where he'd been stretched out on the couch, pulling me into his arms.

"We had fun. Thank you for arranging that. I know you were just trying to help me feel a little bit more comfortable after the other night."

"And because Talia begged me to hang out with you," he laughed, and I felt my cheeks heat. "I think her friendly crush on me may have shifted to you. Not that I can blame her."

"She's pretty cool. I love your friends. And it was handy to have someone to help in the dressing room."

"Oh really?" he chuckled, as he stepped toward me. "What exactly did she help you with?"

"All kinds of things. She was very *hands on*. I already told you I loved your friends."

"And I'm sure they love you just as much as…" he trailed off, but I saw the momentary hesitation in his voice as he tried to play that off as a whole statement, not something that was going to be followed with a confession we may not be ready to make. "Can I see what you bought?"

"Nope," I shook my head, wanting to keep it a secret until the last minute. I was even planning to lock him out of the bathroom tomorrow while I got ready. "You can wait until tomorrow night. A girl must have some surprises under her belt. It might be a garter belt in this case."

"Sunshine, come on," he growled playfully as he leaned down, nipping at my neck. He could try to persuade me as much as he wanted, but I wasn't budging. He could wait, and I knew the anticipation would kill him, which only added to my fun.

THIRTY

Nathan

Boston

Kelly was in a great mood when she returned from her shopping trip with Talia. It'd made me smile as I watched the two of them interact for a few moments until Talia had quickly retreated. It was on the tip of my tongue to ask what they'd talked about, but Kelly would tell me if she wanted me to know. It was clear from her refusal to tell me what she'd bought that she wanted to keep their day private.

Taking a deep breath, I accepted that she didn't have to or need to tell me everything and kissed her neck softly before I leaned back.

"I can wait. I'm sure it's worth all the teasing I know you'll do between now and then."

Although, as she stepped past me, looking adorable in her long black skirt, I couldn't resist patting her on the ass.

"Hey," she giggled as she turned around and teasingly pointed her finger at me. "You back off, mister."

"Just appreciating your lovely skirt." I held my hands up in surrender, tilting my head as I studied said skirt further. Was my naughty girl bare underneath? "Although you seem to be missing something."

"I don't know what you're talking about," she stuttered out, but I could tell from the pink in her cheeks that she'd been caught out.

"Are you wearing panties, sunshine? Because I don't think you are. What exactly happened with Talia this afternoon? Do I need to be worried about my best friend's partner stealing my girlfr..." I cut myself off again as her eyes widened.

"You think I did something with Talia?"

"No," I chuckled, stepping forward and wrapping my arms around her waist. "But quit changing the subject. Where're your panties, Kelly?"

"In my purse."

"And they're in your purse and not on your bottom because?"

301

"I'm not telling you," she giggled as she tilted her head back to look at me. "But other than taking off my bra, Talia didn't touch me."

"She did what?" I laughed, confused at that little nugget of information. "Why did she take off your bra?"

"Nunya," she laughed as my fingers crept underneath the front waistband of her skirt.

"Oh, it's my business," I whispered in her ear, lowering my voice. "You told me who you belonged to, and last I checked, it wasn't Talia."

"Well, I let you put it in my butt yesterday, so I get a free pass," she laughed, unfazed by the tone in my voice. "Quit being nosy."

I growled, reaching down to squeeze her ass cheek, causing her to jump and try to wiggle free. "Hate to break it to you, sunshine. But that pass only lasts twenty-four hours. So, if you want another pass, you gotta let me in that ass."

"You first," she laughed, pulling my fingers from beneath her waistband and turning around. "I recall someone telling me that they'd reconsider one of their soft limits."

"I'm still alright with that," I nodded, fully intending to explore pegging with her since she'd been so open to trying anal. "But it's gonna take some planning."

"Well, you're in luck," she smiled with a naughty glint in her eyes. Reaching around me, she rummaged in one of the paper bags at her feet, pulling out a square package. "I happen to have a brand-new beginner plug right here." She pressed it into my hands with a little eyebrow wiggle and bit her bottom lip as she waited for my reaction. When I turned my attention to the package in my hands, turning it over to check out her new acquisition, she went on. "And, I may have smuggled something out of my brother's closet for you."

Unable to hold in my laughter, I shook my head at her, not knowing she'd taken the pegging vibrator from Evan's house while she was packing. Naughty, naughty little minx. "That just sounds so wrong on so many levels."

"Oh, come on, the package was still sealed. They weren't going to use it. He may let Chase spank him on the ass with a wooden spoon, but I doubt he's letting her shove anything up there."

"This conversation is all kinds of enlightening," I grinned, breaking the seal on the package. "Do go on."

302

"Bite me," she scoffed at my teasing, rolling her eyes. I knew she'd caught her misbehavior because they widened almost comically as she took a step backward.

"We've talked about the eye-rolling, Kelly. Didn't you learn your lesson?" I teased as I stepped forward, causing her to bump into the counter behind her. "And we both know I have no problem biting you. Just tell me where and how hard."

"Do you want a little love bite here?" I continued as I leaned down, nibbling on her collarbone playfully.

"Or maybe you want me to bite those pretty pink nipples?" I said, reaching behind her to set down the package and cupping her breast, my thumb rubbing over one suggestively. She squirmed against me with wide eyes as I leaned forward to whisper in her ear.

"Or do you want me to suck and bite on that tasty clit of yours? You know you love it when I use my teeth."

Ignoring the little gasp she let out in response, I went in for the kill, my lips against her earlobe as I grasped her hips in my hands. "Oh, I know. You want me to bite the back of your neck while I'm fucking your tight pussy right before I fill you with my cum."

She leaned back, panting as I held her captive. "Well, damn. I need to be a brat more often if that's your response."

Dropping my hands and taking a step back, I tsked at her. "Or maybe I'll just let you imagine all those for the next twenty-four hours while you're not allowed to cum."

Her mouth dropped open, her eyes widening in surprise.

"Close your mouth, sunshine. Or I'll fill it for you. I said you weren't allowed to cum, not me." I chuckled, and she snapped it closed before glaring at me.

"You're just mean," she pouted.

Taking a step forward, I grasped her hip, pulling her forward into my chest. "No, you need to mind your mouth, and this is just further incentive to do that." I told her, tucking a hair that'd fallen from her ponytail behind her ear and kissing her nose.

She laid her head on my chest, snuggling in closer.

I took the opportunity to let my hands roam, confirming my assumption from earlier when I traced my palm over her ass. "But you still didn't tell me why you're not wearing panties, sunshine. Such a naughty little slut."

She giggled, pressing her forehead into my chest, but she didn't deny it.

Knowing that I'd pushed her hard with her first scene in my playroom, I didn't try to initiate anything sexual with Kelly, despite her lack of undergarments lingering in my brain. I had to trust she had a good reason, and she was fully covered, so if she wanted to wander around town without panties, I wouldn't try to convince her otherwise. I knew things would likely heat up at or after the party, so I could be patient until then.

"So, I want to call in that promise," she said as we sat on the couch after eating dinner, pulling up Netflix.

"Hmmm?" I hummed as I scrolled through the menu screen.

"You know that note you left on your checklist about the anal limits. I held up my end of the bargain..."

Slowly turning toward her, I could see how tense her body language was, her fingers idly twisting the skirt's material in her lap, her jaw tense. "Relax, sunshine. Ask for what you want."

"I want to..." She made a little hip thrust and poked her finger through a circle she made with the opposite hand.

"If you can't say it out loud, I can't give you an answer." While she fidgeted, I leaned back into the corner of the couch, calmly watching her.

"But..."

"Stuff?" I teased, enjoying how she narrowed her eyes at me and huffed. I was just waiting for the eye roll, but she managed to hold back.

"You think you're so cute, don't you? Making me uncomfortable."

"Don't turn this around on me. If you want something, you need to own it. You need to be assertive and use your words. What do you want from me?"

She took a deep breath, squaring her shoulders and looking me in the eyes. "I want to peg you."

"Good girl, sunshine," I praised, and she immediately ducked her head, suddenly shy again. "Don't look away. This isn't anything to be ashamed of. Talk to me." I grasped her hand, pulling her forward until she settled in my lap. "That was very brave, but now we need to plan what you want. So tell me, what's your fantasy?"

"Maybe tomorrow you can wear the plug while we're at the party, and when we get back home…"

When she didn't finish, after a moment, I asked the question she was hesitant to ask herself. "You can fuck me?" She nodded, but we needed to work on her asking for what she wanted. "If you want to fuck me, Kelly, tell me."

She leaned in toward my ear, her hand grasping the opposite side of my neck. "I want to fuck you after the party, Nathan."

"Fuck," I exhaled as I grasped her hips, turning her to straddle me.

"Not tonight," she laughed, using her fingers to brush back my hair. "But I'm looking forward to it tomorrow."

"Me too, sunshine." And I meant that.

After relaxing on the couch for a few hours, I knew I needed to give her my gift as we got ready for bed. Ducking back into my playroom while she was using the bathroom, I pulled the little black satin pouch out of the drawer I'd hidden it inside.

I'd only ever collared one submissive before, not taking that commitment lightly. Still, even then, it may have been premature because she met someone else and dissolved our contract a few months later. I knew Marisa had wanted me to collar her, often commenting on other people at parties and even wearing a leather choker when we went out, but I never gave her one. It may have indicated she was ready to play, but it didn't mark her as mine.

With Kelly, I wanted that commitment. Not because she was leaving, and I was grasping at ways to tie her to me — sometimes literally — but because she made me feel like I was capable of forming a lasting, loving connection with someone and incorporating play into it. I didn't have to settle for someone who didn't understand all sides of me, and I didn't have to hide my desires to do that either.

She'd been open to learning new things, she'd even asked me about rope resources when we'd spoken about what I wanted in a dynamic, but the fact she wanted to look at training was sexy and such a green flag for me. Kelly wasn't taking this lifestyle as a whim, and she was trying to see if she could fit into my needs. For once, it wasn't just about my submissive and me meeting their needs, she wanted to be a partner, and as a Switch, that was my deepest desire. To have someone crave fulfilling my needs as I did theirs.

It also didn't hurt that the little peeks of Kelly trying to channel her inner dominant energy was sexy as fuck. I'd come so hard the other night when she had her hand over my mouth, using me for her enjoyment. I wanted more of that. I *needed* more of that, and for once, I didn't have a lingering sense of apprehension behind my actions other than knowing that our time together in person would soon be interrupted.

Kelly was sitting on the edge of the bed when I walked back into the room, looking adorable in one of her slouchy sweaters and a pair of pink panties. The pair I destroyed clearly hadn't been her only one of that color, and I wanted to buy her an endless supply — just so I could continue to tear them off her body.

"You look a little lost, sunshine. Everything alright?"

Her gaze snapped to mine, a soft smile pulling at her lips. "I'm good. Just thinking about everything that's happened in the last month. I don't even feel like the same person anymore."

The bed bounced lightly as I sat next to her, the black satin pouch tucked into my pocket. Kelly leaned her head against my shoulder and sighed, and I finally realized that I didn't feel like the same person I was before I met her. This change had been coming for months, and her getting stuck in that hotel room door had been the catalyst.

While she was eager to jump into our dynamic to learn about this lifestyle, I didn't want to be egotistical, thinking it was only so she could be with me, but I knew that it was. Something between us made us want to do things we'd had a hard time doing with others. I'd always been hesitant to let anyone get too close, even in my dynamics, so I'd structured my interactions to make excuses to keep people at a distance on a personal level. Kelly had thrown herself into her career to avoid having to focus on the future, effectively shutting herself off as well.

"I don't feel like I'm the same person either," I admitted, grasping her hand. Her fingers were soft and warm in my hand, their weight helping to ground me. This was fast, but I knew it was the right decision. "I've got something I want to give you."

Her eyes snapped to mine as she shifted sideways to look directly at me. "Should I be worried?"

Humor was her shining trait and her ability to make people smile. I knew she didn't think anyone took her seriously because of it, but it only made me more drawn to her.

"I hope you're not. I'm not," I confessed. Reaching in my pocket, I pulled out the pouch, using my finger to open the drawstring. "Typically, this wouldn't be something brought up this early in a dynamic, but I don't want to wait for some predetermined time. How I feel about you can't be validated because some measure of time is deemed appropriate. We can work our way up to a more permanent one, but I didn't want to wait to give you a symbol of my commitment."

Kelly's breath caught as I raised my hand to her face, my knuckle tracing over her cheekbone lightly.

"Do you remember what we talked about during the card game about collaring? When you were asking me questions about types of collars and what they meant?"

She nodded, her eyes wide, but her fingers gripped mine, so I knew she was listening to everything I was saying to her.

"We don't have to go into that party tomorrow with you collared if you don't want it, but..." Pulling my hand from her grasp, I opened the pouch and dumped the contents into my other palm. "I want you to have this collar of consideration to symbolize what you mean to me and what we're working toward. I meant it when I said you were precious. There isn't any pressure to wear it tomorrow. You can put it on when you're ready, but I want you to know that I'm devoted to this, and I don't want this relationship to be temporary. I know I told you that at first, but I wasn't completely truthful with you because I was scared of rejection. So this is a physical reminder and a promise of my commitment to you on this journey." And something she could take with her to remember me when she left.

When I looked up again, Kelly's fingertips were pressed to her mouth, her eyes glistening as she stared at the small pendant in my palm. The tiny diamond mounted in the gold of the sun charm glittered slightly in the dim light cast from the lamps on my nightstands.

"It's beautiful," she whispered, reaching forward to trace the outer edge of the mandala design. It was an intricate openwork sun surrounded by a crescent moon, with a single diamond in the center.

I'd chosen a thin leather cord for the short necklace, with a gold hoop in the center that the pendant hung from.

It wasn't as blatant as some got with their collars, resembling more of a day collar, but it was clear what it meant to anyone who was looking. Kelly was committed to a dominant, and no one would approach her to play as long as she wore it.

"There's no pressure from me, but it's yours. We can go into that party tomorrow and this will put you under my protection. I want you to wear this as long as you want to keep exploring this dynamic with me," I whispered as I turned her palm over and placed the pendant inside, closing her fingers over it. Her forehead was creased with emotion as I looked back into her eyes, and I watched as a single tear tracked over her cheek, my thumb catching it before it could fall any further. "I don't want you to cry, sunshine."

She sniffled loudly before opening her hand and pushing it back toward me. I had a momentary surge of panic as she offered it back.

"Please put it on for me."

Kelly's breathing was choppy as I shifted back on the mattress, gently taking the necklace from her outstretched palm. My fingers gathered her hair, and she reached back to hold it as I raised the necklace in front of her. I watched as the gold ring settled at the hollow of her throat, satisfaction rolling through me as I fastened the clasp at the back of her neck, kissing it lightly before I wrapped my arms around her waist from behind. "It looks perfect on you. Thank you for wearing it."

"I don't want to take it off," she whispered as her fingers moved up to rub the charm.

"It's yours," I promised as I cupped my hand over the back of hers, enjoying the way she instinctively leaned her head back against my shoulder.

Now, she not only had my heart, she had my mark of commitment to this dynamic as well, and I found myself falling even more.

THIRTY-ONE

Kelly

Boston

My fingers toyed with the pendant at my throat, my thumb slowly rubbing over the smooth facet of the diamond in the center. When Nathan had surprised me with the collar last night, there hadn't been any question in my mind that I would wear it. I knew I was ready for wherever things would take us. I may not have been prepared to tell him my feelings aloud, but I loved him. From what he'd explained to me, this was an entry level collar as my training began, and we could potentially move toward more permanent collars as our relationship grew, but it was the most special gift I'd ever received.

"You ready to go?" Nathan asked as he wrapped his arm around my waist from behind, resting his chin on my shoulder.

His eyes met mine in the bathroom mirror, and as our gazes locked, I felt my nerves start to melt away. I was ready for this, and knowing that I was going there with him, claiming me fully in his life, cemented my desire to keep moving on this journey together.

"I'm ready."

His answering smile was enough to make me want to show him what I'd been hiding under my dress and spend the night in the playroom instead, but I wanted to see how this relationship worked in the real world — in his world — and to do that, I had to trust him.

Instead of leaving his Jeep parked on the street overnight, we took an Uber to Emory's photography studio, silently holding hands in the back seat. I still had a million unanswered questions running through my mind, but I didn't want to make it weird for the stranger driving the car.

"You still with me, sunshine?" Nathan asked as the driver switched on their turn indicator, pulling into a parking spot in front of a brick building with a row of storefronts.

"Let's go." I nodded, taking his hand as he stepped out of the car. The rain from the previous week had finally faded away, but there was a chill in the air as he tucked me under his arm and we made our way toward a darkened storefront.

"Do you want my jacket?" he whispered into my hair as I shivered, but I shook my head.

"I'd rather you kept me warm yourself."

His answering chuckle was worth the cheeky response, and his gruff whisper of '*behave*' in my ear sent a shiver down my spine that had nothing to do with the cold.

As we approached the door, he reached forward to quickly type a passcode into an electronic pad mounted next to it, and a soft click sounded before he pulled the door open, ushering me inside.

"They're probably in the playroom. Let's hope they're not fucking," Nathan chuckled as he glanced down at me, laughing harder at the way my eyes widened. "I was joking, but it wouldn't be the first time they made us late that way. Those two are insatiable sometimes."

"Hmm," I hummed nervously, but Nathan's naughty grin let me know he was on to me.

"Unless you'd like to watch, in which case I'm sure they'd be down for us to be tardy."

"Are you trying to embarrass me again?" I squeaked, hiding my face against the material of Nathan's suit jacket.

"No," he whispered, his breath hot on my neck. "I'm telling you that if you want to watch them fuck before the play party, I can ask them. Chances are pretty good Talia would be into it."

Looking up into his eyes, I shook my head. "I'm not ready for that."

"But you're ready for tonight?" The apprehension in his gaze belied his chuckle behind the words. I knew he was worried that what happened tonight would scare me or make me change my mind about it or him.

"I don't know how to explain it. Seeing strangers doing something and seeing friends doing something are different for me. I'm not saying I'd never want to watch them…"

Suddenly feeling vulnerable, I averted my gaze, stepping toward the curtain that led to the rear of the studio. I didn't know what was back there, but I knew moving forward wouldn't make me feel as nervous as thinking about that line of conversation further.

"Wait." I paused as Nathan tugged my hand, turning back to look at him. "I get it, Kelly. I see you. Don't worry." His lips grazed my knuckles as he pulled my hand to his lips. "Say 'matrix' and I take you home tonight. Don't forget that. If you want to go, we go. No questions asked."

Swallowing past the nerves in my throat, I nodded, following when he pulled me into his chest and kissed my forehead.

"Breathe, sunshine. I've got you."

Talia and Nathan kept the car ride lively, teasing each other as I clung to his hand, my mind racing with scenarios of how the night might play out.

"You're doing great." I snapped out of my daze at the gentle comment from Emory, who was seated behind me in the back of the small luxury SUV. He'd been quiet, only joining the conversation when dragged in, and I could appreciate his thoughtful presence. He seemed to take everything in despite his silence.

"Thanks," I whispered over my shoulder as Nathan squeezed my hand, still talking to Talia, who was seated behind him.

"Just keep an open mind going in. It's not as scary as it seems, and this one won't be too crude. Our host is more into control, and less into dark kinks."

He said that now, but I was still picturing red rooms and dungeons with chains hanging from the walls, even though I knew that wasn't likely as the car turned onto a long, tree-lined driveway. A metal gate loomed ahead, and I took a deep breath as we passed through it and pulled up in front of a large, two-story, brick house moments later.

"You still with me, sunshine?" Nathan whispered as he wrapped his arm around my shoulder and pulled me close enough to kiss the top of my head. Despite my hot girl armor, I felt a little exposed, so I appreciated his reassurance more than I could articulate. "We can go back home if you've changed your mind."

Using his fingertip, he wrapped a curl around his finger and leaned forward so he could look me in the eye. "We can take this plug out, and I'll let you act out your little fantasy." I felt my face heat up when the back seat occupants were silent, Talia likely listening to Nathan's low, suggestive words. His lips hovered over my ear, his voice deep and seductive as he whispered. "I have to

311

admit, the thought of you fucking me is making it hard to keep myself under control."

Blowing out a heavy breath, I turned my face, my lips grazing his before leaning toward his ear. "I hope the thought of me inside you makes you ache."

A rumbling growl built in his chest as he grasped my ponytail, tilting my head backward. Knowing that Talia and Emory were being held captive to witness this exchange made things more exciting. "You're already inside me, but I trust you, sunshine. I'll follow your lead tonight."

Nodding, I breathed out as the car stopped, Talia impatiently shifting in her seat as Nathan reached for the door handle, looking back over his shoulder at me. "You ready?"

"Yup. Let's do this," I nodded, swallowing hard as my heart started to pound.

From the outside, the stately brick mansion in front of me reminded me of some of the older homes in Evanston, but with more of a sprawling colonial façade than the Victorian mansions back home. It screamed wealth and power, and I was curious to see who this Daddy Dom was. He clearly had done very well for himself.

Nathan's hand slipped into mine as we approached the front door. A few other cars were parked in the long circular drive, but the front porch was quiet as Emory stepped in front of us to ring the doorbell. The ridiculously dramatic part of my brain was envisioning either a stuffy old butler answering the door or a scantily dressed woman. When the door swung inward, it was neither.

While Nathan was tall — towering over most men — this guy was bigger, both in stature and build, his muscles bulging in his tailored suit. I'd been around enough executives to know what he was wearing wasn't off the rack, and his suit was tailored to accentuate his biceps and thick thighs.

Glancing to my right, Talia was biting her lip, but as soon as she noticed my gaze, she wiggled her eyebrows, winking before she unsubtly fanned her face. Our host was hot. And he fit the stereotypical mold of what I'd imagine a 'Daddy' to look like. His salt and pepper hair was styled a little shorter than Nathan's, but he had the sides and back trimmed closely, showing off a small tattoo on the side of his neck that led into his shirt collar. A few other hints of tattoos peeked out the bottom of the cuffs at his wrists. While he looked polished and professional, it was with an edge.

"Gage, glad you could make it." His deep voice was warmer than I expected as he reached forward to shake Emory's hand, tugging him along a step. Emory may have had the imposing Dom stare down, but even this guy managed to make him smile.

"Grayson, glad you invited us. Talia's been talking about it all week," he smiled as he looked back to where Talia had schooled her features into a more submissive expression.

"Missi has been excited about finally getting to show off this house. I think the nesting has started," Grayson laughed, stepping back and gesturing for us to come inside.

Emory and Talia led us inside, she a step behind him, holding his outstretched hand with her gaze focused on his back.

Grayson turned his attention to us, smiling widely as he extended his hand toward Nathan. "Nathan Harrison, good to finally meet you."

Nathan tilted his head to the side, frowning as Grayson shook his hand firmly. "I'm sorry, do we know each other?"

"Nope," Grayson smiled, a dark eyebrow arching. "But I need to thank you regardless."

"I'm not following." Nathan sounded a little suspicious, and I squeezed his hand. Emory and Talia waited for us inside the large entryway, watching Grayson and Nathan with matching frowns. They clearly had no idea what this little exchange was either.

"Come in and I'll introduce you to my fiancée. I guess in a roundabout way; you're the reason we're together. Sorry for all the cloak and dagger. I promise Mr. Gage didn't know who she was before my invitation. But I hope you'll all stay for the party anyway. Missi has been exhausted lately, so I doubt she'll stay up for the fun."

Grayson beckoned us inside, closing the door behind us. As we walked into a large living room, quite a few people were already mingling with drinks in their hands, but I couldn't shake the uneasiness that'd taken root with our strange introduction.

"Do you know what's going on?" I asked Nathan quietly as we followed Emory and Talia toward a table set off to the side of the entryway.

"Not a fucking clue," he shook his head.

There was a release form for us to sign that our attendance was consensual and that we gave permission for our likenesses to be captured on film and uploaded to a confidential server. Only the people in attendance tonight would have access to the video footage, but the thought still made me pause. Anyone caught distributing footage would be in violation of the non-disclosure agreement and subject to legal action. It also asked that people not try to film with their phones or personal cameras because they would be escorted off the premises if they were caught.

"There are people filming this?"

"Yeah," Nathan nodded, signing his form and handing it off to the young guy manning the table. "There sometimes are at these kinds of gatherings. You can request not to be included if it will bother you. Everyone here tonight signed one of these, and no one wants to be blackballed from invitation lists, so you don't have to worry about it being leaked anywhere."

I blew out a breath and signed the form, turning back toward the large living space. It was very modern in comparison to the traditional façade of the house; the interior had clearly been updated recently.

Nathan grasped my hand and followed Emory and Talia toward the toward the bar on the other side of the room, gesturing with a raised eyebrow. "Can I get you anything?"

"No. Well, maybe just water. Gotta keep my intake up." I winked as he smirked and shook his head at me.

"Never thought I'd find someone so excited about hydration. I think you're the quickest coffee addict I've ever seen jump ship to water without hesitation."

"What can I say?" I laughed, leaning my head against his arm. "Proper hydration is sexy."

"I think you just like it that I cum more when I'm hydrated," he whispered.

"What a coincidence," I murmured as I used his tie to pull him closer. "So do I."

His lips grazed my ear as he wrapped his arm around my back, squeezing my hip. "We'll make a squirter out of you yet, sunshine. Drink up."

"Mmm, sounds like someone talks a big game."

"If we didn't already have plans for later, I'd say we could get started on practicing tonight. I almost had you there once before. I can do it again." He nipped my ear, lowering his voice even further. "And again…and again."

Looking up at him, I still couldn't believe that he was mine. Bringing my free hand up to my neck, I nervously ran my thumb across the pendant hanging from my collar. "If you're not ready for later…"

Nathan shook his head slightly, leaning down, so his lips caressed my earlobe. "I'm ready. I wouldn't have agreed to it if I didn't trust you and want to share it with you. We talked through it. I'm prepared."

"Just," I sighed, taking a deep breath. "I don't want you to feel pressured because it was something I wanted to try."

"While I truly do appreciate the concern and that you value enthusiastic consent as I do, I promise I'm ready. If this plug in my ass is any indication, I should be in for a wild ride later."

Nathan chuckled at the blush that rose to my cheeks, his thumb slowly traversing the warm skin before he leaned down and kissed my temple.

"But let's enjoy the party first. We've got plenty of time for you to play with my ass later," he chuckled.

I nodded, holding his gaze while his fingers traced down the sleeve of my dress suggestively and the rest of my arm, grasping my hand, interlacing our fingers.

The intense stare was broken by a throat clearing, our slightly intimidating host, Grayson, standing next to us with a woman standing closely behind him. The only indication she was with him was the small feminine hand wrapped around his bicep, a sizable diamond sparkling on her ring finger.

"Nathan, I'm sorry to interrupt, but I'd like to request a moment of your time in a more private setting."

Nathan glanced toward me briefly with a look of confusion before he responded. "Is there something wrong?"

Grayson leaned in closer, his voice quiet. "My fiancée would like to speak with you, and I thought you'd both like some privacy. You're welcome to bring your guest if you'd like."

Before Nathan could respond, the woman standing behind Grayson shifted and Nathan's hand tightened against mine as her face came into view.

"Excuse me," Nathan said gruffly before he tugged me a few paces away.

Emory and Talia joined us moments later, both staring over at Grayson and his mysterious fiancée. I still felt at a loss, but clearly they knew who she was. And gauging the situation by their slightly distressed expressions, this was not a happy discussion.

"Did you know he was engaged to *her*?" Nathan hissed at Emory, his expression angry.

"No idea, I promise," Emory responded as he pulled Talia into his side. "I knew he had a pregnant fiancée but not that the Missi he kept talking about was Marisa."

"I'm sorry I insisted we come tonight," Talia sighed, and Emory pulled her in closer and kissed her temple.

"I don't think any of us knew this was a ruse for her to get me alone," Nathan responded, looking over my shoulder, his face pained. I knew pieces of what had gone down with his ex, but maybe this would be a way for him to put his anger about the situation out of his mind for good.

Nathan turned me toward him, pulling me into his chest and using his finger to tilt my chin upward. "We can leave if you want to. If this is too much for you, we can walk out that door right now. I don't owe her a thing, and she doesn't get to manipulate us to get what she wants."

Out of the corner of my eye, I saw the petite blonde woman cradling her distended stomach, watching the four of us with a somber expression. I wanted to be mad at her, furious that she continued to manipulate Nathan even after their relationship had dissipated. I knew that the way things ended bothered him and that he was concerned for her well-being, not because he still had feelings, but because he was a kind person.

Nathan didn't like to manipulate or lie to people, and I knew she'd hurt him deeply by violating his boundaries. He'd been honest with me about what he wanted for his future. And while part of me would always mourn the child I'd never been given the privilege of meeting; I was at peace with knowing I'd never be a mother. And I knew Nathan would support me as I tried to heal the little broken pieces of my heart that my miscarriage had left behind.

Talia stepped in beside us, laying her palm against my back as she talked to Nathan. "I'll watch over Kelly while you take care of this. I see a few people I can introduce her to. You know Mar won't let this go. If you don't do this now, she'll keep trying."

"It's alright if you want to talk to her," I whispered as I reached up to cup his cheek. His jaw flexed underneath my palm, and I wanted to take all this stress away from him. "She clearly has things she needs to say to you. I'll be safe with Talia. If you want to, go speak to her."

"But..." he trailed off as he closed his eyes, his chest heaving. "I don't want to leave you."

"I'll be fine," I assured him, as I trailed my thumb across his cheekbone.

"Fuck," he sighed as he clenched his jaw, shaking his head before he looked over at Talia. "Don't let her out of your sight."

I wanted to laugh at his possessive comment, but I knew it was only because he was concerned about my reaction to this whole situation. While it appeared from the outside to be an innocent cocktail party, I'd seen enough women wearing almost scandalously cut dresses and various people with collars around their necks to know this was just the precursor of what was to come.

"I can scare away anyone undesirable with my resting bitch face. We'll be fine." She nodded toward where our hosts were still waiting for an answer. "Grayson seems to be watching her every move. I don't think she's going to try anything shady."

Grayson nodded at me as I glanced over at him. I knew he was only trying to ensure his partner got the closure she needed. Maybe it'd help Nathan let go of his resentment toward Marisa. We both deserved to continue this relationship without old baggage weighing us down.

"Look at me, stud," I murmured, smiling at how his eyes softened when his gaze met mine. "Go say what you need to say, and then we can move on, together."

His eyes scanned my face, his jaw clenching before he nodded once, leaning forward to peck my lips. Nathan blew out a deep breath and released my hand, walking quickly toward Grayson with Emory following close behind.

317

THIRTY-TWO

Nathan

Boston

Talia tugged Kelly away from me, walking across the room to a group of people I recognized from some local munches. Even though I was hesitant to walk away from her in a room full of people unfamiliar to her, I knew she was right. I did need to put this in my past. Kelly was my future.

"Let's talk somewhere with a little more privacy," Grayson suggested as he grasped Marisa's hand and turned toward a hallway tucked off to the side of the expansive living room. Marisa clung to his arm as he took measured steps, clearly slowing his stride for her benefit.

"You alright with this?" Emory whispered as we followed them down the hallway side by side.

"Don't think I have an option at this point," I hissed back as Grayson stopped at a closed door and pulled a key from his pocket, quickly unlocking it and pushing it open.

"I guess you hear what she wants, and we'll decide if we leave afterward." Em responded before we reached the door, slipping in after the other two.

"Emory and I will stay here as representatives," Grayson told us as he released Marisa's hand and she walked toward a set of windows along the edge of the large room that appeared to be Grayson's office. "Care for a drink, Mr. Gage?"

Emory squeezed my arm as I turned to follow Marisa, giving me a loaded look that he'd be watching. I appreciated having him here. With both witnesses in the room, one being Marisa's fiancé, I knew she'd likely behave herself. I just wasn't sure if I cared to hear what she had to say.

"You wanted to speak to me?" I asked as I stepped around her toward the windows that overlooked the expansive backyard.

"I know you probably hate me, but I just wanted to tell you that I was sorry," Marisa spoke quietly, staring at the floor as she stood next to me, her voice soft. I couldn't tell if she was playing up her submissive nature or if she was truly repentant.

"I don't hate you. I just want nothing to do with you. What you and Grace did was completely unacceptable. Period. End of discussion."

"I know. It was absolutely terrible," she nodded, finally looking up at me. "But I needed to apologize to you personally."

"To make yourself feel better?" I hissed, feeling guilty momentarily as she flinched, but I was tired of tempering my feelings to please others. "What exactly is the point of cornering me at a party you lured me to under false pretenses to do that? I'm here with someone else. I've moved on. And you need to do the same."

"I know. I've moved on too, but what I did to you and Grace was disgusting. I'm disgusted with myself. My first instinct was to blame it on the hormones, but that's really a cop-out. I was jealous. There isn't any other reason than that. I wasn't enough for you, and it made me jealous that you went to Grace for what I couldn't give you."

"Don't make this about me. You clearly went to other men to get what you needed outside our dynamic. And you wanted something you knew I was *never* going to give you," I said, nodding at her stomach. She'd known going in that children were not in my future. I hadn't lied or misled her.

A large part of me was thankful for having done what I needed to protect myself, so I wasn't tied to Marisa's manipulative behavior for the rest of my life. A smaller part was sad for her, that she'd been that desperate she lied to and manipulated me, and likely Grayson too, in order to get what she wanted — a child.

"You're right. I did. I thought you'd change your mind. And I thought I could be enough for you, but I was wrong about that too."

"We were doomed to fail from the beginning because you lied to me. I was only ever honest with you about what I wanted in a partner."

"I don't want to get in a fight with you. You've clearly made your choice. But you lied to me too," she hissed, her tone accusing. "You never told me about the vasectomy. Ever. Not once."

My jaw clenched at the ire in her voice. But it hadn't been any of her business. Maybe that should have indicated how our relationship was doomed to fail because I'd never wanted to confide in her about it. She didn't know much about my past. And I'd never shared with her about my parents and their toxic marriage.

"Because it should have been enough for you to know that I was upfront about children being off the table. I shouldn't have to justify or explain my life choices to you. Consent isn't just about sex, Mar. You know this."

Marisa took a deep breath, her hand sliding down to cradle her belly. I could tell I was stressing her out, but she knew I wouldn't sugarcoat it. That wasn't who I was. Not when we were together and certainly not after what she'd done.

"I told Grace everything when she contacted me after you left." Her eyes were fixed on the floor at her quiet confession. "She won't speak to me now."

"Good. You manipulated her too. She didn't deserve to be misled like that." As much as I had trouble seeing it at the time, Grace had been just as violated by Marisa's manipulations as I had. It didn't change things between us because I had no desire to rope model for her again, but Grace didn't deserve to shoulder all the blame. She made shitty decisions regarding the false information she was fed, but she thought she was helping in some warped way. I knew Grace had been adopted and was in foster care for a long time prior to that, so I wasn't sure if this fed into her abandonment issues.

"I thought he was yours," she whispered. "I didn't know."

"Thinking and wishing are two different things. Does *he* know you thought his son was mine?" I nodded toward Grayson, who was watching us from his seat in the corner of the room as he sat next to Emory. He didn't seem to be upset by us talking, but he was concerned for his pregnant fiancée. I didn't want to be callous toward Marisa purposefully, but I also wasn't going to lie to her to make her feel better. She'd made some stupid fucked up decisions, and things could have turned out badly for her. Being poly, Grayson seemed to be a better fit for her because she technically hadn't cheated on anyone, but she had lied to and manipulated her partners. If I were in his position, I don't know if I could have been so quick to forgive.

"He does. That's why he extended the invitation for you to come tonight. He knew I wanted to apologize."

"You could have picked a less dramatic way to do that. Kelly didn't deserve to be blindsided by an ex with an agenda." Kelly

320

would have been justified if she'd asked to leave since we were lured here to please Marisa. It'd started her first experience at a party like this on a sour note. I didn't want her to feel self-conscious about being here.

"I didn't know you were going to bring another woman with you," she whispered, and I clenched my jaw at the blatant jealousy in her tone. "You love her, don't you?"

"I do," I confirmed.

"And I saw you collared her? This early? Are you sure she'll be enough for you?" Marisa's fingers fell to the diamond choker at her neck, and I held back the snide comment about the public display of her relationship status. I doubted Grayson's was a collar of consideration or protection, so she understood the gravity of what was hanging around her neck. In our world, a collar like the one she was wearing meant more than any ring on her finger.

I wasn't sure how long she'd been involved with Grayson, but as far as I knew, she hadn't been with him when our dynamic started. While I'd agreed to an open relationship, she also hadn't told me about her other partners. Grayson might have been one of many.

"When you meet the right person, it doesn't matter how long you've known them."

She nodded, reaching forward to cup my elbow. "I'm glad you found that. Truly. I am. But don't do to her what you did to me. Let her go if you think she can't meet what you need in a partner."

Looking down at Marisa, I saw the damage I'd unintentionally caused. Some of it because I saw the warning signs and ignored them, and some of it because she wasn't honest with me. Kelly had already been upfront with me about things Marisa and I never talked about. I knew Mar had been upset by my arrangement with Grace, but she never told me that directly. There hadn't been any limitations when we'd agreed to allow play with other people outside of our relationship.

Not wanting to hurt Marisa's feelings, I just nodded, but I already knew that the dominance I'd craved in a partner was starting to manifest in Kelly. I wouldn't need to find it elsewhere. My sunshine still had a long way to go, and we'd need to figure out where she could train with a rigger in Chicago, but she was open and willing to do that for me. That spoke volumes about her intentions. Mar had never been interested in learning about bondage past letting me tie her.

"I'll leave you alone now. Thank you for letting me apologize." Marisa released my elbow and stepped back, rubbing her hand over her belly. She looked tired.

"Consider yourself forgiven," I told her, "but I'm not likely to forget. Please learn your lesson and stop manipulating people to get what you want. It's distasteful behavior, and you're capable of better."

Marisa nodded, sniffling and wiping the corner of her eye.

Unable to stand next to her anymore, I excused myself, walking directly from the room without a glance toward Grayson. I wasn't exactly a fan of his behavior either, but he was willing to forgive her, so I wasn't dwelling on anything except getting back to Kelly.

Emory fell into step beside me silently and I appreciated that he knew I was done talking about Marisa. Kelly was everything I wanted in a partner, so I wasn't going to focus on the past any longer.

As I turned the corner back into the living room, Kelly looked up, her fingers rubbing the center stone of her pendant as she made eye contact with me. I loved that she'd been doing that since I put it on her, unconsciously rubbing the stone when she was thinking of me. Not stopping until I reached her, I wrapped my arms around her waist, tucking my face into her neck, trying to calm down.

We'd been looking forward to tonight, and I wouldn't let Marisa take that from me either.

"You alright?" Kelly whispered as she leaned into my embrace.

"I will be. Don't let her ruin tonight."

I closed my eyes, soaking in her presence until a loud throat-clearing drew the room's attention.

"Thank you all for coming tonight. I'm going to tuck my beautiful fiancée into bed, but everyone is more than welcome to stay and enjoy the rest of the refreshments or explore downstairs," Grayson announced from the foot of the staircase that led to the second floor, Marisa's hand clasped tightly inside his.

"Want to go explore?" I asked, pulling Kelly away from the small group of people who'd kept talking despite the interruption. Talia gave me a loaded look, ensuring I was alright, but I shook my head. I wasn't dwelling on meddling exes or things that'd happened in the past. I was ready to move forward.

Knowing Marisa wasn't staying for the rest of the party made it easier for me to encourage Kelly to explore.

"Let's go." Kelly nodded, tugging me toward the staircase to the basement. There were plenty of places for us to steal some quiet time down there, most of the guests continuing to drink and talk on the main floor.

Watching her reactions, I could tell she was intrigued. On the outside, it looked like any other basement in a high-end mansion; expensive paintings hung on the walls, elaborate crown moldings, and hand-carved beautifully stained doors. The creative spirit in me could appreciate the work that'd gone into this beautiful house, but it paled in comparison to the beauty I was standing beside.

There was a huge open seating area with a wet bar tucked to the side where a few couples were lounging, oblivious to everyone else. The soft sound of masculine moaning carried through an open door, and Kelly paused, looking back at me.

"The door is open. Go look if you want," I whispered as I squeezed her hand. I could tell she was curious, but I was letting her lead. She knew what she could handle, and I was just here for support.

As we approached the open doorway, the distinct sound of leather meeting bare flesh echoed out into the hallway, and I watched as Kelly's steps faltered, a gasp escaping her lips. Her eyes were wide as she looked toward me again.

"Go ahead." I nodded, letting go of her hand and following close behind her.

One of the couples in the seating area had started kissing, a man now shirtless lounging with one of his arms stretched across the back of the couch while his submissive unzipped his pants. His finger was hooked in the D-ring at the front of her collar, holding her face to his while he kissed her with force.

My own possessive streak roared through me as I stepped in closely behind Kelly, gripping her hips tightly as I leaned in to whisper in her ear.

"Looks like you have your pick of shows to enjoy tonight. Which one will it be? A little bondage and impact play or public fornication?"

Her eyes widened as she looked back toward me, her chest heaving a bit. A little nervous tremor ran through her, but I could see the apprehension mixed with excitement in her eyes. Now was her chance to explore that potential voyeurism kink, and I would enjoy watching her while she did.

She stopped at the threshold, peering through the gap with wide eyes, taking a step toward the partially open door. Such a curious little thing, but I was proud of her for sharing this with me. Watching someone discover their deepest desires was somewhat of a turn-on, and judging from how her nipples were outlined through her dress, she was feeling a similar excitement.

Flattening myself against her back, I placed one hand on her stomach, firmly pulling her back into me. She squirmed, a little gasp passing her red-painted lips as she felt how the anticipation had affected me.

"Go ahead. The door is open. They want you to watch."

Her hand reached up to grasp the back of mine as she took another step forward, but I was right there behind her. If she needed a solid anchor to feel safe, I would be that for her.

"Watch, Kelly. Don't close your eyes," I murmured in her ear when I noticed they had drifted shut.

She let out a shaky breath, stepping forward and opening them.

The inside of the room was entirely paneled in rough-hewn wood planks with a large, black X-shaped frame bolted to the wall opposite the door. A man was strapped to it, his white shirt unbuttoned and hanging open, dress pants pulled down to his lower thighs — tautly stretched across his spread legs. His wrists and ankles were secured to the cross with buckled leather cuffs.

A platinum blonde woman in a short, black, satin dress paced in front of him, a riding crop in her hand. I recognized her as a Domme who donated her services to the kink education circuit on occasion. She was another kinkster who believed in giving back educational content without expectations. While she could be ruthless and got off on her fair share of consensual humiliation, she somehow made it look effortless and sexy.

"Watch how she commands that room," I murmured, enjoying how Kelly practically vibrated with pent-up energy. This was new and scary for her, but judging by the way her pulse had quickened and the flush that had built along the skin just below her collar, she was enjoying it. "He's completely at her disposal, and look how hard he is. He loves how she makes him feel. Does the idea of having me submit like that to you turn you on?"

"Yes."

Kelly's quiet admission had me pulling her closer, my hand slowly sliding up the material of her dress until it closed over the fingers of the hand that was toying with her sun pendant.

"While she works him over, pretend it's me. And that you're commanding my body like that. Can you feel how hard you have me already?"

Grinding into her back slowly, she squirmed as I pressed her hand into her throat, making her gasp.

The Domme turned toward the door, a slow smile spreading over her lips as she looked back at where we watched her. "Oh, look," she chuckled, turning back toward her submissive partner, running the tail of the crop slowly down his exposed chest. "We've got an audience. Do you want them to watch me tease you, pet?"

The man's eyes slowly rose from the floor, widening as he took in Kelly's flushed face and my possessive hold on her body.

"Ah, ah. You're mine," the Domme scolded, quickly flicking the crop against the front of his exposed thigh. She reached out, gripping his hard cock while he groaned. "Don't fucking look at her. You serve me. This cock is for me. She can watch, but it belongs to me."

"Yes, Mistress," he murmured. "Only for you."

"That's right. Your body, and your eyes, are mine."

"Yes, Mistress," he breathed out, his eyes closing while she flicked him with the end of the crop again, the sound of it hitting his skin louder.

Kelly jumped at his tortured moan, and we both watched as his cock bobbed.

"Does the thought of them watching me strike you until you cum excite you, pet?"

He was panting as she slowly dragged the crop between his legs, tracing his shaft with it as she stood off to the side, so she didn't block our view of the show she was directing. Her positioning was as much for our benefit as it was theirs; she wanted an audience and was mindful of their view.

A swift smack to his left pec made Kelly jump, forcing her hips backward into mine. She glanced over her shoulder at me, her pupils slightly dilated.

"Watch, sunshine. They want you to watch."

She nodded, leaning her head back against my shoulder. Every time the woman across the room moved, I could see Kelly tracking her. She was taking everything in with wide eyes and a quickened heartbeat.

The Domme switched implements, taking a soft flogger and teasing him with it while he tried to breathe through the strikes and count aloud. He had amazing restraint, I had to give him that; I wasn't sure I'd be capable of lasting through that much teasing.

"Oh fuck. Please, Mistress, please let me cum. I need to cum," he panted as his arms and legs flexed against his restraints, his hands balled into tight fists. It appeared the sub had finally reached his breaking point. His cock was red and throbbing, the tip leaking and dripping onto the floor.

Kelly was gripping my pant leg with one hand while the other still lay under mine, cupping her throat. The scene was a fervent display of female dominance, but I'd hardly been able to keep my eyes off the woman in my arms.

"Watch as he cums, sunshine. He's so desperate for it, but he's waiting for her. He'd do anything for her. Anything."

"Hmm," his Domme hummed, clearly enjoying his discomfort. "I suppose you may cum, let's see how far it goes." She began to roughly stroke his cock while he threw his head back, the muscles in his neck straining as she pulled him right to the edge and then released her hold on him.

"Now, pet. Cum."

His guttural groan carried out the open door as his hips flexed forward, an impressive arc of cum shooting several feet away from where he was bound and landing on the hardwood floor.

Kelly gasped as she watched his almost violent climax, his cock finally softening slightly as it stopped twitching.

I pulled the door closed as the Domme moved toward her sub, releasing his cuffs and kissing his face softly as she whispered words of encouragement.

"Wow," Kelly whispered as she sagged against me, her body relaxing slightly as she blinked several times.

"Hey," I murmured, sliding my hand to the side of her jaw and turning her to look at me. "Focus on me, sunshine. Breathe."

We'd just been watching, but I could tell seeing something like that from only a few feet away had been a thrilling experience for her. It was always intense to watch other people. Even after all these years, I'd never become desensitized to the rush of watching a scene play out.

"That was intense," she whispered as her eyes focused on mine. "You'd let me do that with you?"

"It's not about letting you, sunshine. Don't be afraid to tell me what you'd like to try and we can negotiate something we'd both enjoy."

As she started to relax, I could tell the sounds of the room behind us had gotten a little more hedonistic as we'd watched the other couple. A glance over my shoulder confirmed my earlier assessment, and the couple who'd been on the couch before were fucking with quite a few observers. The submissive was riding her partner roughly, with his hand wrapped around her neck.

"Whatever I want to try?" Kelly asked as she toyed with the material of my tie, tugging slightly.

"Within reason, but whatever you need from me is up for discussion."

"You might regret telling me that." She slowly wound my tie around her hand, gripping it firmly and turning toward an armchair a few feet away. "Follow me, stud."

Fuck.

I had a feeling things were about to get interesting. Sunshine was ready to play.

THIRTY-THREE

Kelly

Boston

Having absolutely no idea what I was doing but finally feeling like I wanted to figure out how to channel my inner Domme, I pulled Nathan to a nearby armchair using his tie like a leash.

"Sit," I commanded as I stopped in front of the chair, turning him to face me with the chair behind him.

He arched an eyebrow, but I quirked mine right back, nodding at the chair behind him.

"If I have to repeat myself, you're not going to like the outcome," I warned, a thrill running through my veins as I stared him down.

"Yes, ma'am," he replied softly after a few moments, bending his knees slightly as he moved to sit back. I stepped forward, placing a hand on each shoulder and pushing him with just enough force to make him fall back into the chair harder than he'd expected.

"Fuck," he groaned as his hands grasped the arms of the chair, his hips shifting as he took a deep breath.

Not wanting to lose my nerve, I leaned over him, biting his earlobe playfully as I braced my hands on his forearms. "Felt that, huh, stud?"

His eyes widened as I taunted him, knowing that my move likely forced the impact of the plug inside him to be more pronounced. "A bit."

"Good," I teased as I straightened and placed the toe of my high heel on the edge of the chair between his legs. "Unzip your pants."

"Sunshine…"

"I didn't ask you to talk. I said, *unzip your pants.*"

He nodded, closing his mouth as he slowly unbuckled his belt, but I raised my toe, lightly pressing the tip into his crotch, right about where I knew his balls would be. "I never said to unbuckle your belt."

His hands paused, his eyes flashing to mine, his look a mixture of confusion and a touch of defiance with a healthy dose of arousal. He

328

opened his mouth but quickly closed it when I shook my head, his hands releasing his half undone belt. The tail stood straight up from the buckle like I had a feeling his cock would be doing if the bulge underneath his slacks was any indication.

Grasping the end of the leather, I leaned in again, my voice a little stronger as I hissed in his ear.

"I'm going to suck your cock if you can manage to follow directions, but..." I chuckled darkly, listening to the way his breath caught. "You're not allowed to cum. I'm going to use it to fuck my throat until you can't take it anymore, begging me to stop. Then we'll see how quickly you can make me cum with the vibrator in my panties. If you get me off fast enough, I'll let you cum on me when we get home before I fuck you."

Nathan's eyes were dilated as I backed away, his neutral gaze betrayed by the red flush that'd taken up residence along his neck. Pressing my hand against his chest, his heart pounded against my palm, his chest heaving with his now labored breaths.

"Now. *Unzip* your pants."

Nathan nodded, slowly lowering the zipper, then calmly laying his hands on his thighs while he awaited my next instruction.

"Good boy."

His nostrils flared, and I watched his jaw tick, but he didn't say a word.

"Take out your cock."

He shifted his hips slightly as he reached inside the open placket, pulling himself out through the hole in his briefs.

"Balls too." I nodded, loving the little smirk he gave me in return.

I had to admit. Nathan sitting fully dressed in a tailored suit, his hard dick straining while peeking out the zipper was more erotic a picture than I would have imagined.

Part of me wanted to just climb into his lap, shift my panties to the side and take care of it by riding him until we both exploded, but I wanted to hear him beg me to stop. I wanted to see how it felt to be in control of his pleasure.

"Hands on the arms of the chair and don't move. You thrust, I stop."

He nodded, placing his hands where I'd instructed, taking a deep breath and waiting for my next move.

I took a step forward, my hands grasping the sides of my dress and gathering the material until it revealed the tops of my stockings. Nathan's eyes never left mine as I slowly began to pull the material upward, revealing the leather straps of the lingerie Talia had helped me find.

Breaking the eye contact momentarily, I lifted my dress over my head, expecting Nathan to look down, but he continued to watch my face, just waiting.

I knew that some dominants didn't like their submissives to make direct eye contact in a scene, seeing it as a defiant act, but I liked knowing that he was watching my every move — waiting for me to direct him.

"You may look," I said softly as I stepped into the space between his open legs, my hand grasping his hardness firmly. "But you can't touch."

His gaze was almost searing as he studied what I was wearing, his tongue slowly peeking out to wet his lips. His fingers clenched the chair's material, the fabric bunching as his knuckles flexed and turned white.

"I need you to hold still," I instructed as I gripped the end of his tie, pulling it taut in my other fist. "The only word I want to hear out of your mouth is stop. If you cum, we leave, and you don't get to touch me for an entire day."

He nodded, his eyes widening.

I leaned forward, dragging my lips along the outer edge of his ear as I pulled the tie tighter. "I'll spend the entire day naked and make you watch as I touch myself with things from your playroom. I'd hate for you to have to watch but be unable to touch. That doesn't sound like very much fun for you."

A low grunt escaped his lips as I nipped at his earlobe, leaning back slightly so I could look directly into his eyes.

"Wait." His voice was a harsh whisper as he cupped my cheek with his palm.

"But…"

"You don't have to do this."

"But, Nathan, I thought…"

"No," he interrupted. "Don't do this because you think it's what I want. Do it because you want to. Do it because the thought of it is going to turn you on. Don't do this for me. Because I won't enjoy it if you aren't doing it for the right reasons."

"And if I want to?"

"Then, by all means, sunshine. Take what you want," he smiled, returning his hand to the arm of the chair and falling back into his submissive role.

"Oh, I will. Just try not to embarrass yourself, stud. I'd hate for our plans to have to be put on hold. Eyes on me."

Giving his cock a firm squeeze. I kept my grip tight on his tie as I sunk to my knees.

My adrenaline spiked as I saw a few people standing off to the side, watching us, including a woman holding a camera. I took a deep breath and closed my eyes, focusing all my energy on keeping control of this scene.

When I opened my eyes, Nathan was watching me intently, a gentle smile on his lips. He dipped his chin, giving me an imperceptible nod. That was all the encouragement that I needed as I leaned forward, slowly engulfing the head of his dick in my mouth.

Nathan's eyes connected with mine as I slowly worked my way down, taking more and more of him with each pass of my mouth. His chest heaved as I sucked harder, hollowing my cheeks.

The last time I'd done this, he'd still maintained control over the situation — grasping my hair, using that filthy mouth to tell me what he liked — but I was in control this time.

Nathan's dark expressive eyes watched me hungrily as I bobbed my head, pausing to suckle the head of his dick and then slowly suck his length back inside the warm wetness of my mouth.

His whole body was tense as I incrementally increased my pace, his thighs tensing as I broke my gaze and focused on relaxing my throat so I could take his whole length. My eyes watered as I held him in my throat, forcing my mouth down several times before releasing him.

I had to admit, watching him battling to remain still — simply because I'd told him to — made me feel powerful. I'd never thought being on my knees between a man's thighs could be anything other than a submissive position, but as I pushed down and took his whole length again, the head pressing against the back of my throat, I'd never felt more in control.

331

Gripping the base firmly, I pushed up higher on my knees and used the leverage to force my mouth down on him, gagging slightly, which caused him to let out a rumbling groan. His cock throbbed against my tongue as I sucked my way back to the tip, my heart racing as I saw the way his entire body was tensed. He was close. So close, but he still hadn't told me to stop.

He wasn't the only thing throbbing as I sucked him back into my mouth, taking him in as far as I could and twisting my head side to side. My eyes watered as I held him there, and my thighs clenched, my clit slipping along the vibe tucked between my legs.

Part of me wanted to tease him, pull the extra remote out of my bra and turn it on, making myself cum with him in my mouth, but I was focused on him, on his pleasure. On knowing that it would be so much more pleasurable for him later tonight if I edged him just right.

Foreplay had never been such a long, drawn-out process for me, typically only lasting for a few minutes before the main act, but the wait... The long, slow-burn tease was nothing like I'd ever experienced before. I wanted him desperate for me. Like I was desperate for him. All of him. His body, his pleasure, the way he took care of me. His heart. I wanted it all.

I moaned, my heart beating faster as I began bobbing my head, sucking hard at the top before forcing him back inside.

Part of me was thoroughly impressed by his control, but I felt desperate. Sucking harder...moving faster...moaning and gagging with each downward stroke.

"Fuck, fuck, fuck..." Nathan finally groaned, his hips shooting upward slightly as he flexed his thighs and let out a desperate moan. "Stop."

My mouth stilled, his hard flesh pulsing with pent up need between my lips as I slowly released him.

Nathan's chest was heaving, his fingers brutally clutching the arms of the chair, and eyes squeezed tightly shut. His whole body was tense, fighting against the urge to cum.

It was the most erotic thing I'd ever seen in my life watching him struggle to pull in breaths as his hard cock jutted into the air between us.

Slowly standing on shaky legs, I pressed my hands on top of his, loosening his fingers as my hands slowly traveled up his arms, cupping his neck as I whispered in his ear.

"That was fucking incredible, stud. *Good boy.*"

He laughed lightly as his shoulders relaxed, taking a long, shuddering breath before he opened his eyes and met my watchful gaze.

"Sunshine," he murmured, a smirk pulling at the corner of his swollen lips.

"Are you ready for it?" I asked as I reached toward his pocket, slowly pulling out his phone.

He nodded, and I pressed it into his palm before climbing into his lap, straddling his thighs and gripping his shoulders.

"Make me cum," I instructed as I sat back slightly, the backs of my thighs perched on his.

He licked his lips, taking a deep breath as he focused on his phone, unlocking the screen and opening the app to control the toy.

"Oh God," I whispered as his eyes locked with mine, a low rumbling vibration making me clench involuntarily. Sucking his cock has been more than arousing and I was already soaked, wetness visible on the insides of my thighs as I looked down at myself.

He was still hard, his cock bobbing slightly with each sound of pleasure I made as I gazed down at him.

My chest heaved and my nipples were sensitive as he increased the speed, the humming already pushing me close to the edge.

"Can I touch you?" he asked quietly as his free hand squeezed against the arm of the chair.

"Yes, you may," I panted, my thighs rocking against his as the speed of the vibrator slowed.

Nathan didn't hesitate as he pulled my panties to the side, sliding two fingers into me as he pressed his palm against the front of my panties, the toy nestled tightly against my clit.

The people surrounding us disappeared from my notice as he fucked me with his fingers, increasing and decreasing the toy's speed with each thrust of his hand.

"Oh fuck," I moaned as my head fell back, my hips instinctively grinding against his motions, my body right on the cusp of falling. The act of blowing him in front of others had gotten me more aroused than I expected. Clearly my exhibitionist curiosity was confirmed.

Nathan was biting his lower lip, no doubt holding in all the filthy things he wanted to say as I rode his fingers and the toy, my rhythm faltering as he turned it up to the highest speed.

A loud wail tore out of my mouth as I arched backward, a gush of wetness covering Nathan's palm. After turning off the vibrations, he dropped the phone into his lap, gripping my hip tightly in his hand. It was the only thing keeping me from falling off the chair as I pulsed almost violently around his fingers.

My legs were shaking as my heartbeat slowed, my legs collapsing and my weight dropping onto Nathan's thighs.

"Come here," he whispered as he slowly pulled his fingers out, lifting them to my lips. Suddenly feeling brave, I sucked them into my mouth, licking off the mess I'd left on them while he watched; his eyes hungry.

It was official; he'd unlocked the insatiable part of me that was no longer worried about what anyone thought of me. I'd just sucked his cock in front of a room of strangers — likely while being filmed — and shamelessly fucked his fingers afterward until I came. A quiet laugh slipped out as I leaned forward, cupping his scruffy cheeks.

"What are you giggling about, silly girl? Do you find my cock amusing?" Nathan whispered as I looked down at his hard dick straining between us.

"No. Definitely not amusing." Tempting. So tempting. I knew I'd just blown him in a room full of people, but I wasn't quite ready to have full-on sex with him in front of strangers.

"You might as well tell me, or I'm going to get a complex."

"I was just thinking that was the female equivalent of marking my territory. I licked it, and now it's mine."

"Well, if it's yours, sunshine, quit fucking around and put on your dress so we can get home and take care of it."

"Yes,   sir."

THIRTY-FOUR

Nathan

Boston

Kelly was quiet after we left the party. Emory and Talia sent us back to my apartment in the car service. They weren't quite ready to go yet, but Talia had thoroughly embarrassed Kelly before we said our goodbyes. She'd praised her performance, telling her they'd be happy to help her live out her exhibitionist fantasies in the future.

While I appreciated the enthusiasm from my friends, I could tell it'd make Kelly feel self-conscious talking about people witnessing what had happened. She'd been so into it at the moment, channeling something inside herself that literally would have made me weak at the knees if I hadn't been sitting, but I knew how you could overanalyze things once the endorphins wore off. Emotional drop was just as much of an issue after a scene as physical.

"How are you feeling?" I asked as I tilted her chin up to see her face. She'd had herself tucked into my side quietly ever since we climbed in the back of the SUV.

"Was that OK?" Her voice was shaky as her eyes darted across my face. I could tell she was trying to read my expression.

"It was fucking phenomenal, sunshine. Truly. That was the sexiest thing I've ever experienced."

From the way she was practically gnawing on her bottom lip, I could tell that she wasn't sure if she believed me, but it was the truth. I'd engaged in public play before, but that whole impromptu scene was hotter than anything I'd ever done, especially in the submissive role.

"Did you enjoy yourself?" I asked as I slowly traced the pad of my thumb across her cheek, trying to soothe some of the nerves that were cropping up inside of her.

"Yes," she breathed out, her eyes wide.

"Then feel proud of yourself. No one else in that room matters. If they thought that was anything other than an impressive display of your sexuality, then fuck em. I loved every minute of it." *And you.*

"I'm not sure if I should feel dirty. I rode your hand in front of half a dozen people."

"That's what you're worried about?" I chuckled, leaning down to kiss her forehead. I didn't mention it'd been more than just six people who had watched, but I didn't want to freak her out. "Don't you ever feel dirty about doing something you want to do. Fuck other people's expectations. Trust me, every single one of them was wishing they were in that chair instead of me. That was sexy as fuck. And the way you sucked my fingers after, goddamn."

I shifted, my sensitive cock rubbing against the material of my briefs. While I wasn't as hard as I'd been earlier, he still hadn't calmed, angrily throbbing as I thought of what would happen when we got back to my place.

"Do you still want to play when we get home?" I wasn't going to push the issue if she'd had enough fun for the night, but I was anxious to continue without the audience.

"Do you?" she asked as her hand slowly caressed my thigh.

"What do you think?" I grasped her hand, pressing it into my erection as it pulsed beneath the suit material. She glanced toward the driver, but he couldn't see our hands from the front seat. Leaning toward her, I whispered in her ear. "He drives Tal and Em around quite a bit. He's seen much worse."

Kelly squeezed me through the material, and I flexed my hips as I clenched my jaw, trying not to moan.

"You're so hard," she whispered as she looked into my eyes, her chest heaving as her breaths quickened.

Fearing the groan that would escape if I tried to talk, I gave a jerky nod, my gaze locking with hers as the occasional street lamp illuminated her face through the window. While she was visibly disheveled from earlier — with her red lipstick faded because it'd all rubbed off on my cock — she'd never looked more vibrant or gorgeous.

Her hand continued to slowly stroke my shaft through my thin dress pants for the remainder of the torturous ride back to my building, not enough to push me over the edge, but enough that my thoughts were borderline desperate as the vehicle finally stopped at the curb.

Edging wasn't anything new to me, but I needed to cum soon. Especially before Kelly got inside me, or I'd likely go off before we were ready for the night to end. I had a feeling recovery time wouldn't be an issue after the build-up.

"Thank you for the ride," Kelly thanked the driver cheerfully, pretending she hadn't been fondling me in his back seat for the last twenty minutes. If I wasn't so worked up, I might have laughed, but I practically dragged her out of the car, slamming the door and tugging her toward the building entrance.

Kelly followed me quietly, her fingers suggestively stroking my thumb as we walked into the elevator. As soon as the gate was down, she pushed up onto her tiptoes, grasping the hair at the back of my head in her fists as our lips crashed together.

I groaned into her mouth as my hands grasped her ass, squeezing her cheeks as she wiggled against my front.

"Fuck," I grunted as one of her hands left my hair, playfully squeezing my ass as she thrust her tongue into my mouth, causing the plug to shift inside me.

As the elevator platform jumped slightly, coming to a stop at my floor, I kissed her roughly before releasing her, pulling open the cage and yanking on the heavy metal door.

Kelly giggled as she led me down the hallway, bouncing on her toes as I pulled out my keys and unlocked the deadbolt.

Neither of us said a word as we hurried through the door, the heavy wood slamming against the frame as I kicked it closed.

Her fingers were on my belt before I could get my hands on her, making quick work of it and my zipper before she forcefully yanked my pants and boxer briefs to my thighs. With a light shove, she had me pinned against the wall in the entryway, a predatory look putting me at her will.

"Ah, fuck," I groaned loudly as she leaned over me, sucking the head of my shaft between her lips as she knelt on the entryway rug. Her hands clasped the backs of my thighs, pulling me roughly into her mouth, not stopping until I hit the back of her throat.

"Holy shit," I panted as she fucked me with her throat, breathing heavily as she pulled back and dove right back in, moaning around my length.

"Fuck, I'm gonna cum," I groaned moments later, grabbing her ponytail and yanking her backward as I grasped my cock in my other hand. I roughly jerked my length until I came, thick ropes painting the dark material of her dress and the side of her neck.

337

"That was hot," she laughed as she stood, pulling her dress over her head and moving toward the kitchen as she dropped it to the floor.

I leaned back against the wall, trying to catch my breath as she pulled two water bottles from the fridge, tossing one in my direction before she headed into my bedroom.

"Come join me when you're ready. Sit on the bed and wait for me," she called out, glancing over her shoulder as she strutted toward my closed door in her sexy as fuck lingerie. "Don't take too long, stud."

Inhaling deeply, I scrubbed my hand over my face, trying to catch my breath as I pulled my pants up and followed her. The door to the bathroom was closed as I sat on the edge of the bed, loosening my tie and unbuttoning the cuffs on my dress shirt.

I could hear Kelly humming as I stood and crossed to the closet, taking off my shoes and hanging up my suit jacket. I'd need to take it to the dry cleaners before wearing it again. I was sure it smelled like Kelly from how she came all over me earlier. I wasn't complaining, because that scene would be at the top of my list of things I'd imagine in the shower for the rest of my life.

You'd think that when you're moments away from letting the woman you're in love with fuck you in the ass, you'd be nervous, but surprisingly, I was anticipating what she had planned for me. Now knowing what a sensual and attentive lover — and person — she was, the prospect of being pegged wasn't as intimidating as it had once been.

Not wanting to spoil her plans, I finished taking off my clothes from the party, pushing the armoire to the side, and opening the doors to the playroom. For once, I didn't know what would happen in a scene. I knew Kelly had enlisted Talia for help earlier in the week, and like with everything else, I was sure she'd sneakily been doing research. Since neither of us were experienced at this kind of play, I'd told her I trusted her to lead. She knew where my limits were and what my safeword was, so we'd define the boundaries together.

That was the part of our dynamic that needed to develop, and while I loved being the one in charge and introducing her to new things, I was anxious for her to flex her Domme muscles. She'd been sexily confident earlier at the party, leading me around like she owned me — which truth be told wasn't far off the mark.

The door to the bathroom slid open, Kelly peeking around the edge of the frame, backlit by the lights on the vanity. She was still in her lingerie, but she'd touched up her make-up. Her lips were once again painted bright red.

"You ready for me, stud?"

I nodded, dropping to my knees on the carpet and waiting for instructions. Kelly's eyes lit up as she slipped the door open the rest of the way, the rest of her coming into view.

It appeared that Talia had gone all out with hooking up Kelly from her endless toy stash.

"What do you think?" she laughed as she put her hands on her hips and rotated them, causing the small black dildo attached to her new underwear harness to wobble.

I clamped my lips together, refusing to laugh at her antics, not wanting to break character. I may have done the helicopter dance for her one morning when we were back at the farmhouse in response to her, saying the exact same thing, but this was different.

"I know it's not as impressive as what you're packing," she nodded to where my cock was starting to perk between my thighs. "But I think it'll get the job done. Lesbians really know how to design some sexy yet comfortable dick wrangling panties."

I laughed, my ass clenching in anticipation, squeezing on the small starter plug we'd inserted before the party. It'd been rubbing me in interesting new ways all evening, and I was suddenly desperate to see what it'd feel like to have Kelly's little black friend thrusting in there.

Kelly stepped forward, cupping my cheek and rubbing her thumb across my lips. "Hmm, it's too bad I can't feel what it'd be like to fuck you here."

My eyes widened as she leaned forward, shoving her cleavage into my face as she tugged on my cock. Breathing out heavily, I tried to remain still, loving this new seductive persona she'd taken on. It was sexy as fuck.

"But I can't wait to fuck you here," she growled in my ear as she cupped my ass and tapped on the plug with her fingers.

"Such a good boy, so quiet," she murmured as she licked up the side of my neck and grasped my earlobe between her teeth. "On the bed, stud. Get up on your hands and knees."

Part of me was disappointed she didn't lay me across the spanking bench, but I knew the height discrepancy would be tricky to compensate for there, even with the heels. Part of the perks of designing and building furniture was you could customize it. Looked like I'd be adding a stool to the back of the bench.

"Hmm," she hummed as she slowly ran her hands along my hips, tracing her palms up my sides and pressing my shoulders down into the mattress. "Stay like this. Don't move, or I'll stop."

Fuck. I clenched my jaw, fighting the urge to moan as she reached beneath me, giving me a few rough strokes before she leaned back.

"Oh, fuck!" I cried out as her hand smacked my ass, the movement sending shockwaves of pleasure with a twinge of pain through my system.

"We'll get there, stud. Don't be so impatient."

A rumbling growl built in my chest as she rubbed my ass cheeks, her fingers grasping the plug and twisting it inside me.

"Let me hear how much you like it," she teased, and I gasped, moaning as she pulled the plug halfway out and drove it back in. "Don't move. I'll be right back."

Kelly stepped away, and I closed my eyes, remaining completely still as I waited for her to come back. We hadn't even gotten started yet, and I was throbbing, ready to cum all over my bed — correction, *our* bed.

"Such a good boy," she murmured as she walked back into the room, her voice sending a thrill up my spine. "Look at how well you listen. Turn sideways on the bed, keep your face down. Watch me get ready for you."

Shifting against the mattress, I turned, my eyes widening when I saw what Kelly had in her hand. It was the little handheld remote to her panty vibrator. "Don't touch it until I tell you." She placed it next to my arms, running her hand through my hair as she smiled at me.

I had to admit, it'd been a long time since I'd submitted to someone so soft. Kelly's voice was gentle yet commanding, but the predatory, absolutely possessive way she looked at me made me hot. Soft Domme Kelly was impressive.

"You ready?" she asked as she looked into my eyes, tracing my cheekbone with her thumb.

Nodding, I inhaled deeply, trying to calm myself. "Green."

"Good boy. I'm going to prep you now. Hips a little lower."

She grabbed a bottle from the dresser at the side of the room, donning a black vinyl glove and ensuring I watched as she squirted a generous amount of lube into her palm. It was strangely erotic to see her stroking the fake phallus protruding out in my direction from her little panty harness. I was happy Talia had fitted her with equipment appropriate to her skill level. While she'd been intrigued, she wasn't quite at purple double-ended pegging vibrator level yet, and neither was I.

Quietly watching her, I tried to calm my body, taking in deep breaths and feeling all my muscles relax. I knew things wouldn't go as well if I was tense, and I wanted her to enjoy this without worrying about hurting me.

"You look so hot like this," Kelly murmured as she climbed onto the bed behind me. "Hold still while I take this out."

"Fuck," I grunted as she pulled the plug out, shifting across the bed to put it on a nightstand.

Closing my eyes, I took a deep breath, waiting for what she'd do next.

"You're doing so good, stud," she praised, and I smiled as she dropped into her loving Dominant energy. The scared, slightly insecure woman from a few weeks ago was gone, replaced with this radiant, confident partner. "I'm going to use my fingers first. Relax and take a deep breath."

One of her hands stroked my lower back as her lubed fingers gently prodded. Taking a deep breath, I relaxed, moaning into the sheets as she slowly slid them inside, hooking them slightly and rubbing them once they were in.

"Fuck," I grunted as she slowly retreated, pushing them back just as gently as she had the first time.

Part of me wanted to squirm against the pressure, lightly moaning whenever she rubbed against my prostate. Still, she was doing such a good job of directing this I let myself submit and feel it without worrying about actively participating.

341

"Push your ass back, lower your hips toward the bed," she instructed, using her free hand to get me into the position she wanted while wiggling her fingers inside me. "Can you take it harder?"

I nodded, gasping as her fingers slowly pulled out and thrust back inside.

"I need the words, stud. I know you know how to use that mouth."

"Yes, sunshine," I grunted as she used one hand to spread my ass cheek to the side, opening me further.

"Good boy," she cooed, giving one quick jerk of her arm and pushing her fingers all the way inside and wiggling the tips, making me almost delirious with the pleasure it caused. *Fuck.*

"How does it feel?"

Blowing out a few labored breaths, I swallowed, clearing my throat. "It's intense."

"Good intense or bad intense?" she asked, slowing the movements of her arm.

"It's good. So good, keep going."

I could feel my cock throb between my legs each time she hit that spot deep inside me, starting to trigger something I could feel building again. I was so glad she'd made me cum already because I would have sprayed my tension from earlier all over the sheets with how things were going.

"Are you ready for me?" she asked, leaning forward to kiss a spot between my shoulder blades, her warm breath fanning over my skin.

"Yes."

Kelly slowly removed her fingers, leaving me feeling a little empty as she shifted on the bed, and I heard the distinct snap of her removing the vinyl glove on her hand.

"Breathe, stud. Hold still for me, baby."

Not trusting myself to keep in the filthy things I wanted to say to her in response, I nodded, taking a deep breath and clenching the comforter's material in my hands.

My thighs burned from the position I held myself in so she could reach me, but that was just an afterthought as the rounded tip of the dildo attached to the love of my fucking life started to press inside of me.

She'd done a good job of getting me ready for this moment, the pinch of discomfort only momentary, followed by an intense twinge of pleasure as she slipped all the way inside, the fronts of her thighs pressing against the back of mine.

"Fuck. Oh, fuck," I grunted as she pulled out slowly, pressing back inside with a little snap of her hips.

"You OK down there?" she laughed, one palm holding onto the side of my hip as the other caressed my back.

"Yes," I moaned as she slowly retreated and then pressed in harder, making me rock forward against the sheets. "Oh, God."

"You take me so well," she moaned out lightly, and I looked down to the remote still sitting on the mattress beside me.

"Can I use the remote?" I asked with a gasp as she continued her slow torture of my prostate, not quite enough to make me cum, but enough that the sensation was starting to build deep inside.

"Oh," she giggled, her hand smacking my ass, surprising me. "Good idea. Go ahead."

She paused, letting me pick up the little remote, positioning it in my hand securely so I could press the control buttons with my thumb.

"Think I can make you cum before I do?" Kelly laughed as she shifted back, grabbing something from the mattress.

My jaw clenched as I held in my remarks, but she just laughed more, her hips shaking slightly, making the dildo inside me shift in interesting ways.

"You can respond, dirty boy. I know you want to," she taunted as her hand smacked down hard on my ass.

"Fuck, sunshine. Such a bad girl. I fucking love it," I moaned as I turned on the toy, enjoying her startled gasp. I was trying not to top from the bottom, but she'd turned this into a fun little game.

"So get to it, stud. Let's see what you've got," she taunted.

Laughing, I turned it to the highest setting, enjoying how her fingers dug into my skin and the moan that ripped out of her mouth.

"Oh my God."

"Not God," I teased, lowering the intensity. It'd just be playing dirty if I overstimulated her. Sometimes the slow build paid off more in the end. "He's not the one making you feel like this."

"Might want to hold onto something," she laughed as she lowered herself, lying partially across my lower back. Something soft touched the tip of my hard cock, my hips pressing back into her as it covered the end of my shaft.

"Oh fuck," I moaned as she slipped her surprise over my cock, the sensations of the stroking sleeve causing me to press my hips back against hers.

"Someone likes that, huh?"

Kelly used the stroking toy to manipulate my cock roughly as she snapped her hips forward, my breath catching with each thrust.

My fingers struggled to press the buttons on the toy remote as she drove me to distraction, my body building up to something so intense I couldn't even describe it. She was murmuring things into my skin, moaning against my back, and squeezing the hand surrounding me in ways that made stars dance across my vision.

I hadn't anticipated this when she'd suggested she might be interested in pegging. But maybe I shouldn't have been surprised that even this experience with her was intense and wonderful, bringing us both immeasurable pleasure.

Her hand sped, the slick, sucking sounds of the sleeve on my length adding another aspect to the experience, distracting me from the panty toy's controls. Kelly gasped as I pressed the button to turn it to the highest intensity, flexing her hips forward in a rough stroke that I think surprised both of us.

The remote fell to the floor, a loud grunt escaping my lips as I started to feel my balls draw taut.

"Fuck, I'm gonna cum," I groaned, my whole body tightening as a rush of pleasure raced up my spine.

"Yes," she hissed as she sped up her jerky movements, the humming toy in her panties obviously affecting her actions. "Me too, so close. Oh my fucking God!"

Her moans into my skin pushed me over the edge, my release exploding into the stroker in her hand as my vision blacked out.

"Fuck," I groaned, almost collapsing against the mattress with Kelly's limp weight on my back.

"Holy shit," she breathed out with a little giggle, slowly pulling the toy off my cock and withdrawing herself. "Are you alright?"

My face tingled as I sprawled head-first against the mattress. I wasn't sure I was capable of speech yet. I now knew exactly how someone felt when said they'd been thoroughly dicked down from behind.

"Yeah, I'm good," I rasped out as I felt the bed shift, my eyes closing.

I heard some rustling, Kelly's heels clicking against the hard flooring as she walked around the side of the bed.

Warm hands cupped my cheeks, her soft lips caressing mine as she knelt in front of me.

When I opened my eyes, she'd removed her little friend, her bare pussy distracting me for a moment before I looked up toward her.

"You sure you're alright?" she smiled, tracing her fingers over my cheekbone.

"That was..." I took a deep breath, slowly releasing it, a smile drawing the corners of my lips. "*You* were amazing, sunshine."

The radiant smile on her face at my praise was worth the slight discomfort I was starting to feel now that the rush was fading. But I didn't regret a single moment. I couldn't regret any of the moments Kelly spent with me.

The next morning, I groaned, stretching as I reached toward Kelly's side of the bed, my fingers grasping slightly warm sheets. Opening my eyes, I saw the bathroom door partially closed. It was mid-morning, both of us having crashed out from the rush of the night before.

As I contemplated getting out of bed and making breakfast, I heard a soft cry from the bathroom. Unlike when I'd come upon her doing something naughty in the shower, this one sounded desperate and muffled, urging me out of bed and toward the door.

Kelly was sitting on the edge of the large bathtub, her phone cradled in her hand, shaking. "What's wrong? Who was on the phone?" My heart pounded as I tried to figure out how her happy mood from when we'd gone to bed had vanished with one phone call. "Was it another one of those messages? I have a buddy in the BPD; I can have him run a trace. I know you think it's that douche nozzle, Trent, but we can use it as evidence if we ever need to get a restraining order."

"No, I mean yes, but..." Kelly breathed, glancing up and looking into my eyes briefly before her eyes fell back down to where I'd found her staring at the floor. "It was Tom..." she paused, letting out a stuttering breath. "And Deacon. They want me back in the office Monday. A few other women came forward that Trent had been harassing, and they fired him."

"So you're..."

"Yeah, I'm cleared. They closed the complaint against me, and I can return to the office."

"Oh, wow. I thought we…" I trailed off. *I thought we had more time.*

"Yeah," she nodded, turning to the side and wiping the corner of her eye.

"Hey, come here, sweet girl," I coaxed, reaching forward to pull her into my arms. She tucked her face against my neck, and I could feel her body shaking as I held her tightly. I wasn't sure what to say.

"What did the text say?"

"It wasn't as bad this time, but it was from the same number."

She handed me the phone and I felt my pulse quicken at the seemingly innocuous message.

?: You should wear your hair up more, it's sexy like that. Is the necklace new? Blue is a nice color with your skin tone, but I think the leather is my favorite. Someone has been a naughty girl during exile. But I'm sure I'll see you soon.

He didn't need to threaten her again, because he'd been watching, and that was enough to scare both of us. The question was how. Kelly had barely been out of my sight since we'd been in Boston, and the only people who had seen her collar were the people at the play party. Which meant either he was spying on us or he had someone within my network doing it for him. The thing that scared me the most was that now my ability to protect her was going to change, and I wasn't sure how to handle her leaving.

We both knew there was an expiration to being together like this. Her coming to Boston with me wasn't going to be something permanent. I knew she'd been scared to go back to Chicago with the text messages she'd been getting, and I was afraid to let her go.

If I wasn't in love with her while we were in Connecticut, I certainly was now. It wasn't just because we'd physically become closer. That was just an extra bonus that I hadn't expected.

She brought something to my life I hadn't known was possible. My parent's marriage was the furthest thing from healthy, so I hadn't known what a true partner looked like, but Kelly was quite possibly it. She seemed to understand what I needed before I did, instinctively. She had me reconsidering my limits and choices, and how I interacted with people. I wasn't the same man that I was even days ago. My sunshine had helped me find myself again, even when she was utterly lost herself.

And now, I needed to let her go. As much as it would destroy me, she needed to decide what she wanted to do with her future. She was getting her career back, and I'd never force her to choose.

A long-distance relationship wasn't something I saw for myself, but I couldn't stomach the thought of it being over when she returned home. So she'd go back to Chicago with my collar around her neck and her hand around my heart, and I'd hope she wouldn't neglect either of them.

"I don't want to leave," she whispered as she played with one of the buttons on my shirt.

"You know you've always got a place to stay with me," I whispered. She didn't just have a place to stay, she had a home, but I was trying not to make it harder for her to go back to Chicago. "The first vacation days you can get, I'll come to you, or you can come here."

"Mmhmm," she nodded, but she still sounded as devastated as I felt.

"I wish you could stay with me here, but I know your job is important to you."

She sniffled, clinging to my chest, and my heart swelled with emotion. I knew I'd had a terrible habit of keeping women at a distance because of my own emotional issues, but this little firecracker — my own personal sunshine — had split my heart wide open.

Taking a page from her book, I traced a finger down her back. I knew what she'd been spelling on my skin after her first scene, but I'd been too afraid to admit it at the time. Once I said the words or acknowledged to her that I knew, it would change things.

Her choppy breathing stilled as I very deliberately traced a large V from one shoulder, down to the dip at the back of her waist and back toward her other shoulder.

Without looking up at me, she traced an E with me against my pec, pausing briefly before we both traced Y, O and U against each other. Her finger may have well been a brand against my skin.

"I love you, sunshine," I whispered quietly into her hair, closing my eyes, and waiting until she responded.

"I love you too, stud."

347

And I knew that whatever happened next, we knew exactly where we stood with each other.

THIRTY-FIVE

Kelly

Chicago

"You sure you've got everything you need?" Tom asked as he leaned against the doorframe to my office. He wasn't officially back from paternity leave yet, but he'd come in today to babysit me. I'd told him to stay home, but I was getting the kid gloves treatment. Nathan had been concerned about the last text message I'd received right before Tom had called, which mentioned our attendance at the play party. Since he couldn't accompany me back to Chicago, he'd enlisted my friends to keep an eye on me.

Sam and Christine had met me at the airport a few days ago, helping me get back to my apartment and inviting themselves to stay for dinner. I wanted to be insulted that no one thought I could take care of myself, but it was nice to have them around.

They'd escorted me to and from work yesterday, making sure I got into my apartment safely before they left, promising to be back in the morning. Sam had offered to take me to work this morning, but they'd settled for letting me drive since I still needed to grocery shop for my barren refrigerator. They'd hopped on a bus to get to their office and told me they'd meet me after work and go shopping with me. Apparently, I couldn't even be left alone to grocery shop. I doubted the mystery texter would attack me inside a Kroger, but my friends took their protection duties seriously.

I knew I should have unpacked my suitcases the first night, but they were still against my bedroom wall. I'd flopped face-first onto my covers last night after getting off the phone with Nathan, but I'd passed out after I fruitlessly looked for my tablet. I was certain I'd stashed it somewhere in my hasty packing before I'd left less than a month ago, but I was sure it'd turn up sooner or later.

"I'm fine, Tom." The look he gave me certainly didn't look like he believed me, but I didn't care. No matter how happy I was to be cleared from the false charges against me, I didn't want to be here. I wanted to be in Boston, cuddled up in bed with Nathan. "You don't

349

need to hang around here all day. I'm sure you have better things to do. Charley will hate me if I monopolize your time."

"Charley definitely isn't going to hate you," he laughed, rubbing his fingers along the scruff covering his jaw. He wasn't quite Nathan's level of fuzzy, but it was obvious he hadn't had much time for personal grooming with a newborn at home. "I think she was getting tired of me being home all the time. She keeps sending me out on bullshit errands so she can nap without me hovering."

"Seriously, I'm good. Deacon already dropped off my files and caught me up to date on the projects he wants me to work on for the next few weeks."

"Don't let him overwhelm you. He was thrilled with your productivity while you were gone, and I'm a little afraid for my job with how he was raving about the work you did for his clients."

"I'm just happy to have an office to come back to," I sighed, even though it still felt foreign. I found I preferred my slouchy sweaters and leggings — and the company I'd had over the last several weeks.

"Deacon still feels terrible about things, but at least we were able to get *him* out of the office." He pursed his lips, his face suddenly more serious than I was used to seeing him. "Have you gotten any more of those texts?"

"No, just the three before I left Boston. The phone number doesn't have a name attached to it that we can find. I don't even know for sure if it was Trent."

I hadn't received any more since the night of the party, but I'd also thought they'd stopped after the second one. Trent was enjoying drawing out this little game he was playing. Some people he'd been friendly with in the office said he'd left town, but every time I left the building, I felt that I was being watched.

The truly paranoid part of me thought that someone had been in my apartment, but the door was locked when I got home, and other than my misplaced tablet, everything was where it was supposed to be. At least from what I remembered.

"Just be careful. We don't know that it was him, but Charley remembered Terri saying she was receiving creepy messages from an unknown number a few months ago. It was different from what you sent me, but I'm still worried."

"While he's a gigantic douche, I don't think Trent wants to hurt anyone. He was trying to intimidate me. I just stood up to him."

Tom sighed, shaking his head. "Alright, but don't stay here by yourself, and please make sure that a security guard walks you out to your car if Sam isn't here."

"I'll be fine. I've got my guard dogs, and honestly, Trent should be more scared of Christine than Sam anyway. Go home to your wife. Or at least get a haircut or something. You look like a slob."

"Oh, thanks," he chuckled. "Way to make a man feel good about himself."

"Yeah, we both know that's not my style." At least not with Tom. Part of the beauty of our friendship was that we didn't placate each other. He looked exhausted, and I was sure his equally exhausted wife would appreciate him taking care of himself without her having to remind him.

"You still need to come out to the house this weekend to see Porter."

"I know," I nodded, staring down at the stack of folders on the corner of my desk. While I'd been anxious to meet him when he was born, I hated that the thought of holding a baby right now just made me want to cry. Maybe if Nathan were here, I'd feel different, but I couldn't dwell on the fact that I had no idea how we would make this relationship work long term. "Just let me get settled back in, and I can drive out. Maybe Sunday?"

He nodded, seeing that I was still a little out of sorts. Tom wasn't aware that I could never have children, but he was there when I'd started bleeding in the office during my miscarriage. He'd seen the look of panic in my eyes as he helped me get packed up and in my car.

We had a big meeting with a prospective client that day so he couldn't go to the hospital with me, but he knew something had happened. But I hadn't fully confided in anyone here or otherwise. Nathan was the only one besides Tyler who knew what transpired. Christine and Sam had relocated after Tyler was long gone, so I'd just pushed down the memories and moved on.

"Go home." I gestured for him to leave, and he finally complied, letting me sink back into the backlog of work I had waiting for me.

My phone chimed with an alert hours later, and I blinked hard at my computer screen, finally noticing that it was much later than I'd

351

thought. 5:00 pm had passed by without me noticing, and one glance out my office door showed that most of my colleagues had left for the day. No one usually stuck around after the workday ended, so the halls were eerily dark.

Sam and Christine had told me they'd be here around 5:45, but by 6:20, I still hadn't heard from them.

Unlocking my phone, I cursed at the line of missed calls highlighted in red in my call log. Christine had been trying to get ahold of me all afternoon, but my phone had been in 'do not disturb' mode. Shit.

Pulling up the most recent voicemail, I looked at the text transcription, and my eyes widened. Scrolling down to the first message, I held my phone to my ear.

"Hey, Kell. I really need you to answer your fricking text messages. I've been trying to get ahold of you for the past hour and got no response. Nana fell getting out of Piet's pool, and they transferred her to Boston to have surgery." She sighed loudly. "Sam and I were able to get tickets out on the last flights tonight, but we can't meet you after work. I'll keep trying, but please let me know you got this."

Each message sounded a little more frustrated, and I felt like a shitty friend who hadn't been paying any attention to my personal phone while I was wrapped up in my computer.

After listening to all of them, I tried to call her and Sam, but their phones went straight to voicemail. No doubt they were already at the airport, if not in the air.

The sea of cubicles in the main area of the office was empty, only the lights in the main hallways still on. I knew a cleaning crew would be through here in a few hours, but it appeared I was alone for now.

I tried to call Nathan, but he'd been busy getting caught back up on his own projects, and I didn't want to disturb him. He'd also gotten a call that the garage door of the workshop appeared to be damaged, and he needed to drive down to check that out sometime this week too. I knew we'd said we would make time to talk to each other every day, but I could already feel our lives pulling us in separate directions.

When his phone went to voicemail, I left a message while I packed up my bag to go home. "Hey, it's me. Kelly. It's Kelly."

God, could you get more awkward? He knows it's you. "I'm just heading out of the office, but I wanted to let you know Sam and Christine are headed your way. Nana is having emergency surgery, and I guess they'll be there for a few days. Can you get the number of a place where I can order flowers there?"

Locking the door to my office, I tried to finish up before reaching the elevators. "I'll try calling again once I get home, but I know you're busy. I love you. Talk to you soon, stud. I miss you."

The empty elevator stopped at my floor, and a frisson of unease swept through me as I boarded the car alone. There were guards at the security desk in the main office, so I knew not just anyone had access to the elevators, but I hated riding them alone.

I scrolled through my personal email as I leaned against the back wall, my heart jumping as the car stopped a few floors down. My pulse hammered as the doors opened, and I breathed a sigh of relief when I noticed an older woman standing there with a file box. Someone else had been working late.

I returned my attention to my phone and didn't look up as the car resumed its downward motion. Movement in my peripheral vision had me glancing up, noticing that the woman hadn't boarded the elevator alone. A tall man in a pair of worn jeans and a hooded sweatshirt was standing next to the control buttons, and his hands were shoved firmly in his pockets. It was weird that he was wearing his hood inside the building, but he was just standing there silently, so I tried to convince myself that I needed to stop being paranoid.

The elevator stopped a few more times, the stragglers in the building finally heading home for the day. It wasn't packed shoulder to shoulder like it could be first thing in the morning, but the hooded man stepped directly in front of me as more people joined us.

Not wanting to be completely creepy, I stared at his shoes, trying to figure out why they looked familiar to me. It wasn't like most people wore tennis shoes to work, but these sneakers were black with black soles and red stitching along the sides. A vague memory of seeing them at the company picnic last year lingered at the edge of my consciousness, but I thought I must be losing it if I focused on people's shoes.

The elevator stopped at the main lobby, and most people exited the car heading out onto the street. The guy in the hoodie stepped back, bumping against me as he moved for people to get out. He didn't look back as I tried to step around him, my bag brushing against his arm as I tried to get out of the way. *Dick.*

There were three levels of underground parking, and unfortunately, I hadn't been able to find anything on the first two levels this morning. Hoodie guy and the woman with the file box remained on the elevator to the parking levels with me. She pressed the button for the first level, looking back at me. "What level are you on?"

"Three." The man in the hoodie flinched at my voice, and I frowned as he reached over and pressed the number two on the panel. He hadn't talked and had barely moved since he got in the elevator other than trying to step on me.

As the car started again, that feeling of unease I'd felt since I arrived back in the city multiplied, even more so when the elevator stopped, and both of the other passengers filed out. The man in the hoodie headed toward the door to the stairwell, and I frowned, watching the woman go out the other exit from the small elevator enclosure.

The car stopped on the second level, and I quickly pressed the close door button when I didn't see anyone waiting to board. I tucked my phone into my pocket, grabbing my key and sliding it between my pointer and middle fingers. I knew I couldn't do much damage with a blunt metal key, but I was officially freaked out when the doors to the lowest level slid open. I should've taken Tom's advice and had a security guard escort me from the main lobby.

I blew out a shaky breath when I stepped out into the little enclosure outside the elevator, glancing toward the door to the stairwell as I turned to head in the opposite direction.

Calm down, Kelly. You're just being paranoid.

My phone buzzed in my pocket as I started to head toward the ramp I'd parked on, and I looped the keys on my finger as I pulled it out and looked down, frowning at the alert on the screen.

Airtag Found Moving With You

Shoving my phone back into my pocket, I checked the area around me, the dim lighting of the parking level looking much more sinister than I remembered it appearing before. I knew I was being overly suspicious, the stress of the last month catching up with me, and this being the first time I was truly by myself in weeks.

As I passed the door to exit the garage directly from the stairwell, I felt my bag jerk backward before a hand clamped down on my wrist.

Before I could scream, another hand closed over my mouth and hauled me backward into a solid body, my arm twisted behind me.

"Don't even fucking think about it," a deep voice hissed, and I felt tears forming in the corner of my eyes as he dragged me back toward the door to the stairwell, my fingers clawing at the back of his hand that covered my mouth.

The door slammed into the concrete wall, echoing as he pulled me back into the stairwell and turned, pushing me against the wall with my face smashed into the rough surface.

"Where's your bodyguards now, *sunshine?*"

My eyes widened when I recognized the voice, my pulse hammering as I tried to figure out how Trent knew what Nathan called me. Only a few people in Boston knew that he called me that, and none of them knew Trent.

"What are you doing?" I whimpered as his chest pressed against my back, his hand holding my wrist in a painfully hard grip. "Why are you calling me that?"

"Oh, I'm sorry," he chuckled as he leaned in close to my ear. "Is my brother the only one allowed to call you that? Guess you only let guys who fuck you in public give you sweet little nicknames. Never thought you were dirty enough to be into that BDSM shit, but you looked hot in that strappy leather get-up you had on."

What the fuck?

"The video I downloaded was pretty fucking raunchy. Could have done without seeing my brother's dick out, but I just put my thumb over that part of the screen. Who knew you were a gusher? That part was fucking hot."

"What are you talking about? What video?"

I knew people had watched us, but I hadn't realized the photographer had filmed it. And how had Trent gotten ahold of that video?

"You really should find a building with better security. I was able to hack your electronic deadbolt pretty easily. Missing something?"

Fuck. My tablet.

"And it's pretty reckless to leave yourself signed into your email account on all your devices. What if something got stolen? What if someone read through all your personal emails? Looked at videos people sent you encrypted links to access? Talia seemed to think you wanted to see yourself get finger fucked after you blew my brother. It'd be a shame if that video ended up on the internet," he chuckled, his sour breath fanning across my face. "You made it pretty fucking easy to figure out where you were when you had your tablet save the password for your bank account."

"And made it easy to see who you're fucking, apparently. So how was it? Is sleeping with my brother everything you thought it'd be? I've heard he's into some pretty racy shit, never pegged you for the type to be into that too."

"What are you talking about? I didn't even know you had a brother," I whimpered as he pressed his shoulder forward, the concrete scraping my cheek as he leaned in.

"Oh, Nathan doesn't talk about me? I'm insulted. He forgot I existed like the rest of those assholes who share DNA with me."

My heart hammered in my chest as I tried to connect the pieces. Nathan had said that his brother's name was Bradley.

"But his last name is Harrison. How can you be his brother?" I asked, my eyes darting across his features as he leaned around, finally showing me his face. My eyes scanned over him quickly, trying to find the similarities. Nathan had dark hair and dark eyes, while Trent had sandy blond hair and striking blue eyes. Trent was shorter than Nathan, his shoulders not nearly as broad, but I could see the same strong jaw and full lips that looked so different on Nathan's face.

"Bradley Harrison the third died when my grandfather did," Trent growled. He yanked me backward, spinning me around and slamming my head against the wall behind me as he roughly grasped my neck. "At least I'm sure my siblings thought he did. I haven't heard from them in years, not that they gave a shit to begin with."

Trent pressed his hand harder against my neck, and I gasped for air, my hands clinging to his, but he didn't release me. "I legally changed my name to my middle and mother's last name trying to get as far away from the family that resented my existence almost as much as I do theirs."

I couldn't speak as he held me captive, my head pressed tightly back into the concrete wall of the stairwell.

"But I'm not here to tell you my sob story. Since I know you'll only believe his side anyway. Did he tell you his mother refused to adopt me?"

He dropped his hand, slapping both his palms on the wall on either side of my head. I took in a shaky breath, my fingers touching the tender skin of my throat. "She was mentally ill."

"No, she abandoned me, an innocent two-year-old, just like my parents did," he hissed. "She was a selfish bitch. Which is why her husband fucking cheated on her, to begin with."

"But your grand..."

"My grandfather was a workaholic who tried to use what time he didn't dump me in daycare to turn me into my father. My father was a dick, so you can see how well that turned out."

While his tone was menacing, there was an underlying pain that made me feel a shred of pity for him. Their father's actions had left some deep scars on both Nathan and Bradley — Trent, whatever identity he was going with.

"That doesn't explain why you're targeting me. I didn't do anything to you."

"Didn't you?" He chuckled darkly, picking up a strand of my hair and rubbing it between his fingers. "I seem to recall someone refusing to sit next to me in staff meetings and turning me down when I offered to buy you a friendly drink after team-building exercises."

"You've always been terrible to me," I insisted, but he narrowed his eyes, and I pinched my mouth closed.

"No, I was terrible to you after you decided I was beneath you. Didn't stop you from fucking my dirty construction worker brother, though. So maybe you only spread your legs for men like that."

"Men like what?" I frowned.

"Who charm women with false promises and don't care who they fuck over. He not only looks like our father. He acts like him too."

Shaking my head, I clenched my jaw, gritting out, "Nathan is a good man."

"A good man that abandoned his pregnant girlfriend," Trent scoffed.

"She's not his girlfriend," I countered. I knew they'd been in a dynamic until February, but they hadn't been together romantically in months. "And that isn't his baby."

"Could have fooled me," he grinned, turning the phone in my direction. It was a photo from the other night that I hadn't seen. Marisa was cupping Nathan's cheek, and she had her hand grasping his elbow, her large belly pressing into his stomach.

"I was there too. They aren't together." I'd been with Talia in the other room, but Nathan had only talked to Marisa privately for a few moments.

"Hmm. Our father told my mother all kinds of lies too," he remarked darkly. "And she died because she believed him." He stared at the wall above my head, my trembling form still cowering away from him.

"I'm sorry that happened to you," I said softly, but it only made him angrier.

"You think I want your fucking pity?" Trent growled as he grasped the hair at the back of my head and yanked, causing me to cry out.

"Why are you doing this?" I whispered as tears formed in the corners of my eyes. "I didn't do anything to you. Just because I wasn't attracted to you doesn't give you the right to threaten me and attack me. I don't owe you anything."

"Because his father took something from me. So now I'm going to take something from him."

"Please stop," I whispered, my tears finally spilling over.

"Oh, what's the matter, Kelly? Do I not pull your hair the way he does? Don't worry, I don't fuck like he does either, but you clearly like it rough." Trent taunted as he yanked my hair harder, using it to turn me toward the door leading back into the parking garage.

THIRTY-SIX

Nathan

Connecticut

It'd taken me most of a day to start clearing out the debris that'd blown into the workshop from the smashed-in garage door. Nothing was seriously damaged besides some tools carelessly thrown around my workspace. My security system and cameras would need to be replaced because of the two-by-four taken to them, but overall, it could have been much worse.

What scared me the most was that I kept thinking about what could have happened if Kelly and I had been here when the vandal broke in. I was already worried enough about her going back to Chicago without me.

I knew that it was an irrational fear and that she had Christine and Sam to support her, but something didn't sit right with me. She seemed to be settling back into a routine in the few days she'd been home, but I didn't like knowing Trent was somewhere in that city. Whether she wanted to admit it, she was being targeted, and I had no idea what this guy could do.

Even though Kelly had asked me not to, I'd gone ahead and had my friend with the Boston Police Department run a full background check on the guy, but I knew it'd take a few days. I just wanted to see if anything in his history was a red flag.

My phone buzzing in my pocket startled me, and I pulled it out, frowning at the three missed text messages and the missed call from Evan within the last ten minutes. I knew they were back at the house, having just missed Kelly as she flew out the other day. They said everything had looked normal when they got in last night.

I was sure Kelly would call me if she'd heard different, but I hadn't heard from her since earlier in the day. I knew she was playing catch-up at the office and working long hours, but I didn't want her to burn herself out the first week back.

When the phone in my hand started buzzing again, Chase's contact information scrolling across the screen, I quickly connected the call.

"What's up?"

"Oh, thank God. You answered. Have you heard anything from Kelly in the last half hour? Evan tried to get ahold of you, but neither of you answered."

Tapping the button to put it on speaker, I opened up my missed calls, scrolling through the list. Kelly had called. "Yeah. I guess I missed one about an hour ago. I haven't listened to the voicemail yet. I talked to her this morning on her way to work, but she had meetings all morning and met with Tom this afternoon. I was trying to give her some space since I knew she was busy and hadn't called her yet."

"Shit," she hissed, and her muffled voice carried through the line as she talked to someone in the background. "Where are you?"

"What's going on?"

She took a deep breath, cursing again. "Evan and I are trying to get on flights out of Hartford tonight. She hasn't tried to contact you after your call?"

"No." But I was starting to get fucking worried. I'd anticipated talking to her later tonight, but now I seriously fucking needed to listen to that voicemail.

"He got a text alert twenty minutes ago that her phone had sent out an alert to emergency services. His parents got the same alert and headed into the city to see what's happening, but her phone is now going straight to voicemail."

Bile churned in my stomach as a wave of nausea crawled up my throat. "Where was she?"

"The map showed her office building, so I guess she must have stayed late at work, but we have no idea what's going on."

"Fuck," I growled, clenching my jaw. "It could be that fucker, Trent. Are there still tickets left on the flight you booked?"

She held the phone away from her mouth again, talking to Evan in the background. "Yeah. Looks like there's a few."

"Text me the flight details, and I'll meet you there."

I dropped the tools I'd been cleaning and moved over to the damaged door to inspect the frame. Hopefully, I had enough time to get it boarded over before I needed to leave for the airport. I'd intended to stay in the Airstream overnight, but my suitcase was still packed, so I just needed to take care of this and hop in the Jeep. The airport was only a half-hour away, so I could get there quickly depending on when the flight was scheduled to depart.

"Why would you drive to Hartford all the way from Boston?"

"I'm not in Boston. Someone vandalized my workshop a few days ago. The neighbors told me that the garage door was damaged, so I came down to assess things and take pictures so I could file an insurance claim."

"Oh my God. Why didn't you say something? We could have come to help you."

"You literally just got home from your honeymoon. I should have just left it and gone to Chicago with Kelly. I had a terrible feeling all morning that something was off."

"Evan said something about some text messages. Why didn't you guys tell us what was going on?"

"Because they stopped, and then Kelly had to go back to work so she wouldn't lose her job. I don't think either of us was thinking clearly."

"Fucked each other senseless," she laughed, but I stayed silent because I wasn't in a joking mood. "Sorry, not the time. I texted you our itinerary. Do you need us to come to pick you up?"

"No, I'll meet you there," I assured her and quickly said my goodbyes.

Rushing around for the next half hour, I quickly screwed some plywood into the garage door frame. It'd have to do until I could get it repaired or replaced. Honestly, they could burn the whole fucking workshop to the ground, and I wouldn't care as long as I got to Chicago to find Kelly.

I hoped we were all just being paranoid, but as I repacked the Jeep and Kelly's phone was still going to voicemail, I was starting to get freaked out.

The airport in Hartford wasn't huge, but we'd managed to secure seats on a direct flight that got us into Chicago O'Hare two and a half hours later, so I had to hope we'd have some answers by the time we landed.

"Do you know anything about this guy?" Evan asked as we settled into our seats on the plane, Chase sandwiched in the middle seat with me sitting on the aisle.

"I had a cop buddy run a check on him, but he hasn't called me back yet, and I tried to do an internet search and just came up with a private Instagram account. A random article from a university in Chicago mentioned him in the graduating class from their graduate school in computer science, but nothing before that."

"I mean, she told us about the harassment, but she never said anything about the text messages other than in passing the other day. Do you think this is related?"

Clenching my fists, I tried to scan through the timeline of everything mentally. It was far from coincidental that the person sending the threatening text messages knew where we'd been and what we'd been doing. Clearly, someone was watching us, or someone was feeding them information.

"I hope she just accidentally set off the alarm and dropped her phone or something, but I can't shake the feeling that this guy is a little unhinged. He just got fired for harassing multiple women and has potential charges pending for stalking one of the other women in their office. I don't want to consider the possibility this could all be related, but there's no telling what he's capable of."

"This flight is taking too long," Chase sighed as she checked her watch for the tenth time in the last half hour. "And I'm fucking starving."

Evan handed her a package of almonds and water, and she blew out a deep breath, suddenly looking a little pale.

"You alright?" Evan asked as he rubbed her back. While she'd been worried when Evan was missing last year, she'd kept her shit together pretty well. "I've got those ginger chews in my bag if you need one."

"I'm fine. Just a little lightheaded," she sighed as she sat back and pressed her hand into her abdomen. My eyes drifted to Evan's and back to Chase's, and they both smiled guiltily.

"Yeah," she laughed. "Came back from vacation with more than a sunburn on my ass."

Evan laughed, shaking his head as he looked over at me. "We haven't told anyone yet, but now hardly seems like the time."

"Congratulations. That's great. I'm sure your families will be thrilled." Kelly would be. I knew she'd love having a niece or nephew.

"Yeah," Evan nodded, his hand covering Chase's. We sat silently for a few minutes, my knee restlessly bouncing as I thought about how Kelly would feel upon hearing their news.

"I should have stayed with her." Running my hands through my hair, I tugged, the pain helping distract me from the immense amount of guilt running through my system. "If he hurt her, I'll fucking rip him apart."

Chase gasped, but Evan nodded seriously, making direct eye contact, which I knew wasn't something that he was typically comfortable with. "And I'll help." Under normal circumstances, I would've laughed because he was a big cinnamon roll, but I nodded, knowing that I'd do anything for my sister as well.

"Let's hope we're all overreacting," Chase responded, trying to break the tension, but we were all likely to be on edge for the rest of the flight.

Since none of us had checked a bag, we took off through the airport terminal toward the rental car area with our carry-ons as quickly as possible, Evan continuing to try to contact Kelly.

When we got to the rental car desk, he cursed, answering his phone and holding it up to his ear as he stepped out of line. "It's my parents. I'll be right back."

Chase and I awkwardly stared at him while he paced back and forth next to the elevator doors, his eyes widening at a few points and his body language indicating he was visibly upset. Part of me wanted to rip the phone out of his hand and demand answers, but I knew he loved Kelly just as much as I did, and we were all in this together.

"She'll be alright. It's Kelly. She could kick this douche bag's ass if she needs to."

I chuckled at Chase's attempt to be encouraging, but the longer Evan was on the phone and the more agitated he became, the more my stomach tied itself in knots. "I really fucking hope so because I don't want to go to prison for tearing this guy apart with my bare hands."

"Calm down there, killer," Chase laughed, but we shared a loaded look as Evan ended the call and shoved his phone back in his pocket.

"We need to get to the hospital..." My pulse started pounding in my ears as he talked, my anxiety likely rivaling his at that moment.

"My mom said they were on the way there now, but they'd weren't allowed to talk to Kelly because she was being evaluated for a concussion in the emergency room and they need to run some tests."

"Fuck," I sighed, choking back the swell of emotion that ran through me. Chase reached out to hug me as my eyes welled with tears, causing a few to spill over.

"She's stubborn as hell, Nathan. I have no doubt she'll get through this. You know Kelly probably put up a fight. I'd hate to see the other guy if she's in the hospital."

"She better be alright," I choked, hating that I wasn't there for her. This would have never happened if I had just gone with her like I'd wanted to. "Because I'll fucking kill him if she isn't."

"Let's just get in the car and get to the hospital instead of playing out worst-case scenarios."

Evan secured the keys for the rental car, but I knew he shouldn't drive. His face was pale, and he looked eerily like he did before his panic attack last year.

"Maybe we should just get an Uber instead," I suggested, but Chase snatched the keys from her husband's hand, nodding toward the escalator.

"Nope, I got this," Chase assured as she pulled up the map app on her phone and calmly handed it to Evan. His hands were shaking as he entered in the information for the hospital.

"Are you sure you should be driving in your condition?" I asked, and she rolled her eyes at me.

"I'm pregnant, not an invalid. Give me some credit here."

The three of us quickly found our way into the rental car lot, piling into a nondescript dark sedan. The sun had already started to set, and the sky outside was lit up with a brilliant show of oranges and purples as we left the airport and headed toward the city.

It'd been years since I'd been to Chicago, and I'd never wanted to return under these circumstances. Kelly should be with me, safe and smiling and giving me a hard time, not all alone in some hospital on the other side of town.

Chase drove through traffic like she'd been racing a formula one car and lapping the slower stragglers, but at least we weren't fighting with rush hour as we made our way from the outskirts back into the city. I watched as we whizzed past other vehicles while I waited for my phone to turn back on. With my phone clutched in my hand, I sighed as it loaded, waiting for any news.

A text from Talia scrolled across the screen saying our friend at the Boston Police Department had been trying to get ahold of Kelly.

Talia: Call me as soon as you get this. Trent isn't his real name. He changed it 5 years ago.

When I didn't respond, she sent a follow-up that made my pulse race and my eyes widen.

Talia: Trent Alsop was legally born Bradley Trenton Harrison III. You need to tell Kelly he's your brother. What are the chances?

Fuck. I always knew Brad had a temper, but I didn't know him as an adult. I knew that was my fault, but my grandfather had never been disrespectful to women. How did Trent, Brad, whoever…end up being such a terrible guy?

I tried texting Kelly's phone, just in case and was surprised when I got a response back within a minute.

Nathan: Please let me know you're alright. Chase, Evan, and I are headed to the hospital to meet your parents. I love you, sunshine.

Kelly: She just went down for a CT scan. I'll keep you updated on her progress. She's a special young lady. I'm sorry I didn't prevent this sooner.

Nathan: Who is this?

Kelly: Deacon, her boss. She unlocked her phone so that I could contact her parents. She slurred to call a stud and fell asleep before the nurses took her down, but I wasn't sure who that was.

Fuck. That meant she was having trouble staying conscious. Or she was at least disoriented.

Nathan: I'm headed to the hospital with her brother. We should be there soon.

Kelly: See you soon. Her parents just arrived.

"She's getting a CT scan," I announced, my voice strangely hollow. The longer we waited to get to her, the more my concern grew. I was glad that she had her parents and boss with her, but I was scared. And I felt like I'd failed to protect my sunshine. She'd been in danger, and I just let her go. I could have gone with her, but I'd blindly wanted to let her stand independently. That was a fucking mistake in this instance.

The conversation about us truly being together was going to happen sooner rather than later. While I'd never previously considered moving, if it meant I was there when Kelly needed me, I'd find another job. It wasn't like commercial construction was geographically restricted.

"How did you find that out?" Chase asked as she glanced back at me through the rearview mirror.

"Her boss texted me back on her phone. He's there with her, and your parents just showed up. How much longer?"

"Like five minutes. I'll drop you and Evan at the door."

"No," I shook my head, not wanting to leave a pregnant woman to park a car by herself in the dark. It was too soon. "Drop Evan off, and I'll walk you inside."

"But," she started, but I interrupted her.

"No, I wasn't asking. Just get us there soon."

She sighed loudly, but Evan gave me a grateful glance over his shoulder. I could tell he was torn over worrying about his injured sister and concern for his pregnant wife.

Chase pulled up under the Emergency room overhang at the hospital a few moments later, assuring Evan she was quite capable of parking a car. He still looked visibly shaken as he got out, but he was keeping it together.

On the other hand, I was freaking the fuck out as Chase pulled into a parking space.

"You gonna be OK?" Chase asked as I held out my hand, helping her from the driver's seat.

"I'm not worried about me."

"She's gonna be alright," Chase reassured me, reaching over to squeeze my palm.

The walk through the parking lot seemed to take forever, both of us lost in our thoughts, her warm little hand still held in mine. I wasn't sure which one of us was comforting the other. I knew Chase put on a good show about being tough, but she'd gotten attached to Kelly.

Evan was pacing next to the elevator as we walked in through the sliding doors, waving us over quickly.

"Everyone is in the trauma care waiting room upstairs. She's getting stitches now, but it looks like she only has a serious concussion. They couldn't find any bleeding on her brain, just some swelling they want to keep an eye on. But they gave her a sedative to keep her calm."

Fuck.

Part of me was glad she only had a concussion, but she should never have gotten hurt in the first place.

"Am I allowed in there?" I asked as the elevator doors closed, and the car started moving upward.

Evan frowned at me. "She's your girlfriend. Of course, she'd want you there."

"But with your parents, and…"

"Knock it off, Nathan," Chase scolded, shaking her head as the doors opened. "You know Kelly won't let them keep you from seeing her."

I swallowed heavily, walking behind the couple a few steps back as Evan led Chase toward the waiting room.

As we crossed the threshold of the small room, I saw Evan's parents, who I recognized from the wedding, sitting with an older man wearing a suit.

"Oh, baby," the woman cried as she stood and crossed to Evan, pulling his head into her shoulder. I could see his chest shake as his mother embraced him, and my eyes started to water. Suddenly, I didn't feel worthy of being a part of this given I'd failed to protect their daughter.

Kelly's dad looked toward where I stood with Chase, frowning for a moment before he stood and headed in our direction.

"Chase, thank you for getting him here."

"Of course, Ian," she smiled sadly as she reached forward to pull him into a hug.

"Who's this young man?" he asked as he leaned back with an expressionless face. I knew I wasn't exactly young, but he was a few decades older than I was.

Chase responded since my throat was suddenly dry. "This is Nathan. He's a friend of ours from Boston. He's dating Kelly."

He's going to marry Kelly was what I wanted to say, but I extended my hand instead. "Nice to meet you, Mr. Stineman. I wish it were under different circumstances. I love your daughter very much."

Chase's eyes widened, but Kelly's dad smiled faintly, squeezing my hand before giving it a firm shake.

"We should be able to see her soon. It's nice to meet you. Our girl is a tough one."

Nodding, we followed him toward the seating area. I sat at the far end, but I saw Kelly's mom giving me appraising glances from her seat between her husband and son.

When the nurses came in and said Kelly was cleared for visitors, I shook my head when Chase gave me a significant look as she stood up with Kelly's parents. Family should be first.

After they reappeared, Evan went in with Deacon, who wanted to say his goodbyes to Kelly. "Evan would have let you go in with them," Chase scolded me as soon as they disappeared.

"I can wait."

"Stop beating yourself up."

Chase knew I felt guilty, but she didn't know half of it. I saw the messages. I knew how scared Kelly was despite the brave face she put on. And I let her talk me into her going back home alone.

"My brother is the one who put her in the hospital. I'm not sure I deserve to be here."

Her head comically swiveled in my direction. "What the fuck? I thought your brother lived in Hartford?"

"Not that one," I responded quietly, feeling guilty I'd never truly considered Bradley my sibling. Maybe if I'd been a better brother, he wouldn't have turned out this way.

"OK, I'm gonna need storytime."

Evan reappeared in the doorway before I could tell her my whole sordid family history.

"She's asleep, but the nurse said someone can sit with her," he told us as he took his seat next to Chase.

"You go," she urged, pulling on my elbow. "I need to find food anyway or I'll start hurling again. I'll see her in a little bit."

Evan told me the room number, and I followed the long hallway to a partially cracked open door.

When I pushed it open, the tears I'd been trying to hold in slipped down my cheeks as I took in her tiny body curled in the sheets. Kelly had a bandage wrapped around her head, a small dot of blood visible through the thick gauze near the side of her head. She had dark purple bruising on her wrist and forearm, the side of her face was slightly swollen, and her lip was split.

I dropped heavily into the chair next to her bed, taking her warm hand into mine and leaning my head forward.

"Oh, sunshine. I'm so sorry."

THIRTY-SEVEN

Kelly

Chicago

As Trent used his foot to kick open the door to the stairwell, I felt a moment of panic overwhelm me. This might be the last time anyone ever saw me if he took me somewhere.

"You don't want to do this."

A dark chuckle escaped his lips at the clear desperation in my voice. "Of course, I don't, *sunshine.* But what choice did any of you leave me? I started over entirely once already. And now, I might end up in jail for harassment. What choices do I have left? My career is toast. My family doesn't exist, and everyone thinks I'm a monster."

"I don't." A jolt of pain ripped through my scalp as I tried to shake my head, but it was nothing compared to how it'd felt earlier when my head hit that concrete wall in the stairwell. There was still a dull throbbing at the base of my skull that had nothing to do with his grip on me. Once the adrenaline wore off, I worried about what it meant.

"Spare me the dramatics, Kelly. We both know you'd be happy if I went to jail."

"If you don't do this. If you stop right now, I promise you I won't press charges."

"That flew out the window the second I put that tracker in your purse. Do you know how long I waited in this garage this afternoon? I had originally intended to just put the tracker on your car when you didn't come out at six, but then you fell right into my lap when I was coming back from using the bathroom."

"So you're going to hurt me because you think you have to? You can choose to stop now before you can't take it back."

He stopped walking, his grip on my hair relaxing for a moment. I didn't dare move, afraid of what he would do if I did.

"Wait, you're serious?"

"Yes. If you promise me you'll stop and get yourself help. I won't go after you."

"God, you really are delusional," he scoffed and pushed me forward. I stumbled, still a little dizzy. "Just get in the fucking car."

My heartbeat thrummed in my ears as I walked toward my car. My phone was still tucked in my pocket, and I wondered if he'd notice me taking it out. He was distracted, his eyes darting all over to make sure no one else was down here.

Deciding to chance it, I reached into my pocket and pressed the side button five times before glancing down. The bar to activate the emergency alert flashed across the screen, and my eyes darted back to Trent before I slid my thumb across the screen.

A loud screech tore from my pocket as the alarm sounded, and Trent growled as his hand grabbed the back of my neck, pushing me forward into the trunk of my car.

"What the fuck did you do?" he hissed as the weight of his body pressed me into the warm metal.

My breath was choppy as he pressed his forearm into the back of my neck, pinning me in place.

"Why the fuck did you do that?" he shouted, and I gasped as the pressure against my neck made it hard to breathe. I knew sending the alert was a risk, but I didn't want to think of the alternative. Now there was no way for him to get me out of here. Someone would find us. They had to.

My phone started buzzing in my pocket, and Trent pulled it out, angrily swiping the screen to disconnect the call. It immediately started humming again, and I coughed as the weight of him holding me down disappeared.

"Fuck. Why won't they stop calling?" he growled as he tossed my phone on the ground, sending it skidding across the concrete toward the driver's door.

"Get in the car," he growled as he yanked me backward by my hair, his other hand grasping my upper arm tightly.

"Stop," I cried as he squeezed harder, trying the door handle to the back seat, but it was still locked, my keys in my pocket.

"Unlock the fucking door, Kelly."

I hesitated, seeing movement from the door to the elevators.

"Give me the damn keys," Trent growled as he reached into my pocket, his fingers grasping the key loop as he held me close to him.

As my boss' figure came into view with a female security guard standing next to him, I knew this was my chance as they turned to head toward the executive parking area.

"Get the fuck off me," I screamed, louder than I normally would have, but it did the trick, Deacon's head swiveling in our direction.

I didn't see his response as Trent's hand pressed hard on the back my head, slamming my forehead into the metal.

"Shut the fuck up," he hissed, pressing down and making me wince.

The blinding pressure was only momentary before I heard a clicking noise, and Trent's hand was gone. His body twitched violently against the side of the car beside me.

"Stay down, you piece of shit," the female security guard growled as she held the taser out in Trent's direction. When he stopped spasming, he tried to push himself up, and she pressed the button again, Trent hitting his head on the side of my trunk on the way down to the concrete floor of the parking garage.

"Kelly," Deacon gasped as I slumped against the driver's door, my body sliding down the metal with a squeak as my vision blurred. I brought my fingers to my temple, wincing as they encountered wetness. "Shit, call the police," he instructed as he knelt in front of me in the confined space between cars. "And an ambulance."

"Is she alright?" the security guard asked, the sound of zip ties loud in my ears.

"Kelly," Deacon said softly, snapping his fingers in front of my face, but I was staring at the blood on my fingertips.

I blinked hard, having trouble focusing on him as I looked up, intensifying the pain in my temples. Closing my eyes, I leaned my head backward, wincing as the tender spot where he'd pulled my hair touched the hard metal.

"Stay with me, Kelly," Deacon said, his voice louder and more panicked.

"S'ok," I mumbled, opening my eyes and wincing at the strange orange brightness from the overhead lights. "I'm just gonna rest my eyes."

"You need to stay awake until the paramedics get here."

Deacon kept talking to me, but I was too distracted to listen, his voice sounding wooden in my ears. Sirens echoed off the walls of the parking structure, making me wince and hold my hands over my ears. My eyes opened and I could see Deacon's mouth moving, but I couldn't tell what he was saying to me.

Moments later, but it could have been longer, a man in a dark blue paramedic uniform knelt before me, grasping my uninjured wrist and pressing his fingers to my pulse point. Static filled my ears as he pulled a penlight from his pocket, studying my eyes and gently touching where the cut on my head was with his gloved fingers.

He placed his hands underneath my armpits, slowly lifting and turning me, pressing my shoulder lightly until I leaned back onto a waiting backboard.

Deacon's concerned face flashed in my peripheral vision as I was lifted onto something, flashing lights strobing across my blurry vision. My ears rang as my head was secured in place.

My consciousness started slipping as several faces entered my field of vision, a pinch in my arm causing my eyes to widen. I knew they were asking me questions, but I couldn't understand them, my tongue feeling heavy.

The lights were brighter as we entered the hospital, more faces rushing around me as I tried to rest my eyes. Deacon was gone, replaced with a concerned-looking doctor who used another light to look in my eyes.

"She's got a concussion for sure. Let's order a CT to rule out bleeding or a skull fracture since her face is starting to swell. Do we need to start a rape kit?"

"No," Deacon's low voice called out from within the room. "It didn't get that far."

"Alright," the doctor nodded. "Empty her pockets. Are you next of kin?"

"No," Deacon answered again. "I'm her employer. I was with one of the building security guards when we found her in the parking garage."

"Check her phone for me to see if there's an emergency contact. A nurse will give you some forms to fill out while we try to reach her emergency contacts. Did she have a purse with her?"

"I've got it," Deacon answered.

The doctor looked back toward me again, "I'll get you down to CT soon. I can only give you a very mild sedative until we know what kind of head injury we're dealing with."

I tried to nod, but my head was still strapped in place. "OK," I rasped but felt my stomach turn, wrinkling my face.

"Get me an emesis bag," the doctor said to someone outside my field of vision, tilting the board I was strapped to forward slightly.

She held the blue bag to my face, the contents of my stomach emptying into it while she said encouraging words to me. Not that it was much since I skipped lunch. How embarrassing was it to throw up in front of your boss?

"Get that sedative going and make sure her orders are rushed. She's clearly in some pain, and I can't start pain meds until I know what's happening there."

The doctor left my field of vision, and Deacon grasped my hand, speaking softly. "I'm still here, hun. Is there anyone I need to call? You've got about two dozen missed call notifications on your lock screen."

"My parents," I rasped quietly. "Can I have my phone?"

He pressed it into the hand of my uninjured arm, and I awkwardly tried to hold it up so I could use the facial recognition. It didn't work, the passcode screen popping up after it'd failed. I tried to type in the number sequence a few times, failing, until Deacon took the phone back.

"What's your code?"

I read off the numbers for my passcode, and he unlocked the screen, my head suddenly feeling heavy. He started talking, but I drifted off, listening to his deep concerned voice.

"OK, your parents are already on their way here," he said louder, his voice right next to my face. "Is there anyone else you need me to call?"

I opened my mouth to answer as someone else pulled the curtain of my cubicle aside. "Let's get Ms. Stineman going. You've got a slot in CT."

Deacon talked to her, squeezing my hand as his kind face leaned over me. "Who else do you need me to call?"

"Stud," I slurred, my eyes slipping closed. "Call Nat..." my voice drifted off as my eyes fell closed, and I finally slipped into unconsciousness.

THIRTY-EIGHT

Nathan

Chicago

Kelly remained asleep for a few hours, her hand lying softly inside mine on the edge of her bed. The doctors came in with her parents and presented the CT scan results, thankfully with no bleeding or skull fractures visible. She still needed to be monitored for a severe concussion and some swelling, but she was lucky. He hadn't caused any lasting damage. Once her cuts and bruises healed, she would recover. I knew it wouldn't be an easy road, knowing that surviving an assault like that didn't go away overnight.

I emailed my boss, applying for an emergency leave of absence. I still had some vacation time left, but I wasn't leaving sunshine's side until I knew she was alright. My brother had left a shitshow in his wake, and I had to clean up his mess. I needed to call my sister and other brother. They at least should know what had happened.

I wanted to hunt him down and murder the fucker, but he was in police custody, pending Kelly's decision whether or not to press charges. She better be pressing fucking charges. He deserved it, family or not.

Kelly continued to sleep after the doctor left, and Chase convinced her parents that I should be allowed to stay while the four of them headed back to their house. Chase pulled the pregnant lady card, and Mrs. Stineman looked torn, but wanted to care for her guests. They finally relented, leaving me with their phone numbers in case things changed during the night.

The nurses brought in some sheets and blankets, but I knew I wouldn't sleep. My mind was restless as I kept watch over her from her bedside.

The following morning, Kelly woke up groggy at first, but quickly perked up when she noticed me sitting in the chair next to her bed.

"Hey, sunshine. How're you feeling?" I asked as I pressed the call button to alert the nurses she was awake. They'd monitored her

374

vitals throughout the night, quietly coming into the room to check on her, but she hadn't been fully conscious since she talked to Evan and Chase last night. While she was awake when the doctor had come in the previous evening, I doubted she remembered a word he said through the haze of pain meds.

The nurse quickly assessed her, asking her questions and having her fill out a meal request card for breakfast. It was still early, the sun barely peeking over the horizon.

"Finally," she yawned as they left the room, reaching down to grasp the back of my hand. "We need to talk."

"We don't need to worry about anything right now," I assured her, turning my hand to interlace our fingers. I wasn't going anywhere. "You need to rest."

"I want to talk about coming back to Boston with you."

Shaking my head, I grabbed her water bottle, placed it gently on her lap, and nodded toward it. "Drink."

"Yes, sir," she winked as she slowly lowered her mouth toward the straw, a mischievous smile on her lips.

"Behave, you're in no shape to be doing anything," I scolded, my lips twitching as she pursed her lips into an exaggerated pout.

"But you'll still obnoxiously insist on me being hydrated."

"You are correct," I chuckled, enjoying the little flare of defiance in her gaze. "You need to rest and take care of yourself. I'm worried about you, Kelly."

She nodded, swallowing hard, her eyes becoming suddenly glassy. "OK, quit distracting me. I'm coming home with you when you leave. How long are you here?"

"As long as you need me."

"Then you can help me pack once they let me out of here."

"Kelly," I sighed as I held up my hand, but she didn't stop talking.

"You're not talking me out of this. You have family in Connecticut. I have family in Connecticut. My parents have been talking for years about moving to North Carolina to be closer to my aunt and uncle. I think the only thing keeping them here was me," she explained, but I didn't want her to jump into a decision like this.

"You don't need to make this decision now. I know your career is important to you, and I don't want to pressure you. We can figure it out. You need to rest and heal first."

"I don't want to figure it out." Kelly reached forward and cupped my cheek.

"Oh...that's..." I felt my heart drop as I tried to determine what she meant.

"Because I want to go home *with* you. Not just to visit for a weekend. I want to stay. With you. I love you, Nathan." My heart warmed as she smiled at me, still so beautiful beneath the discoloration on the side of her face and the bulky bandage.

"I love you too, sunshine. So much. But this is a big decision, and I don't want you to make it because you're scared. I can't ask you to walk away from your job." I didn't deserve to. While I wanted her safe, I wanted her happiness more. If that meant I came here, then I would. I opened my mouth to tell her as much as she laughed, holding up a finger.

"You don't have to. It can come with me. Deacon told me I can continue to work remotely."

"But that's not a long-term solution, and you've got Tom and Charley, and Sam and..." I pointed out. We couldn't live in limbo as we waited for them to call her back to Chicago. What happened when the guilt over what happened wore off, and her boss wanted her back in the office?

"Do you not want me to move to Boston?" she frowned.

"It's not that. It's just..."

"Talk to me, stud. Tell me what you want." I wanted her — forever.

"I want you with me. But I don't want you to do it out of obligation." It'd kill me if she uprooted her life and decided she didn't want to be in Boston with me.

"Since when have I done anything because I felt obligated?" Kelly laughed. "I want to move to Boston. To be close to you. And to be close to my niece or nephew."

Chase and Evan had shared the news with her when I'd gone to the cafeteria to get dinner last night before her family left. I hadn't wanted to leave her alone.

"But what if you decide you don't want me?" That was my biggest fear — being abandoned. I knew it stemmed from my adolescence, with how things had fallen apart after my father's death, but it was something I could never seem to shake.

376

"I'll always want you, Nathan. Always. Because I don't think I'll ever love anyone as much as I love you. I don't feel like this is my home anymore because you're not here." Her voice was quiet, but I could tell she meant every single word.

"But my brother. He hurt you, and I couldn't protect you." Trent's actions weren't mine, but I didn't want it to be something that drove a wedge between us.

"Your brother needs help. And we're going to make sure he gets it. You were both damaged by your father, and I know you don't think I should forgive him. But he has felt alone his entire life because of your father's actions, and we need to step up and show him he doesn't have to keep lashing out."

"I still think you should press charges for everything." I traced the bandages on Kelly's head. "He could have killed you, and he broke into your apartment."

The police had come to speak to Kelly's parents right before they left last night. Trent had confessed everything, hoping for lighter sentencing.

"And I think that's the last thing he needs. He needs family. And he needs you to show him that not everyone in his life abandons him. You've both let your childhood trauma define you for too long, and it's time to stop letting it. You help family when they need it, and Trent...Bradley, he needs help, not another family member casting him aside."

"I don't know if I can ever forgive him for this. If Deacon and that security guard hadn't shown up, he could have..." He could have done so many terrible things to her, and we were lucky it hadn't come to that. I wasn't sure I had it in me to help him.

"I don't think he wanted to hurt me. He just felt desperate."

"Stop making excuses for him," I barked, pulling my hand out of hers. She needed to hold him accountable for what he'd done to her.

"I'm not making excuses, I promise, but I think he just needed to feel in control of something. What he did was terrible, and under different circumstances, I could agree with your anger, but he's so broken. I want to help him."

Her kind heart was both an asset and a curse, it seemed. "You're a better person than I am."

"Well, yeah," she laughed. "But seriously. We need to make sure he goes somewhere he can get help. And sitting in some prison for years isn't that place. If you don't try to help him, we're reinforcing that your family hates him. While you were a teenager feeling like your family fell apart overnight, he was just a toddler who lost his parents and felt like his entire family resented his existence."

"You're pressing charges," I told her, unwilling to let him off that easily. He committed assault, stalking, breaking and entering, and intimidation. He was a criminal.

"I will, but I want to propose that part of his sentencing involves getting help at a psychiatric facility."

"He needs to go to jail. He's dangerous. He was preying on women and he assaulted you."

She sighed, rubbing her thumb across my beard. It'd started filling in again since I hadn't shaved after she left to come back to Chicago. "I don't want to let him off easy, but I want to make sure he gets the help he needs. You don't think he deserves it, but he's your family."

I nodded, clenching my jaw, knowing she wasn't going to give in.

"So Boston?" she asked, a smirk on her lips.

"You know you've always got a home with me," I told her, placing my hand over hers and feeling myself calm at her touch. She was safe, a little banged up, but safe, and that was all I wanted.

We'd have to figure out all the details if she was coming back to Boston with me, and the selfish part of me didn't want to press her about it being the right decision anymore. I wanted her with me. We were bound together now, and I would never willingly release those ties.

"You just had to get yourself put in the hospital the same week as Nana, didn't you?" Christine asked as she marched into Kelly's hospital room the second day after she'd been admitted. The symptoms of her concussion had greatly diminished, but she was having issues with balance and she was sleeping a lot. The doctors said it was normal, so I tried not to worry too much. She was scheduled to be released in the morning, and I think both of us were ready to get out of the hospital even if it meant we had to get back to reality.

"Yes, because I clearly did this to inconvenience you," Kelly scoffed as she tried to turn herself to climb out of the hospital bed. She hated being confined to it, and she hated the walker they had been making her use even more, but I wasn't willing to risk anything. The second set of CT scans didn't show any additional swelling or any bleeding on the brain, but she'd still been knocked around quite a bit and was fragile. Her bruises were angry looking — dark purple with yellow smudges around the edges. It made my blood pressure rise every time I saw the outline of Trent's fingerprints on her neck and her upper arm.

"No, don't get up." Christine waved as she approached the bed, Sam following close behind. He looked concerned for Kelly, and I appreciated that the two of them had done all they could to watch out for her. It really did come down to shitty timing. Trent had shown up at exactly the wrong time and none of us had been able to protect her. As much as I wanted to place additional blame, mostly on myself, it was all his fault. The best way to avoid being assaulted was for the person perpetrating the assault not to be a gigantic fuckwad, not anything else.

"How're you feeling?" Sam asked quietly as he took a seat in the chair next to the window that overlooked the parking lot. Kelly had joked that she had the typical Chicago deluxe view, but I knew she was done with hospitals for a while.

"I've clearly been better," Kelly smiled as she motioned to the bruises that still littered the side of her face and neck. "But nothing that I can't handle."

"We're sorry we weren't there," Christine sighed, her face pinched with worry.

"You had no way of knowing that he'd come after me like he did. I don't think anyone expected this to be his next step."

"But we were supposed to be there." Christine frowned as she reached down to grasp Kelly's hand. She still had an IV for anti-nausea medicine and to keep her hydrated. She'd been tapering herself off the pain medication.

"How's Nana?" Kelly asked, clearly wanting to change the subject. She'd been trying to deflect the conversation away from herself today, hating that her parents — and me — had been hovering. They were just scared for her, as was I, but her attacker was still in jail, having been denied bail until he was arraigned. He'd apparently gotten himself considered a flight risk when they found out he'd recently been in Connecticut. We couldn't prove anything yet, but it looked like he was the vandal who'd broken into the workshop. It didn't seem so random any more.

When Kelly told me what he'd said to her in the parking garage, it seemed finding out about us had escalated his behavior. I knew she was right, and he needed help, but it made me sick to my stomach that he'd attacked her because being with me had triggered him.

"She's alright. Driving Piet insane with trying to bribe nurses into breaking her out of the hospital, but her hip surgery went well. She'll be OK after a few months of physical therapy. Nothing is going to slow Nana down. Mason showed up once she was out of surgery and she asked to be transferred to a private suite that doesn't allow unapproved visitors — her son included — when my mother tried to sneak in with him."

"I love your Nana," Kelly laughed as she reached over to squeeze my hand. "But my parents would lose their shit if I didn't let them visit. You'd think I was terminal from the way they've been hovering. Thank goodness Chase's morning sickness finally made an appearance or they'd never have left."

"I'm sure Evan is loving the extra attention," Sam chuckled as he sat back in his chair, Christine joining him in the seat next to it, the two interlacing their fingers as they chatted with Kelly. I hadn't spent much time around them, but I knew they'd been good friends to Kelly over the last few months. "But I can totally picture him playing tea party."

"Like you're any better," Christine laughed, pushing her shoulder playfully into Sam's.

"So about that favor you owe me, Christine," Kelly started as she squeezed my fingers, smiling widely.

"Oh frick," her friend laughed, cringing before she looked over at Sam, who clearly had no idea what the two women were talking about judging by the frown on his face. "I knew you wouldn't forget about that."

"Don't worry, it's not that bad," Kelly laughed. "Have you two given any thought into upgrading from a one-bedroom apartment? I might have a lead on a good opportunity for you to pick up a two-bedroom condo in your neighborhood at market value."

THIRTY-NINE

3 MONTHS LATER

Nathan

Boston

It took two months for Kelly to settle all the details of her move and get her condo sold to Sam and Christine. They were more than happy to do a quick sale to take over her mortgage, and Kelly was anxious to get out of Chicago. Deacon was more than accommodating, giving her a month of paid leave to get herself packed up and settled. He wasn't as resistant to the move as I'd feared he might be, telling Kelly he was more than happy with her work while she'd been gone, so he didn't see any reason why her working remotely couldn't become the norm.

She'd still need to make the occasional trip back to Chicago, but I fully intended on traveling with her, and she had Christine and Sam to keep her safe if I wasn't able to. Tom and Charley had also offered up their guest room if Kelly didn't mind a screaming baby for a next-door neighbor.

After meeting with the Cook County prosecutor, Kelly had convinced them to give Trent a plea deal. He'd spend eighteen months in jail for the assault and stalking charges and another six months in a psychiatric center to satisfy his incarceration terms. If he had any issues while he was locked up, they could revoke the early release, but he seemed remorseful when the lawyers had all met with him. He was facing over five years in prison if his case went to court.

Despite not wanting anything to do with him, my older brother insisted on paying for his lawyer, knowing that while Trent had made some colossally big mistakes, the formerly Bradley Harrison the third was still our little brother. My sister had broken the news to our mother, and thankfully she hadn't relapsed, instead telling my sister that she was sorry things hadn't turned out differently. I knew she always harbored some emotional guilt for refusing to take

Bradley in as a toddler, but she wasn't fit to care for him then and neither was I.

"Come on," Kelly insisted, tugging my hand as I locked the Jeep doors and stepped over the curb to the sidewalk. "They're waiting. You know how Em feels about tardiness."

"He can keep his pants on. We're not late yet."

"Quit stalling," Kelly pouted as she dragged me toward the door to the photography gallery at the storefront of Emory's studio.

I knew she was right. I was stalling, but I still had trouble accepting that she was ready to start her rope training. She'd been a quick study with knots, tying up all our furniture in her spare time after unpacking her boxes in the apartment, half of her things going into storage.

She'd had me build her a small desk nestled into the living room window, taking up residence there or on our bed while I was at work. I worried about her being by herself all day, but Trent was serving his time, and I knew my building was secure. It also gave me the incentive to work normal hours, not burn myself out as I used to.

"I'm sorry, sunshine. I know you're ready." Leaning over to kiss her cheek, she smirked at me, reaching back to tap me on the ass. She'd convinced me to slip in my little friend before we left the apartment, and I was anxious to see what it felt like while I was partially suspended.

Emory had agreed to mentor Kelly as a rigger, and the two of them had been working on partial suspension techniques for the last several weeks. Today was the test of her skills, so I was her rope model, even if it made me nervous. It'd been a few months since I'd done suspension work, and the memories of my last scene with Grace weren't ones I wanted to revisit despite forgiving Marisa for her behavior.

I'd also been finding it hard not to be extremely protective of Kelly. Talia had introduced her to her friend Max, who was a crisis counselor. She'd been amazing at helping her work through some of her residual trauma from the attack. It killed me to see Kelly suffering from insomnia and crying after the first time she'd initiated some intimacy between the two of us since the assault. I'd let her lead, not wanting to risk triggering anything, but I knew she was frustrated by some of the things she'd liked prior to the attack now making her skin crawl.

The first time I'd jokingly tugged on her ponytail she'd ended up on the bathroom floor sobbing. I'd felt like shit for days afterward, keeping my touches with her wholly gentle, but she'd been upset I was holding back from her.

Over the last few months it was a balance between her pushing her boundaries in the safety of our bedroom and letting herself heal without extra pressure. Surprisingly, we'd discovered that light impact play helped her start to enjoy my touch again in the playroom. She'd also been taking the lead more and asking to top and regain some of the control she'd lost over her body.

"Thank you for agreeing to help," she smiled as she opened the door, holding it for me to enter, and then flicking the lock on the front door behind us. I turned the sign that indicated the gallery was closed and followed behind Kelly as she parted the curtain to the photography studio.

"Of course, sunshine," I whispered, squeezing her hand and leaning over to kiss her temple. "You know I'm here however you need me. I have to admit I've been anticipating this for a while now."

She smiled, pressing her forehead to my arm as she snaked her arms around my waist. It'd likely still take some time, but I was content to let her go at her own pace while we continued to develop a deeper emotional connection. The fleeting thoughts of marriage I'd had while she was in the hospital were still there, but I was waiting for her to let me know it was something she wanted. There wasn't any rush.

Music carried from the back playroom, Talia's voice sounding through the door.

"We're here," Kelly shouted over the music, pausing before she peeked around the door threshold. While neither couple minded, Kelly had walked in on them accidentally mid-scene a few weeks ago and had been cautious ever since.

"Finally," Talia laughed, peeking around the corner with a large metal dildo in one hand and a polishing cloth in the other. She didn't even pause, pulling Kelly into a hug and pointing her large metal friend in my direction. "You were cutting it close."

Glancing at my watch, I saw we still had five minutes until we'd been ordered to arrive. "He can keep his panties on."

383

"You know how he feels about those," Talia joked as she tugged Kelly into the playroom, stashing her toy in the large cabinet of toys. Their collection was much larger than mine, but I also didn't get them all for free.

"Well, I left mine at home, so no worries there."

Kelly smirked when she looked back at me, knowing that there wasn't much underneath my athletic shorts. She'd edged me on the way here, suggestively rubbing me while I tried to concentrate on driving through the light weekend afternoon traffic. I knew when we were done here she wanted to play.

"I've got your harness ready," Talia nodded to the large leather bed in the center of the room. Em's space was quite impressive, and I was almost jealous I didn't have a larger apartment. My playroom was tiny in comparison, but still capable of meeting most of our needs.

Kelly released my hand as I crossed the room, pulling off my shirt before stepping into the harness and quickly tightening the straps. She wasn't quite ready to make rope harnesses for suspension work, so this would support the ties she was working on today while keeping the pressure evenly spaced on my upper legs.

"We ready to get started?" Em asked as he came out of the back room, using the pulley system to lower his suspension grate.

"Yup," Kelly chirped, grabbing a bundle of rope from Talia's hands and starting to unwind the outer rope coil.

I quietly listened to Emory and Kelly moving into position under the grate. My friend calmly instructed my partner as she worked on binding my chest, learning how to use the pulley system and secure her knots before moving on to the next section of the complicated suspension tie.

Not wanting to interfere, I listened to her quiet instructions, moving as she guided me, letting her lead. It was hard for me to submit the control in something that felt like second nature, but watching my mentor working with Kelly flooded my system with an intense sense of pride and satisfaction. She didn't have to learn how to do this, she wanted to, and she was taking it seriously.

When she got to the point where the rope could hold my weight, I couldn't keep the smile off my face as she gently pressed me back into the hold, watching my reactions and checking the grip of the knots.

"Are you doing OK, stud?" she asked as I felt myself testing the tie, flexing my shoulders and my hips as the ropes gently bit into my bare skin.

"I'm perfect," I smiled as I watched the smile slowly grow across her face. A little under a year ago, we'd met briefly, and at the time, I hadn't known what my life was missing. But circumstances had brought us back together again, showing us what could be. So when we finally had time to explore our attraction, we knew it wasn't something either of us could ignore. "And so are you, sunshine. I love you."

THE END

BONUS CHAPTER: MORE THAN WORDS
Book 4 of The Words Series

ONE

Isobel

Boston

My heels made an annoying clicking noise as I took off across the main lobby of my office building. I was late, and my Uber driver would bail if I didn't get my ass outside in the next two minutes. My rider rating couldn't take a hit, or I'd be pushed back down with the idiots who drank too much and puked all over someone's seats or the people who got dinged because they were morally opposed to basic personal hygiene. Since I'd sold my car, I relied on having a good rating to get to and from work most days on time.

"Finally," the young driver sighed as I slid into the backseat of his waiting Toyota and pulled the door closed. "Took yah long enough, lady. It's rush hour, and I can't have yah killin' my rides for tha rest of the night."

"Sorry," I huffed, trying to straighten out my long pencil skirt. Changing had been out of the question after my meeting with the executive marketing team had run long. Those lucky bastards didn't have to go to this ridiculous team-building that Sloane, my boss, had arranged with the publishing house genre heads. "Missed the elevator and had to run barefoot down ten flights of stairs."

"Bet that was somethin' ta see," he smirked but quickly averted his eyes at the glare I returned. Men. This was why I was keeping to myself lately. No matter the age or walk of life, men were constantly judging me based on my looks. Apparently, tall, blonde and dimpled warranted the male population of Boston and the surrounding tri-state area to think I was a ditz or a whore. Or both. Never mind that I worked my ass off in High School to get out of my shitty midwestern town and earn a scholarship to an Ivy League university.

And it couldn't possibly register with them that I worked three jobs — and no, none of them were stripping, although it might have paid better — during undergrad and grad school to pay for what my scholarships didn't cover. Which was a lot when you lived halfway across the country from your family, who pretended you didn't exist because you left behind the family farm to do something they considered pointless.

But none of that mattered because if you had a vagina, you clearly couldn't be taken seriously half the time. I hated that my career was seemingly at a standstill. I hated that the genre I chose to edit was constantly being trashed despite the millions of dollars of revenue it generated for the publishing house each year. None of that mattered because I was cute, blonde, and female. But fuck dwelling on what I couldn't change because those bastards could lick the sole of my one pair of Louboutins if they had a problem with me being an empowered woman.

I could survive in Boston just fine without a support network. I had friends, sort of. And I had loyal co-workers, well…I had dedicated interns. And I had the support of my boss, who was an inspiration to women in the publishing industry everywhere.

"We're here," the Uber driver announced quietly, looking warily at me in the mirror. Maybe my stony glare and ten minutes of silence had changed his decision to make smartass comments about my appearance. But I wasn't expecting miracles. He just wouldn't say them to my face.

"Thank you," I sighed, plastering on my biggest smile and quickly gathering my things to make my way into the ax-throwing bar. I was already late and didn't want to stay any later than I had to.

"Alright," Sloane called the group to order once I'd settled in at a barstool, my coworkers quieting down. "The teams are as follows. Chloe and Roger are in bay one against Logan and Ryker. Amanda and I are in bay two against Julia and Mark. Kyle and Zuki are in bay three against Grant and Hilla. Fred and Reilly are in bay four against Donna and Jacob. And last but certainly not least Lorenzo and Kate in bay five against Isobel and Adrian."

"Oh, joy," I muttered under my breath as Adrian made his way through the crowd toward me.

He was objectively handsome, tall, with broad, muscular shoulders, light blue eyes, and hair as dark as ink. The first time I'd seen him, I'd stopped short, my heart beating erratically in my chest as I watched him verbally berating the copy machine on our floor. He'd somehow managed to get sheets of paper stuck in every single place it could jam inside the machine. That's what he got for trying to duplex print an entire manuscript on there instead of ordering a bound copy from the printing department. Rookie mistake.

I'd thought it was adorable, the scowl on his full lips, the muttered curse words thrown into his thick Bostonian accent, but then he'd noticed me watching, delivered one extremely sexist come-on, and I'd disliked him ever since.

He was arrogant. He was an asshole. He treated some of the interns like they were worse than gum stuck on the sole of his expensive Italian leather shoes. He was a genre elitist. And despite all that, he was annoyingly good at his job. I'd never seen another editor quite as good at plucking obscure authors out of a submissions pile and getting them to the top of all the must-read charts. He often saw potential in authors that others overlooked. It made me simultaneously in awe of him and constantly befuddled when he continued to curate this persona of a crude playboy.

And worst of all, he was easily the most attractive man I'd ever seen when he kept his mouth shut. There was something about the set of his mouth and how his eyes crinkled when he was about to say something stupid. He *knew* half the shit he said would get a negative reaction, but he said it anyway. The man had absolutely no filter.

He was also a misogynistic jerk. And did I mention arrogant?

"Hey, Is," he greeted. The polished professional façade fully in place. This was the face most people saw. They didn't see the strong Boston accent and the sarcastic quips I'd spied when he interacted with people outside the office. I was certain the phrase 'wicked smart' had never passed his lips on company property. And his 'yous and yeahs' didn't sound anything other than crisp and enunciated perfectly.

When he was in work mode, he was on. Impressive degree with honors, deep voice with perfect inflection, every strand of shiny dark hair precisely in place, expensive suits with expert double Windsor knots in designer silk ties.

Once, just once, I wanted to see the veneer crack and see the real Adrian. The one he'd buried deep under this giant douche persona he showed everyone else. I knew there had to be more than met the eye, or the ear, but he was so insistent on cultivating the office asshole persona that he never let anyone see past the bullshit.

"Adrian." I nodded, hating that the hair on the back of my neck stood on end as his arm brushed against mine.

"Are you sure you can handle doing this in those shoes?" he asked, leaning in toward me so only I could hear his words. "Not that they aren't amazing, but I can't see three-inch heels being good for your balance."

"Are you sure you can handle this with the three inches you're packing below the belt? I mean, I'm sure you think it's amazing, but it can't be good for…well, anyone." I hissed as I stepped away from him. I bumped into Lorenzo, grimacing as his drink sloshed over the edge of his glass.

"You alright there, Isobel?" Lorenzo asked as he reached over to steady me with a hand on my elbow.

"She's fine."

Adrian's calloused fingertips closed over my other elbow, and I wobbled as my eyes darted between the two handsome men who towered over me.

"No thanks to you, I'm sure," Renz muttered as he narrowed his eyes at Adrian. There was no love lost between the two rival editors. Where Adrian was an asshole, which most of the interns, including my own, called Dickhead. Lorenzo was the office eye candy, and the interns ogled his selection of snug dress pants.

Lorenzo *was* nice, but his nice-guy personality left nothing about him to the imagination. A good heart wrapped in a pretty package. While that should have been attractive, especially to a woman who was well into her thirties and should be thinking about settling down someday, it seemed a little anticlimactic. What you saw was what you'd get. All that you'd get.

There was no mystery there, no spark. No passion simmering under the surface. No secrets to uncover that no one else knew about. Maybe I'd been editing romance novels for too long and had become immune to the 'nice guy.' After all, the toxic hero seemed to sell, and women swooned over an asshole by the millions — especially if he had millions. Too bad the asshole in my real life wasn't going to be pulling a redemption arc anytime soon.

"I'm fine," I told them both, clearing my throat. "I'll be fine. Thank you."

"I have some sneakers in my gym bag if yah need em," Adrian whispered as he leaned into my personal space again. My eyes flashed over to Lorenzo, but he was already deep in conversation with his partner, Kate, a non-fiction editor who had as much personality as wallpaper paste — and was just as in demand as an antiquated wall covering adhesive.

"I'm good, thanks," I responded, glancing at his polished leather shoes. His feet weren't huge, but they were also substantially larger than my size nines.

"You sure? I'd hate to see those affect your aim."

Turning to face him, I paused, taking in the lone curl of hair that had fallen onto his forehead. I'd rarely seen his hair looking anything but like it belonged on a Ken doll, and my fingers twitched with the urge to push it back into place.

"My aim will be just fine."

He hummed, nodding before bringing his glass to his lips, taking a sip of the amber liquid inside while maintaining eye contact with me.

"Want to place a wager on it?"

"I'm not betting on ax-throwing with you. You're bigger than I am and stronger…" His grin grew as I kept talking, and I had the increasing urge to dig one of my heels into the top of his foot.

"No, no, keep going." He smirked as he did that masculine thing where he was clearly undressing me with his eyes. "I'm interested in all this sudden praise you're throwing out."

My nipples pricked with how he paused when his gaze was aimed at my cleavage. Pig. "Eyes up here, big boy."

He chuckled, tipping his glass in my direction before leaning in close to my ear. "Which one is it? Do I only have three inches, or am I a big boy? Surely they aren't exclusive, or your boyfriends have been seriously lacking in what they're packing."

I clenched my teeth together as I fought the shiver that ran up my spine at how his warm breath felt as it fanned over my bare neck. He smelled good, fresh, and alluring, with a hint of wood smoke and something vaguely floral.

Considering he spent most of his lunch breaks in the corporate gym on the bottom floor of our building, he always surprisingly looked perfectly put together.

I hated running into him because my fair skin only turned bright red with physical exertion. Genetics had ensured I didn't get that glow some women got when they exercised. I looked like a hot mess with an excessive perspiration problem. No amount of dry shampoo would save me from an hour of preparation to put myself back together to head into the office.

"Hmm," he hummed before he leaned away. "Care to make a wager on the outcome of this evening?"

Turning toward him, I frowned. "We're on the same team."

"I'm aware." He nodded and took another sip of his drink, his eyes clocking the nervous shifting I'd been doing since he'd set his sights on me. "Total points, bonuses for bullseyes."

"You going to keep score?" I asked, narrowing my eyes. I didn't trust him not to cheat.

He shrugged, lifting his chin toward me. "Don't trust me?"

"Should I?"

He'd given me zero reasons in our history as coworkers to trust a word that came out of his mouth, in a professional capacity or otherwise. He was constantly bragging about his authors and their rankings to anyone who would listen. Didn't help that his department had the largest share of the advertising budget. I could put a few of my authors on the Times list with that kind of exposure.

"Fair point," he laughed, stepping in and placing his free hand in the center of my back. It wasn't somewhere inappropriate, but the jolt it sent between my legs hadn't gotten the message. "You keep track. My math is shit. But I'm sure you can handle it with that impressive Ivy League education your parents bestowed upon you."

If he only knew my parents were grain farmers who cared more about crop yields and the newest corn hybrids on the market than whether their youngest daughter got an education at one of the top English programs in the country. I may have dressed the part, but I wasn't some elitist snob like he perceived me to be. My upbringing was probably less glamorous than his. He'd likely never been asked to mix organic fertilizer by hand in his life. My job during high school had literally been shit-stirring. And not the kind he engaged in.

"Because you're clearly lacking in educational pedigree."

"According to some," he laughed, dropping his hand and stepping around me as Sloane motioned for us to move toward the cages where we'd be doing the actual ax throwing, not just the lobbing of verbal ones. I'd missed the entire demonstration, but how hard could it be?

Hold ax, aim at the target, pretend bullseye is Adrian's face and throw.

"You ready for this?" he asked as we stepped inside the enclosure. Kate and Lorenzo were standing against the opposite side, clearly planning their strategy.

"What are the stakes?" I asked quietly as my fingers trailed over the handle of one of the axes in the hanger on the wall.

"What do yah want?" Adrian chuckled, his palm settling in the center of my back.

"You to quit disparaging my authors. It makes you sound like an arrogant douche when you go off on how other genres are beneath you."

"I never said romance was beneath me, Is. I said that the market share wasn't as deep."

"Quit comparing the two. You stay in your lane. I'll stay in mine."

"But it's so fun to veer into your lane and cause some chaos." I could hear the smirk in his voice without needing to turn around.

"What do you want?"

He paused, his fingers flexing against my back. "I don't think you're ready for what I want."

"Try me." The smoldering look he had aimed in my direction may have worked on other women, but I wasn't some naïve intern.

"One kiss."

Rolling my eyes, I turned around and placed my hand in the center of his chest, pushing until he stepped backward. "Done. No tongue."

"Deal."

He abruptly stepped back, taking an ax from the holder and stepping up to the line.

"You mind if I got first throw, Renz?" Adrian asked as he titled his neck from side to side and rolled his shoulders back. I tried not to stare at the way his dress shirt stretched across the broad expanse of his back, but his little warm-up had made it difficult to look away.

With a quick wink over his shoulder, he staggered his feet and brought up his hand. With a quick snap of his arm, the ax flew through the air, wedging itself into the center of the target with a solid *thwack*.

I had a feeling I'd just been played. Smug bastard.

As the night wore on, the soreness in my feet grew, but I refused to admit defeat as I stepped up to the line to throw my final ax. If I managed to get it clearly in the bullseye, I could tie Adrian. But I knew he'd stopped actively trying to win a little while ago. He didn't think I had a chance and was teasing me with the close score. And I was taking the bait because my competitive streak couldn't let me admit defeat.

Kate and Lorenzo had lost interest, checking their phones as Adrian and I continued to bicker between shots.

He seemed to think Red Sox fans were more devoted than Cubs fans, and I was educating him on how despite their recent World Series win, the Cubs fans were diehard loyalists who would celebrate their team until their dying breath, even if they never made another series run in this lifetime.

"Oh, come on. The Sox're one of tha originals. How can you not love the legacy of one of the first franchises in American baseball?"

"I didn't say they weren't loved. I said Cubs fans were more devoted."

"Bullshit," he chuckled as she shook his head, picking up his glass of scotch and swallowing the remainder. I tried not to stare as the muscles in his throat flexed, but judging by the smirk, I failed. "Fenway is so much coolah than Wrigley. There's history heah in Boston."

I smirked at his accent slipping through, and his eyes widened, a frown crossing his features. "No, I get it. Architecturally Fenway is nice, but I think it's easier to be a fair-weather fan than one who is enthusiastic for the underdog, even when they're beaten year after year."

"After year, after year, after year," he smirked, and I kicked my foot backward, my heel poking him in the shin.

"Don't be a dick," I laughed.

"Ah, but I've gotta live up to my name."

"At some point, you could just stop being a dick, and maybe the nickname would die out."

"And what fun would that be?" He winked. Of course, he liked that people called him a dickhead, not always behind his back.

"Quit distracting me."

"You're the one who keeps bringing up your mediocre baseball team." Turning around one last time, I fixed him with a glare, but his cocky smile just widened. "You gonna throw that ax or just tease its poor shaft all night?"

Kate gasped at his crass question, Lorenzo's face pinching into a frown as he looked between the two of us. Our team had already won. At this point, my last throw was just a formality. And it determined whether Adrian got that kiss he wanted.

"Maybe it likes to take it slow."

"Maybe you're stalling because you know you'll lose," he taunted.

Gritting my teeth, I took a deep breath and focused on the center ring, pulling my arm back and breathing out as I released my weapon toward its target.

My eyes closed before it hit, my body jolting with the sound of the impact.

"Nice throw," Renz cheered, and I opened my eyes, surprised that I'd managed to hit dead center on the target.

"Thanks," I smiled as I looked back in his direction.

"You were a formidable opponent," Adrian drawled as I turned toward our side of the range and wiped my sweaty palms down my skirt. "Guess it was a draw."

"We both know you let me catch up. Does that mean we're both winners?"

As much as I wanted him to quit being a dick to my authors, I wasn't sure I wanted his lips anywhere near mine. That seemed like a terrible idea. We worked together. He was an epic asshat, and my attraction to him was solely to his body, not his lacking personality.

"Nah. I don't need a pity kiss. We're good."

"If you say so." I nodded, relieved.

"Well," Sloane said from the opposite side of the fence, smiling widely at us. "Looks like the two of you scored the most points tonight. Guess you're my lucky team."

"We were keeping score for something other than bragging rights?" I asked, glancing over at Adrian. He shrugged, looking back toward our boss.

"Well, I didn't tell anyone ahead of time. But the team with the most points gets to represent Vivid at the New England publishers conference next month."

"I have to go with Adrian?" I asked, trying to sound less annoyed than I was. While he'd been tolerable tonight, I didn't want to be trapped in Eastern Maine with him for a week. While I liked going to trade conferences, I knew we'd have to spend time together if we were being sent to represent Vivid. And I'd have to pretend I didn't despise him.

"I was secretly hoping it'd be the two of you, with the press Adrian got for Stone's last release and the articles you've been contributing about the resurgence of romance novels into mainstream media with streaming services greenlighting movies, I think you'd be good representatives. Neither of you has any releases that conflict with the conference, so it seems like a perfect fit."

Glancing over at Adrian, I tried to gauge if he was dreading this as much as I was, but his eyes weren't focused on our boss. They were focused squarely on my ass. Great.

"I'm sure we'll have a great time. Have Chloe send over the itinerary to Sam so we can make sure all the edits on my plate are covered, but I'm in."

Sloane smiled, reaching over to squeeze his arm. He grinned at her in response, and she cleared her throat before she looked over at me. Of course, she'd fall for his bullshit. Everyone seemed to. "Think you can make it work, Isobel?"

"Do I really have an option? Neither of us has any conflicts, and it seems like a great opportunity." I tried to tack on a smile at the end, but I wasn't sure I was successful with the slight frown she directed at me before she stepped back, plastering a smile on her face.

"Great. I'll get you all the details this week and have travel book your accommodations. I know the venue shifted, so we need to get on booking rooms."

Yeah, there had better be rooms, plural. While I'd shared accommodations with female co-workers in the past at conferences, I was definitely not sharing the same hotel room with Adrian for a whole week. I'd rather sleep in the rental car.

As Sloane walked away, Adrian stepped forward, placing his hand on my back as he deposited his empty glass on the high-top table in the corner. "Don't worry, Is. I'll make sure we have a good time. Maybe you'll lighten up a bit outside the office."

"Ugh. You're such a dick," I hissed as I stepped around him. "Just because I don't fall on yours doesn't mean I'm an uptight bitch."

"Hey," he chuckled, holding up his hands as he stepped to the side, holding open the net for me. Kate and Lorenzo took off while we talked to Sloane, and the rest of our co-workers had taken off or headed toward the bar down the street. "I never called you a bitch. I happen to think wicked smart, opinionated women are sexy as fuck."

"You lost me at opinionated. Sorry that standing up for my authors and my *chosen* genre makes me opinionated."

"I thought we were calling a truce," he chuckled, seemingly unaffected by my hostility.

"We tied. And you said you didn't want a pity kiss, so I thought that meant I'd be the recipient of your closed-minded, sexist, crude, incorrect, and often offensive commentary."

"I can keep up my end of the bargain, I'll try to watch my mouth, but I don't want you to kiss me if you don't want to. I'm not that much of a dick."

"You sure about that?" I scoffed and pulled out my phone, ordering a ride as he followed me toward the door. I would try to escape him outside, but it was still raining and dark.

"Trust me, Is." He smirked as he stepped in close and tucked a few loose strands of my hair behind my ear. "If you're not begging for it, I'm not interested. I can be patient."

"You're likely to be in the ground before that happens," I growled as the alert that my ride had arrived popped up on my screen. I didn't look back as I pushed through the door and jogged across the sidewalk to my awaiting car.

As I looked back toward the door, Adrian watched me through the glass, a smug grin on his face. Pressing my hand against the car window, I flipped my middle finger, hating that he had turned me into this person.

His smile widened through the rain-streaked glass, and he held his hands over his heart as I narrowed my eyes and faced forward. I was going to fucking kill him for baiting me into competing against him. It was his fault I would be stuck going to that conference with him, and he seemed to be looking forward to tormenting me the entire time.

BONUS CHAPTER: MORE THAN WORDS
Book 4 of The Words Series

TWO

Adrian

Boston

As I stood at the bar window and watched the car pull away, I couldn't help the smile on my face. I knew Isobel didn't care for me. If the constant narrowed eyes and look of disdain painted across her face weren't an indication, the very heated conversations we tended to have every time we were in the same room together should probably clue me in.

I knew why she didn't like me. It was my own fault, but I couldn't seem to turn it off around her. This bullshit polished professional persona was my armor. The protection from the real world that I'd strapped on at sixteen and had never taken off. At least not around anyone but my family. I was pretty sure my Ma would beat the shit out of me if she knew half the things that came out of my mouth.

My twin brother and I may have grown up without a dad past kindergarten and holes in our shoes, but we'd been taught manners. Too bad being the nice guy didn't get you shit in the world. It sure as fuck didn't get you respect, and it definitely didn't remove the target from your chest around the good ol' boys club. But I was as good an actor as I was an editor.

I'd spent half of high school with my face buried in a book and the other half with a bat in my hands. Those were the only things that were gonna keep me outta the military or a factory. My brother hadn't been so lucky. He used to joke that I was the brains and he was the brawn, but things had changed a lot since we were kids.

My phone started buzzing in my pocket, and I pulled it out, frowning as his face scrolled across the screen. Where I was all flash and good looks, he was rugged and, well...hairy. Chin-length dark

397

hair sprinkled with grays and a full beard had covered up the scars I knew he still carried from his time in the Marines.

"How's it going, Hutch?"

He huffed, probably ready to tear into me for how I could mask my accent. He'd never been able to master it, and despite his now effusive use of random jarhead slang from his time in the service, I don't think he ever would. Not that he needed to; despite two tours of duty, he was still pretty much a townie.

"This fuckin guy, Jesus fuckin Christ, Ad. Where are yah?"

I'd told him this morning I had a thing after work, but something must have happened at home for him to be calling me.

"Where's Pops? You need me to find him?"

A rough cough came through the line, and I winced, hating that every little thing seemed to be harder for him since he'd gotten home two years ago. He'd come a long way, but his body had taken a lot of abuse at the hands of others in the last ten years.

"Yah. If you can pull yah self away from whateva cake eater shit you've been doin. That old fuck told me he was goin to Dunkies and took off. I already called there, and the packie at the end of the block, and nobody's seen 'em."

"Does Ma know he's missing again?"

"Are yah fuckin kidding me with this? I'm not fuckin tellin her shit," he laughed, then lowered his voice. "She's on an overnight. I don't want her to worry when she can't get home anyway."

"There's a Pats game on. I'm sure he's down at the bar," I sighed, grabbing my bag and heading toward the door. I knew if it weren't raining, he'd go after our grandfather, but his chair wasn't the best in the rain, and he couldn't use the cane with the sidewalks this wet. I also knew that he wasn't always the soberest once he took his final dose of meds. He was careful not to drink, but I knew some of his painkillers packed a steady punch. It also tended to make his Bostonisms a little more pronounced. There was no doubt which side of the bay he came from once his mouth opened past 8:00 pm.

"You're a fuckin gem, Ad. You know I wouldn't call unless I was worried."

"I know, Hutch," I sighed, tucking my face down as I jogged toward the parking lot where I'd left my car earlier. "I'll find 'em and get him home. You need anything? Did you eat?"

He growled, and I knew I'd hit a nerve. He didn't like me babying him or feeling sorry for him, but I knew he didn't have the best track record of taking care of himself. "I'm fine. Just find Pops, and we're square."

"I..." the line disconnected, and I clenched my eyes shut as I pressed the button on the remote to my car, the chirp of the doors unlocking echoing despite the steady downpour.

I bet Isobel wouldn't think I was quite the dick I acted like if she knew exactly how I spent most of my time. I may flirt inappropriately or say sexist things at work, but it was all bullshit. I spent half my time babysitting my senile eighty-five-year-old grandfather and the other trying to figure out how to make my twin brother's life easier because I felt guilty my life had turned out so vastly different from his.

Maybe things would be different if his last tour hadn't gone so far off the rails, but I'd always felt this lingering sense of guilt that I'd gone to college and made something of myself while he spent his youth devoted to a country that'd cut him loose the second all his body parts weren't intact. He'd missed out on a lot in the fifteen years he'd been in the service, and I knew it ate at him that his sacrifices had all fallen apart with his injury.

But he'd really kick me in the nuts if he knew I was still feeling so intensely guilty because he was proud and tough and didn't want anyone to pity him for anything. But I still had a hard time seeing past the imagery of him lying in a hospital bed overseas with part of his leg missing and bright red scars littering his face.

"Hey." The bartender, Jeanette, nodded as I pushed open the door to the neighborhood bar that Pops had treated as a second home since he'd retired twenty years ago. "He's in the back with the other old fucks. They're playin cards. He's behaved himself tonight."

"Do I need to close out his tab?" I asked, bracing myself for how much it'd be. Based on how much he'd drank, I could usually tell what kind of mood the old man would be in.

"Nah," she smiled, waving my hand away. "He paid for the two he had in cash and has been nursing a watta."

Thank fuck. I wasn't in the mood to have to wrestle him down the sidewalk in the rain if he was past the point of being belligerent. Pops was pretty good-natured most of the time, but if he was deep into the whiskey, sometimes things got ugly.

399

I knew most of the people at work thought I worked out so much to look good and because I was vain, and to be honest, I did like the appreciative looks I got because of my physique, but it was mostly because of Pops. The old man was the same height as me, even though he appeared a few inches shorter because of how he stooped when he walked, but he was a wiry thing. And I'd also bulked up when Hutch was discharged because I knew Ma couldn't afford to have someone else come in when she was working, and I needed to be able to lift him.

He wouldn't let me touch him now, but before the prosthetic and all the physical therapy he'd done in the past year, he'd needed the help. Now he got around mostly fine, just not when it was raining.

"Thanks," I mumbled, lightly patting the bar, shooting her a wink before I wove through the tables toward the back half of the bar, where the old man coughs, and dry laughter rang out despite the late hour.

"Ad, my boy," Pops laughed as he clapped his hands, clearly happy to see me. So it'd been a good day. Some days he didn't recognize me, and those were the hardest. Those were the days I fucking hated dementia and what it did to people. Telling elaborate lies to a man I'd spent my entire life admiring just to get him to walk home at night even made me feel like shit.

"Alright, Pops, time for yah beauty sleep."

His cronies chuckled, and some patted my arm as I walked around the table to lend my hand to Pops. He'd never admit it, but he wasn't as spry as he used to be, his boxing days squarely in the past. It was hard to watch him get older, but I was glad he was still around. I knew he'd been lonely since my grandma passed on, but there were still enough of his old neighborhood buddies alive that he kept himself busy.

"Yeah, I guess yah right, Ad. Us O'Neill's have to keep these mugs lookin' good for the ladies. Wouldn't want them to miss out with having to look at all these ugly old fucks. Isn't that right, my boy?"

"Yeah, Pops. It's all for the ladies," I laughed and shook my head. My grandfather hadn't looked at another woman since the late fifties. Even dead, my grandmother was the love of his life. But our family did have a reputation for being pretty boys, which had made running around the neighborhood as a teenager kinda fun. Especially when there were two of us. Hutch had been more the heartbreaker between us, but neither of us had ever had to work much for female company. Sometimes it was the same female, but that had been years.

"See youse assholes tomorrah," Pops yawned as he patted the shoulders of a few of his buddies as I cupped his elbow and led him away from the table. I knew he'd stay here all night if I let him, but then Ma would be worried, and she hadn't worked her ass off for decades for the men in her life to give her grief. She'd already had enough heartache to last a lifetime when my father was killed.

"Bye, Jeannie," he called out, winking as the pretty bartender waved in his direction. I knew she had a soft spot for Pops, and with her cousin technically being my ex-sister-in-law, we were almost family. In the five degrees of separation way that many of the original families in the neighborhood were.

I led my grandfather to the covered front stoop of the bar, instructing him to stay put until I pulled the car up to the curb, we could have technically walked home, but I wasn't making him do that in the rain.

As soon as I pulled up, I cursed and grabbed my umbrella, hurrying around the car to shield him as he rushed as fast as he could move toward the passenger side. "Oh, I get car side service now?" he joked as I held the umbrella over his head and pulled open the door.

"Careful with the drop," I cautioned as he gripped the handle inside the door and lowered himself into the seat with a shaking arm.

"I can handle gettin' in a fuckin car, Adrian. I'm old as fuck, not a toddlah."

Biting back a sarcastic retort, I let him get himself buckled and closed the door, rushing back to the driver's side.

"So who sent you out after me this time?" he asked as I settled in his seat, turning the wipers back up and checking my mirrors before pulling away from the curb.

"Hutch," I sighed, hating that this was where we were. Pops felt like the rest of his family was always trying to keep him on a leash, but we'd had enough late nights calling around the neighborhood when he didn't come home that night to scare all of us.

"Well, can't say I blame 'em," he sighed, folding his hands in his lap. "Last week was kinda bad. I know I scared your Ma. Thought she was my Aileen and acted like a shit toward her when she came home one morning."

Ma was an ER nurse, often pulling overnight or double shifts and then taking care of my brother and my grandfather during the day when she wasn't sleeping. I told her she should think about getting a placement in one of the doctor's offices closer to the house, but she told me she'd be bored out of her mind without the grueling pace of working in trauma care. I didn't see the appeal, but I also fainted at the sight of blood, so we clearly weren't cut from the same cloth.

She excelled at fixing the messes of people's bodies. I excelled at fixing the messes of people's words.

Hutch was more like her, a field medic for years before he'd gotten Raider training.

"You know she understands, Pops," I sighed as I pulled up to the curb at the modest row house that I'd grown up in.

"Yeah, I get it, Ad. But sometimes, I feel like it's not fair that I'm still here and she's not. Your Ma is stuck with the three of us, and on my bad days, she doesn't even have me."

"Well, you're stuck with us for the time being, old man, so quit your bitchin."

"You know, if you'd quit acting like a prick, maybe she'd have another woman around."

Fuck. Getting my balls busted by the elderly now.

"She has Pen around. I don't think Ma cares if I settle down."

"Hmm," he hummed as he turned in his seat to face me. "You know that she always told me she wanted a house full of grandkids when she was little."

"Then maybe she needs to ask Hutch for another one."

"Or maybe you stop running from your problems and settle down already. Maybe I'd like to see one of your kids come into this world and put you in your place like Pen has done with your brother."

My ten-year-old niece was a little ball-buster, but she was only around on the weekends. Still, I knew she had a special bond with Pops. It wasn't that I didn't want kids. I was a work-a-holic who didn't have much time to meet women, and being dubbed the office Dickhead didn't leave much room in the office dating pool. Not that I hadn't thought about a certain feisty blonde a lot over the last five years we'd worked in the same office.

"Just somethin' to think about. When you grow a pair, you let me know."

He didn't wait for me to get out of the car, opening the door and stepping onto the sidewalk. The rain had settled into a gentle sprinkle, and I found myself staring through the streaky raindrops on the window as he pulled himself up the front steps using the handrail. My brother swung the door open before he got to the top, his middle finger extended in my direction briefly before he helped Pops in the front door and pushed it closed.

I knew I should stick around and see how things were going, but I had a lot of work I needed to catch up on if I would be out of the office for a week. Part of me was dreading keeping up the act with Isobel the entire trip, but the other part of me wondered how she'd react if I didn't bother anymore.

"Are you fucking kidding me?"

My eyes widened as I stopped midstride at the outburst coming from the partially open office door at the end of the hallway. I'd intended to stop by Isobel's office and confirm the itinerary for our travel plans, but I wasn't sure if I should just come back.

"Fuck, fuck, fuck me. God fucking dammit."

My lips pinched together as I listened to her little mini tirade. I could hear things being slammed around on her desk, and I could just imagine the little pouty look she got on her face when she was irritated — which was admittedly a lot when I was in her presence.

If her intern was in there, I didn't want to step on the hornet's nest, but as I crept forward and peeked around the edge of the frame, the table across from her desk where her guard dog often worked was empty. Maybe I could avoid a conflict with both this morning and return to my office to ensure my files were all marked for my copy-editing intern, Sam. He was typically on top of things without much interference, but I had this compulsive habit of micromanaging.

It was probably an older twin thing, but I was the planner, and Hutch was the one who often blew those plans to smithereens. I knew Sam thought it was weird that my files were all meticulously organized, but the only way I survived school was to make sure I had every single aspect obsessively covered. It was easy to let things go and backslide, but that made my skin crawl. We all had our tics, and an almost compulsive need to organize things was mine.

"What the actual fuck," Isobel sighed loudly as I watched her, throwing her phone onto her desk with a dull thump. Her forehead fell to the messy pile of papers in the middle of her desk, rising and falling a few times before she sighed again and sat back into her chair, facing the ceiling with her eyes closed.

I watched her face soften as she took a few deep breaths, the tension draining out of her shoulders.

"What do you want?" she asked in an exasperated exhale. "And quit staring at my cleavage."

Biting back the quick response, I went with something neutral, not taking the bait and getting myself in trouble. I'd been more fixated on the soft motions of her throat as she breathed than the few buttons she had unfastened on her blouse.

"Just wanted to make sure we were on the same page for tomorrow. Do you need me to go pick up the rental? I don't mind. I've got some time open this afternoon."

"Fuck," she sighed as she sat forward, scooting her chair closer to her desk and picking up her phone. "About that. There won't be one. Travel just sent over an email. They weren't able to get a car. Something about the reservations not being put in for the correct dates. We'd need to come back Tuesday, and with the closing reception not being until Thursday night, there's no way to make it work."

"What are they proposing as an alternative?"

"They were going to try to get some plane tickets figured out, but then we'd be stuck in the airport all day and still have to mess with a rental on the other end. So basically, we'd lose most of tomorrow when we could just drive there in less than four hours. Corporate travel is so stupid sometimes."

"If you're up for it, I can drive. I mean, I've got a car. Or we can take yours, or…"

"Except I don't have one." Isobel frowned as she finally glanced up and made eye contact with me. This was probably the longest we'd been in the same room together, and I hadn't managed to piss her off yet. I was sure my dumbass could come up with something quick without even trying.

"Then it's settled. I'm giving you a ride whether you like it or not."

The corner of her mouth quirked, a naughty little smirk forming as she did a slow glance at where I stood across from her desk. "Well, I have to say your tactics need a little work, and I can see how you manage to get laid as often as you do with that confidence. But probably shouldn't tell the lady she won't like it. Seems a little counterproductive."

Fuck.

Blowing a breath, I tried not to take the bait, but as she crossed her arms over her chest, the movement pushing her breasts together enticingly, my brain short-circuited.

"Well, if I were giving you that kind of ride, there wouldn't be any doubts about your enjoyment. But you would need to make sure your arms and legs were holding on tight because you might hurt yourself if you fall off."

She pinched her lips together, but she couldn't hide the smile or the blush. I knew it was a fucking stupid line to say to her, but I couldn't take it back now, and the more she fought with me, the more I craved the attention, even if it was for me being a chauvinist asshole.

"It's cute you think I am interested in riding the kiddie rollercoaster but don't worry, I'm sure someone will enjoy your quick and mediocre thrill ride."

Do not engage.

"Right." I blew out a breath, fighting back a retort because I didn't want to say anything else that she could turn around on me or completely offend her if we were spending hours in a car the next day. "Just email me your address, and I'll come to get you in the morning. Do we need to stop here before we head north?"

"No," she shook her head, returning her attention to the chaotic stack of papers on her desk. "I'll make sure Christine has all the files she needs before I leave today."

I must have made a face at the mention of her intern because she narrowed her eyes and pointed toward the hallway.

"You know the way out. I'll email you if there is anything else we need to go over. I'm sure you've got things to take care of for your precious best sellers."

I couldn't shake the sense of unease at her comment, hating that things always seemed to sour when we were in the same room. I thought we'd come to a mutual agreement to try to behave around one another at the team-building exercise, but she still despised me. I wanted to say the feeling was mutual, but then I'd be even more of a liar.

I didn't want to hate her as easy as it would be to do so. But the walls I'd constructed around myself ensured that we'd never be more than colleagues who barely tolerated each other.

She'd made her distaste for me known regularly over the last several years, but I still couldn't deny I was attracted to her.

I never dated within the office, but I'd shamelessly flirted with enough women to get a reaction out of her that she thought I was a manwhore.

That wasn't a word I'd use to describe myself. I never went more than a few months between partners, but I was far from having a revolving door of pussy.

I didn't have the reputation that Hutch had when we were younger but being the identical twin of the school Casanova who was nicknamed *Big O* when we were fifteen, wasn't easy. It also meant that having the same face meant girls came after me due to his reputation alone. I wasn't proud enough as a teenager to turn down willing partners, even if it was only my face they were interested in.

It also hadn't hurt in college that I got a lot of leeway from some of my more privileged classmates because I was attractive and an athlete. They didn't know the only reason I was even attending college was because of the scholarships I'd managed to obtain and that I lived in the dorms all four years because I couldn't afford not to. Ma would have been fine with commuting into the city every day, but Southie was a haul from Boston College, and I needed the time to study before and after classes and practice.

That was another thing I found hot about Isobel. We seemed to both love baseball. Despite her choice of teams being a little lacking, it still intrigued me. But she was from the Midwest, so I could see why she was attached to the Cubbies. My fascination with the Sox started when I was barely old enough to hold a bat.

When I got back to my office, Sam was busy working at his small desk in the cubicle right outside my door, going through one of my mystery writer's newest manuscripts. I'd read the first four chapters, and the plot was solid, like Evan's manuscripts typically were, but something about the character's interactions seemed clunky. Maybe Evan had spent too much time in seclusion the last several years and had forgotten how to interact with people. Not that he was too keen on social interaction in general.

"How's it going?" I asked as I leaned against the opening of his workspace. Sam sighed loudly before scrubbing his hand over his face and turning in my direction.

"It's not good. He's gonna hate it, but several chapters need total rewrites. I don't see any other way around it."

"Fuck." Rubbing my fingers along my chin, I tried to think of the best way to approach this with Evan. He typically didn't require much hand-holding, but I didn't want one rough storyline to tank his series of best sellers. "Just do a full developmental edit on it and send me the notes before you say anything to him. I know he's been showing signs of burnout lately, and I don't want any criticism to throw him off his game."

"Alright," Sam nodded. "I'll start over from the beginning and start creating a developmental file to send you."

"Just make sure you send it to me before you say anything to him. Dealing with Evan requires a little finesse." Sam smirked, shaking his head. I knew what he was thinking. "I'm capable of dealing with my authors, asshole. You can wipe off that douchey look on your face."

"Right on, boss," he laughed, putting his earbud back in and returning his attention to his tablet. I knew he thought I was an asshole, but he'd been a college athlete. He knew how things worked in that environment. He wasn't exactly a golden boy.

ACKNOWLEDGMENTS

Thank you so much for joining me in another installment of The Words Series. It's been a crazy ride since Chase & Evan were created, and getting to know all the truly amazing bookish people who love my book babies has been so much fun.

As always, huge thank yous to Danielle, Miguel, and Kelly G for being my backbone and telling me 'go write, bish' when I'm moody and insecure. Also, for helping me sift through stock photos to find the right cover model even though I'm endlessly indecisive. I couldn't be on this journey without you guys.

Many, many thanks to my alpha readers. Lizzie, for always being the most enthusiastic cheerleader as I post my sometimes rough chapters for you to go through. And for helping craft the plot twist in Bound because it made Trent's character arc that much better. Talita for being frank and insightful when I need it and always encouraging our little tribe of book people. Kelly S licked Nathan first, so you'll have to fight her for dibs. Thank you for always giving a fresh reader's perspective when you go through the rough draft. Tara for always being willing to jump on a rough draft and find my plot holes. Miguel, for sending dozens of hot emojis and begging me to find you a Nathan. I know if you approve that I've created another great book boyfriend, also for encouraging me to drop in just a dash of angst to add tension to the story.

I wanted this book to stand out and not be just another one that sensationalized this subject matter. So I truly appreciate the time that Alison took as a sensitivity reader to help me fine-tune this book and make the characters and their world as close to life as possible.

To the creators of the game they played in chapter 21, *Funishment,* for allowing me to borrow your words to make Kelly's transition from research to play less intimidating. Go get your copy at: https://funishment.squarespace.com/ and follow them on Instagram.

Once again, thank you to Vanessa and the team at Cherry for bringing another book baby to life. Jonathan, thank you for making my words pretty. And Pair, thank you for making my book heroes look dreamy on the cover.

And last but certainly not least, thank you to my family for putting up with me hiding so I could write. Also, to my husband for distracting my four minions so I could get edits fixed and chapters proofed without 1200 requests for snacks. And a special thank you to my mom for loving and supporting me through this transition into writing. Just don't ask me about research again.

There are a few more stories in this series to be told, so look out for More Than Words toward the end of the year for more on Adrian and Isobel. And next year, there will be a prequel story from Emory and Talia.

Follow me on social media:

Instagram: @elkoslo_writes

Facebook: E.L. Koslo & E.L. Romance Writer

Tiktok: @elkoslowrites

To check out details on the series, please visit ELKoslo.com and sign up for my newsletter.

(I will also always post content warnings on my website, so check there if you have any questions)

Feel free to join my reader group called The Dirty Words Brigade on Facebook. I post previews and updates on what I am working on and occasionally remember to facilitate games.

Until next time and thank you for being wonderful, supportive readers.

E.L. Koslo

Did you enjoy Bound By Words?

❤

Leave 5 stars and a nice comment to share the love!

You didn't like it?
♠

Write to us to suggest the kind of novel you dream of reading!
https://cherry-publishing.com/en/contact/

Subscribe to our Newsletter to stay up to date with all of our upcoming releases and latest news!
You can subscribe according to the country you're from:

You are from...

US:
https://mailchi.mp/b78947827e5e/get-your-free-ebook

UK:
https://mailchi.mp/cherry-publishing/get-your-free-uk-copy

CANADA:
https://mailchi.mp/96b9df3ed1ca/newsletter-canada-cherry-publishing

AUSTRALIA:
https://mailchi.mp/f7093b3c6c1a/newsletter-australia-cherry-publishing